Harper Errant 1

The Dragon Ring

Maggie Secara

Come away, O human child!
To the waters and the wild
With a fairy, hand in hand,
For the world's more full of weeping
than you can understand.

— William Butler Yeats

First Popinjay Press edition February, 2017.
This Popinjay edition has been re-edited and corrected. As a result, it is slightly altered but is otherwise unchanged from the original 2012 edition published by Crooked Cat Books.

ISBN 978-0-9818401-5-4

Quoted material

"Anglo-Saxon Rune Poem", from Runes and Heroic Poems, by Bruce Dickins, 1915. Ben's version is my variation on Dickins's translation.

"West Country Girl" by Chris Caswell, 1984. Used by permission.

Please visit the author at www.maggiesecara.com

Popinjay
Press

for
Ari and Robin
my favorite wizards
and Kris,
who can be a wizard too,
if she wants to

Wonderfully engaging

Intelligent and entertaining

A magical journey

A beautiful blend of history and folklore

A wonderful blend of the contemporary and arcane

Lyrical... Completely masterful...

A strong literary bent making for an artfully crafted tale, both serious in its execution and beautiful to read.

Sunday

Monday

Tuesday

Wednesday

About the Author

Acknowledgements

The Dragon Ring owes more than I can say to quite a few people. To begin with, the multi-talented Professor Ari Berk, not only for his many years of friendship, but also for inspiration: long funny chats, tales of his adventures on Dartmoor, the splendid, jewel-like stories in *The Runes of Elfland,* and the adorable goofiness of *Goblins* (both with Brian Froud, whom I also owe for those and *Faeries,* too).

Thanks also to Ari's wife, the splendid Dr Kristen McDermott and their son Robin, for providing all unwitting a model for Ben and his family. To the wise and funny Glen Kranzer, in his occasional guise of Jacob Peachbottom, without whom there would have been no Jack Greengage. And to the inimitable Conn MacLir for providing a pattern for Guthrum the Dane.

Some people have a proper writing circle, I have a Treehouse: Deirdre Sargent, Joel Reid, and Scott Perkins whose encouragement, cheerleading, and the occasional kick in the butt I needed.

Among the rest of my Facebook friends, I must remember Rebecca Roberts, Sandy Hoskin, and Christine Taylor, Melinda Sherbring Nan Earnheart, and Gereg Jones Muller, who read various drafts and provided excellent notes.

Not to forget the enthusiastic cadre at the several incarnations of the *Worlds of Maggie Secara* group on Facebook who read the first draft as it emerged over the frantic weeks of November, 2009. For advice and advanced brain picking in matters musical I am indebted to old friends Darren Raleigh and Tracie Brown, both real harpers with tremendous knowledge of their music and their craft, and the good humor to indulge an aging chorister.

Characters have their models and so do places. I would be remiss if I left out the people and village of Ilsington (not Islington!) at the edge of Dartmoor in Devon who, under the quizzing glass of Google, gave me the model for Iveston on the Moor, especially the school, church, and local legendry. If you felt someone reading the Village Meeting Minutes over your shoulders, that was me.

Many kisses to you all, and to the legions of Faerie—they know who they are.

Maggie Secara
March 2012

Addendum

Respectful thanks to Laurence and Stephanie Patterson at Crook Cat Publishing who took a chance on an unknown, un-tried, middle-aged author, and helped to bring Ben and Raven into the world.

M.S.
April 2017

Dramatis Personae

IVESTON ON THE MOOR

BEN HARPER, organizing guru, overworked author, popular host of reality show "Now or Never" specializes in helping people organize their homes and their lives.

MELLIS POWELL, professor of music and tolerant wife

SPARROW HARPER-POWELL, their fragile son

MRS SATTERLY, the postmistress

MR DAY, landlord of the local pub, Day's Star

DINAH AND TOM SHORLAND, MORGAN TYLER, BRIAN DYMOCK: Members of Faerie Reel, a popular local ceilidh band

OF FAERIE

AUBREY KING, who is also Oberon King of Faerie

LADY GRACE, who is also Titania Queen of Faerie.

RAVEN, one of Oberon's principal gentlemen

ODIN (WOTAN, etc.), the All Father, etc., now in service to Oberon

PAULY (ONYX), one of Titania's minions

GAEZEL, a succubus of uncertain alignment

Various fae great and small, seen and unseen, and a wee man

WESSEX 876 AD

ALFRED, King of Wessex, eventually to be called The Great.

GUTHRUM Sitricson, a war leader intent on becoming a king

HRAFN ALFSIGR, the king's shield bearer

BRAND HARPER of Ivarstanehaugh, the king's harper

LADY CEOLWEN, the magistrate's elf-ridden widow of Bydford

FATHER DAMIANUS, a timid priest

BISHOP WULFHERE, Alfred's self-righteous chaplain

Numerous thegns, Danes, priests and supernumeraries

LONDON, 1599

SIR FRANCIS BROWNE, a gentleman in service to Lord Aubrey

LORD AUBREY, a fellow of infinite jest

THOMAS GARRARD & ANDREW PENNY, a pair of prosperous goldsmiths

TIBBIT, a girl with something to sell

JACK GREENGAGE, called by some Jack Plough, lately come to London

MISTRESS PENNYFEATHER, an unreliable widow

NED & MERWIN QUINEY, two unreliable fellows

MARCUS TANDY, a master goldsmith

AVERIL TANDY, his spending wife

RAFE, an idle apprentice

IVESTONE ON MOOR, 1763

MR CORBIN, the village schoolmaster

MRS CORBIN, his wife

MR RAWLEY, the assistant schoolmaster

MIDGEN & WIGGENS, a faery pair of King Charles spaniels

MR FORDHAM, the vicar

MISS PRISCILLA DAY, an plain but potentially wealthy woman

CAPT. JASPER JARVIS, a fortune hunter

Various schoolboys called Blackhurst, Powell, Dymock, and other familiar names

The Dragon Ring

Thursday

1
Iveston on the Moor, Devon, England

❋

The King's Raven soared up out of Faerie, spiraling between banks of summer storm and into the sun over Dartmoor. The veils that cloak his world from ours fell together behind him like a crystalline song. Icy wedges of air streamed past the sharp eyes, poured across the stretching wings as he reached over the horizon for the moon's white disk. Then pivoting on a night-black wing tip, he turned and powered towards the ground, flipping barrel rolls for joy, because he could. Just as he flattened out to skim the granite-crowned tors, a glint of sapphire glittered at him from somewhere below.

Reluctant but obedient, he tumbled out of the sky over tiny Iveston village, stalled, and came to rest, wrapping hooked talons over the fence that defined the well-ordered yard of a country pub from the wild moor lands beyond. For a moment, he was a laughing young man sitting on the fence in black jeans and shirt. Then the elegant gentleman who had called him snapped an order, clearly expecting to be obeyed.

Vulgarly impertinent, the boy was the raven again. His head bobbed once, and again, in case his lord had missed the courtesy. (He hadn't, and couldn't resist smiling.) Shouted a territorial caw, in case the ordinary *corvidae* in the neighborhood had missed his arrival. Then he sprang up with a noisy clap of wings to settle on the roof peak of the pub called Day's Star. On guard, eyes bright, he settled in.

Inside the lime-washed and serviceable Star, its dark interior redolent of time and beer, things were not so poetic. Well, not entirely. A pair of old men bent over a chess game in a corner under horse brasses and framed headlines from the Great War. Another, content to sit alone with his Kindle reader and a short whisky, took up the seat nearest the bar, occupied by his father and grandfather in their turns. Quiet enough, then, excepting the click of the e-reader paging, and the occasional muttered "Check!" There's a bit of poetry in all of that, maybe.

Mr Day, the landlord, added a metallic clank and thump to the mix, fitting a new keg in under the bar. But the sound that rang up to the sharp-eared Raven on the roof was none of these: less content, much younger, and utterly American.

"I said no, Peter, and I meant it! Just no!" Ben Harper had been reviewing galley proofs of the new book all day and had come down to the pub for a sandwich and a pint. "I should never have picked up," he muttered.

"What's that, eh?" said his agent.

Ben sighed and let the other man go on. It was an agent's job to keep the magic going, and wild ideas that worked were Peter's specialty, yes. He was the one who had turned Ben's knack for efficiency and clear thinking from a cottage industry into a career. So he was grateful. Really. The man earned his percentage, but there were limits. There had to be!

Ben drained his pint and gave up.

"Peter, stop. Could you stop? I said, no castles. No US locations. Maybe next year."

"Just let me finish, mate! This is brilliant! You'll love this."

Ben set the cell phone gently on the table and raised his empty glass and a meaningful look to Mr Day, who nodded back.

"Sorry? Sorry, Peter, you're breaking up!" Ben shouted, and with guilty satisfaction, tapped the call closed. Most of Dartmoor didn't even get cell service. Calls got dropped here all the time. It could be minutes before Peter noticed and rang back. A few blessed minutes, Ben thought. Maybe longer.

A fresh pint of Day's Best Bitter appeared in front of him, tiny bubbles rising through the gold to a thin, creamy head. When a second one materialized next to it, he looked up again, confused.

A quick flare of sunlight flooded the window over Ben's head, rendering his benefactor more or less invisible.

"Hope you don't mind."

The pleasant voice might have come out of the air, or from another world, there was no way to tell. Then a cloud, or something, softened the light again, and the comfortable shadows returned. The voice became a shape, then a man, and a whole new problem. Harper blinked and dropped his glasses back down to his nose.

Wary, he tipped his thanks with the fresh pint. "I don't usually accept drinks from strange men."

It was part of Ben's nature to notice, catalog, file, and he did it now without thinking. The tall, lordly type in beautifully tailored jacket and a silk shirt of pale but uncertain color smiled at him, then dragged up a chair and sat down opposite. Black hair curled loosely on the man's shoulders framing a sharp-featured face. Celtic, perhaps, or more exotic than that. Eurasian, maybe. High cheekbones touched with warmth, fine features, dark eyes so deeply blue they matched the sapphire that winked in one slightly pointed ear. A tendril of smoke spun up from the cigarette he held cupped between long manicured fingers.

Ben shot a questioning look back towards the bar; Mr Day just shrugged.

"Aubrey." The accent was plummy and posh, like the manner, if perhaps just a touch foreign. Not from around here, no. "Aubrey King."

"I'm sorry—Oberon? Not a name you hear a lot."

A cloud slipped off the sun again, and a stray sunbeam highlighted the planes of the face. He might almost have been posing for a magazine. Or an album cover. Ben suspected the guy was aware of the effect he created.

The fellow lifted one sable eyebrow, chuckled lightly as if he heard that all the time, the picture of aristocratic ease. The old wooden chair didn't even creak when he settled back in it.

"Aubrey," he corrected. Aubrey took a deliberate drag on the cigarette, then carefully let it out over his shoulder. "Been following your career, Ben Harper. Have a proposition for you."

Ben rolled his eyes, manners collapsing altogether. "Oh, of course you do."

Conversations that started like this invariably involved a unique opportunity he didn't need and couldn't afford. For the sake of distraction, he nodded at the cigarette. "Y'know, you can't smoke in here."

"Ah!" said Aubrey, his glance flickering to the cigarette with a grace note of surprise that might even have been genuine. "Quite right. Old habits."

He made a show of pinching out the cherry, then folding the stub into his palm. With a gesture like a stage magician, he fanned open the fingers again and it was gone.

"My 7-year-old can pull a quarter out of your ear."

We know the Sparrow! Yes, we do!

Listen!

Silly human!

What the hell? Tiny voices like a pack of munchkins were giggling somewhere, maybe under the window behind him, or just outside the door that stood open to the car park.

"Pfft," said the guy, Aubrey. "Pixies."

"Yeah, okay," Ben said. "Or kids." But he did wonder if the school had let out already. He had to pick up his son today.

In fact, he thought, it was probably time to go. Yeah, he should go. He tipped back his glass for a last appreciative swallow, and set it down a bit harder than he intended. By all rights it should have sloshed beer over the rim, but it didn't.

He stared at the glass for a second, then stood up. "Sorry. I really have to go." Feeling churlish but in suddenly desperate need of open air, he flung himself away from the table.

An enigmatic smile hovered around his lordship's mouth as the dark eyes tracked the American. "I think you'll find it's not the kind of proposition you expect."

"It never is, mate. But whatever it is, I really don't have the time," Ben said over his shoulder, and added with the barest courtesy, "Thanks for the beer."

He ducked under the low doorway to emerge, striding out across the pub's postage stamp front garden. Before his eyes had even finished adjusting to the light, the clouds parted then closed an instant later. Dazzled, running shoes skidding on the wet grass, Ben drew up short before he could slam into a picnic table still beaded with rain.

Vision cleared, and there was Aubrey.

He stared, then flung a look back over his shoulder towards the doorway he'd just come through. The man still appeared to be sitting at the table, calmly sipping his beer.

Again he looked to the rail fence where Aubrey couldn't possibly be but manifestly was. The double-take might have been comical if it weren't so bloody impossible. Ben pushed his wire-rimmed glasses up his nose with one finger. Who was this guy?

"Okay," he said carefully, backing away from the table, and the stranger. "Nice trick. I'm sure your idea is utterly unique, won't cost me a thing, and will make me rich."

A thin smile lifted Aubrey King's eyes, but he just put his hands in his pockets, shifted his weight, and said nothing.

"But could you just, y'know, call my agent, okay? He vets brilliant ideas all day long."

Like a criminal seeking sanctuary, Ben was edging backwards toward the pleasant darkness of the Star. He had taken no more than a few steps when a huge bird dived out of nowhere with a harsh cry, cutting the space between the two men. Ben stumbled back as a night-black wing tip nearly clipped his nose.

"Hey!"

The bird banked, traced a figure-eight around Aubrey, and soared back up to the roof. It snapped its beak and trained its black eye on the American, then gave a throaty croak, as if having the final word.

There was that childish giggling again.

"Aw, come on!"

Ben stared around, a little frantically. Still no children. Behind him, the figure with the beer had gone. And Aubrey just stood there by the front gate, calmly looking back at him. There was something else about the guy, despite the casual pose, that Ben couldn't quite put a name to. An air of...what?

Ben shivered slightly, then sighed again. If this was what stress was doing to him even before the new series started shooting, he was in serious trouble.

"Damn," he breathed.

And then he started to laugh—at himself, at the day, at life. Shaking his head, he gave up and walked back across the grass with a rueful smile. As he put out his hand, his gaze for the first time rose to meet Aubrey's long blue eyes, dark and strange as the sea.

"Look, I don't know what's going on."

"Going on?" said Aubrey.

Ben said, "Sorry," and realized he meant it. "I'm listening. What can I do for you?"

Aubrey put his hand in Ben's, accepting the apology with a nod.

"It's going to take some explaining," he said. "And some time. Ah! I know, that word again. But time is not really the problem, Ben. At least, not in the way you think."

"Oh, now you're just being mysterious."

The aristocratic smirk again. "You did leave a pint of perfectly good beer on the table. Shall we go in?"

Pushing a fringe of sandy hair back out of his eyes, Ben looked at the man, really looked at him. "Are you glowing?"

Well, he was. Not in any vulgar, glittery way but a glow indeed—an aura maybe—pale in the watery, unreliable light.

"Am I?"

That eyebrow lifted again with amusement and something else Ben couldn't guess at.

When the clouds moved again, it was gone. "Hmm, maybe not."

Stress, Ben thought. And sunlight bouncing into his eyes. English springs are notorious for bright intervals of sun and shadow. And technically, it was still spring for another week or so. If the yard seemed perceptibly darker, that would be the trailing edge of the earlier storm slipping by on its way to Surrey.

"Curious," Aubrey said. "So. Drinks?"

Time appeared to be the recurring theme of a day growing

steadily more odd.

"It's— I don't know." Ben checked his watch, then turned to look down the street toward the sixteenth century clock tower and past it to Iveston School. "Damn it! I've got to get my son from school. Would you mind—?"

"May I walk with you?" Aubrey King gestured with grace.

"Uhm, okay."

Compartmentalizing out of habit, and because he saw no other choice, Ben set the weirdness aside and crunched down the driveway and into the road, with the tall, fae gentleman strolling easily at his left hand.

The half-timbered pile that was the Star (est. 1621) sprawled at one end of the village. The school in serviceable red brick lay, wisely, at the other. As Iveston was one of Devon's smaller villages, the two ends were not all that far apart, with little more than the vicarage and the consecrated breadth of St Michael's church (est. 1528) between them. As they passed the ancient lychgate leading to the graveyard, Ben felt more than heard the other man take a step back, then cut behind him with a rhythm almost like a dance step, to walk on the other, sunnier side of the street. The green smell of the moor washed over them as he moved, and a light scent of violets.

"Issues with the Church?" Ben asked with a curious grin.

"In a manner of speaking," the other man said, without elaborating. A raven, probably not the same one, called from somewhere. "Indeed," he added obscurely, smiling.

They walked on with Ben expecting a hard sales pitch at any moment. Instead, the man was humming a clever little tune he'd never heard before.

"Who are you?" said Ben suddenly. "Really?"

Aubrey's face lit up, as if he had been waiting for this question, then appeared to reconsider. Finally he shrugged and said slowly, "What if I told you I was Oberon, king of Faerie?"

Ben snorted. "I'd look around for hidden cameras. Or the men in the white coats."

"Yes, I suppose you would. Still, it might be true. This is Dartmoor, the heart of England's magick, and there are stories.

The fae, it's well known, cannot lie."

"So they say," Ben allowed. "But come on, who are you? What are you? Reporter? Rock star? I know, super hero. Is this your secret identity?"

That made Aubrey laugh out loud. "I knew I liked you," he said without answering. When they finally stepped onto the sidewalk in front of the low wall that protected the school from the street, he faced the American soberly.

"The real question, Ben Harper, is who are you? An efficiency expert who has no time? A musician who never plays? An actor of more than ordinary charm who's content to be a TV star writing housekeeping manuals?"

"Hey!"

The voice was light, almost mocking, but the expression was serious. "What other gifts are you neglecting? Don't you wonder?"

Ben pushed his glasses up again. It's not like he hadn't been asking himself those very questions lately. Lately, and for a while, in fact. But having someone else fling his doubts in his face, doubts he'd barely begun to share with his wife, was something else again.

"Hey," he repeated, and felt stupid when he did. Not exactly a devastating comeback for the man's too-accurate assessment. A few yards away, the clock on the school wall ticked over another loud minute before Ben said, annoyed: "So, what is this, a rescue? Some kind of intervention? Are you the ghost of Christmas Yet to Come? Who put you up to this?"

His new friend, if that's what he was, stiffened slightly. So much for his more than ordinary charm. It sounded insulting even to Ben.

Those pixies, or small children, were laughing at him again or maybe it was the wind in the oak tree just over the way.

"Okay," Ben said as the strained silence lengthened. "Just tell me what's going on."

Now the man did crack a smile. "You're collecting your child from school, I thought. What's his name again?"

The awkwardness shifted.

"Uh, Sparrow. He's called Sparrow."

Ben pushed open the chain link gate to join the cluster of waiting parents applying their x-ray vision to the smoked glass doors for the first glimpse of their kids. Alas, parental super powers were on the fritz today. All anyone could see were their own fun-house reflections.

Aubrey considerately stayed behind, leaning his back against the wall, paying attention to the village instead of making the other grown-ups nervous. Well, maybe that was the motivation, but when Ben looked back he had that feeling again, of some kind of power restrained and contained. For all the relaxed elegance, the man stood like a soldier on guard, scanning for trouble. Who was this guy?

Abruptly, the flat buzz of the school bell jangled the country quiet, and the question slipped away. In seconds the tiniest children burst shrieking through the double doors in a bobbing river of robin's egg blue, and slammed into parental knees. Before they'd quite cleared the hallway, a half-dozen 7- and 8-year-olds came barreling through, their gap-toothed smiles as sunny as summer days.

Next week—no, tomorrow, Ben realized—was the last day of term. No wonder they looked so especially cheerful. They'd be free, and two weeks later he'd be back at his London desk, living on fast food and coffee, the willing architect of his own depression. Willing, mind you. Which brought him back to Aubrey King and the favor that hadn't yet been asked. King of the faeries, oh yeah. Still, there was something.

Where the hell was Sparrow?

A light glimmered behind the tinted doors, a child skipping, tow head bobbing like the bird that had given him his nickname. You'd never know, most of the time, how delicate he really was. As he pressed through the doors, cheerful but paler than usual under the sunny hair, Ben noted with worry the signs of strain on the kid's face. Something had happened—an asthma attack? How severe? The medication usually worked, but now and then Sparrow pushed himself too hard to keep up with the other kids. Things happened; Ben made the effort to stay cool.

The teacher was bringing him out, one hand on the slender shoulder as if trying to keep him from floating away.

"Daddy!" Sparrow started to break away but the restraining hand caught him back. He squirmed while Daddy exchanged a few words with Teacher about chronic illness and activity levels. Daddy took his hand.

Might be worse, the grown-ups agreed. Might still be living in Los Angeles.

Impatient, Sparrow squiggled, bounced, and danced, still tethered to Daddy but distracted by everything, humming some little hum that wasn't quite a song. Unless it was. The pixies had been singing with him at lunchtime today, before the asthma started up, and now he heard the tune again, all twisty and strange. Two or three of the pixie folk were pulling at him, dragging at his shoelaces, and babbling in their tiny voices. One of them squeaked and pointed, until he looked up.

A wee man just about the size and shape of a garden gnome stood on the wall wearing a curious coat of leather and leaves, with a red feather in his pointed cap like a safety flag. Sparrow giggled, as he always did, for the wee man's nose was so long and curved down that it almost touched his chin, and his chin was so long and curved up that it almost touched his nose. They'd met before. And he was chatting familiarly with a tall, dark haired man wearing a golden crown and a sober expression.

The man said something. The wee man roared with laughter. It hopped on one foot three times, spun around, and vanished with a *pop!* Sparrow gasped. The kingly man looked down and met the child's awed gaze.

Sparrow knew better than to talk to big strangers, even faerie ones, so he whipped back around at once, suddenly shy, and tightened his grip on Daddy's hand. He had meant to give a loud, impatient sigh, but forgot.

Finally, Miss Martin went away, and it was time to go.

"How now, gentle knight," said Ben, giving the boy his complete attention—finally. "Your charger awaits. Will ye ride?"

"Good my lord, so shall I," Sparrow cried, because he was his father's son.

2
Iveston School

Ben swung his son up off the ground and into a noisy, nuzzly embrace that brought a giggle and squeak to be put down. Instead, he flipped the boy around so he rode high on Daddy's shoulders, and pushed out through the school yard gate where Aubrey stood at ease just a little ways away.

"Sparrow, this is Mr King. You may shake his hand."

"How do you do, Mr King," Sparrow lisped politely, and bowed from his chivalric height like any courtier.

"Well met, sir knight," said Aubrey, taking the little hand. "I'm well pleased to make your acquaintance, Sparrow."

"I know what I want to be when I grow up."

"Do you? And what is that?"

"A wizard!"

The grown-ups carefully did not laugh, though Aubrey was grinning broadly. "A wizard," he repeated.

"Yes. Daddy will be one, too. We can be the wizards, and Mummy can be our servant."

"Oh, really?" Now Ben did laugh. "I wouldn't tell her that. Can't Mummy be a wizard too?"

"No," Sparrow said earnestly. "Wizards are men. She could be a sorceress, but they're mostly bad."

"I see," said Aubrey King. "What sort of a wizard, then? You mean like in the cinema?"

The child bestowed a withering glance that plainly said he'd expected better from a lord of the Fae.

"No. A real wizard. We'll make things, you know, like magic rings and songs that are really spells—Mummy can help with that part. She's a musician, you see," he added confidentially, in case Mr King didn't know. "And we'll learn stuff from the pixies and the moor folk, and other stuff, too."

Where had all this come from, Ben wondered, sharing a look with Aubrey.

The gaze the man returned held a tinge of curiosity, and something else less comfortable. "A very special child, this child. Keep him safe," Aubrey said, sounding quite serious. "And now, I must leave you, I fear."

"But—"

"Do me a favor, Ben." The peremptory tone was quite unlike a request. "Get Sparrow home at once, without delay. And if you can, be on Raven Tor at twilight or thereabouts. Can you do that?"

It was Ben's turn at last to shoot an arch look, which made Sparrow giggle and cover both Daddy's eyebrows (and incidentally both eyes) with his hands. "Yeah, I guess. But... Hey, kiddo, quit wiggling! And move your hands, I can't see." He reached back to latch onto tiny wrists.

"Do it now, please," said the imperial voice, then all was breezy silence and bird song, and the music of the chain link gate clanking in its frame. Sparrow squealed with delight.

Ben blinked when he could see again, but Aubrey King had gone. Gone. Not walking away, not climbing into the nearest Mercedes, just poof! disappeared. "Where'd he go, sport?"

He could feel the boy's hands let go as he shrugged, rocking on his chivalric perch, then grab Ben's face again. "Don't drop me, Dad!"

"Never. Did you see where Mr King went?"

"Well," Sparrow drawled thoughtfully. "Into Faerie, I think. It was rather quick."

An active imagination is a wonderful thing in a child. Of course it is. Unless you need an actual report about the actual world. The adorable British accent made up for a lot.

"You're getting too big for this game, little bird," Ben said with a groan. "Time to walk."

Sparrow clambered down and took his father's hand. A few steps later, and Ben was carefully looking both ways to cross the road though there was seldom any traffic. Errands to run, as usual.

"Dad, Mr King said we should go straight home."

"Mr King didn't know we have to get groceries and pick up the mail first. I'm sure he won't mind if we dawdle just a little, okay?

3
Post Office

The post office was a cluttered counter at the back of Satterly's Sundries as it had been for a hundred years. The post mistress, who was also Mrs Satterly and smelled of talcum powder, always called Ben "Mr Harper" when they came in, and said to Sparrow in her broad Devon brogue:

"Hallo, Robin! Or is 'ee Bluebird? Or Plover?"

And each time Sparrow said stoutly, "I'm Sparrow, Mrs Satterly."

Most days, the whole shop might have no more than two or three customers at a time. Today after two days of rain there was a line that snaked back through the aisles between canned goods and shipping materials, local cider and a computer station for hire by the hour. There was no home mail delivery in the villages of Iveston Vale. If you wanted your mail, you had to come get it, so most people had been content to let the bills wait in their boxes. They made up for it now by queuing in the shop, Ben among them, getting rosy and damp as the temperature rose with the population.

For all the delay, there was nothing much for Ben's household but flyers for local dance parties, the parish newsletter, and a handful of catalogs and a couple of scholarly journals addressed to his wife, all bound in a rubber band.

Rural junk mail, Ben thought. Okay, a postcard from Chris Caswell telling him to check in to Facebook more often; that made him laugh. And the glossy folder for the Devon Midsummer Folk & Roots festival—that made him sigh. And then it got worse. Slipping the elastic from the catalog roll, he practically dropped the full color annual from Telynau Teifi in

Wales—harp porn of the first order. He half expected his hands to start shaking, it had been so long since he'd set finger to harp string.

Flipping longingly through the hard glazed pages, he almost missed walking into the leggy blonde in the tiny green flutter of silk and cashmere. Almost, but not quite.

Her platinum hair fell in long straight strands like icicles to her waist. The perfect skin was only a shade more rosy. A snow queen in a new spring frock, she stalked through Satterly's like it was Harrods, gathering looks by turns both admiring and amused. So no one but Ben was surprised when, narrowly avoiding old Arthur Leere's cane, she practically marched into Ben's arms.

Ben looked up with a startled grunt, wondering where the hell the Amazon had come from. Before he could stop her, she had somehow bounced off his elbow, banked off the tinned pies, and caromed shrieking towards the Cadbury's display with the jeweled stiletto heels of her sandals skidding on the cracked linoleum. Shocked but chivalrous, Ben grabbed her arm. "Watch it!"

"Watch your bloody self!" she snapped, and twisted away from him, flinging back the platinum hair. The flying ends stung Ben's cheek like an explosion of ice as she put a steadying hand through a box of wine gums.

He stepped back, blinking.

"No problem. Yo, Sparrow. Ready?" he called.

But she wasn't done. Pushing off again, she had stumbled somehow against a screeching metal rack of post cards, which fought back by hooking onto her pearl-buttoned cardigan. Her yelp and the crash as the rack hit the floor brought the whole room to silence.

Swearing, she stopped where she was and with crimson manicured fingers smoothed the cashmere—miraculously unharmed—along with her composure, more or less. Then she proceeded to walk peevishly but with perfect grace through the scattered views of Dartmoor now littering the floor.

"Jesus," Ben cried, and moved in once again to divert her. Sparrow was sitting on the floor right in the path of her pin prick heels. Ben grabbed her elbow, swinging her smartly around.

"Honey, are you okay?"

"Oh, gods above, an American." The glittering eyes rolled. "Yes, sweetie, I am perfectly well, thank you." Her gaze moved pointedly to Ben's hand still printing her white arm.

He removed it, of course, and gladly while noticing, irrelevantly, that her flesh under his fingers was dry and cool, though everyone else in the room was sweltering.

"Actually, I was speaking to my son," he said, and looked down at Sparrow. "Everything all right?"

When the lady followed the look, she met wide eyes with her own leaf green ones, and smiled. Like the coming of spring on the moor, her demeanor altered, blossoming. Though nothing obvious had changed, she was all at once younger, softer, infinitely sweeter, though to a trained eye like Ben's, no less dangerous.

Her voice went up half an octave, Ben judged, as she breathed with surprising tenderness, "Oh my! What a lovely child!"

Sparrow was holding quite still.

"This is your little boy? It's Sparrow, then, is it? That's your name?"

Sparrow only nodded.

"Yes, it is," said Ben.

"That's a wonderful name." With perfect grace, she sank to her knees so her eyes were at the boy's level. "Your daddy nearly pushed me over you, didn't he?" she cooed, and with a gentle finger pushed his hair out of his face. "Bad daddy. But oh, Mother Goodness, aren't you a handsome fellow! How old are you, my love?"

Sparrow, ordinarily fearless, glanced to his father for reassurance that it was all right to speak to the strange, very strange woman. Ben gave him a wink and a nod.

"I'm seven, Miss."

"And do you live here in the village, Sparrow?" He nodded shyly, reluctant to give anything up.

"You know," she said, leaning forward. Her voice went low

and conspiratorial, while her smile somehow cheered every heart in the room, even those who couldn't see it. "I believe you have some very special gifts, don't you, my Sparrow? I think that you can hear the bells of Elfland. You can, can't you, my love? Yes, I see you know what I mean. Tell me, sweeting—"

"Excuse me," Ben said, sounding harsh and uncouth in his own ear after the measured beauty of the lady's voice.

She glanced up at him, and suddenly Ben Harper understood what a terrible mistake he'd made. She meant no harm. How could he have been so awkward? So boorish? Even the neighbors were shaking their heads. What an idiot he was, not to see at once that she was everything noble and refined in the world, while he was nothing but a vulgar TV pitchman, stammering and stupid and...

"Daddy?"

Sparrow's voice came from somewhere far away. Ben shook his head, clearing his throat. "I'd rather you talk to me, Miss—"

"Lady," she corrected gently. "Lady Grace." In a single fluid motion she spiraled up from the floor to her full height, radiating trust and friendship, and exquisite.

Oh, damn. She was glowing.

A startled laugh burst from Ben, and the hypnotic suggestion or magic spell or whatever it was, snapped, shattering in icy shards he could almost see. Or was that her hair? Oh, no, not again. Around him, the room, the village, the world returned seamlessly to normal. Someone laughed and Mrs Satterly called for the next customer.

The woman, however, appeared to teleport away from him in one angry move.

"Are you laughing at me, you... " You could see her sorting through a mental arsenal before launching the worst: "Colonial!"

From every corner, merry Iveston eyes were crinkling and lips twitching. Someone fancied herself, didn't she? Eh, the Yank could handle it.

"Why yes," Ben said with exaggerated good cheer. "I believe I am."

The scarlet lip curled just slightly. "A bad choice, Ben Harper. I might have been your friend."

He didn't wonder how she had picked up his name—he was a little bit famous, after all—but he didn't care.

"Nice bumping into you, too, milady. Come on, son, we're done here."

He never saw the gesture her fingers formed, or the change in the glow he had sensed more than seen, but someone else did.

"No!"

Faster than thought, one of the numerous Satterly nephews stepped out from behind the counter, or somewhere, and thrust out a hand to stop her. All the neighbors turned to look, including the snow queen, bleak now with contempt.

"What?" she said, biting off the word.

"I mean, no, Lady Grace," said the nephew, more diffidently this time. A pretty boy of about sixteen, he tossed a raven's wing of black hair out of startling blue eyes, and added, "Looked all over in back. No postcards of Raven Tor at twilight. I can sell 'ee an instant camera, take your own, like?"

She sniffed and brushed past him, tossing her hair one last time. A moment later, she had gone, and the whole shop breathed normally again. Like a dozen Sleeping Beauties waking from a dream, the neighbors fell at once to chatter and awkward laughter, not quite sure what had happened, or even what they had seen. If, indeed, they had seen anything at all.

Still grinning, Ben tucked the mail into the canvas carry-all Mrs Satterly had already filled with the bread, milk, and apples for him. A moment later he had sidestepped the devastation and was out of there with Sparrow's warm little hand securely in his. The bell tinkled as they passed through, and the double-glazed shop door creaked, hissed, and clicked shut behind them.

It was a good half mile or so from the village green to silver-thatched Diamond Cottage. The Raven who had been calling challenges from a tree nearby stopped in mid-caw to observe his charges crossing the road, then launched on a following course. If today was like other days the pair would look at bugs, examine leaves, groan over awful riddles, maybe even sing, and so come at last to home. If they noticed him, well, what harm? Watching was the easy part of his job

.

Maggie Secara

4
On the road

"Well," said Ben. "That was interesting."

It was also enough. The rest of his errands could wait. Moving along with purpose now, they skipped the village hall and the rose-covered teashop he had meant to visit, and dived directly into the long nameless road that led to the cottage. Whoever that woman was, however random an encounter that might have been, Ben found himself wishing for his home ground and a locked door.

"She was a sorceress, wasn't she, Daddy?" Sparrow said as the tree-lined road started to rise. It was less a question than a request for confirmation.

"Could be." Ben didn't like to encourage snap judgments. "Maybe she wants to be nice and just doesn't know how."

"Maybe." Sparrow thought about that for a minute, then shook his head firmly. "No. I'm sure she's a sorceress."

"Ha! I'm sure you're right. Do you know which nephew that was? The one that stepped in?"

"He's not one of the nephews, Dad."

"No?"

"No, silly." Grown-ups could be so dim. "He was like Mr King. Didn't you see? So was that lady."

Ben looked down quizzically. "What do you mean, sport?"

The boy shrugged as if any fool could plainly see, and decided to sing for a while as they walked the sun-coined path. He was fine, obviously. A little weirded out, but hey, so was Daddy. As always, Ben found it slightly astonishing how easily kids recovered. Taking the hint, he jumped into the song when his part came around.

On the second pass through *Row, Row, Row Your Boat,* a third voice joined in light and cheerful, if a little rough, somewhere behind them. Ben turned, walking backward and ready with a smile, but the road was empty. A little spinning dust devil was catching up leaves and dust and dry things beside the foot path, but that was all. Apparently, even the big raven that usually saw them home was busy elsewhere today. Companionably, the disembodied voice bounced gently down the stream with them.

Ben was beginning to have serious doubts about this whole day.

"Who is that?" he called. Someone had to be pacing them just out of sight among the trees. Can't have been easy, keeping to the tune and the uneven, sloping path at the same time. "Walk with us, if you like."

No reply, just the tune. The longer the round went on, the more it began to winkle at Ben's senses. The sky had opened up at last to a perfect afternoon on the clear blue edge of summer, but the world felt dark.

He shivered despite the sun. As the path crested the next rise on a sharp curve, he caught his breath, and halted, skidding slightly on the pebbled earth. Straight overhead summer ruled, but before them the way lay grey and blind. The notch between the low hills that led down to Diamond Cottage, the road, even the cottage itself where it stretched like a hobbit house along the river bank were blanketed, cloaked, drowned in dense, roiling fog. As he watched, even the chimney pots disappeared.

Ben spun around, muttering. Behind him, the same shapeless wall rose thick and grey.

"Hang on, little bird," he said quietly, not wanting to alarm the boy. The song never faltered, the piping voice unwilling to let it go, and the stranger with him. Sparrow kept marching forward, unafraid or unaware, into the mist.

Row, row, row your boat.

Ben ran two or three steps to catch him up, and put a hand on his son's shoulder. "Sparrow! Hold!"

Apparently alerted by the familiar command in his father's

best podium voice, Sparrow stopped walking at once. Even so, the song went on, though the tune had collapsed into a kind of monotonous drone.

Merrily, merrily, merrily, merrily

Fine, Ben thought. Bizarre, but fine. He could ignore that. What he couldn't ignore was the fog.

He'd lived here for almost ten years, and knew the country well enough, for an outsider. He'd seen a wet mist like this spring up out of the ground before. Out on the open moor, such quick fogs could create devastating Hound of the Baskervilles terrors. He'd been caught in one himself a time or two. But this didn't feel the same. It felt— He sought for the words that were the tools of his trade. It tasted wrong.

Ben shivered, willing the discomfort to stay where it was and not churn to pointless fear. In a day as odd as this had been, what was one more thing? All he had to do was get Sparrow home and out of the weather. How hard could it be?

Life is but a dream!

Eyes closed for a moment, trusting the native intuition he had always relied on. And there it was, like a homing beacon, reaching out and bringing him in. That way.

"Okay, got it." He opened his eyes, and grinned down at his son. "Here we go."

Then Sparrow looked up at him. The pale, pointed little face was etched with panic.

"Merrily, merrily, merrily, merrily," he chanted dully.

Ben stooped to pick the boy up and slowly started down the curving hill. The fog closed over their heads with a sound like a muffled gong.

"Merrily, merrily, merrily, merrily."

This had to stop.

"Sparrow, stop singing."

Mid-merrily, the little voice broke off, and the tow head dropped to his father's shoulder with a shuddering sigh. His breathing sounded hoarse and hollow. He'd lost his emergency inhaler somewhere.

He'll be ok, Ben thought, but for how long?

"Guess Mr King was right, eh little bird?" he said, trying to sound jolly. "If we'd gone straight home we'd have missed all this, wouldn't we? Probably more adventure than one boy was meant to have in an afternoon."

The third voice had kept on like a faithful dog. Now it broke off, screeching with laughter.

"Merrily, merrily, mortal boys! Be we merry yet? Yet shall we be merry, hey ho! Nobody home!"

"Nobody's home, all right," Ben muttered, and kept going.

The road was old, hardly more than a macadamed horse track lined with willows, and just wide enough for a moving van if the driver sucked in his stomach. The footpath at the verge was no better, and worse in the terrible fog. It was like walking in a dream, plodding forever with no sense of getting anywhere, except… Except he knew where he was, forty yards from his garden gate. Thirty-five. Thirty.

Though he placed his steps carefully, an acorn wobbled under a heel and made him catch his weight and Sparrow's on the other foot. A woody creeper snaked out and grabbed at his jeans. Drooping willow branches whipped his face and tickled Sparrow's nose.

"Step lively now!" called the voice, harsh and mocking behind him. "That's the way, busy mortal. Hey! Hey!"

"What are you?" Ben shouted, clutching Sparrow more firmly. "What do you want?"

"A question! A question!" the voice cackled in front of him. "Tidy timely pennies for such timeless tidy thoughts, hey-hey!"

"My tidy thought is that you're pissing me off, mate."

From the left now, swaying above him from a willow branch: "Ooh, a fighter, he! Come and get me, busy mortal, tidy man! Mind you bring the kiddy, too." And now from off to the right. "My lady wants a piping wee mortal to be her singing boy. You can clean her stables."

"Shut up!" he shouted, and deposited Sparrow on the ground with a thump. "Stay," he ordered, and turned ready to find that mocking mouth and smash it, whatever it was attached to. "Show yourself!"

"Ben." Another, milder voice spoke gently at his shoulder.

"Listen," it said. "You know how to listen."

His jaw clenched so hard his bones ached. "I won't…" he began, then stopped, feeling the difference in the voices—one mocking, the other earnest. There was no compulsion, no illusion, just advice calmly delivered. No will moved him but his own.

So he listened.

The wind was moving, ruffling his hair, rattling the willows, balmy and sharp-scented with marigolds. Leaves rustled overhead in a familiar dry snap. Out there somewhere, a dog barked. A tune at the edge of his hearing threaded the air, high and sweet—a flute, maybe or no— A keening fiddle reeled out an aire so simple it might have been made at the dawn of the world. Ben started humming, trying to match and catch it. He could feel the harmonies shaping in his mind, stirring old habits long neglected. His fingers twitched for the harp strings that would capture it, build on it, and fling back variations.

It faded and trailed away, and with it the mocking voice. "Very well," it cried from far away. "Ah, ah, ah, you have friends, I see, in strange places. Well played! Another time, busy child."

"Sir?"

Ben whirled around, scuffling on the tarry surface of the road hot with summer. Blinking and dizzy, he whipped off his glasses to press the heels of his hands to his eyes as the last wisps of mist dissolved. Combed shaking fingers through hair damp with sweat. Mellis would be making him cut it soon, he thought with adrenaline-fueled irrelevance.

"Sparrow?"

"Here with me, sir," said the kid from the shop, the kid that wasn't a nephew. He was holding Sparrow's hand—a happy, relaxed Sparrow who only looked at his dad with tilted, bird-like curiosity just where the path split off to home.

"Where were you, Dad? Were you lost?"

Ben took a deep breath and let it out in a rush. The next second, he jumped aside as a dozen swiftly racing bicycles and their grim-faced riders pounded past, yelling at him to get out of the bloody way, and left him staring in the crazy swirls of dust and detritus that trailed in their wake. A perfectly ordinary day. Oh yeah, sure.

5

Diamond Cottage, teatime

Sparrow and the kid from the shop claimed to have been waiting for Ben while he walked half way back to the village, then came back muttering to himself. Of the panic, the fear in his son's expression, there was no sign. Ben shook his head, bewildered. After a minute, he thanked the kid and let him go, still without catching his name. Sparrow seemed untouched by the experience, almost as if nothing had happened.

And well, what had happened? What did he think, the child was possessed or something? Away with the faeries? Ben knew he'd been working too hard—traveling, speaking, writing—but for some reason, not making music. He shivered a little, knowing it was only going to get worse. When he threw open the kitchen door, Sparrow just tumbled into the house, carefree as ever.

Mellis had left them a note. Had to go up to Exeter for a meeting, then stop and see her mother. Might be late. Kisses. Carry on.

So Ben made tomato soup and grilled cheese sandwiches for their tea. There were further speculations about wizards and pixies through that and bath time, then magic was set aside for a session involving most of the Lego blocks in Great Britain, some pencils and a rubber band. Bedtime at last, Ben picked up *A Child's Garden of Verses* and read aloud:

> *In winter, I get up at night*
> *And dress by yellow candlelight.*
> *In summer, quite the other way—*
> *I have to go to bed by day!*

Which made Sparrow giggle, since it was practically Midsummer, and the days were so very long he really did go to bed by day. At half past seven, Mummy called to say she was on her way. A quarter of an hour later, he was yawning, and by eight o'clock, he was fast asleep.

Ben stood in the bedroom doorway smiling softly and cataloging the curious afternoon. A mysterious man, a crazy lady, and a teenager who seemed to be everywhere. A hallucination of the very first order. And in the end, domestic bliss. Yeah, he could live with that.

And speaking of living, the last proof pages for the latest volume of household organizing brilliance were waiting on his desk. It was time for the efficiency guru to earn his keep. It might not be the career he had intended, but my god, how the money rolled in.

With a sigh, he flipped on the baby monitor next to Sparrow's bed, then turned and jogged downstairs, humming the bawdy old tune under his breath.

> *My daddy makes book on the corner*
> *My granny sells second-hand gin*
> *My sister makes love for a guinea*
> *My god how the money rolls in!*

As an emblem of his success, Ben thought as he opened the office door, Diamond Cottage was a good one. The foundation was a few hundred years old, and the whole thing was bigger than it looked, stretching back along a fold of the land toward a twist of the river like some kind of hobbit mansion. One room had just been tacked on to the last as it grew. The office had been added at the bottom of a narrow staircase sometime around the second world war.

A big picture window and garden door in the eastern wall, the brainchild of a later owner with an artistic bent, filled the space with light. In the last year or so, he had traded endorsements with Alan Titchmarsh, and now a soft, fragrant garden where stone paths draped with lilacs led down to a low gate and the mill stream that marked his property line, and the distant view up the moor to Raven Tor on the horizon. It was just a bump from here, but worth keeping.

As he entered, he thought he heard whispers and something like his name. It stopped him in his tracks for a moment, wary after the day's adventures. Then he grinned and shook his head, knowing it was only the draft from the open door sighing across the strings, all the many strings in the room. Strings he had been neglecting.

On a stand beyond the serviceable sofa stood a battered old Gibson, his best friend since college, and the black, square-topped Martin 12-string that sang like chimes at midnight. That one he had bought with the check from his first big magazine sale. Nestled into a shelf on the book-crowded wall opposite sat the sweet-faced mandolin his fingers were almost too big to play. And near the window, where daylight would catch the bright-work, the Irish harp he had named Moytura.

Regretfully, Ben paused by the harp for a moment to touch the interlaced Viking dragons carved into the pillar, inlaid with gold and bronze and copper. She was the most beautiful thing he owned, and he hadn't set finger to string in months.

"I'm sorry," he said softly. "Soon, okay?"

A loose phrase of a song, a flutter of notes in the fog, skittered through his brain just out of reach, and vanished. Well, it would come back to him. Probably. Maybe.

In the meantime, there was also the proof copy to review, a virtual spindle full of phone calls, and an Inbox full of emails demanding his attention. He sighed. It was not where he wanted to be on a summer evening.

And well really, who would? The window showed a sky still filled with light. There would be enough to read by until almost eleven. The path up to Raven Tor was a familiar one and he wasn't yet so prosperous that he'd grown bored with country rambles. Today, he thought, his mind had been exhausted; he was too tired to work, too wakeful to sleep.

"No," he told himself sternly, and said it out loud to make it true. "Work to do."

In two weeks, when he actually needed a clever ima-gination, he'd be brainstorming with the "Now or Never" production team on the new schedule, and the book had to be ready for the tie-in sales before the first episode aired. Besides, he couldn't very well run off and leave Sparrow alone.

On the other hand, curiosity had begun to gnaw at him a little more with each weird encounter. Twilight, Aubrey King had said. And glowing or not, something was going on, and the guy was part of if not the actual source of it. Was it magic? The real thing? And what if it was? If Ben had just listened to him this afternoon, maybe— Okay, maybe his day would have been just a little less adventurous.

Don't go there, he thought, sliding behind the desk at last. Just don't.

The view out the window drew him, even as he opened the computer. There was a conversation waiting for him out there on the tor. In the middle of the night. On the moor, clear now but only a day away from a summer storm, boggy and liable to sudden mists. Irritably he slapped aside the whim and with a sigh, clicked the email icon, feeling virtuous in the electronic flicker of a glow he understood.

Then he stopped, suddenly mutinous. He only had two weeks of freedom left. What harm in stealing a couple of hours?

Sparrow'd be fine. Hell, Mellis would probably be pulling up the drive even before he left. Home any minute! Safe as houses, this house, in this tiny village. Ben was back in the nursery almost before the program had finished powering up.

In seconds he had selected the baby monitor app on the mobile phone, setting it to ring the sat phone if Sparrow cried out or anything else made a significant noise in the room. He placed it on the night stand next to the man-in-the-moon nightlight, and kissed his son's downy cheek.

Below in the office, he threw on a battered leather jacket, dropped the sat phone into a pocket, and headed out through the garden into the long, clear twilight. When Mellis got home and found the quiet house, she'd know where he was. She wouldn't even be surprised.

The sky over the moor was high, clear and still a pale, watery blue. An ancient tune in his head jostled and bumped around till it found a shape, and he was singing as he crossed the footbridge.

"Jog on, jog on the footpath way
And merrily hent the stile-a!
Your merry heart goes all the day
Your sad tires in a mile, ah!"

6
Raven Tor

The track wound around the hill, an easier grade and safer going than striking straight for the top, and Ben was in no hurry. At each turn a new vista laid out a crazy quilt patchwork of fields and hedges, green common land dotted with sheep. A bit higher and he could wave at his own patch of garden, see his lighted office window flashing back at him, unsuccessfully broadcasting guilt.

A couple of hundred yards later, nearing the top, the ancient spiral itself began with the first low stone, blue and grey, no higher than a milking stool. Simple, unprepossessing as it was, seeing it always made him breathe a little differently, as if the air had changed, or the world. The first layer of his melancholy dropped away. Beneath it, a curious sensation of possibility, of options. There was a door standing open somewhere just waiting for him to notice and walk through it.

Passing the stone, he reached out just grazing the rough surface with the pads of his fingers. Music, or the recollection of music, sounded in his head, as if he had touched the strings of his harp. Was this what that Aubrey guy had wanted him to see?

And speaking of Aubrey, where was he?

Was that laughter? He turned in place, looked up and down the path, frowning; right, left, no one. Another burst of giggles and silly whispers, like children playing hide and seek, but not very well. Little lights flickered on the edge of his vision: lightning bugs, maybe, or faeries?

Greetings!
Well met, fellow!

Hail!

Shakespeare? At least the hallucinations were getting more literate.

He took and held and let out a deep breath, pointedly ignoring the little voices, and the ripple of movement through the grasses, and sat down on the ancient stone.

Mice. It would be field mice.

The chill of the granite under his bum seeped cold into his bones as he gazed out across the valley, mundane now and ordinary. That open door felt both imminent and more lost than ever.

What now? He stood up and considered the options. It was mid-summer in England, which meant he had a good two hours of daylight, maybe more. The next of the standing stones was within sight, and the rest were beckoning. Why not—

Ben Harper*!*

He jumped a little at that, "Aubrey?"

Ben Harper!

"Now stop that!"

Nothing but more stupid laughter. All right. It wasn't that he didn't believe in the pixies, or piskies, as the locals called them. He wanted to believe in them. But, he had lived here a long time without seeing even one, aside from the souvenirs at the Frisky Piskie Tea Shoppe in the village.

By way of warning, he added: "I'm good at finding things, y'know. Sort of a gift. So if you're hiding, whatever you are, I'll find you. I always do."

Heading up hill again, he continued to the next slightly taller monolith, and the next, lightly touching each as they spiraled up the crown of the hill. And he continued addressing his invisible friends, smiling in spite of himself.

"I can find the keys people mislay, pull the missing contract out of a pile of someone else's bills, and talk a homeowner into getting rid of mementos of an old, dead relationship before it destroys the new one. Which means," he went on, touching the next cold stone. "That if there were pixies on the moor, I would see them."

The giggling stopped at once. A few consulting whispers

whistled after, then there was nothing but the wind soughing across the grasses. On the other hand, he had to consider that he'd never looked for them. And just because he'd never looked for them, didn't mean they weren't there.

The circle at the top of the spiral path was complete even if the stones were mostly broken. At its far edge hulked the unlikely tumble of boulders known as the Raven's Eye, which some said was the granite core of the hill with the top soil worn away by the constant wind (it was), and some said was a door into Faerie, and who could say? It was like a door. From two sides, slabs of granite had fallen or perhaps been laid by giants against and on top of each other, leaving a low squarish archway just big enough for a grown man and his son to sit under without banging their heads. Not so long ago, women had come up here to be passed through the arch when they wanted to get pregnant. On school holidays, teenagers came up here to get high.

Just now, Ben Harper sat on the ground in that archway and contemplated the view. He listened to the breeze hum through the sparse grasses and furze, imagining the men who had so long ago raised this spiral singing to the sky.

A slight grumble of earth and stone made him shiver. Louder, the sound coming from directly beneath him. To a California boy that's not especially alarming, except that earthquakes seldom happen in Britain. Dust and grit sifted down from the stones over his head, though, and that made him jump. The air shimmered around him as the rumble grew louder. And the earth shook more seriously now.

A California boy also knows when it's time to get out of the building. So he was on the other side of the circle, breathing hard, when the rumble became a sound like pounding hooves, like moor ponies teased by elf riders to a gallop, like the planet rifting open. And as he watched it, the space under the stone arch fell away with a hideous crack, and as the dust settled a ramp could be clearly seen sloping down into the hill.

Out of somewhere impossible, a stocky grey Dartmoor pony hauled itself up into the clear air and shook its mane, looking fat and well fed. Behind him came a pair of spotted ponies, white and black, and a bay with black mane and tail, nudging a bright-eyed foal. Six or seven more, the last two bearing riders with limbs so long and slender and with faces so wild there could be no mistaking them for human.

Ben stared and shook himself, knuckled his eyes to be sure of what he saw. The ponies cantered past him and came to a rest just outside the stone circle, as if it were the most ordinary thing in the world. In moments they were all calmly grazing and frisking amongst themselves, snorting their pleasure at being again under the familiar sky.

The two almond-eyed riders leapt to the ground, graceful as Minoan bull dancers, and with a few melodic words and a friendly smack or two encouraged the ponies to wander towards home. That done, their pointed faces alight with humor, they each threw Ben a mocking salute and strolled fading into the long twilight over the brow of the hill.

Still stunned, Ben blinked, looked again at the Raven's Eye, and there it stood, still and whole, no different from when he had first come here today, or last week, or ten years ago. The earth was solid, the ponies—who could not have run through that opening, no taller than a seated man—wandered calmly grazing as if they had always been there, which they must have been.

He sat down shaking just slightly and wished he hadn't left the house. Had he fallen asleep? Then he smiled a little, feeling foolish. Of course. In the Devon twilight, anyone might mistake ponies grazing on the far side of a stone circle for ponies who came out of nowhere with elven riders and who knows what else.

"Merlin, too, maybe," he grumbled.

"Not Merlin," said an old man's dry voice nearby.

For the second time today Ben was startled to find himself in company when he'd thought himself quite alone. If it was that Aubrey guy, well, it was about time. He turned to find the speaker staring at him with a pleasant grin.

"And not your pointy-eared friend, either. Just me."

"And who are you?"

The man was tall but sturdily built, broad shoulders like

a fighter, and looked as if he had seen a battle or two. Army? The military installations were nowhere near this part of Devon, and the tor was in no one's jurisdiction but the national park system.

"Nor army neither, son, at least not lately."

He was dressed in colorless old jeans, plaid shirt and a long top coat, with a slouch hat pulled low over one eye. His hair in a long, iron grey braid was slung over one shoulder, and he leaned slightly on a walking staff almost as tall as himself. The biggest raven Ben had ever seen fell silently out of somewhere and perched on the old man's shoulder.

"Ah!" cried the bird, cocking his head in Ben's direction. "Wake up!"

Then it sailed off to sharpen his beak on the lintel stone of the Eye.

"What?" Ben took a step back, then recovered. Right, he thought. Like parrots, ravens could be taught to echo human speech, but, "Hey, I know that bird. It…"

The thought trailed away, pointless.

An odd feeling rolled over him as it had earlier of a door standing open and leading… where? It was a little like being stoned, a little like a headache, and a little like the suspended moment when the conductor's baton goes up, just before the orchestra begins, when the whole world catches its breath. Mostly it felt like the weirdness was just never going to end.

He tried to meet the old fellow's bright grey eye, but his gaze kept slipping away to the black bird, grinning at him. "Do I know you?"

"A little, I think." It was the oddest accent. Dutch, maybe?

Well, he wasn't giving in to this. Vibrating with annoyance at a full day of totally psychotic everything, Ben said. "Look, mate. I don't want to be rude. No, that's a lie. See ya."

And he started to turn, but the firm, friendly weight of a hand on his shoulder changed his mind.

"Would you believe me if I told you?"

Something Scandinavian, maybe? In any case, the hand was removed.

"Told me what? Your name? Sure. Why wouldn't I?"

The man's chuckle was almost a growl.

"They used to call me Wotan in this part of the world. Or Woden. Most people have forgot that. Odin's good, too."

"Bloody hell!"

Spooky fog, disembodied voices, elves driving ponies up from the bowels of the earth, and now a forgotten Norse god. Was he having some kind of psychotic break?

Whatever it was, he was running out of synonyms for bizarre.

"Come on, son!" said Odin. "Can't you see it's me? Walking staff? Big hat?" He lifted the edge of the brim to reveal his face. "One eye? Even Gandalf didn't have that!"

Ben turned back, crossed his arms and just stared, tight-lipped.

"Son, you know perfectly well you just saw Molly Downing's ponies brought home from grazing beyond the fields you know. And you know what you saw this afternoon, and what happened after. Herself, she didn't take to you at all, so the Raven boy says."

When Ben still said nothing, the old man shrugged, giving a nod toward the rocky gateway. Where the black bird had been, a cocky teenager in black jeans and t-shirt sat dangling long legs over the edge of the lintel stone. He flung a wing of sooty hair back from his face, bent his mouth in a thin smile, and flipped a two-fingered salute.

"Nice manners, your people," Ben observed, realizing that he'd already known that the bird and the boy were the same. When he blinked, there was only a Raven. "Assuming I believe any of this."

"It would be best if you did, son. You've already accepted our help twice today."

The silence between them lengthened while the water-color sky in the east went a little more purple, the western edge a little less pink, till it looked like a new bruise. Finally, Ben stapled his determination to his sense of what was possible, and made up his mind. He walked away.

Two steps, and he turned back with a frustrated cry barely

escaping through whatever it was welling up in his chest. Started to speak and stopped, his throat tight with some emotion that had snuck up on him out of the Raven's call and the angle of light. He'd half believed in Faerie his whole life. Every time he touched his harp, he knew the truth of that magic, and yet he kept setting it aside.

All day he'd been fighting a creeping understanding, and something that tasted in his mind like nostalgia, but for places he'd never been and songs he'd never sung. It was too late now to be skeptical.

"Okay," he said, still rebellious. "Fine. Now, what. Do you want. From me?" The words snapped off, echoing slightly among the stones.

"A small thing, his lordship says, that only you can do," Odin said. "Saving the world, maybe."

If that was meant to shake Ben's composure, such as it was, it didn't work though he did laugh a sharp, hard bark.

"Right," he said, shaking his head. "It must be Faerie. I can't get a straight answer. I suppose he'll be wanting my soul, now, too."

"Your soul?" That tickled one-eyed Odin like a new riddle. "What would he do with it? Nay, if anything, he may help you find it again."

He could feel his face growing taut and warm. What was it Aubrey had said about talents he'd been ignoring? And here he was, teetering on the edge of a fairy tale of his very own, and,

"Stop!" Ben threw up his hands. "I believe you, I do. But it doesn't matter."

And turning it down.

His chest hurt, his eyes stung. It was too late. He was too old for this. "I can't. You'll have to tell him, I … You don't understand. I have no time."

And ignoring the tiny gasps of surprise and dismay, which he absolutely did not hear all around him, he turned for the absolute last time and started for home.

"I'm too old for this," Ben grumbled, scuffing pebbles out

of the path. At least the mocking laughter had stopped.

Yet the tightness in his chest had eased as soon as he walked away, or at least it had settled into its usual level at Yellow Alert. He could breathe. If his eyes still stung, that would be the dust in the wind. It made his nose twitch too, so what? He was doing the right thing, the responsible thing.

"Crap, I'm only thirty-five. I'm too young to be this old. But God dammit, fairy tales?"

He moved quickly, rejecting the call to adventure as just one more burden to avoid. Work to do. Calls to return. A book to finish. A relief, really, to leave the magic alone, no matter how real. The magic of television would do him well enough. The faster he walked away, the quicker it would be over.

The light was good enough and the path was easy, all downhill. Still, you have to pay attention on the moor, even when you know your way. Even when you're staring right at the ground as you go. So when the track under Ben's boots went soft as a Persian rug, accompanied very faintly by the sound of crystal chimes, he stopped. His head came up, tossing the hair out of his eyes, blinking at the change of light. He pushed the glasses up his nose and, violently, sneezed.

7
Diamond Hall, 1762

Disoriented, Ben stepped back, turned around and around again till he felt like a character in a cartoon. Too old for enchantment or not, he had unmistakably walked off the moor and straight into the dust-choked leather-bound library of what had once been a very fine house indeed—once upon a time, whenever that was.

As big as a church and crowded with shadows, it had clearly been shut up a long time, for the air was warm and thick with the must of old cigars and dried glue of old bindings, with old flowers and old furniture, and a fairly new Turkish rug of vast dimensions. Where a stray sunbeam fought past a pair of thick, velvet drapes on the only window, dust motes danced in sudden swirls, stirred by his entrance.

Open mouthed, eyes gradually accommodating the light, he ventured further into the room, more curious than afraid. On one long wall, locked behind beveled glass, seemingly endless shelves held books of the sort people used to buy to show they could afford books they didn't care to read. In between the cases, fly-specked and hazed with dust, and throughout the room in fact, stood rows of glass-faced display cases filled with curiosities: bones, fossils, bronze spear points, painted Persian jars. The kind of thing you usually find in a museum labeled *Provenance Unknown* because it's so rude to say "stolen."

Ben glanced into each one where the light allowed. Every now and then he stopped to wipe a clear space with the edge of a fist and stare, fascinated. God save the British Empire, he thought. And the antiquarian passion for picking up bits of junk from everywhere.

But everything, even the most precious, was smothering in dust, draped in cobwebs, or buckling under a rising damp. As a museum it was a disaster; as a home, it was unlivable. Ben the Organizer felt an atavistic urge to bring some kind of order to the chaos, to catalog, label, and Jesus, rescue it all! He had a crew that would eat this place up—respectfully, of course— with a spoon!

The room had clearly stood unattended a long time and yet he could hear, faintly, a harp being played lightly and well. Some kind of illumination, too, warmed the room though the source was uncertain. It was, Ben thought, more like a film set than a place people had ever used.

Film set. Of course.

A tight smile turned up the corners of his mouth. The saving-the-world thing was a joke, then. Okay, he got it. A distraction. Odin, pixies, mysterious meetings by moonlight— all an elaborate joke! Was this the great idea Peter had been trying to sell him? A Halloween special? Served him right for not listening. Somebody should be here, though, standing by. His production assistant, at least, hiding in a closet or secret passage or something.

"Elaine?" he asked tentatively, peering into shadowed corners for the telltale red dots that meant cameras were running. "Anybody?"

A young person cleared his throat just about two feet behind him, and the air stirred. Ben gasped, then gagged on a sirocco of dust.

"Are you all right, Ben Harper?" said the boy from the shop, who was the Raven boy at the tor. Only now he sported a snappy public school accent and totally looked like Gainsborough's Blue Boy. His long hair twisted to a crisp white collar in curls as intensely black as the shadows behind him. The Gainsborough effect, all blue satin knee britches and bows, was complete and gorgeous. No honestly, gorgeous. And he was, yes, glowing just slightly.

The boy bowed like a *maître d'* and said "Pray be seated, sir. Let me fetch you something to drink." And by fetch the boy meant serve from the pitcher and tall glass that appeared on a silver tray in his hands. And ice. "Americans always want ice," Blue Boy added, setting the tray down on an inlaid table.

Wide-eyed, Ben stumbled back and collapsed into a tall wing chair, and sneezed when still more dust exploded from the upholstery.

"What are you, Doctor Who?" he asked, and stared at the drink in his hand. He looked up doubtfully.

"You may call me Raven, sir," said Raven.

Something tiny and foolish giggled under the chair. Oh good, at least that hadn't changed.

"Thought, or Memory?" Ben said, playing along for the moment.

"Sir?"

"Odin's ravens. Which one are you?"

The pointed chin lifted and Raven indulged in a lofty smile. "I see what you mean, sir. Neither one, sir. Or possibly both." In another minute he would be Jeeves. "My lord thought you would find me easier to talk to than the All Father, who is inclined to mysteries. There is much to talk about that must be said plain and orderly."

"I like orderly. I'm good with plain, too. Can I ask a question?"

"Of course, sir."

"Who's paying for all this?" He really, really needed it to be a joke.

"Sir?"

"Lights, camera, action?" Ben suggested, looking about the room significantly. "It's okay, I can dig it. This place definitely needs my help. Where do we start?"

The kid ignored the question, politely, waiting for the correct cue. The slightly tilted blue eyes framed in sable lashes reminded Ben of someone. Aubrey?

"Okay, but y'know, this kind of total immersion improv is harder than it looks. I never say no to ..."

He used to never say no to the offer, Ben thought, chagrined even though that experience was long ago. If this was for the show, he was being a poor sport. If this was Faerie, as Odin had suggested, he was being a bad guest.

So he gestured with the iced glass in his hand. "If we're in Faerie, or Asgard, the Summer Lands, whatever it is, is it okay for me to drink this, or will I be bound for a certain term to serve somebody?"

Betraying just a touch of surprise and even a little annoyance, Raven said, "This house is in the past, sir, not in Faerie, as such. You may eat or drink anything without compulsion or consequence."

Ben thought about this a moment, then put the drink to his lips, and almost choked in surprise. Lemonade! Proper American lemonade just the way he liked it: sweet enough but not too sweet, no fizz. Elaine, his production assistant, would know that. She had to be here somewhere. "It wants a touch of Jameson's, yeah?"

Raven nodded slightly, and Ben tasted again. Oh my, there it was, sharp and strong. How had he missed that before? Power of suggestion? Another sip or two wouldn't hurt, just to be sure. Yeah, still there.

"All right," he went on. "And what is this place?"

The boy frowned in the most well-bred way, as if slightly disappointed. "I was told you see things, sir."

The American waited, and the boy took a breath.

"Very well. It is 1762. The house is Diamond Hall. In a way, sir, it is your inheritance."

Ben knocked back the rest of the lemonade, appreciating the dark strength of the whisky, and forgetting that tea had been half a sandwich and a beer an hour ago—maybe longer. Or that the glass had refilled on its own while he was talking. He set it down with a click on the little table that appeared when he needed it, or had always been there. Must have been.

Jumpy, he thought he might be better on his feet, where the smell of dust and mildew wasn't so strong. "See things? I'll tell you what I don't see, kid. I don't see my team, I don't see a camera, and I don't see the point!" He hollered down the room. "Cut!"

The special effects—pixies, music, laughter—all halted, shocked into silence as the echoes faded. The kid waited opposite, his face composed, letting the silence lengthen.

"Hmm," Ben said at last, and gulped, his temper checked as quickly as it had blossomed. "All right, then. Let's see." And now he was looking, really looking. Coming up dusty but empty, he pursed his lips and thrust his hands into his pockets.

"So." He drew the syllable out slowly, still scanning the room, still nothing. "Okay. No cameras, then."

He met the strange eyes of the Raven boy, and felt that sensation again: an open door, a waiting carriage, an offer.

"Magic?"

Raven nodded, looking less deferential and just a bit dangerous, more like the fae lord he probably was.

"And Aubrey is ..."

"The Lord Oberon, sir."

"The king of ..."

"Faerie, yes, sir."

And there was the tight chest again, and the longing. He cleared his throat, feeling awkward and uncomfortable. A second offer? It had been hard enough to walk away once.

Finally, he shook his head. "Nope, can't do it. I need to go home. Please tell His Majesty that whatever he needs, I can't help."

"Best you tell him yourself, sir."

And on that note, the boy bowed with grace and walked away in his buckled shoes, fading to nothing before he got to the double doors at the far end of the room.

8
Lemonade

"Hmph," Ben snorted, reaching idly for the frosty glass. If this was really 1762—and there was no point in arguing about that anymore—he was stuck here until they sent him home. All he could do now was stare into the displays, and twitch over the deep level of clutter and loss.

Spindly-fingered pixies in their nut brown caps and weedy clothes peered tentatively from behind curtained paintings and out from under display cases.

Something popped suddenly into the room, and two twiggy creatures with enormous tufted ears expanded like balloons and bounced from ceiling to floor, zoomed round the walls and disappeared with a double pop.

A creature with hummingbird wings and a pointed face like two twigs from a holly bush hovered in front of Ben's nose till he batted it lightly away.

Finally, a warm voice, already familiar, and a rush of scented air like violets made him look up.

"If you see anything labeled EAT ME, DRINK ME, or SMOKE ME, be sure to leave it well alone."

As expected, the equally gorgeous but somewhat more believable Aubrey had entered the room, this time dressed for the office, if by office you meant the executive cabin of a very private executive jet. The silk suit, subtly green, was Italian tailoring; the boots looked expensively comfortable.

He came forward smiling and took Ben's hand, as graciously businesslike as his costume.

"Sorry for keeping you. I have something I want you to

look at," said the king of Faerie, as if picking up the conversation from where they had left off, and perhaps he was. "Then we'll see whether you can do what I ask." A sideways glace. "And if you have the time."

Ben grinned nervously, which surprised him. He'd never had a nervous professional moment, not even when he'd met the Prince of Wales. This wasn't the same. "Of course. Sir. But—" The king of Faerie paused, raising a curious eyebrow. "Forgive me, sir, but what do I call you?"

A genial smile creased the aristocratic features. "When used with courtesy, any name will do. I already know my titles. Perhaps Aubrey would be best."

"Cool. Okay. I'm honored, sir. Really." He really was, if still tentative.

"To business then, shall we?" Opening a painted wooden cabinet, Aubrey carefully withdrew a wide loop of carved and braided gold. A bracelet of some kind, or an ancient torque; larger than one, smaller than the other. "The beginning and end of the task is this."

As he reached for it, Ben thought he saw, or maybe heard—

The hair on his arms lifted, gooseflesh rippling under the sleeves of shirt and jacket. He half expected a charge of electricity to snap across the gap, and quickly withdrew his fingers. Feeling foolish under the king's patient gaze, he simply took it.

The body was a twist or plait like a knotted rope; the ends, two red-gold finials, snarling dragon heads scrolled, engraved and carved like the ones on his harp. No question, a kind of energy, a pulse almost, tingled where the cool gold rolled through the palm of his hand. Foolish perhaps, but the oddest impulse came over him to raise the thing to his ear like a sea shell and listen for the breathing tide. No, it was more than that. If he just focused his attention, he thought, he would hear a voice singing or maybe chanting the story of its creation.

There! There it was! A kind of sonorous rumble in words just beyond the edge of his understanding, like a sleepy grandfather reeling out a story in the next room, or in another time. Suddenly it stammered, skipped a beat, like a hiccup or an old LP skipping a track. If he could just step through that door and listen to it.

Aubrey cleared his throat.

With a jump, Ben swallowed as a quick shudder ran through him and the story slipped away.

"Ah, hmm," he said. Get it together, Ben. "Viking, yes? Wow."

The other man smiled slightly though what he meant by it was hard to judge. "Seventh century, or at least it came into your world in the 7th century."

"Is it, you know," Ben asked uneasily. "Enchanted? Or anything?"

"Do you mean, is it cursed?" The smile broadened as the American thrust it back at him, a touch too quickly. "I realize you've been brought up to believe in nothing, but I trust you'd be able to tell if the old perils were still active."

"How would I know that?" But he did know. Something like but not quite a vibration hovered at the outer edge of his consciousness as if a magic had been there but was gone, like a deep spell bound onto faerie gold, now loose and faded. Yes, it was safe, which certainty did little to quell a quick surge of panic. Maybe he should have paid closer attention to the lemonade.

Aubrey set the ring down and went on gently. "You sensed something before you touched it. Even more, when I put it in your hand. That's part of your gift, you see. Oh, not the one for tidying up other people's messes, although that is excellent; I have no idea where that comes from. No, the other one, that lets you hear the little ones on the moor—or, behind the sofa."

Something hedgehog-like near Ben's foot looked up, blinked and, curling into a ball, allowed the king's boot to tap it lightly away.

"It lets you see what you called a 'glow' that marks me walking in your world." One or two piskies bounced into the room like helium balloons, and out the other side. "To hear the bells of Elfland is a rare gift and fair. One that until lately you've hardly used and, for the most part, denied."

"But that's— I mean, it's—"

He stalled with no idea what he meant to say. Something had appeared, then just as quickly vanished, and the words just wandered off. Sick with weirdness, he sat down hard and bent over his knees.

It wasn't possible. None of this was possible. For a whole day, Faerie had conspired to demonstrate to practical, organized, reality-show host Ben Harper that what had been set aside with other childish things was—

Hitching the sharp creases of his trousers, his grace crouched as he might in front of a child, wrists loosely draped over his knees, and met Ben's dazed expression.

"It's magic, Ben Harper. Just magic. Wonderful, not impossible."

Ben sat up a little, clasping his hands. He tried to speak, and when the words caught in his throat, imagined for a shaky moment that something was preventing him.

"Are you reading my mind?" he croaked.

Aubrey rose sharply, the picture of slighted pride.

"Of course not. Do you think I've never had this conversation before?" Then quickly as it flared, the irritation died. He tipped the amber contents of a crystal flask into a fresh glass and handed it across, saying, "Sip this, human child, and listen."

Numb, Ben had no idea what it was he touched to his lips. Like amber dipped in honey scented with roses and sandalwood, a warmth slid through his veins like fiddle music on a sunny day; he could almost hum the tune.

"Better now? My metheglin often has that effect. Very well," Aubrey said, pacing a little as he talked. Where he stepped, Ben noted in the finicky corner of his mind, the dust never flew. "Your particular gifts are three: of Clear Sight, of True Direction, and of Music."

"Three. Of course," said Ben agreeably, and stood up just to see if he could. To his surprise, his mind steadied as well as his legs, and his vision cleared. Though the lighting hadn't changed, everything was sharper, clearer, as if he were seeing it all for the first time. His emotional world felt steady and reasonable, too. Well, enough. He sat again.

A pair of gremlins, or whatever they were, were doing back flips at the top of the room, weightless as astronauts. Ben could hear them giggling whenever they bounced and spun off the baroque ceiling ornaments.

"I could do without these interruptions, if you all don't mind," his Grace remarked pointedly. A badminton racquet appeared in his hand; he stepped onto a chair, and batted each one out, or rather through, the velvet draped window. From the lawns below came the shrieks of children's laughter.

Stepping down and seating himself, the elf king crossed his legs and threaded his hands. Ben, a little giddier than he knew, thought the fae lord looked like an expensive shrink, sitting there all handsome and wise, and all. Mellis would think he looked like Rupert Everett with long hair.

"Such gifts can be a mixed blessing, that's true."

"Uhm."

"Just listen. The first of your gifts we have already discussed. For the second: Have you ever gotten lost on the moor? Have you ever gotten lost at all? No," he said when Ben looked merely thoughtful. "Even this afternoon, bewitched though you were, your gift found you. Thirdly, you are a musician of more than ordinary skill—more skill than you appreciate. The first two talents will set you on the path, the last will permit you to walk it. Still with me?"

Ben nodded, flattered, and pushed up his glasses. "Sure."

"The task is easy, but only you can perform it. The rewards— Well the rewards will be exceptional."

"Odin said you'd help me get my soul back," Ben said. Humor always helped.

Aubrey only nodded, re-crossing his long legs. "I will be in your debt. And Faerie keeps sharp accounts, I assure you."

With a gesture, he called the dragon ring into his hand from a side table cluttered with painted miniatures in ugly frames, a music box, and a chunk of pink-veined marble labeled "Temple of Zeus, Patmos".

"This arm ring is missing from its place in the ninth century. It has been lost for generations beyond the questing of many men. I found it here, in this house."

"I don't see…"

"Listen. It is here now, but there is one place and time where it must be, and for some reason is not. That must be remedied."

Ben looked doubtful but forbore, for a change, to speak. That smart mouth had gotten him into more trouble than it ever got him out of, and likely would again. Listening, yeah, okay.

"Where I need you to go," said Aubrey, "is the war court of King Alfred the Great. What I ask you to do is return to him this token, which he has given his word to deliver. And where that court and that king are, it is Christmas in the year of grace eight hundred and seventy-six."

More relaxed than he meant to be, Ben let himself snort just a little. He was dealing with the weirdness rather well, he thought.

"If you can send me, why not just go yourself? Sounds like a party."

"I am forbidden from meddling in human history, human child, even to keep it in its proper place. Only mortals can do that."

Ben Harper sat back in the chair, suppressing a laugh. Meddling was certainly a human trait. "Go on."

"I need you to return this to Alfred, king of Wessex and incidentally to his mortal foe, Guthrum, who leads the largest pack of sword Danes now threatening his kingdom. It is the only thing on which Guthrum will swear his treaty oath. Yes, that means I need you to travel in time."

"But—" Ben stared at the ring, the doubts of a lifetime fighting to return. "It's already happened."

Aubrey had anticipated this and waved away the objection. "Time is a mobius strip, Ben. Try not to let it give you headaches."

"Mobius strip. Okay, but," he tried again, settling on a purely mundane objection. "Won't they just go to war again in the spring, anyway?"

"Of course they will! The question you should ask is why

is Alfred called 'The Great'? This treaty, even though it fails as all treaties fail, is a pivot point, a marker around which other events turn. The success of this day, however brief, gives him the heart to begin—just begin, mind you—to set events in motion that will transform this island. Your legal codes, the tradition of literacy, even the survival of your language owe their existence to him. Light and shadow, what do they teach in the schools these days?" he muttered, flinging himself from the chair.

The frosty gin-and-tonic that appeared in the royal hand just as quickly disappeared down the royal throat leaving behind only a broken wedge of lime, then just the glass, then nothing at all. "It's more complicated than that, of course."

He turned the ring over in his graceful hands as if looking into time, which perhaps he was. As he held it up, the twisted gold flared, its light undimmed by the centuries.

"This ring is a token Guthrum will recognize, or his lore master will. He demanded it because he believes it cannot be produced, and if it is not, he will storm off into red war with every appearance of being mortally offended, even while he's laughing his head off." Then more grimly, Aubrey added: "Ben, it has to be done. The treaty must be made. The ring must be there."

"But," said Ben. Even with a clearer head, he felt as if he was asking all the wrong questions. "Why does it matter to you? Your realm doesn't depend on human history."

"Doesn't it? Well, you know best."

With a broad gesture, the heavy drapes flew aside. The westering sun flooded the room, and now when light struck the ring, need fires burned in the jeweled dragon eyes. The king of Faerie turned it in his fingers, sending flames shooting into the shadows, breaking rainbows through the display cases and across all the dusty treasures. But though Ben nearly gasped in wonder, Aubrey wasn't happy.

"Come over here, if you please, Ben," he said with traces of a frown. "There's more here than I remember."

Blinking, Ben joined the king, patting his jeans and jacket until he remembered his glasses were on his face. The tiny folk were laughing at him, but he was starting to enjoy it.

"What is it, sir?"

"Runes."

"Really? Wow. Runes on a piece of Norse jewelry, fancy that." Then he peered obediently at the thing, and said, "Sorry. Is it something special?"

"Look here, along this strand inside, do you see? Here it says *the child made me*."

Ben took the ring, accepting the vibration or chanting or whatever without being drawn into it. A smooth space in the inside of the curve was marked with angular letters deeply incised.

"Sure, okay. I see," he said, handing it back. "Wasn't that there before?"

"I'm not sure."

Now it was Ben's turn to register surprise. "I thought this was an old familiar piece?"

"It is. Or rather," said Aubrey, clearly puzzled. "It was. I wonder... Never mind. I have told you everything. Will you accept my commission?"

Ben froze, frowning. How could he answer? His life was not his own. The whole proposition was impossible, whether he believed it all or not. He'd already turned it down once, and meant it.

"What if... "

"If Alfred fails," the king said testily, "England will remain a tribally splintered island, a colony of Viking kings, famous only for bad cooks and second rate mercenaries. No Robin Hood. No Agincourt. No Shakespeare. No Churchill. Look!"

He flung an angry gesture across the blazing window. Like silent newsreels, images splashed across each mullioned pane describing a land bereft of grace and vital pursuits. In dizzying succession, Ben saw a country that had never faced down an Armada, spearheaded a religious revolution, or given the world its greatest plays. No colonies in the New World, no empire, for good or ill.

And then, two figures that might have been Ben Harper and Mellis Powell crossed paths in the dreary streets of some anonymous city without even a glance. Ben's eyes narrowed at the impossibility of that. Head down, he turned away, cold reason kicking in at last. He could feel his consciousness change gears as the processing, however belatedly, began.

"Ben?"

"Give me a minute!" he returned, holding up one hand. "Wait. Sir."

No longer confused or awkward, gears were turning. Everything he'd seen and everything he'd heard over the whole long day tumbled through his mind, sorting and resorting into boxes and folders and racks of ideas, cross-referencing, footnoting, discarding duplication, fears, and arrant nonsense until from two disparate niches, one phrase surfaced, terrible in its music.

"The Bells of Elfland." He looked up, meeting Aubrey's stormy eyes. "That's what she said to Sparrow, that woman, Lady…" Then he squared his shoulders, coming on guard as he made the connection at last. "Titania."

Aubrey nodded grimly. "My loving queen, yes."

"She sent the fog. And the voice."

"And the spell, yes," said the king. "I did tell you to go straight home."

"You knew she was in the village." Ben's jaw tightened. "The voice said, 'my lady wants a wee mortal to be her singing boy.'"

"I can keep him safe."

"She threatened my son!"

"By the time you're back, she'll have forgotten. She gets these—" Aubrey waved it all aside. "Enthusiasms. They pass with the weather."

"Do they? Because she seemed pretty enthusiastic this afternoon."

"Ben Harper," said Aubrey sharply. "When I gave you fair warning, you ignored it. My Raven pulled you out the first time, and had your back the second. If you had done as I asked, none of it would have happened. She would not have found him there."

"Bullshit!" Ben said tightly. Then a fist slammed to the

table. "You mean if I had gone to my room like a good boy, and hidden away, the scary lady would have left us alone—this time. Damn it, Aubrey, even Sparrow could tell what she was!"

"Enough!"

Nothing could have prepared him for the transition as the avuncular academic became swiftly and completely a king alive with anger, weary of being continually crossed. But Ben, too, had come into his strength, and he was just as bloody-minded.

"Get bored do you, you immortals?" he snarled. "Is this how you keep yourselves entertained? Manipulating time and human lives?"

"What!"

"This is just some perverse, bloody little game you play with your wife?"

The fire in the king's glance should have told him he had gone too far.

"Game!" Every pane of glass, every artifact, the plaster in the ceilings vibrated with the sound. "You think the future of your world is a game?" Shimmering with power, the air crackled with fury that lifted strands of the shining hair like a sudden storm.

Ben Harper's temper had shattered beyond self-preservation.

"The past can take care of itself, milord, but nothing—you understand? Nothing on this earth would keep me from my wife. No time, no history, no tide of fortune, and no game of yours will touch my son!"

As if he had planned it, a chorus of trumpets suddenly blared; somewhere cymbals crashed; cannon exploded. And the bells of all the churches of Moscow rang through the treasure room in the final bars of the "1812 Overture".

That was his ring tone.

Why was his phone ringing?

The air swirled, summer hobs dived for cover, and someone really should answer that phone! He shouted over the crash of his own anger, over the roaring in his ears.

"And as for your trashy props?" He grabbed up the chunk of pink-veined marble from the temple of Zeus and raised it over his head.

"Ben, no!"

With a sobbing oath, Ben slammed the stone down once, twice across the golden ring. Both finials snapped away, and three pieces spiraled up like pinwheels and vanished into the shimmering air.

Nearly frantic, Ben Harper snatched the persistent phone out of his jacket pocket and flipped it open, but before he could shout into it, he had disappeared.

In a leafy corner of his kingdom, the most noble Oberon, three thousand years crowned king of Faerie, who is also urbane and scholarly Aubrey King with a sea-dark sapphire glinting in his ear, collapses with a sigh into his chair of carven narwhal ivory and buries his face in his hands. In a moment, he sits up, and with his fingers combs the hair back from his narrow face.

With a thought he exchanges the stupid, bloody, god-forgot business clothes for raiment rich and fine. He calls for his musicians, and a long, thin clay pipe, and a serious drink. He allows some pretty dryads to fuss over him for a while.

"Oh well," he says at last. "What's life without a little melodrama?"

After a while, he finds a Miami supper club in 1965 where a two-toned Ricky Ricardo jacket and a pencil thin mustache makes him the object of every woman's sighs long into the night. It is good to be king. Complicated, but good.

9
Diamond Cottage

Ben landed face first at but not quite on the shallow-set flagstones of his doorstep. Perhaps there was some disconnect in the orientation of physical space in the past, or in Faerie, or in dreams, or perhaps he had simply stumbled down from the tor in a deeper than usual fog. Hard to say. It was dark.

"Ben? Ben, where are you?" Someone was shouting at him from very far away.

One eye opened. Hmm. Still dark.

Okay, the flower bed under his cheek was his—probably. Drunk? He considered the possibility, which turned out to be great. But no, not drunk, exactly, though the ocean was roaring through his head like a freight train. Or was it the other way around?

Both hands were outstretched in front of him as if he had tried to catch himself before hitting the ground, and sort of failed. One hand still clutched his mobile phone, which may or may not have been the source of the shouting.

"Ben, are you all right!"

Ah, yes. Yes, it was.

"Uhm, Mellis?" That couldn't possibly be his voice!

"Ben?" Getting louder now, and a bit clearer.

If Mellis was talking to him, Sparrow must be all right. Hey, if Mellis was talking to him, it meant the world hadn't ended, his life hadn't changed, and that Aubrey guy was so full of shit! Somehow he dragged the phone to his ear.

"Uh, honey?"

"Ben Harper, where are you? And good lord, Ben, what are you doing on the ground!"

Disorienting him further, if that were possible, the voice of alarm still buzzed through the phone while it shattered the air, uhm, mainly above him. A pair of familiar hand-painted sneakers took up a position just in front of his gravel-scraped nose, attached to two of the shapeliest ankles it had ever been his pleasure to know.

With a grunt and several well-placed groans, Ben dragged himself into a somewhat girly pushup, then rocked back onto his knees and beamed up at the love of his life, who was pointedly not beaming back.

"Hi, honey, I'm home."

Gently but with a certain constrained ferocity behind it, she reached down one forefinger and pushed his glasses back up his nose.

"So you are," she said in her adorable accent, refined but touched with the local Devon brush. "And for a limited time only, you are welcome to come within and regale me with the tale of how you got here at this hour and in this state."

"Thank you," Ben said meekly, and completed the operation that involved getting up. She was gone by the time he'd gained his feet.

There was not much point in merely dusting himself off. He did give his jeans a desultory pat as he went round to the mudroom, stumbling a bit under a curiously starlit sky. Better to at least clean up a bit, and dab a cloth at the scrapes on his chin before coming in through the kitchen.

Scowling into the dark, he missed the Raven watching him from the rafters—again.

It did occur to Ben, washing up, that he might have behaved rather badly back there, wherever there was. How often is a man given one chance to be a hero, never mind two? How often, he thought with some belated wonder, does Faerie ask for help? And instead of appreciating the grace and favor, he'd gone a little mad. He could have just said no, as he had to Odin, and walked away.

Sparrow, though, and the faerie queen's enmity. That had torn it. Powerful immortals who shouldn't even exist threatened his family. So yes, he'd gotten a little hysterical, a little insulting, and Aubrey—*Oberon!*—had flung him out on his ass. Well, the guy wasn't a parent, was he? How could he possibly understand?

Ben winced, hearing the clank of a cliché he despised, even as it rolled through his thought. As punishment, he flung a last double handful of cold, oh very cold water over his face before reaching for a towel.

Oberon, for godssake! Time travel, magic rings! The king of bloody Faerie! There was scope, a breadth of vision no mortal mind could— Even clichés failed him. Oberon's acquaintance with humanity must be long and deep, and his understanding profound. And Ben Harper, who for his whole life rather imagined he might have a hero in him, had lost his cool. First challenge in the epic journey, he thought with deep chagrin, had been an epic fail.

Well, he was out of it now. Aubrey could find another hero. A proper hero. Titania's whim would pass. His family would be safe. The only immediate problem now was how to account for himself to Mellis when the truth was patently crazy.

He leaned in the doorway between kitchen and front parlor, gathering his thoughts while drying his hands. His lady, like Goldberry among the lilies in flowing green trousers and tunic, was sitting with her feet tucked up in the wing chair on one side of the empty fireplace. The distaff side, as they say, though the spinning wheel in that corner now only commemorated a moment of whimsy, the distaff gathering dust. Her music and the playing, writing, and teaching of it, had won out in the end. Ben's had somehow lost.

He set that thought aside, yet again.

A sturdy teapot and cups waited on the coffee table, fragrant and steaming, but he ignored it, watching her. A bulbous glass of red wine cast a garnet shadow across the room as she flipped through the score for some student project. The shadow bobbed gently as she stopped on one page and hummed a little of the soprano line, conducting with the wine glass in her hand. Stopped and scribbled a note. Turned the page. He could tell she frowned even with her golden head bent over the work.

Barely kissing 35, Mellis Powell's golden hair, cropped short and tousled like a Botticelli angel's, had begun to show a silver thread or two, but she fought back with a good will. Village women muttered darkly about "Hollywood" and "dye job" but Mellis, whose family had lived here as long as any of theirs, just laughed. She'd earned those grey hairs, she said, from every student who had ever mangled a simple chord progression. She'd also earned the right to please herself.

He watched her, barely breathing, and knew he'd made the right decision, if not the exciting one. To lose her or his son in some over-wrought faerie melodrama— well, no. Just no. They'd find someone else to save the world.

In a moment, he knew, she'd jump up and carry the score over to the piano. Her fingers would arch over the keys and come down, following the indicated dynamics, and never mind the hour. Sparrow had from the womb spent his whole life with guitar, bodhran, zither, even a didgeridoo vibrating through the house at all hours, so no mere piano could wake him.

In fact, Ben thought, it might be good to pop upstairs now and see how the little fellow was doing. He'd just take a minute and do that, would Ben. Yes, just tip-toe quietly through the hall and up the—

"Dominic's fine, sweetheart," said Mellis, without looking up.

He jumped, startled without really being surprised. Then she added, "Nancy said you sounded a bit strange when you called, and hopes next time you'll give her a bit more notice."

"Oh, ah, well good, I thought I'd just—What?" He hadn't called the babysitter. Should have, of course. Which probably meant someone else had. And Faerie kept sharp accounts.

"I looked in on Dominic when I came home." Only his mother and the school nurse called Sparrow by his legal name. "And about an hour ago. And again before I rang you. Again."

Mellis turned in the chair, finally, and folded the music away. With deliberate care, she removed her reading glasses and placed them with the score on the end table. When she looked up, she was smiling. "Are you going to tell me about your adventures? There's tea, and I do love a good story."

Ben straightened where he was and sighed. This sort of mind reading he was used to and it didn't bother him at all.

"Lady Mellisande," he said with a slight but courtly bow, and kissed her hands. "I thank you."

"And is his lordship at all drunken?"

He thought about the question, doing a quick inventory of aches and pains as he poured tea and spooned sugar. "Y'know? I don't think I am!"

The surprising golden brown eyes twinkled when he took the chair opposite hers, somewhat gingerly. No way she could miss that.

"Excellent. I called at the Star on my way home, by the way. They hadn't seen you since this afternoon."

"Oh, well, no. I haven't been there, since… what time is it?"

"Almost eleven."

He winced, and swore a little. How could it possibly have been that long?

"Dinah and Tom came by and left a note while you were out. They wanted a harp and someone to play it tonight in Exeter, but you weren't here."

"Damn! Why didn't they call?"

"They did. You didn't answer. And then there was Peter."

"*Meh*, I'll call him in the morning." The tea, sweet in his mouth, tasted strong, bracing, and utterly ordinary. "I needed to think. I went up on the tor to think. Music would have been better."

The look she bent on him was thoughtful and grave. "I rather think music is what you've been needing, love."

"Really?"

"Yes, really. But that's not the point right now. Go on. Mr Day said you were talking to some 'foreigner' this afternoon. Dressed like a Londoner, he said. Maybe a movie star, or one of those big directors. Are you thinking of becoming a movie star, Ben?"

"Ah, well yes." Her eyes went wide. "I mean, no! That is,

yes, I met a guy, no on the movie star." His hands were shaking. Why were his hands shaking? Best to put the mug down. "Why? Was I acting funny?"

"Not that he said. Of course, he might not have wanted to worry me, what with you being loony and all. Sad enough me not being married to a proper Dartmoor man."

Even her most tolerant smile lit up a room, and her teasing one— Ben basked in it, grinning back.

"I suppose you want to know how I got down from the tor in the dark and ended up in a face plant on the doorstep without getting pixie-led around the moor or run over by Teddy Blackhurst on his motor bike."

She nodded and picked up her wine. "As long as it's funny."

That was their motto. No matter what the trouble, if you could find the funny, it would be all right. But where was the funny in this? She'd be justified in thinking he was drunk out of his mind or just plain crazy. And really, wasn't he?

"Well," he said, his voice a little higher than normal. "I don't know how funny. Okay, let's see." It would be useful to go through the events, in order, for his own sake. "I picked up Sparrow."

"After talking to the movie star."

"Hey, he bought me a beer. I had to be polite." The giggle was not a good touch. "Ah, yeah."

"Who was it, then?"

Oh no, no, no, not yet. Broad outline first. "Aubrey something. Good looking, I guess. Kind of a Rupert Everett type, with an earring."

"Rupert Everett! And you didn't call me?" She was laughing. Good sign.

"Oh yeah, but with long hair. Not your type at all." No need to go into that just yet. "Anyway, went and got Sparrow. Stopped in the village and, *erm*, picked up the mail." The Titania incident could certainly wait. And the mist. "Sparrow says he wants to be a wizard when he grows up, by the way."

"That's nice, dear."

"And a whole nother conversation, I agree. Anyway, tea, Legos, bath, bed, done!"

A stern no-nonsense look settled around her mouth. The one her students hated, especially when a project was late and the excuse was insufficient. "Done for Dominic, not for Daddy."

"Yeah, well, I went down to the office. I've got galleys to look at. A bunch of calls. And the stupidest proposal ever from Peter. Halloween special! No seriously, all singing, all dancing. Ya-da-da-ta-da-da! Ya-da-da-ta-da-da" He mimed the Warner Brothers dancing frog till she threw a book at him. He dropped his hands and looked somewhere else. "I ran away."

"You ran away." She already knew he was lying.

A moment ago, the funny had been in the palms of his hands, now it fled and nothing, no clever words, nothing was going to get it back. She watched his eyes roll up and away, calling on memory and deciding what to tell her.

Mellis leaned forward and poured more tea, the lights in her hair shining like faerie gold. As his stillness continued, she got up and fetched the Jameson's and a pair of glasses.

"Ben?" she said.

"You know, I may never drink lemonade again."

"What?"

"Mellis?" And he met her eyes at last with love and something like fear. "You know I love you."

"I love you too, Ben. Tell me what happened."

Maybe coming at it sideways would help.

"Okay, you've lived in this part of the world most of your life, right?"

"You know I have, except when we were at university." Her stern look was mutating into a worried frown.

"And when you were little, you believed in pixies or piskies or whatever, and faeries and marsh wiggles and all like that, right?"

"I suppose."

"There were fairies at the bottom of your garden?"

"Dartmoor was the bottom of our garden!"

"Exactly. I mean, he said I was brought up to believe in nothing. That's not true, exactly. I've never... The part about the music, of course, but, well, you have to be rational. I mean, Titania and Oberon, they're just characters in Shakespeare!"

"Of course," Mellis said quietly. "Around here, the names are completely different, and no one talks about them. Why do you think Teddy Blackhurst drives his motorbike so fast across the moor?" A sip of wine. A second thought. "Who said you believed in nothing?"

The black bird no longer watched from a branch outside the window. Instead a shadow, just one among so many the lamp light pushed away, lingered near the cold stone hearth, small and watchful.

Ben swallowed rather momentously, then blew the delivery.

"Oberon," he said, or mumbled, okay more of a whisper, sort of. She wasn't fooled.

Of course she didn't believe him. Who would? If a shadow could be said to show emotion, the one on the hearth registered wry disdain.

With an admirable economy of motion Mellis whisked away the liquor, laughing uneasily as she did so. "Oberon? I see. Is that the production company? Or... Oh, Ben, you did not go into Newton Abbot and get foolish with strangers, did you? You haven't invested in anything without talking to... Did you buy something?" No laughter, no reply. "Oh my god, what did you buy?"

Oh, if only it were so simple. Wouldn't it be easier to say he'd been drunk and stupid and bought the Tamar Bridge, instead of being drunk and stupid and called the King of Faerie a perverted, role-playing poser. Not to mention risking The World As We Know It.

"No," he said, retrieving the whisky. He knocked back a serious shot and winced. For the first time ever, the good stuff just didn't seem as good as it should.

Well, he's done me no favors there.

He stood up and set the glass down on the table that was always there whether he needed it or not, and went to her with open hands. A flicker of something by the fireplace caught his eye; trick of the light, nothing more.

"No, I didn't buy anything. I didn't even buy into anything, which may have been a mistake. Sweetheart, Oberon isn't a surname, and it isn't a company. It's a guy. A real guy. The Rupert Everett guy, Aubrey? He's Oberon."

"Oberon," she said flatly.

"Yeah."

"The king of the faeries."

"That's the guy. He proved it to me." As the color drained from her face, he placed a soft kiss on her cheek, and moved to the piano where he picked out three notes C-D-G, and held them till the tone died.

Mellis took and held a deep, thoughtful breath, but Ben wasn't watching her now.

He spun away from the piano and stopped to stare instead at her wavering reflection in the night-filled window. "Or he could be Odin. Or they might be the same thing, I'm not clear how this works."

His mind was racing, or it was filled with jello, he hardly knew which. The room was too small. A man couldn't pace properly. That's what was wrong with the World As We Know It! No pacing room! Yet somehow, he managed. He took the few steps back to Mellis, who was still staring. Back to the window, the piano, to Mellis again, bouncing off the distress in her eyes; he touched each marker like a talisman, like a man running bases, banging out words as if speed alone would make it all add up.

"He said his name was Aubrey, see, to start with, but there was this woman in the shop, she was Titania. And Sparrow was…"

"Sparrow!"

"It's okay, nothing, I took care of it. And there was this fog, see. But it was okay, because I don't get lost!"

"Ben," Mellis said sharply, and when he passed her, she reached out for him.

He touched her hand, grateful for any gesture, and kept moving, getting louder and more agitated with each halting round. He never noticed her edging towards the credenza and the telephone.

"Then there was this really old house, and it was— No, it used to be— and this kid who looked exactly like—"

"Ben!" More anxious than angry, arms crossed tight against her body, she watched him spiral in.

"I swear, exactly like him! And then it got really crazy, because…"

"Ben Harper, you stop this!" and stamped her foot in frustration.

The shadow on the hearth wasn't too thrilled with him either.

"But no, see, he really is Oberon, see, and maybe… well anyway, he's got a mission. For me." Anxiously he stopped at the window again, and turned at last to face her, chest heaving. "A quest, y'know? A quest!"

If he hadn't been so frantic, he might have seen the shadow that slipped across the floor and merged almost with his own, flickering like candlelight against the walls.

"Ben, if you're going to lie to me, at least make sense!"

"Sweetheart, god, if I was making this up, wouldn't it make sense?"

"Yes," she said, quietly now, and lifted the phone off its charger. "And that's how I know there is something very wrong. I'm going to call someone. You remember Terry Hoskins, at the college. You've got on well with him at faculty things. I can get him to come out tomorrow, I'm sure I can."

"Terry the Shrink?" he whined at her back. "No, Mellis, honey, I'm fine. A little dizzy, yeah. 'Cause I didn't believe it either, at first. And like I said, I was pretty rude. I said some things I shouldn't have—you know me—then the phone rang. *The phone rang!* In 1762! Wow, that's what it was!"

Trembling fingers combed through disheveled hair. For a moment his whole mind lit up with the revelation. "He didn't throw me out, the ring-tone did! It's the music, Mellis, see? You were right! It's all about the music! And you— you called me home from Faerie!"

Ben never felt the honeyed breath that whispered across his forehead, and by the time he'd heard the tuneless melody crooning in his ear, it was too late, or possibly just in time. Fortunately for his marriage, his eyes rolled back in his head and he lost consciousness. Whether it was the stress, the metheglin, or the horns of Elfland ringing in his ears he would never know. Happily, as he dropped, the Raven boy guided him so that Ben landed on the sofa's cabbage roses instead of the sharp corners of the coffee table. All gods knew he'd been tempted to just let the man fall.

All Mellis heard was the muted thump and creak of springs. With a sigh, she put down the phone. Cheeks flushed but still somehow dry-eyed, she stood over him for a minute, utterly unaware of the extra shadows in her house, or the faerie presence at her shoulder, the voice in her ear.

No need to wake Terry at this hour. Ben has been under a lot of stress, lately. Maybe he really did get lost on the moor.

Except Ben never got lost, never. Misdirected maybe, and he might wander a bit before getting his bearings. Pixie-led, as they say. But never lost.

It was Dartmoor. Anything was possible.

"Anything," she murmured, regarding her beloved with a gimlet eye. "Except twilight encounters with the king of the fairies!"

Then she leaned over him, smoothed the hair off his face, thinking "haircut." Tugged the glasses off his nose and folded them on the coffee table. And because she really did love her husband to distraction, she even pulled off his shoes and lifted his feet onto the sofa, then pulled the crocheted afghan down to cover him. She kissed his brow, surprised at how cool it was, not at all the fevered flush that promised a hangover. Then she went up to bed.

10

Midsummer Dream, Act 2, Scene 1

Enter, from one side, Oberon, with his train; from the other, Titania, with hers. Each is clad in sumptuous array of silks and brocades of shifting hue. Titania, queen of love and beauty, perilously fair, wears upon her glimmering head a crown carved of a single diamond. Lacey wings almost transparent but for the glitter of silver and golden veins, scroll above her bestirring the air with sweet perfumes. Where she enters this green and leafy grove, primroses spring from under her feet, preserved from the vulgar earth by gilded sandals. Joyous music surrounds her and yet, her lovely face is sad. She sighs, laying a trembling hand to her bosom as if all the gorgeous panoply of her court is naught but grief and endless sorrow.

Oberon whose twisted features betray a nature harsh and cruel marches forth, surrounded by his train all armored for the hunt. His clothes are rich and thick with embroidery, but fouled with the gore of his bloody enterprise. The only music of his coming is the harsh cries of hunting horns and the baying of red-eyed hounds, the whine of insects. The only perfume is the iron smell of death that rises from the creature slung from a sapling and borne by four broad-shouldered rangers. No wings beat the air but those of bats, vampires, and the demon grotesques that wait in his service.

Where Dian's moonlight strikes full in the midst of the wood, they meet, she in fearful dignity, he the testy suitor.

"Ill met by moonlight, proud Titania," declaims the noble king of Faerie.

Drawing herself up, she answers out of pride. "What, jealous, Oberon? Faeries, skip hence: I have forsworn his bed and company."

As she turns away, his rough hand clutches her wrist, purpling it with bruises, and she gasps. "Tarry, rash wanton: am not I thy lord?"

Coldly, she examines his hold on her, and he releases it. She curtsies in her dignity and replies, "Then I must be thy lady."

What does that mean? Ben Harper's eyes are frozen open and he cannot move nor can he speak, witness to this scene. The lady is serenely gowned in sea-blue silk and creamy piles of gauze like the foam of a wave. Her lord, a brute in Italian armor, bears the scar of a sword cut across one eye, and his mouth is an open wound. He threatens and upbraids her, she resists and weeps.

But that's not him, Ben thinks in his dream. Who is that guy?

"These are the forgeries of jealousy!" she cries, and Ben thinks yes, they are. The queen's tender delicacy begins to crack. "How dare you chide, when I know your infidelities, can count them in the wasted fields, the dying children, the evils of the world. The human world grows warm while you revel in unseelie pleasures."

"The progeny of evil arise from our dissension."

She nods her agreement. "We are their parents and original."

"Do you amend it then," saith he, mildly now, pulling her into his embrace. "It lies in you: I do but beg the little changeling boy to be my henchman. Fight me not but give him me, and all shall be restored. Why should Titania cross her Oberon?"

She snaps now, the truth of her temper finally on display. "The faerie world buys not the boy from me!"

The trembling hand, the pale countenance are gone, all gone, replaced with snarling fury to match his own and better. The dainty attendants singing and sighing beside her vanish leaving behind a pale, sickly boy of about 6, though Ben has the feeling he is much older. The boy starts to cry.

Freed from invisible bonds, Ben finds he is holding the child, looking from one powerful contender to the other, uncertain of his role. Images change without cause or direction, and he knows it is a dream. Since it is a dream, no choice truly matters. If it is a dream within Faerie, then no choice is safe.

The eyes of both king and queen turn to Ben. "Bring him to me," says the faux-Oberon, only now the eyes are soft and lit with care. "Only I can save him!"

"Nay, he is mine!" the queen cries, then calms at once and lowers her tone to match her lord's. "This is how it happened, don't you see? Everything you have heard about my lord is false. The boy is my god-child, my little Indian boy, as that mewling poet said. His mother was a votress, a votary, a— " But she has forgotten her lines, choking on the lies.

"Enough," the king says quietly, looking rather more like Aubrey than like the Horned King. "I will not let you play your games with him. Leave him alone."

It is not a suggestion. Mounted now, he turns a gaily caparisoned stallion into the wind and urges it to the sky, the milk white, red-eared hounds of the Wild Hunt baying beside him and following in his wake.

Ben looks down at the fragile child in his arms, and flinches as it squirms and bawls and stares back at him with eyes rimmed in blood. It opens its mouth and screams, and the mouth is filled with fangs like needles. In horror, Ben leaps to his feet, flinging the monster from him. It faces him like Gollum at the pool and screams again, then bounds into the wood on four limbs, slashing at the greensward with ragged talons.

"It was a mistake, Ben Harper," she says with wonderful sweetness. But he is not fooled, having heard this song already. "A mistake not to come to you, I see it. He has the gifts to be a prince of Faerie, almost immortal, and when he comes into his power, yes, my Champion. Nor will you suffer for it. Come to my Court. Live beside him under my care, and play for me. Such pleasures can be yours, only do not defy me!"

A whirlwind engulfs him in glittering air and images of such blossoming beauty as Ben has not imagined. Elfin ladies beckon him to play with them, mermaids wreathe him in songs of love no human can withstand, a spreading oak tree garlanded with silken ribbons drips with gold and jewels like ripe fruits. He has only to reach out.

His mind reels, beset with songs and tales all playing out before he can process them. Past and future slam together and splinter and knock him to the ground. Visions of wealth and wine bear him toward a golden shore. And in none of them, none of them, do his wife and child appear.

"No," he says, cold and quite clear.

All is still. He is laid out flat and motionless on the damp and *dusky earth.*

"Know this, human child," a sweet wheedling voice says beside his ear. Titania, her other-worldly face sly, her tone intent, speaks as softly as a prayer of vengeance. Pale curls caught in golden bands beside her face break on the ground like icicles, the color of her eyes. "I will have the child. I will stand between Oberon and his plans for no more reason than to thwart him, and I will have the Sparrow to be my knight!"

"No!" The word croaks out of him on will alone.

A twitch at the sides of the lustrous mouth betrays some slight dismay, surprise perhaps that he has broken her constraint. But she has brought the wrong coin to tempt him.

"My, my, it is clever, isn't it?" She is further away. "But it defies me at its peril. I know the jewel the king would have you seek, Ben Harper, and I know where it lies. Give me the Sparrow and I will give it thee."

There is no question in his mind, sleeping or awake. "Never."

"Give me the Sparrow and save your world!"

"Not for your faerie fucking kingdom!" Ben shouted, and sat straight up in darkness.

Rain sheeted down every window, and a crash of thunder rattled the dishes in the sideboard, followed in the instant by a massive crack of lightning. He jumped when it did, looked around wildly, surprised to be indoors. A headache beat at his temples and he could barely breathe, then understood that his cheeks were wet. Either he had in fact been out of doors— somewhere—or his face was damp with tears. Both were likely.

11
Queen's move

He was shaking as he reached for a lamp, grateful when it went on and flooded the homely room with light, warm and golden. His skin was clammy, his hair full of leaf litter, and his sweater smeared with mud and something he hoped was not blood, whether the monster child's or his own. And somehow he knew Sparrow was in danger.

Impulsively he checked his watch, scratched a bit but still on his wrist. A little past 5AM. Mellis would be up soon, getting Sparrow ready for school. It was Prize Day, last day of the term, parents in attendance. Lots of children, lots of parents and aunts and uncles from everywhere, strangers all over the village hall and play yards. How was he supposed to keep a child safe in all that mayhem? Maybe he shouldn't let them go.

That's it, he thought. Keep them both at home.

He sat up, thinking hard, and reached for his glasses. Oberon had misjudged his queen, probably not for the first time. This whim of Titania's was unlikely to pass, no matter what choice Ben Harper made.

Rain was coming down in buckets. When had that started? Perfect! It would be too wet and nasty. They'd have to cancel. Except he was thinking like a Californian. In England it was never too wet to go anywhere.

Okay, maybe he should call the police. Tell them he'd gotten a tip there was a kidnapper, a child molester, a terrorist plot to bomb the school! That would get them out here. Then at least there would be... what? Witnesses? A body count? Terrorists in Iveston! Why would anyone believe him?

More to the point, what could the police possibly do

against the hosts of Faerie? How on earth could he protect his child when he couldn't even explain the threat!

Another rumble of thunder boomed, another crack of lightning, and all the lights in the house flared and went out. A shriek exploded from the floors above.

"Ben!" That was Mellis.

"Daddy!" *Sparrow!*

Pound up the stairs, burst into the room and wonder why the door is blocked half way open. He could hear a groan, and realized there was a body lying crumpled between the door and the wall, revealed in a sudden sheet of lightning.

"No!"

Titania in long green gown, her hair like slivers of ice, was leaning over Sparrow, laughing and crooning like a playful parent. The storm—this was her storm, following her from Faerie.

"Daddy!" Sparrow squealed and gasped, trying to get a-way, trapped in his corner trying to breathe. "She hurt — Mummy! Make her —go —away!" The rest of his words turned into breathless sobs.

"Get away from him, you bitch!" Ben screamed.

But when he moved to stop her, she gestured vaguely towards him, and a wall sprang up of honey-smelling air and scrolling roses white and red. He beat on it, threw himself against it, but the roses had thorns like knives, and they tore and scratched him at shoulder, hip, and fist. Pain and sickly sweetness filled his head and turned his stomach, but his anger only grew.

"Pretty bird," the pale queen sang, weaving symbols and patterns glowing in the air around the boy. Sparrow's breathing slowed, the panic withdrawing as the spell took hold. "Will you be my nightingale, will you sing for me in Faerieland? Such a lovely voice you'll have. Such a pretty boy to be my warrior, my hero. Come, Sparrow come. So pretty a fool to sit on a stool and sing. Dame Margery dies in a corner there, but you shall live forever!"

"What are you doing? Leave him alone! Sparrow!"

"He weeps and he wails," she chanted over her shoulder,

fixing a mad and spiteful gaze on Ben. "And tears down hail, but nothing him avails, little Sparrow."

Bored of cajolery and of waiting for the child's cooperation, surprised that it did not come easily, she reached out a long white arm and smirked. "Stupid poet. Stupid children. Who are you to defy me, Ben Harper? But look you, I am a gracious queen. Ah-ah! You do not dare to doubt me!"

The wheedling tone did nothing to soothe. "I offer an honest trade. Faerie always keeps a bargain. I shall take this Sparrow, and you shall have another. When the sun rises—" An ugly giggle broke her voice. "—Why, your new poppet will rise as well! May you have joy of him! For as long as he lasts!"

It was too much. Locked and lost and held too long in terror, despair exhausting hope, Ben suddenly knew where his only answer lay. Falling to his knees he pounded the oaken floor three times with his bloodied fist, and raised his voice above the storm.

"Lord Oberon!" he cried out. "Help me!"

Lightning cracked, and in a glimmering swirl of oak leaves and a towering rage, Oberon was there. His dark hair snaked out around his face in the snapping ozone, and his eyes were black with fury. Titania froze. In an instant he had taken up Sparrow over his shoulder, snapped two fingers in Titania's direction, and all three vanished leaving only the echo of the queen's howls ringing in Ben's ears. Leaves, flowers, music and the maelstrom itself simply stopped. Flying toys, thorns and rose petals thudded to the floor, along with Ben, sobbing uncontrollably.

Finally, slowly, he found the strength to rise and find his wife. Mellis lay sprawled on the floor where she had fallen, slammed into the bedroom wall by the power of Titania's whim. Oh my god, thank god, she was breathing, if shallowly.

He shook her lightly, and called her name, then shook her again and though he frantically kissed her cheeks and hands, even slapped her dear face, there was no response. No blood, no bruising, but no waking either, as still as Sleeping Beauty.

Racked with misery, he picked her up and carried her to Sparrow's narrow little bed under the window, where predawn light was chasing the clouds across the ever-changing moor. The Raven's Eye stared back, gleaming dully in the middle distance. As he laid her down and was smoothing her night dress and straightening her limbs, weeping, he cleared aside his little boy's toys to make room: a bear, a handful of green plastic pixies, a shabby wooden puppet.

"Fucking pixies," Ben thought bitterly. And as he flung the toys aside, the puppet bounced up under his hand again. "What the hell is this?" He tossed it to the floor.

It was crudely carved, hardly more than a block of wood with a wooden ball for a head, the face painted in flat unlikely colors. The limbs were nothing but wooden sticks, strung together with waxed linen thread, or with… what was that stuff?

And as the sun rose and thin grey light crept over the landscape, he watched the puppet began to change, and grow, and as it grew the colors filled out and the spaces filled in. Twigs thickened to childish arms and legs, the ball head softened with features, a button nose, a rosebud mouth that opened on the pearls of childish teeth. The chest began to fill and rise. And Ben's throat closed in horror as it took on the shape and form of his child, his only Sparrow, in the school clothes he had worn the day before. And when it woke with a rosier cheek and sounder chest than Sparrow had ever had, breathing easily and smiling, Ben backed away and whimpered.

"Good morning, Father," it said, with no light in its eyes at all. "I am ready for school."

Maggie Secara

Friday

12
It is the Road to Fair Elfland

"Titania," Ben spat, and her name was like a curse in his mouth. "Lady bloody Grace. This is not over."

The now-familiar sound of crystal chimes clashed in his mind's ear, and in the window overlooking the rain-washed moor, a raven landed on the sill. It croaked once, forcing Ben to look at it while light and color shifted until it was the boy from the shop, from Diamond Hall, from Faerie. Dressed in severe black doublet and hose, ruffed to the ears like an Elizabethan gentleman, there was no denying what he was. Blue highlights gleamed in his black hair, though one lock over his left eye flared pale gold like Sparrow's, as if in tribute to the child.

"Where's my son?" Ben demanded. "Why did he take him!"

"We must go quickly, before your lady wakes."

"I'm not going anywhere. I'm not leaving her here with, with this thing." He spared a glance for the changeling, then looked away, gorge rising in revulsion. Harmless and horrible, it sat primly in the middle of the leaf-strewn floor, a warm and breathing ventriloquist's dummy, as if waiting for a cue.

"Never mind that, sir." The Raven boy had his orders. He stepped down into the room, his expression set, and stood over Mellis, mindful of the fear that rose from her, unconscious though she was. "She is well enough where she is."

He held up a white hand to stall further objection. If he couldn't lie, he was also not obliged to say all he knew, or all at once. "She is safe for now, and Sparrow—"

"Sparrow!" Ben leaped to grab the boy by the shoulders, longing to shake the supernatural complacency off his face.

"Damn you, where's my son?"

"He is safe," Raven said, delicately extracting himself from Ben's grip. He was stronger than he looked. "And better protected than you could keep him, for all your loving care. My lord asks you to trust him, and come to him—now." An appraising glance eyed Ben's disarray with distaste. "Get dressed, sir. The hour groweth on apace, and while we have some time yet there is none to waste and much to do."

Desperate and already exhausted, Ben stared a moment then shot from the room. He wanted nothing to do with changing or bathing or anything but finding his child. But he had to calm down, he knew, if he was heading into a, well, call it a quest. Adventure felt crass, as if it were an internet game he had joined on a whim. He couldn't hit Save and come back later. There was far too much at stake. There was...

"One thing at a time, man," he muttered. "Focus!"

Bathroom first, clean water on his face and hands, the back of his neck. The sandy beard he'd been neglecting for days could just carry on by itself.

Then fresh clothes that hadn't been ripped up by weird freaking supernatural creatures. Black jeans and the good boots. The tooled leather belt with the silver Navajo buckle, Sparrow's gift at Father's Day. The first t-shirt out of the drawer was the one that said Music is a Force of Nature, which he threw over his head like a talisman. The sturdy old black leather jacket. If he didn't feel much like a hero, at least he could look heroic. Maybe it would help.

One thing at a time. Out of habit, he grabbed the cell phone he had left behind less than 12 hours ago. Mechanically he cleared the apps, set a vacation response for email, and shut off alarms and reminders, while the thought kept repeating: *If only I'd listened. If I'd asked for help! If I'd kept my head!*

Stop it! With ruthless efficiency, he shut such thoughts away. Slipped the phone into the pocket of his jeans.

"Hey, I grabbed one of Sparrow's inhalers. You think..." he said, striding back into the nursery. Then stopped dead. "Hey!"

Raven knelt beside the little bed with his hands moving

above Mellis's still form, singing a wordless tune that twisted and coiled like a living thing around her. Finally, he intoned three or four strange words and placed one hand over her eyes. The look he turned over his shoulder Ben could not begin to read. The manner though, when he spoke, was less cocky than it had been.

"The queen's spell was more complex than I anticipated," said Raven, coming smoothly to his feet.

"Tell me," Ben said grimly.

"The queen's heart is engaged all out of proportion, only my lord can guess why. Her power is older and far greater than mine. When I tried to end the song, I made it worse. In saving her life, I nearly lost her mind."

What color was left in Ben's face drained away, but speech, at last, failed him.

"I can't break the spell, but I have done what I can to re-tune it," said the boy, just as if the words made sense. "With luck, all will be resolved before—"

"What?" Even the instant's hesitation was more than Ben could stand. "Come on, before what? Before she dies?"

"No, before it does. The stock, that is the changeling, is only true for a few days, then it sickens and soon dies."

"And then what?"

"Please, sir." The tight expression returned. "My lord has all your answers. If you're ready, we must go."

"Right." Still fighting to master himself, there was one last stupid question. "Ah— Do I need to bring anything? Y'know, like a gun, or a sword, or anything?"

Raven lifted a straight black brow over a withering look that was much too much like Sparrow's, and said nothing.

"Okay, good, because I don't have a gun. And I left my swords in California. C'mon, let's go."

"Make your farewell, and follow me."

He had been avoiding looking right at Mellis, but there was nothing left to do. The kid had accomplished something, he could see that. There was hope. Fresh color touched her cheeks, her chest rose and fell with deep and normal sleep. She looked as fresh as Snow White in the crystal casket.

He wanted to reach out and touch her, to lie down beside her and hold her, to share whatever dream-state she was lost in. It wouldn't help. Better to back away now than be caught up in misdirected emotions. So he threw her a kiss from the doorway and whispered, "I love you. I'll find him."

Then dragging his gaze from the gamin face, he turned and jogged down the stairs. No questions, no confusion. Whatever he had set in motion, he would fix it or die trying.

Outside he found Raven waiting with a pair of grey moor ponies, lightly saddled, and shod with silver, patiently cropping the potted greenery by the kitchen door. They were sturdy creatures and short legged, and Ben was fond of them. Raven asked, "Do you ride?"

"Been awhile, but yeah," said Ben, and mounted up. Shortly, and without another word, they were trotting up the road to Raven Tor just as the first true colors of dawn began to fill the eastern sky.

At the crossroads where the Iveston Road broke off for Widecombe, Odin saluted Raven with a pull on his broad brimmed hat and fell in beside them. He strode along easily, twirling the massive staff between two fingers like a baton.

Unable to restrain a double-take, Ben had to ask: "Aren't you— I mean, I thought you guys were— Aren't you and Oberon the same person, just, y'know, avatars or something?"

Raven allowed himself a mysterious smile and trotted forward a little, but the one-eyed god in his slouch hat and ratty top coat let out a mighty guffaw. "Nothing in Faerie is so simple, Ben Harper."

More than that apparently he had no need to say. Mysteries, Raven had said.

"Odin," Ben said, further on. "All Father?"

"That's my name."

"Where is my son?"

"Safe. Where he is, the queen cannot touch him. And nor, if I have sung the runes aright—and I always do—can she find him, at least for now."

Could old gods lie?

As the path rose with the dawn chorus of moor birds

calling around them, the ponies carried them swiftly round the rising spiral right up to the Raven's Eye.

Pausing briefly in the mists that hover between the worlds, Raven raised a silvery voice and sang a simple phrase. The earth rumbled and fell away under the stone archway as it had before. Ben, taking a deep, awe-filled breath, urged his pony down the ramp and into the realm of Faerie.

"I got that much right," Ben said, mostly to himself. "The magic. It's all about the music. Old Thomas the Rhymer, he knew." The old song winding unbidden through his head suddenly made sense.

> *Oh see ye not that bonnie road,*
> *That winds about yon ferny brae?*
> *That is the road to fair Elfland,*
> *Where thou and I this night maun gae.*

For the first little way, the path through Faerie looked a lot like eastern Dartmoor, rolling and rocky with a high, granite-hearted waste on one hand covered with gorse and heather; on the other, a burbling spring marked by the darkness of clustered trees, bordered with blackthorn. The light was different, though; sharper, the colors truer.

The path crossed an ancient stone bridge over a rushing brook where nymphs splashed in the water or sat on the rocks. Like pretty girls with tiny wings fluttering between their naked shoulders, they stopped their singing to look up startled as he passed. Then they waved and giggled, calling out to the pretty mortal, blowing kisses.

Ben started to wave back, but Raven smacked his hand down. "Sir, don't. Just don't."

Further on, and from another direction, the strain of a hurdy-gurdy beat against girlish laughter, undercut with the hooting of boys at play.

"Fauns," said Odin. "It's like Disneyland around here, some days."

Disneyland, yeah, Ben thought. On an E-ticket ride. Without comment, he stopped twitching and started paying attention.

Moorland gave way to a wood of rattling aspen and silver birch. The stream dived underground on one side of their path, and a clear pool overhung with willows opened up on the other. Red-breasted robins gave place to stellar jays. A voice singing a wordless, melancholy tune set in an ancient mode disappeared behind them. At each change he sensed more than heard the faintest crystal chime. Sometimes he even felt something, a *frisson* of energy that raised the hairs on the back of his neck. Not unpleasant, just odd when combined with that feeling of passing, finally, through the doors that had been standing open for him.

"The hour groweth on apace, my ass," he muttered, then added in his best outdoor voice: "I don't want anyone to think I don't appreciate the tour. But, are we there yet?"

"Behold, Master Harper," Raven said with a flourish. And in that moment, the wood opened into a vast wide lawn. The kid pulled his mount aside and bowed like the Chamberlain of the Court. "You are well come and welcome in the King's Great House of Faerie."

"House" was not the word for the confection that seemed to have grown alive from the meadow and woodland behind it, nor was it exactly a fairy-tale palace. It was more like a friendly inn, the best sort of inn, where the taps never run dry, and the party never stops.

Ben shut his mouth as soon as he realized it was standing open, and rode forward.

13
The King's Great House

The main building did appear to be a substantial multi-storied thatched cottage roughly the size of Kensington Palace, but somehow smaller, or larger, or sort of folded in on itself, merging into frowsy woodland at the edges, and elsewhere billowing into roundel windows and fanciful verandas. Fae folk of all sorts and sizes fluttered and feasted, danced on the greensward or played games with color and harmony.

It wasn't a palace, he thought; it was elvish summer camp.

Though it must have been at least a half mile away, they closed the distance between two heartbeats, as swift as a dream. Here a pair of long-limbed elf lords were using crystal wands to draw glowing, colored shapes in the air that swirled then interwove, so that each intersection chimed when touched. Directed with slight touches and a whispered word, they passed on and through each other, till harmonies rose up like soft voices from their engagement. When a particularly sweet chord combined, those around them turned to applaud and praise.

Overhead, silken banners that teased the eye in fragile shades of green and silver, heliotrope and gold, draped and looped through the tree tops, sometimes merging with them, sometimes sparkling into pools far below like water, or as water, Ben couldn't say and wouldn't ask. Framed by house and enchanted forest lay a meadow, manicured like a lush green lawn left ragged at the edges, suitable to the king's more rustic folk. A light breeze stirred the air as cool and sweet as true love, perfumed with fruit and flowers.

Ben, transported, closed his eyes and found his lashes wet.

It was a little like a dream, a little like exquisitely realized CGI, and a very little bit, in the corners, like that Renaissance festival they used to have in Marin—all really and truly there, in front of him. The isle, he thought, was full of noises.

Unless it wasn't.

He blinked, now, and looked again, really looked. Yes, much of what he could see with his own eyes was something he could touch with his hands, and many of the wonders—the multi-state draperies, for one—were delicately true. The rest was at least partly illusion. So was the food, and most of the population. Or was that their nature?

It hurt his brain to think about it, and he had enough to worry about already. This ability to see through to the true nature of things might be useful, but it was giving him a headache.

"Ben? Ah, excellent!" Aubrey's voice said from somewhere.

Dismounting, Ben handed his pony to one of the long-haired horse boys he had seen on the moor last night, at least he thought it was one of them. And he thought it was last night. Ben also thought the fae smirked, but it might have been the normal set of a fae complexion. He had no time to care.

"Take me to my son," he said sharply to the empty air.

"I wish I could," said Aubrey, putting down his wand. The musical puzzles fell into sparkling dust and air.

Ben said with a sigh, "You just love doing that, don't you."

"I do, what can I say?"

He was dressed now as Ben expected of the King of Faerie, with a richly modest band of wrought gold crowning his hair, and something medieval to wear: silver tights, a brief tunic of damask silk, pleated and belted, with high collar and long, dagged sleeves dotted with ermine and diamonds. At the end of each flame-scalloped dag, tiny bells tinkled sweetly as he moved, but he made them go away.

"Pretty for dancing," he said. "Annoying for talk. Love the T-shirt, by the way."

The American wasn't about to be distracted by magic or flattery. "So when can I see him? He's here, isn't he? In Faerie?"

"You believe in us, at last."

"What choice do I have? Now where is he?"

"Sit down, Ben. Have a beer. We'll be here a while. And you can't go to him, I'm sorry. That's part of the protection. But I can show him to you."

When they sat, it was in gilded chairs with velvet cushions at a table under the trees. Graceful attendants brought food and tankards of ale, but Ben looked at none of it.

"I'm not eating your food, sir, if that's okay with you. Now, what about Sparrow?"

"Here," said the king of the fae. From a pocket in the air, he pulled a mirror of black stone so polished and so black that it soaked up as much light as it reflected. A nod, and images appeared like video on its face, but better: a pretty glade like this one but much, much smaller.

Sparrow was there, laughing and doing something with a branch of holly under the instruction of a stout older gentleman in a violet gown covered with stars. The boy too was robed in standard wizardly gear. A table nearby was set for breakfast, with tea and marmalade and toast in a silver rack. There was no sound, but Ben could watch his son wave the holly wand once, twice, three times over the tea things then poof! An explosion of sparks and oily smokes.

"He's learning to brew a tempest in a teapot," said Aubrey.

Ben was grinning through his relief. "He's learning to be a wizard. He'll hardly know I'm gone." He risked a stupid question. "Is that Merlin?"

Aubrey lifted that long eyebrow as he had done before. "Better. Taliesin. Merlin is a legend."

"And the purple outfit?"

Smiling, the king said, "It's the boy's fancy, and the magister doesn't mind. He is in good hands. A few hours ago, not so much. Now Sparrow is hidden from Titania and nearly everyone else in a twist, you might call it, of Faerie. Only Odin truly knows where and how it is hidden."

"And you're not Odin."

Enigmatic smile. "He is as safe as I can make him, you have my word."

"And is your word any good?" said Ben, and blanched.

"Sorry," he said weakly, swallowed, and stopped.

But the king only met Ben's eyes with his lofty, elegant smile and said, "The Fae cannot lie. Prevaricate, dissemble, mislead betimes, or withhold the whole truth, but never lie. That is a human trick. But the truth can be perilous, human child. And expensive."

"Expensive?"

"Have a beer, Ben. I tell you the child is safe and you are my guests. You may eat and drink anything in this realm without compulsion or consequence." The words Raven had used in the old manor house.

Ben nodded and for now, pulled the tankard toward him.

"And Titania?" At this Oberon did deign to look a little troubled. "Don't tell me. You can't govern your wife."

The king snorted. "Can you? There's an expensive truth! Well, I have done what I may, and confined her to her own house for a time, but her temper is, ah, as you have seen. She'll be sending her folk against you, now, for no better reason than to square with me. Which will make your task that much harder."

At this Ben tried to smile, then remembered something. He pulled the inhaler out of his pocket and placed it on the table.

"I brought this for him, sir. But I guess you can't get it to him."

Answering a glance from his lordship, someone whisked it away.

"We'll keep it anyway. He won't need it where he is, and you have enough to keep track of."

"And now the task, sir."

"When you broke the ring," Aubrey said, dropping into lecture mode, "the pieces were flung away into time, governed by forces I won't try to explain. And here is where it gets tricky, much more than if you had simply accepted the bloody thing to begin with."

"And traveling in time is the easy part, I suppose." It might even be true, thinking about the field trip from the Raven's Eye.

"Judge for yourself. You must go to each one first at some point in the past, wherever it's gone. Listen to its song, hold it if you can, then leave it. That will allow you to find it again in your own time, whatever it has become. When you have found them all, call for me. And that's it. Complex goal, simple resolution."

He plucked a chocolate-covered cherry from a golden dish at his elbow, and popped it into his mouth, smugly pleased with the economy of his explanation.

"Simple, sure. But what about, y'know, paradox?"

The pleasure faded almost before the cherry liqueur. Clearly, the man on whom so much depended was still fighting him, worried about temporal mechanics he'd learned from Rod Serling! That would never do. Clever, creative, intuitive Ben Harper's whole mind had to accept the realities, whether or not he understood them, or all was lost.

"Ben, I don't know if you're worried about stepping on a butterfly, or about causality, or wormhole physics, or something else, but you have to stop it. You cannot let mere reason dictate what is possible and what is not. All of history has happened and is happening now, all at once, yes, and yet some things may be changed. Nothing light or trivial touches the time stream, any more than a pebble dropped into the river diverts the Thames. But in order for an event to have happened, it has to happen." His new henchman's eyes were crossing. "That is your task. You are yourself a part of the story now, don't you see?"

The mortal man took a breath, nodded, and said, "I broke it, I have to fix it, I get that. Time is a mobius strip, sure. The rest I will take on faith."

"Thank every god," said the king.

"But shouldn't I just bring the pieces to you?"

"No! You put the pieces into the time stream. They have become, or are becoming, part of people's lives—a family heirloom, a religious icon, a tiara set with diamonds, half a dozen coins saved for a dowry—part of their stories. Who knows what might be affected by pulling any one of them out again, until you can hear those stories for yourself."

"I just leave them where I find them."

"Exactly," nodded the king. "You will know them in your present, no matter what form they've taken, because of the stories they tell when you find them. And they will give up those stories to you because of the connection you forged with the dragon ring in Diamond Hall."

"When I smashed it," said Ben, sheepishly.

"When you smashed it." The sea blue eyes glittered.

"Then you take the present bits and remake the ring, so I can take it to King Alfred et cetera, et cetera?"

Aubrey nodded.

"This makes no sense whatever."

"Welcome to Faerie, Ben."

Ben smiled wanly and sat back, daring at last to lift the tankard of ale to his lips. Like the liquor at Diamond Hall, it was extraordinary, but whether it was sweet or bitter, light or dark, though he knew it at the time, was ever after beyond him to report. It was good, that was enough.

Rubbing lightly at his bearded chin, he considered the problem while Aubrey drew patterns of jeweled light on the table with one idle finger.

The awesome prospect laid before him, Ben thought, was terrifying, and wonderful, all swirled together. If he allowed fear to overbear his mind, as any rational man might, he'd be frozen in place till the world ended. Instead, while he sipped mellow ale at the heart of Faerie, he listened, just listened. Bird song faded, harp song stilled, and the sigh of sweet airs moved in a silence that vibrated with life and power. Breathing in the magic, he began to feel the threads forming that might yet become a plan. Threads to be twisted into cord, or woven into a story. Or a song.

Aubrey had said it. Ben the Efficient had been letting mere reason govern him for too long. He had put limits on the possible, boxed his imagination like a decorative but useless memento. He was done with that, he thought, and knew it was true.

Meeting Aubrey's placid gaze, "I'm not a hero," he said at last.

"No one ever is," said the king.

So Ben took a deep breath and put the tankard down carefully. "Then how do I start?"

Now Aubrey looked thoughtful, collecting himself for the next phase.

"Only you can tell. However, I can offer two tools to aid you. I'm sending Raven with you, for one." And there Raven stood, in green and buff leathers, booted and spurred for travel, at the king's right hand. If he didn't look pleased, that was hardly news.

"I can't tell how much help you'll need, if indeed you need any at all, but my power is greater and less in various times and places. If you call, I may not come. Raven, though, is often strong where I am not. If nothing else, you'll have a guide."

"To keep me from being an idiot in foreign places?"

Aubrey nodded. "That, and to provide translations, as required. While he is by you, you will speak and hear whatever languages are needful where you are." He paused for a moment, then added, "It will help, I must tell you, if you speak plainly and without the charming Americanisms."

"Dude!"

The eyebrow went up but the royal countenance remained neutral. "Mmm. If you need money, he will have it. You will doubtless need to be somewhat other than yourself—again, your call. Raven will help you adapt. Listen to him, then follow your gift."

"And the other thing?"

From a pocket Ben could not imagine in the skin tight tunic, the king pulled a battered book about the size of an ordinary paperback, covered in soft sueded leather with the remains of gilt tracery on its face. When he flipped through it, the pages appeared to be blank.

He glanced up. "You want me to take notes."

That amiable, kingly shrug again. He didn't give away much, Oberon. "If it pleases you to do so." He nodded toward the book. "But look again."

Now a dozen or so pages were covered with writing, some scrawled, some in a neat copperplate hand. Some pages were splashed with blotted inks, some other stains that might be blood, and the oily prints of someone writing during an all-you-can-eat spaghetti feed.

One page appeared to be a crude map with rivers, land-marks and principal settlements marked but not named. Interesting. For the most part, the notes themselves were impossible to read, often scrawled over each other on successive layers. One note, outlined in red, was hopping from page to page as he turned the leaves, as if trying not to be overlooked. Startled when he realized it, Ben slammed the book shut and slapped it back on the table.

"What the hell is that?"

"A diary, for lack of a better word. It is very old. And of course, also very new. Some of my people are being, hmm, helpful, now that they know it is for your use."

"And how do I use it?"

"That's another thing you'll have to discover for yourself."

"Oh fine. Any clues?"

"There are clues within the diary. First, though, may I make a suggestion?"

Gingerly, Ben reached out and ticked open the cover with one finger. There it was again, that note. He flipped the book closed.

"I'd appreciate it, sir, I really would."

"Get some sleep."

"Sleep!" Ben snapped, the crisis returning in full force like a slam to the chest. "How the hell can I sleep?"

The king continued without pause. "I told you that time was not the issue you thought it was. Here in my house, where time moves at my whim, there is somewhat less urgency, more space for you to rest and think. Look over the diary. Talk with Raven, if you like. Consult any books or any of my people who might be helpful. Borrow what you need. But mostly, sleep. My lady's grace has taken much from you. I should like to see it restored, as far as it is within my power."

And in the moment, Ben was snoring, his head laid on his crossed arms at the table.

When he woke eight hours later in a spartan but well

appointed bedchamber, he breakfasted with Raven and the king, enormously refreshed. If he was minded to be cranky about having his options shortened, steak and eggs straightened that out right quick.

By the time, whenever it was, that he and Raven stood again in the faerie king's meadow, he had read and consulted, thought and imagined, and borrowed a few things that would come in handy, and the haversack to put them in. He'd played some music and listened to more, and looked in on Sparrow one more time. Composed and ready, he had a strategy if not exactly a plan. He also had a song in mind to charge the magic which, somehow, would come from him; a song he knew so comfortably in its endless verses, it would leave the rest of his mind free to do the hard stuff, the navigation.

Now he threw a leg over the silver-shod pony and felt for his bearings. The thread which, he had realized, connected him to the thing he sought tugged faintly but surely as if it were tethered to his chest. North, and a little east, and some other direction that had no name. All he had to do was follow.

"I think," said Ben, turning towards it. "No, I'm quite sure. That way." He nodded off to his right in the direction of a holly hedge.

"How can you know that, sir?" Raven asked. Whether he was mildly curious or mildly skeptical was hard to say. It wasn't his gift they had to follow.

Ben said, "I know. And what's more, your grace—" The corners of his mouth turned up with irony, as he patted the diary tucked into his jacket. "I have a feeling I'm going to meet your friend Alfred sooner than you think."

The king betrayed no surprise uncommon to him, but gravely took Ben's hand, warm and firm in his own.

"That should be interesting. Keep your wits about you, human child. Remember your manners!"

Ben nodded. "Good my lord, so shall I." Then he turned at last to Raven. "You'll let me know if I'm doing this wrong."

Ready now, he gathered the reins and sang out in his clear, pleasant baritone:

O'er the hills and o'er the Main,
Through Flanders, Portugal, and Spain,
The king commands and we obey
Over the hills and far away!

He caught Oberon's grin in the corner of his eye, and touched two fingers to his forehead in salute. Then caroling merrily, he turned the pony's head to the north and a little east, and set off through the enchanted wood. Raven followed in haughty silence.

Within a few paces, Ben felt something pass over him like a veil of silk or of falling water. The light changed, and a path opened under their ponies' hooves, littered with fallen oak leaves and squirrel-shattered acorns, edged with meadow grasses gone to seed. His focus held.

A minute later, rocking with the pony's ambling gait, he modulated the song into a new key, and another barrier he couldn't see raised like a barbed portcullis. The path was now chillier, and the meadow gave place to woodland, and the smell of oncoming snow.

"And if that phone rings," Oberon shouted just before they faded on the brightening air. "Answer it!"

"Now I wonder, " he wondered, addressing no one but the attentive gentlemen of his train, poised to make themselves useful. "Should I have mentioned the three tokens he'll need in the end?"

As he shook the thought away, the bells on his sleeves chimed prettily again. "He'll work it out."

Saturday

14
Kingdom of Wessex, Yule, 876 AD

❄

They rode out of Faerie through a riot of bluebells and hawthorn blossom that gradually gave way to an autumnal shower of golden leaves and a sky loud with migrating geese. Finally with some meandering they emerged on a hilltop at the edge of a frozen winter woodland stitched with barren trees, piled and layered and silent with snow. Nothing but foraging animals and a pair of red-eyed wolves would ever realize that their hoof prints had come out of nowhere.

Where the hill broke to a shallow cliff, the wood thinned and broadened out under layers of leaden sky into the tree-studded down lands of ninth century Wiltshire, at least Ben thought it was Wiltshire, where a light snow was falling. There they halted, surveying the land spread out below.

"Wow!" His voice shook with the sudden cold and the plain wonder of what he had done, and where he was. "Just, wow!"

"Well done, sir," Raven said, drawing up beside him. "I've never come through the gates quite like that before."

"You want to lead?"

They were a thousand years—a thousand years!—in the past, and he, Ben Harper, had brought them here! He couldn't stop grinning. They were also, Ben guessed, another frozen hour's ride from their goal—plenty of time to arrive as weary travelers in some plausible way at the fortified house or whatever it was. No, not a house exactly. A hunting lodge, or what his pioneer forbears might have called a fort. He had a sense of wooden palisades, but nothing more detailed. He only knew that somewhere down there in the densely wooded valley of the Avon, one fragment of the dragon ring had landed.

Clad now in the tunics and gartered hose of royal servants, armed for the road, both Ben and Raven were bundled in double layers of furs, woolen cloaks, hoods, and scarves appropriate to the age and the weather. Even their sturdy ponies had grown a shaggy winter coat, and their breath steamed under coarse blankets.

Ben puffed frosty breath and settled the reins in his gloved hands.

"Cold?" the raven boy asked.

"Kind of warm, actually," said Ben, finally noticing the costume change. The history buff buried under the efficiency expert beamed with pleasure. "But good! Great, even! Good thing I'm not allergic to wool."

"You have your skills, I have mine."

Ben couldn't stop staring around, though the pony was getting restive. The countryside lay so still and unreal, if it hadn't been for the piercing cold, Ben would have thought they stood in a film set, or in a painting. He listened, really listened to the silence, and wonder swept over him again. Except for the hiss of their breathing, and his own heartbeat drumming in his ears, nothing stirred, nothing at all. Nowhere in his own time was the mark of the modern world ever utterly absent— this absent. No underlying electronic hum, no distant highway rumble, not in the whole world. And when the winter night fell, it would be utterly dark under the overcast, lacking even starlight or moonshine or urban glow.

He sat back in the saddle with a dopey grin stretching his face in awe, touched with a little fear.

Raven noticed, and cuffed his shoulder lightly. "No gawking, sir, if you please," he said. "Y'know, you might have brought us in a little closer to the mark, if you don't mind my saying so."

"Are you kidding? And miss this?" Ben pounded the saddle horn with sheer glee. "I mean, seriously! Wow!"

"The ponies are getting cold, sir."

"Oh, right."

As they turned to pick a path down from the cliff edge,

Raven added. "You do have some idea where we are, then?"

The shout of Ben's laughter rang in the frosty air. "The Middle Ages?"

"It is, yes," said the boy, patiently. "And we are in England. I believe that will be Chippenham." He waved a hand in the general direction of a smudge away over the horizon, a smoky patch of sky, as always, indicating a living community. "If we can get down from here without breaking our necks, we'll be somewhere on the Roman road from Bath—the A4, more or less. And it's just about..." He drew a deep breath as if tasting the air. "Yes, Christmas Eve."

Ben just kept grinning, though the snow was swirling and the temperature dropping, and Raven sighed. "Are we there yet?"

"Soon, yes. Very soon."

When they found the road, they urged the ponies to a quicker step. He was humming the ancient tune that had brought them here, which wouldn't be written for another six hundred years, and was for a while completely, thoughtlessly happy.

The world was not only silent, he noticed, but remarkably empty. They passed now and then the odd steading dug in against the freeze, its presence betrayed only by a thin stream of hearth smoke. Here and there rose other signs of human use, sometimes no more than a herdsman's bothy, abandoned for the season, squatting like a dirty snowball in a hazel brake. But no traffic, no people.

Away south across the frozen river, clinging to the swell of a hillside, a monastery and its low, stone church huddled with its back to the road, keeping its stinks and its treasures to itself. A single iron bell clanged a few sorry times, breaking the air.

Raven flinched a bit at the sound. "They'll be ringing for Tierce," he muttered. "And what else?"

He didn't look happy.

"Is it true," Ben asked, seeing the reaction., "that the fae can't bear the sound of church bells?"

"Only when they're out of tune. Stop talking, will you?"

The Dragon Ring

All the wry humor had gone from him like pinching out a candle.

"What? Why? I'm enjoying—"

"Hark!" the boy snapped, and Ben stopped, attention focused. They waited, Raven with his head tilted, birdlike, listening.

"What is it?" Ben whispered at last. "What do you hear?"

"Breathing, and something else."

"I'm breathing."

"Please, sir! Dogs, maybe. No, wolves—two or three of them. And the queen's magic out of tune."

"Shit."

"Quite." The boy shook himself, took a long look back over his shoulder, humming a pattern of five or six notes breaking crisp in the crisp air.

Ben watched him, noting how the youthful patina fell away as one by one Raven threw off all the useless scarves and pelts, and the glimmer of Faerie intensified around him. And when he turned to look ahead again, three massive black wolves, red-eyed and grinning, blocked their way. His giddy happiness vanished, and his mouth tasted of ashes.

Sleek and well fed in spite of the bitter season, one paced the width of the road, whining, disturbed by the Romans' iron road buried long beneath the snow. One hunkered down, as wolves do when stalking prey, one watching behind. The largest sat staring at Ben from the middle of the path, secure and quiet as a watch dog. Ben's pony backed nervously.

"Do you know how they used to hunt the wolf, Ben Harper?" said the raven boy, drawing the shining long sword at his side.

"How's that?"

"With traps and snares, and dogs. Today, I am your dog. Draw your sword."

Fumbling briefly through the bundling layers, Ben felt the hilt come into his grasp with an ease he did not deserve. It had been too long since he'd last handled a sword, and never one like this. The blade gleamed as he brought it up into position, easier in the hand than he expected. Light spilled off its sharpened edges.

"I don't know if I remember how."

"I don't expect you to use it." The fae's eyes never left those of the animal before them, though he had marked the other two to right and left. "But I want it in your hand. Your job is to find the artifact. Mine is to keep you alive to do it. So when I say ride, you ride, d'ye understand? You'll hear things behind you, but do not look back. And whatever else you do, do not leave the iron road."

"What about you?" Ben's voice, unlike his companion's, trembled more than he liked.

"I believe," said Raven, thoughtfully. "I shall sing. Now ride!"

The boy's sword point prodded the terrified pony's flank, and it sprang forward, flying over the thick bodied, bandy-legged leader with a leap seldom seen in a moor pony. It came down, skittering in the icy track until it found its footing. Ben clung to the reins, and felt his thighs grip what was now a sure, swift saddle horse. The wolf's jaws snapped as it leapt for a perch on the great horse's back. He lashed out with the sword and felt it connect. The beast yelped with a voice that sounded like a human curse, and tumbled away, only to gather itself for the pursuit and start again.

Behind him Raven fought magic with magic. His vision filled suddenly with light, and the bump of power that came with it rocked him forward in the saddle. But the monster was still there. Ben could all but feel it breathing in his ear, imagining the vicious snap of jaws, the red heat of its mouth, the deep desire to crush bone and rend flesh, the radiating hatred not of a hunting animal but of something almost human, but quite alien.

A piece of Titania's consciousness must be in there, Ben realized. She would be watching, somewhere, through the wolf, directing it, reveling in the chase.

Ben rode hard, urging the horse into a flat out gallop, even knowing the danger on the frozen path. They spun up rooster tails of snow as they went, following the road as it followed the river, and the winter wood closed about him.

What was Raven doing? He thought he heard another horse behind him, keeping pace. He desperately wanted to turn and look but knew it would only slow him down He had only a few miles left, sure, but how long? And then what? Turn and make a stand? Hope Raven would be there? Hope, perhaps, for aid from men he didn't know, who—he imagined frantically— might not even see the wolves out of Faerie. And what if…

Sword gripped in one outstretched hand, reins in the other, bent low over the saddle and pounding through the forest of oak and ash, Ben found himself pushing panic aside and reaching out for the thread, the harp string he must follow to his goal. What would happen when that thread took him off the road, as it surely would?

It didn't matter. It didn't matter, and there was nothing else to do when at last the path to his goal veered into a wide dirt track flanked by holly trees. Daring to slow down, though sensing still the monster behind him, Ben did what he had to do, and when the turning came, pounded off the iron-bound Roman road. And nothing happened. Ben swung the horse around, bringing up the sword, praying it would answer his command when called.

The wolf stood there, staring up at him and snarling as if it had been waiting instead of chasing him down.

Then it threw back its massive head and let loose a weird, keening howl followed in its echoes by a voice strained and distorted.

"You will die, human child! And I will take your wife in thrall to be my kitchen maid, unless you tell me where the child is."

He gulped, fighting down whole new terrors. A wind rose out of the leafless wood, bearing with it hysterical laughter, disordered threats, cajoling, entreating, a jangling chorus like voices in a madhouse. Snow swirled up, getting in his face, into his nose and his mouth open to say "Never!"

Then the wolf gathered and leapt, snarling, not for the horse panting under him, but straight for Ben. And without thought, the sword swung round, thrust up with both hands on the hilt as the beast came down, and took the monster in the throat, spitting it through skull and brain. Blood gushed from mouth and eyes and around the blade. The enormous weight nearly broke his arm, but he used the momentum to swing the body overhead flinging brains and blood in a scarlet arc, and let it drop.

Mortally silent, it slid from the blade to the snow almost in slow motion. When it touched the earth, it vanished, and the whirlwind of voices ceased in the instant. The horse didn't like this at all, but stood, trembling and overheated.

Shaky himself and drenched with sweat, Ben dismounted and ripped away the layers of clothing and furs he hadn't had time to discard, now drenched in gore. Then he used a woolen scarf to rub down the horse, who had served him with so great a heart. It accomplished little but would have to do. More would have to wait on good stabling or, perhaps, faerie magic.

"What did I tell you, human child!" Raven scolded, flinging himself from his shaggy pony. The mantle of his power had diminished but not his rage. "What did I tell you about straying from the road? Did I say, do not leave the road?"

"What was I supposed to do?" Ben shouted back, trembling as the adrenalin rushed away.

"Keep riding, dammit!" The boy delivered a petulant punch to the shoulder that hurt, but oddly warmed.

"I did keep riding, dammit! It's this way!"

"Did you not hear me calling you? I took care of the other two as fast as I could, but this monster wanted nothing to do with me. I've been right behind you for miles. Thirty seconds, Ben. Thirty seconds and I could have spared you."

The fear and anger was draining out of him too, and he looked almost as spent as an ordinary mortal.

Both horses were exhausted, so Ben and Raven took their reins in hand and faced up the broad path that led to King Alfred's hunting lodge. Many men and horses had passed here recently, and the way, sheltered and trampled, was a mass of frozen mud and wheel ruts, but little snow. So they walked the rest of the way, faerie magic gradually resupplying whatever set dressings had been cast aside.

"So what happened?" said Raven at last.

"I'll tell you later," Ben said, getting the tremors under control.

"Okay."

"Pepper spray might have been in order."

Raven chuckled, "Or a shotgun."

15
Outside Cheltenham

By the time they emerged from the holly way and stumbled almost literally into King Alfred's deeply fortified vill at the raveling edge of his kingdom of Wessex, they had been marked by no less than half a dozen pairs of watchmen, but offered no aid. What they could see of the walls under the snow was turf-covered earthen ramparts braced with timber fronting a stout stone wall, and a watchtower but no gate.

"We're here, but how, y'know, how do we get in?"

"Mount up. Just keep riding. There will be a gate and welcome," said the raven boy with almost jaunty confidence.

"They've seen us, I think."

"That's good, sir. We're supposed to be here. Just keep moving."

"It's only a hunting lodge, how big can it be?"

"A royal hunting lodge, Ben Harper. As big as the king wants it to be."

They picked up the pace and followed the path skirting the palisade and ditch. It took another twenty minutes' cold slogging round the perimeter to find the gate where indeed, a heavily armed and curious welcome was waiting.

When the challenge came, Raven raised a hand. But before he could do whatever came next, Ben called out to the men at arms on duty.

"I am the king's own gleeman, Brand Harper of Ivarstanehaugh. Let me in, or by Our Lady's grace I'll put you into a satire!"

Raven shot him a look, and said under his breath, "You got that all worked out in your sleep, did you?"

"Hush. Of course not. I looked it up," Ben hissed.

"What, on the Internet?"

"Later!"

"You are well come, lord," said the guard who shoved back the gate against the snow. "Eh, who's this, then," he added sharply, peering at Raven.

The boy flashed a winning smile, and the man stood back, blinking. "Of course, lord, forgive me. I'd know you anywhere. Come in both of you, and get along quickly to the hall."

"Christ's blessing on you, fyrdsman," Ben said heartily. "We heard wolves in the wood a while back, and the king will be sore in sorrow if his favorite gleeman is meat for wolves on Christmas Eve!"

The man gave him an odd look but waved him on. It was too cold to worry about gleemen's funny talk. Thankfully he failed to notice that while Ben's breath frosted on the air, his companion's did not.

Ben noticed, though. "Aren't you cold?" he asked when they were clear of company.

"No, Brand Harper," the boy said mischievously. "Nor am I sweating under all these layers, but warm I surely am."

"Must be nice."

The yard between the gate and the hall, a good hundred yards away, was filled with the barracks and workshops, barns and storehouses of a garrison, across a white expanse of frozen exercise ground, as well as the general trappings of a Saxon mead hall.

"You looked it up?" Raven repeated. Snow was falling again, with a wind behind it like the wind off a glacier.

"We could have been here sooner," Ben said. "But I was reading. Did you know Ivarstanehaugh was the Saxon name for Iveston, where I live?" When Raven just stared, he went on. "Okay, have you ever tried to read while opening options in time and space—on a moving pony?"

Raven shrugged in that eloquent faerie way. "You've picked up the trick of traveling through the gates very quickly."

Ben smiled thinly, pleased with himself. "It's in the music, isn't it?"

"Yes."

"I heard you singing over Mellis, and then at the Raven's Eye. I may look like a mild mannered TV presenter… Well, all right, I am, but not entirely. See," Ben chuckled, searching for the words. "It's like there's a story, or something, that sings from every magical object. I mean, every magical object has its own story, like a song, y'know? And if I listen for it, focus on it, I can hear it, or feel it, or something."

He shook his head in frustration. "I'm not explaining it very well. But as soon as I understood what it was, what I was hearing, or feeling, or whatever, when I really got it, I could pick the thread of it out of the air like, like plucking a harp string. And once I touch it, I can follow it, see. The story that sings from the dragon ring led me here to King Alfred's hall. The thread is really tight here, you could say, like it's anchored to a tuning peg in this place. Does that make any sense?"

They reined up at last at the steps of the king's hall with its carved and gilded wooden columns. Wooden steps led up to pillars carved with interlaced images of rearing bears and writhing dragons flanking doors as barbaric as any Viking's; among them, too, the cross and thorny crown of Christ, and other images Ben couldn't place. Hopefully no one would ask him for songs about any of this stuff.

Raven must have been hoping the same, but he said only, "When we get inside, human child? Can you do this?"

Ben grunted, unpacking his gear from the saddle with frozen fingers. "The diary. Apparently, if I can read it, I can use it. I just hope I've puzzled out everything I need."

"And how are you going to convince them you're a harper?"

"I thought that was your job, to match us to the place and time."

They stopped to answer the door ward's challenge. This time Raven spoke, and the replies came easily, and apparently in the right form, for the door ward, clearly anxious to get the doors closed and barred in a hurry, let them in with deference and set them on their way.

"And so we do," Raven went on when they were clear. "But I can't make you a musician."

"Fear not, my lad. I'm musician enough. I just hope—I mean, what do I know from ninth century minstrelsy? With luck we should be just so much background color and noise after the…"

In an antechamber they stopped to throw off a couple of layers of wool till they were fit to make a decent entrance upon a king and war lord in his hall.

"But if they call for a harp tune, harper, what then?"

"I did think of that, so I borrowed one from his grace's music room. I don't suppose he'll mind. It's called Dariole."

"You what?" Raven coughed.

Ben lovingly patted the bundle he had slung over his shoulder, a loose triangular bag about two feet long, painted in interlacing floral patterns. It jangled a little as he shifted it. "He said I could take what I needed."

"You took the king of Faerie's harp!" As they entered the mead hall of Alfred King of Wessex, the sound of Raven's laughter rang across the rafters. "Oh sir, you are so dead!"

16
Harper Errant

It was warmer in the hall than Ben expected. Waves of heat rose from the huge log fire burning at the center of the room, vented by a brightly painted smoke hole over head, and glowing braziers stood along each wall. Add the heat as well of the horde of sturdy thegns, each one with a mail shirt chiming between his brightly dyed and embroidered tunica, and the padded arming shirt and linen camisa. It was warm enough to distract him from Raven's breaking character for a fit of laughter. On the other hand, who exactly was Raven's persona, here and now?

Every day a new adventure, he thought. With the heat and the glimmering light of fire and torches on lime-washed walls, and the glistening sweat on so many winter-pale Saxon faces, Raven's faerie glow would be effectively masked, if any were here that could see it.

So what exactly was he looking for? A bit of a golden arm ring a few inches long: one of the heads or the smashed and flattened body. Would it be just lying around, kicked under a bench, hung up on the wall? What if he was wrong? What if had flown into the fire? What if it wasn't here at all?

"Listen!" a stranger said to his neighbor in passing. So Ben listened.

And there it was. He could hear it. If he tuned his senses just under all the chatter and clatter, it was there like a deep growl, a rhythmic rumble that grew slightly stronger as he focused on it. In that bass rumble was almost the beginning of words, almost a chant made by a monk in a faraway cell. The story of its breaking was here, and thus the artifact itself, that was certain—but not in this room.

He started to move casually through the crowd, accepting a cup of mead, laughing at a joke half heard, greeting those who greeted him, and passing on. The fragment should be easy to find. If only he could get into the side rooms with his magical GPS. Then there'd be a chance to examine it, read its story as Aubrey had said. With Raven's help he should be able to get the time he needed.

The harp in its gilded bag shifted on his shoulder, and the jangle of muffled strings rang as it had before.

Someone nearby perked up and whispered to his neighbor. "Gleeman!" The word began to sail through the room almost faster than he could think, and he wondered how much Beowulf he could summon up.

No, nothing. Drawing a blank.

Then a sudden silence fell, and all turned as one to face the back of the hall, Ben and Raven looking as eagerly as the rest. Two page boys entered, and the king's chaplain, then Alfred the king, thin and looking ill. He was dressed more or less as the warriors in the hall, his rank picked out by a simple crown of golden wire. With him came the tonsured bishop—that would be Wulfhere—head to head with Alfred in earnest conversation. A double string of priests and men at arms brought up the rear but no one noticed them, for as soon as Alfred entered the room, a great roar went up and a stamping and thumping of trestles from thegns and housecarls shook the hall, although the ealdormen, Alfred's earls, looked grim.

With a majesty that belied his youth, the king occupied a solid oak chair that was not much more than a bench with two arms and a back to it; not quite what Ben expected of a throne but clearly the seat of authority. The heir of long-domesticated mercenaries, refugees, and pirates, Alfred had at 25 survived a series of defeats at the hands of the latest marauders; and yet for the most part retained the loyalty of his thegns, even in these dark days huddling behind their walls. Their fear of the Danes and their own love of power, buttressed by sworn oaths of loyalty, gifts, and one massive victory, were enough to keep them together for the defense of Wessex. For now.

And yet by all accounts, Alfred wanted only peace and safety for his people to farm, to pray, to ask for justice and receive it. Today, apparently, in a midwinter truce, there was breathing space enough to give audience, hear complaints, dispense justice. And meet an enemy.

Before Ben could remark to his companion, Raven had moved through the crowd as only the fae can move and bent his knee to the king.

"Great lord!" the boy said, loud and clear. So much for background color and noise. "Forgive me, I pray, I have left you too long without my service."

Alfred stopped, exchanged looks with the bishop, then down at the dark haired youth. Ever stylish, Raven had dressed himself for court in a black woolen tunic swarming with leafy embroidery along every the edge.

"Hrafn Alfsigr, my foot-loose shield-bearer! And where have you been wandering this fortnight since I sent you forth with my loving queen, the lady Aelswith. Making merry with the wenches in Winchester, no doubt."

Raven blushed, to Ben's utter astonishment, and the bishop snorted.

"We'll be getting you married before long, boy," Alfred went on. "It would be better to resist such temptations. We will pray together later. Now say what messages you bring me."

Well. This was nice. Well done. Without effort, Raven had inserted himself seamlessly into the timeline where they needed to be. Now all Ben had to do was get out of the hall to start the search. Had to, for Sparrow's sake.

Using the royal distraction, Ben pretended no one had noticed the harp, and just kept walking, keeping to the walls, avoiding clusters of people who were looking at him, *right at him*, with expectation. And Dariole jangled again, as if demanding to be played.

"Shut up!" he muttered. The harp rattled louder and practically leapt off his back.

"Brand Harper!" said Raven, his beautiful voice urgent at Ben's elbow.

"Not now!" Ben hissed. But Raven was not here to whisper.

"Lord, the king commands your presence and your harp. Which you have to admit," the boy added less volubly, "is trying to tell you something."

So Ben nodded to fate and gave in. He relaxed away from the whispering at the edge of his consciousness, letting the performer in him take over. With sure hands, he unslung and drew out the king of Faerie's harp as he strode across the creaking, rush-strewn floor. When he met the grave, fair face of the king who clearly knew him well, he went to one knee and bowed his head. A flash of color caught his eye as he did so, the damp edge of an oak leaf, dragged in on someone's heel, poking out from under the top layer of rushes. And the leaf was the fresh grey-green of summer. Curious.

King Alfred's voice, surprisingly light and pleasant, said, "How do you expect me to dispense justice, Brand Harper, without your music? Take your accustomed place, now that you've remembered where it is. But by Our Lord's most precious blood, man, play something soothing so we can continue. We'll have the heroic measures after we take our meat."

17
Lawgiver

Ben nodded and rose easily, plucking up the oak leaf and slipping it into his belt to share with Sparrow later. Then he took his place as he was told. Someone brought a stool, and while he settled himself below the king's left hand, a fluttery flighty jabbery sort of female sort of noise rose up and motivated from the edge of the room to its center. The path of its progress was marked by large men making way for a tiny middle-aged woman flinging back layers of veils, shuffling out of massive furs, probably someone's mother.

"Justice, my king!" she was shouting high and shrill. "King Alfred, justice!"

Others tried to prevent her, but the king smiled and gestured her forth. "Stay her not, my lords, but let her come to the king," he said. Or so it sounded to Ben. He may have been romanticizing.

"I am Ceolwen of Bydford, most noble king," the woman said with a deep curtsey. "I am the magistrate's widow of that benighted place. And I beg your help. When God's Church can't help me, surely it is the King who must."

The priests all frowned but the armed men in the hall chortled in their beards.

"Nothing is beyond God, my lady, but what service can I do you. Hrafn, lad, bring a stool and let the lady Ceolwen sit."

Her frantic hands went to her face in amaze. "Oh! Oh, to sit in the presence of the king!"

She settled herself for a moment, then leapt up, pacing, kicking rushes and tripping on the wet, embroidered bands of her richest violet gown. The pale blue and cream layers of her wimple and veils whipped about her shoulders, barely hanging on to her modesty with golden pins.

"Nay, sire, nay, I cannot sit, I can't sit. I'm much too upset to sit, not denying the honor. It's the *alfr*, you see, your highness. Elves! Oh!"

She wailed in frustration and anger, wringing her busy hands or waving them about in the air as she paced. "Oh, how I hate them! In summer, they lurk in the plowed furrows in my fields, you see. And at midwinter they creep into my byre and bother the kyne. And when my men tend the fields or milk the kyne, the little arslings shoot at them with their little elf darts. They're all over sores and blisters, my men are. Every week, half of them are sick with it and cannot work! Now you may say it's nothing, and you may wonder if I haven't prayed enough, but I am a good Christian, and so are all my household and all my tenants, too. Sire, I've had my priest go down twice to say the masses and do the blessings. My neighbor, Bjarni Bjarneson, read in the priest books himself and found the necessaries, but it doesn't work. Twelve masses, Sire, that's what it's taken. Twelve masses each time, and the holy water and Mercian beeswax, and oh I don't know what all, and that takes treasure, your grace, hard money!"

Out of breath at last she paused and sat a moment to compose herself, re-pinning her veil automatically. Finally she folded her hands in her lap and sighed. "I'm a poor widow, sire, with a son to keep the manor for until he comes of age, and hold off the Danes, too. Danes! By Our Lady, sire, bring on the Danes but rid me of these elves!"

By now the hall, and Ben too, were roaring with laughter, but though Alfred's eyes watered, he held on to his air of regal detachment. "My lady, tell me," he said at last, hoping she was ready, and encouraged, she launched again.

"I will, Sire. Do you know what else, sire? Mine is a modest holding, truly modest, sire, with barely the villeins to work it, and forest on every side. I'm surrounded by forest. Forests! Don't you think those elves would want to live there and frolic happily in the greenwood? But nay, sire, they have to live in my fields. Sire, I am begging you, as your loyal bedeswoman and your mother's second cousin, to aid me!"

Raven, standing just behind the king's chair, leaned down to pass something to Ben and whisper in his ear. So Ben sobered enough to beg Alfred's attention with a touch. And when the king looked round at the harper and nodded, Ben rose and took stage, pitching his voice so all could hear.

"By your leave, my king. This young man," nodding at Raven, "is too modest in his youth to bring this to your attention himself. But I have here a token from Aelberic his father's farm. Now this farm I know to have been plagued with elves for many years."

With great formality he laid a silver coin stamped with the king's profile into the king's hand.

"And yet it is beset no longer. I have it on Lame Aelberic's oath, that if the lady Ceolwen will let her priest but bury this token in the midst of the worst part of the, *erm*, infestation, along with three leaves of holly and, ah…" He glanced briefly at the bishop who was turning purple. "And cause a Mass to be said for the king, her elf troubles will be ended."

The king's pale eyes looked out of his strained, narrow face with some doubt. "You're sure of this?"

"As I am sure of my hope of heaven, Sire."

As Alfred gave the widow Ceolwen the coin and his blessing, and saw her returned to her retainers praising the king and his wisdom and roundly cursing the heathen *alfr*, Raven caught Ben's eye and nodded with a small smile. The coin, the holly, and the Mass, while edifying, were only to ease her mind, of course. Whatever goofy faerie pests were bothering her, they would be gone before she got home.

"Happy Christmas," Raven said.

And then the fun was over. The lady Ceolwen had called on the Danes by name, and by god, here they were. Answered by a shout and an angry roar from every throat, the great double doors to the hall slammed back, war horns blared, and every man in the hall surged to his feet sword in hand. For here came the enemy, Guthrum the Dane who wanted to be a king, that had fought them two long years to this truce.

18
Rune with a view

Incandescent with fury and pride, Guthrum strode into the hall with his shieldthanes, his housecarls, and his herald. The cheek plates of a helmet carved with writhing serpents masked his face, topped with a white horsetail of the Viking clans.

Alfred stood to meet him, his own men forming up along both sides of the hall and behind him, Ben on his left hand and Raven behind his right shoulder. The chaplain and his priests melted back to the wall and the shuttered windows, clutching their pectoral crosses, though the bishop remained, if not nearby. Midwinter was sacred to heathen and Christian alike, and the truce, for now, would hold. Should hold.

"What is all this!" Guthrum bellowed, dragging off the hideous helmet and tossing it to his boy. His face was clogged with scars. "You start without me? You put this woman's little troubles before ours! You there, widow! I'll send three of my *godhi* to your farm, Thor's priests. They will take care of your elves. And then!" He roared again, taking in the whole company. "In the spring I'll burn it to the ground!"

Lady Ceolwen screamed and fled the hall with her serving men and waiting women scrambling behind her.

An ugly laugh erupted from Guthrum's men.

"Heh, Saxon women," he sneered. "Like Saxon men, they scamper from me like rabbits! You, Alfred King! Do you apologize for this affront to my honor?"

While Alfred faced the man mildly, Ben stood his ground, his heart in his throat. He really didn't have time to die in the ninth century.

"Enough of your bluster, Guthrum Sitricson!" Alfred the

king shouted back. "You were delayed. My people look to me for wisdom in peace as well as in war. No affront was intended, in Christ's name."

The older man grunted and scanned the Saxon court. "You are either very brave or a fool, king, to face me with your skald and your hearth boy before your housecarls."

"My gleeman I would set against yours were he three days in his grave. And the boy..." The look Alfred threw at Raven seemed to say he knew more than he said. "My shield bearer in his youth is the match of any other of my men and two of yours in the flower of their manhood. Now peace! All of you, put up your weapons. Hrafn Alfsigr, have a chair brought for Lord Guthrum. Father Damianus! Documents here, now."

So the business of diplomacy began, the Norseman's requirement for bluster and boasting satisfied, at least to the limits of Alfred's patience. Trestle tables were set up and benches brought. The two kings sat in their chairs of authority at either side of a table spread with parchments handsomely written out in Latin with notes in the vernacular, and scribes read aloud, interpreted, noted, and corrected while monarchs, priests and lawyers wrangled, and everyone else got lightly drunk. Most of the agreement had been thrashed out over the past week by proxy, but nothing was settled.

Ben, trapped at King Alfred's side, could do nothing but what the king commanded. Which, if the situation weren't so dire, he would have given his left arm to do. He had never held such an instrument in his hands, nor in such company, in his life, or been asked for such music.

The immediate challenge was that notions of melody have changed a good deal to the common ear in twelve hundred years. So many of the songs he knew for the harp would have sounded bizarrely alien to anyone in the hall, which would draw attention he did not want. Forced to leave the classic Irish pieces behind, he simply let the elven harp take the lead. As he sat with Dariole between his knees, the silver strings sang and so, from time to time, when it came to him, did he.

A rune poem opened to him in bits from somewhere, probably the diary:

Feoh byþ frofur fira gehwylcum (he chanted)
sceal ðeah manna gehwylc miclun hyt dælan
gif he wile for drihtne domes hleotan.

Wealth is a comfort to all men
yet must every man bestow it freely,
if he wish to gain honor in the sight of the Lord.

Riding seems easy to the man sitting indoors;
To the one who travels the high-road
    on a stout horse,
an act of courage

The torch is known to all who live
by its pale, bright flame;
it always burns in the room where princes sit.

An open hand brings credit and honor,
    supports a man's fame;
it gives help and sustenance
to broken men who have lost all else.

Gyfu gumena byþ gleng and herenys,
wraþu and wyrþscype and wræcna gehwam
ar and ætwist, ðe byþ oþra leas

And though his music and wisdom went largely unre-
marked, it seemed to Ben that tempers which would have been
huge and brittle on both sides remained calmer than expected,
and more good work was done than at other times. Still, he
didn't trust the Danes. And nor did the Saxon king.

19
Alarums and diversions

Eventually, cooking smells began to waft through the room as the two bullocks and five great boar turning on spits spilled fat into the fires of the cooking house, attached to the main hall by stone walled corridors. Stomachs grumbled, mouths watered, and those who had sat in one place too long began to feel their piles turn hot and their thighs sweat under their woolen gowns and furs and mail. Alfred had been thrifty with his winter ale, too, among the diplomatic corps, such as it was, and thirsts were raging. Of all in the room, only Raven remained awake and alert, and even he was immersed in maintaining his persona, flirting easily with a serving maid, teasing a long blond braid out from behind her wimple.

Tenderly Ben lifted his fingers from the harp and stilled the strings. He had to take a break and surely, things must be winding down. How difficult could it be to agree to stop fighting and exchange a few hostages? And if it was so easy, why was Oberon so worried about it?

At last the king stood up, looking drawn, and nodded to the harper that his timing was perfect. "Are we finished then, Guthrum Sitricson?" he said.

Guthrum smacked the trestle with an open hand, startling the room and waking those who had dozed off.

"It is not for you to say so, Alfred of Wessex," he grumbled. "We are done when I say we are done!" Hot eyes scanned the room with a challenge as grim as when he had arrived.

"Well?" said Alfred, showing neither fear nor impatience nor any attitude at all.

"It remains still to swear our oaths as I told you, on Odin's ring."

Oh here we go, Ben thought, shoving the exquisite harp into its leather bag. It's here somewhere, but it's broken, and it's all going to go to hell. In a moment it would be all over.

Then Alfred smiled his stately political smile, an expression few men master so young. With a snap of the fingers, one of the mousy priests stepped forward looking uncommonly smug, and placed a slender, silk-wrapped box in the bishop's hands. Wulfhere threw aside the covering, and suddenly the dragon ring's voice that had been muffled and dull was in Ben's mind as clear and strong as digital playback.

Bishop Wulfhere could be forgiven for the superior smirk he brought to the table, and all at once Ben knew why. At his shoulder, Raven swore eloquently, and added, "The bastard!"

Wulfhere was smiling because the gold and crystal reliquary he placed on the table was clasped with a golden dragon's head, snarling like the ones on the ships the Vikings came in.

Guthrum was swearing too.

"Fiends of Muspelheim devour you!" he snarled. "You swore you had the dragon ring!"

Now the bishop spoke in tones exactly as disdainful as his smile.

"This is all that remains of your heathen talisman, lord, for we found the one part only."

"What!"

It was so clear now! That was it! Hungrily, Ben listened and looked and followed the lines of the interlace engraved like tattoos about the snarling face, the rune for Victory carved between its slitted eyes. That was it!

Raven's hand was on his arm. If he could only get clear enough to take two steps, they could collect the horses; two seconds more and they could be on the road home!

"Indeed, all that remains is this vile demon, a spawn of Satan, a monster of the heathen world which Christ confound." Signs of the Cross fluttered along the dais. "We found it indeed

to be marked on its neck with signs betokening the uncon-
quered son of God. Within the box is a precious finger bone of
the holy Saint Swithin, which your heathen beast now guards
as an angel with a flaming sword guards the gates of Paradise."

"Traitor! Defiler!" Guthrum bellowed, and the room
exploded with threats and oaths.

And as he did the hall grew suddenly cold, as if the fires
had all died, as if snow piled in the corners. Another voice
joined in, wild and high, shrieking over the building chaos.
Every door crashed open, and the outer doors to the hall as
well, and a blast of cold and ice flew in swirling to the ceiling.

"Liars and oath-breakers!"

The sound was like a woman's grief but more horrible, a
Valkyrie screaming on the wind, and when all eyes looked
upwards, they saw her floating, hovering at the painted roof
tree: a tall, mad-eyed woman with skin as white as snow,
raging mouth the scarlet of heart's blood, and hair that snaked
around her like a storm at sea, as white as the doorway to a
frozen hell.

Titania, screaming, lashed out with beams of cold that
turned first the smug young priest and then another to pillars
of ice.

"It is the harper's doing, Guthrum the Dane!" she shrieked.
"It is he who has betrayed you, and the boy with him. The
harper destroyed your heirloom, the gift of mighty Odin to
your long fathers. Destroyed it with a blow in the name of the
White Christ!"

Dumbstruck Ben stared open-mouthed. How on earth did
she know that? How had she found him?

Enchantment swirling about her in great swathes of wind
and frost, she reached out a hand towards him and Ben froze
on the spot, pinned like an insect while Guthrum's men moved
to take him, and Alfred's men stood powerless even to draw
sword.

"Raven!" Ben choked through teeth glued shut. "Two
seconds. I need two seconds!" Then he snatched at a tune in his
head, and he made it his anchor.

And sable-clad Raven, the only one of Alfred's court still

mobile, thrust up his fist towards the mad queen and punched the air.

"*Haegtesse*! She-witch! Demon!" he called, and released his fingers. One two three balls of black air whirled from his palm one two three, and slammed her up against the ceiling. She howled her surprise and fury! Raven had nothing like her power, but his blows were distraction enough.

"Ben, now!" Movement came.

It was like walking in jello, infinitely slow, but he had his music and his direction. Two steps attained, the third was easier and by the fourth he was running out of the hall and out of the world with Raven's hand clutching his sleeve. Whatever mess they had left behind would have to take care of itself.

"We'll clean it up in editing." He laughed a little wildly, then mentally slapped himself for his childish sense of timing.

Another step and the rush of air around them resolved into things: huge dark and spicy trees with rusty bark, a rushing brook, a ferny floor and streams of mist-filtered sunlight. They skidded to a halt on a dirt path that smelled of sugar cookies and pine.

Ben felt as drained as if he had just given a major presentation to a producer followed by singing the Friday night set at the Star with two encores. He was nearly as winded as if he had run all the way down Raven Tor. If only he could get his breath, he would swear long and creatively, but for now, it was enough just to breathe.

In a minute, in a minute, okay two minutes, he might be able to think. At least the faerie queen had not chosen, or perhaps had not been able to follow them, and for now it felt safe, just barely safe to rest.

"Can I ask you something?" Raven said, quite calmly.

His head tilted way, way back looking at a patch of blue sky. Somewhere a bird warbled, but he couldn't put a name to it. Pretty though. And the slender-boled trees just went up and up and up a hundred feet before the first branches reached to catch the mist.

"Sure," said Ben, still bent over, hands bracing his knees like a marathon runner, gasping though his companion, of course, was not.

"Where are we?"

Ben stood up and looked around, gulping air and more than a little amazed, and realized with astonishment just where he had landed them. That's what happens when you put panic to work for you.

"Uhm, well, let's see. These really tall red trees are California redwoods—you know, sequoias, the coastal kind. And those sort of Christmas trees there are sugar pines; you can tell from the smell of vanilla in the air. Off hand, I'd say somewhere in the Santa Cruz Mountains. In fact, oh god!" He gestured back through the trees more or less the way they'd come. "My mom and dad's summer cabin is about 5 miles that way. This is Fall Creek."

It was Raven's turn to look thoughtful. "You are good. But there was no music. How did you do it?"

"Oh, man, the music was everywhere! I'd been playing all afternoon, and the artifact itself was like some kind of a Gregorian chant. Well okay, it was in my head, wasn't it. The whole time."

The boy looked uncommonly impressed. "What was?"

Thank goodness the ground was padded with fern and the spongy detritus of a redwood grove, because Ben was giggling helplessly as he collapsed to the forest floor. "Springsteen, man! *Born in the USA!*"

20
Above Santa Cruz, California

As the laughter died and the rush of flight receded, Ben realized his face was hot and his whole body clammy; sweat gathered in his hair and made his scalp prickle, and he felt a little sick. He desperately wanted to go home to his own comfortable cottage and the family he loved and even the work he was sick to death of. But as soon as he thought of it, he knew that home wasn't there, not properly: just a horrible simulacrum of his son, and his wife caught in some kind of nightmare.

It was easier just to lie there staring glassily up at the blue hole in the otherwise evergreen canopy. Ben's lungs burned with the transition from past to present, from frozen woodland to green mountain side, from medieval winter to a summer eight time zones and more than a thousand years away. Still, it wasn't as if he'd actually run the whole way. The narrow escape from a strange and frozen death had simply overwhelmed him.

A minute more, and he managed to pull himself together sufficiently to sit up again and drag the harp onto his shoulder, and think about asking politely if Raven happened to know how to get to Dartmoor from here. The thought slipped away as by common consent they started walking further into the fragrant trees, following the river, breathing easily at last. Another half thought made him reach behind the silver belt buckle that had traveled in some form or other to the ninth century and back.

With two fingers he slipped out the oak leaf, damp and fresh. Why had he kept it, he wondered, twirling the stem. To show Sparrow, he had told himself at the time. But why? An oak leaf in a forest hall, no matter the century, was hardly newsworthy. A green leaf in winter, maybe, but still.

He sighed with resignation and muttered, "Must be a good reason," then tucked it back behind the buckle. Then he added, more conversationally, "That woman is seriously deranged."

"Yes," said Raven. The boy was still dressed for Alfred's court and admiring the scenery. Any passing hikers, if they thought about it at all, would think there he was a refugee from a medieval faire. It was Santa Cruz. It could happen.

Questions were starting to bubble to the surface as Ben's mind relaxed, freed from panic and character improv. "Okay, how do you do the thing with…" How to ask this?

"What, sir?"

All right, the boy wasn't reading his mind. "They knew us—King Alfred, the bishop, the thegns—everyone who was meant to. We were familiar faces to them. I didn't expect to be noticed, much less recognized and put to work. Who were we? Really?"

The raven boy took a moment to consider, and said, "When you said you looked it up, what did you mean?"

"I told you, there are amazing things in the diary."

"And who wrote the diary?"

"Uh… You?"

That small, enigmatic smile. "I don't keep a diary."

"Raven!"

"It's complicated, sir. You can track your missing jewel through time and even space, and you can play the harp—that harp!—with more skill than you admit. I, among other things, can manipulate, well, things. It is one reason my lord sent me with you, along with the languages and so on."

Ben considered this, walking now along the sandy edge of the creek rushing into shadows. Raven was whistling, and exchanging calls with a blue jay.

"I have two more pieces to find. Are you staying with me?"

"To the very end, sir. Assuming…"

"Assuming what?"

"Assuming my lady Titania doesn't kill me along the way." He held up a hand to stall Ben's reaction. "Never fear, sir. She's had her tantrums before. True, the last time it took me, oh, longer than I liked to get back. But here I am."

As if the day hadn't already been weird enough. "Where from?"

"Nowhere, sir." The boy looked uncomfortable, which really wasn't like him. The sun seemed to be setting, the light golden in their eyes.

"You can't tell me?"

"Just nowhere, sir. It wasn't pleasant. The queen and I are not... friendly." Raven paused, whistled a single low note, and smiled. "And here we are, sir."

Wide-eyed, Ben whipped around, reorienting whether he liked it or not from Pacific coastal woodland to "Dartmoor!"

The light, the sounds, the smells had all subtly shifted as they ambled along the creek path and out of a California springtime, across a corner of ageless Faerie, and into the long summer twilight on Raven Tor. A high wild shriek echoed behind them so ferociously that he flinched, but it was only a hawk, hunting in the peach-streaked sky. Listening close, he could just make out the muffled roar of a car down on the motorway, the underlying hum of the modern world, and the evening air sighing through the Raven's Eye.

"You're good, kid," said Ben.

"You wanted to be home, and your song took us to your childhood home. You need to be at your present home. This is as near as it is wise, I think, to simply appear out of nowhere. Your house is..."

"That way, I know. But we're not done. I mean, shouldn't we get be getting on with it?"

"Go home, Ben Harper," Raven said, and smiled. "Read in the diary. Eat and drink. The food of my country does you little good, and my queen kept you from a feasting... for which we should probably be grateful. Salt beef, unhopped ale, and not a salad anywhere. Very virtuous, but not very festive."

Ben laughed with the realization. "Are you suggesting, Hrafn Al-whatsit, that they're all so cranky because they're constipated?"

"Almost certainly."

The Dragon Ring   125

"But I can't go home! What about my wife? What's happening with Sparrow, and..." He shuddered, flinching from the thought. "And that thing that looks like him?"

Out of the utter silence of the high moor, and more to the point, out of the deep front pocket of Ben's jeans, a cell phone chirped. Man and Fae exchanged startled looks.

"My lord did say..."

It kept chirping while he scrabbled to drag the thing into the open. Caller ID said ELF KING. Funny.

'Your lordship!" Ben laughed into the phone.

Aubrey's genteel voice came through over sweet bell-like music low in the background. Well, the line was probably not any of the usual carriers. "So you were successful. Well done."

"Raven did his part too, sir. Thanks, but ..."

"Go home, Ben. That comfortable study of yours is well protected. And I've put a glamour on it. Mellis and the changeling cannot enter. They will not try. Even your friends won't think to call on you there, unless you ask them to."

"But sir!" A massive yawn overtook him before he could quite finish saying whatever he had already forgotten. He could imagine the amusement creeping across the almond-eyed face, and yawned again.

"Whinging is unbecoming to a hero," said the king of Faerie. "Let me talk to Raven."

Still astonished, he handed the phone over to the kid, who frowned. "Just take it. And no whinging."

The boy in the medieval tunic put the instrument to his ear and strolled away, saying nothing. A few minutes later, having measured out the perimeter of the clearing with even steps, he returned with a curious expression, and held the sleek black phone out to Ben.

"He says to take care of the harp," said Raven.

Their hands touched.

That was all.

21
Diamond Cottage

Ben opened his eyes. For good measure, he tried again, which was harder than it sounds since one eye was blinkered by the arm across his face. So he put his trained, analytical mind to the problem and hit on a solution. Yes, indeed, raising the head from folded arms first proved the better plan.

Home, then. In his own office, yeah, leaning on the work table opposite the desk with a blanket over his shoulders and with aches in muscles he'd forgotten he had, primarily in his backside and thighs and, oh yes, his hands. Raven was gone. Getting up and into a steamy shower seemed a laudable but unlikely goal.

"I knew I was too old for this."

But he yawned, stretched, letting every joint take its time to crackle and pop while he took stock. Something, he realized, smelled wonderful, better even than the roasting bullocks in Alfred's hall. A thick ham sandwich on fresh country bread, home made crisps, and a bottle of Bass Ale were waiting in front of him, with a napkin and everything. The books and papers and sheet music that usually drifted across the table had been neatly stacked and set aside.

The king of Faerie's harp, precious in its painted bag, sat in the corner of his broken down but too cool to throw away old sofa, vibrating to some inner airs of its own.

He was again wearing the clothes he had left in, except for the leather jacket, which was brushed and draped over the back of his chair. His glasses appeared to be neatly tucked in the breast pocket, and the faerie diary lay opened to a page with a botanical drawing of an oak leaf. The penny dropped.

Weary as he was, he started to laugh.

"I have a Brownie! Brilliant! Brownie, if you're listening, I, uh, I appreciate it."

He remembered just in time that it will not do to thank a Brownie, if you want them to return. After that, the smell of food put practically everything else aside in service of his hunger.

The diary kept him company while he ate. The first pages, ones he'd already read and used, had settled down. The inks were fading along with the bad jokes in the margins. Perhaps the "little ones" were bored already. But no, as soon as he turned the first new page, the action began again. There was a sketchy and slightly sarcastic write up of events so far, with his name reported as "Ben-Hoopy", and Raven called "Crowsfeet" throughout. Bloody goblins.

From between two pages where it had been tightly tucked, he unfolded a printed paper torn from some old book—the *Journal of the Wessex Antiquarian and Archæological Society, 1888*, apparently—a drawing of a Saxon reliquary with its dragon's head and finger bone of St Swithin matching the details he had soaked up almost 1200 years before. Even as an old engraving, hardly more than a pencil sketch, the dragon finial alone was beautiful beyond words. Carefully he folded the journal page and slipped it back into the book.

Another page turned, and this time the mustard on the hand-made paper was from his own thumb. Well, fine. His household Brownie—did they have names?—had known exactly the right mustard to use and exactly how much. Ben, bodily assumed into gustatory heaven, fought to keep his attention on the book when there was so much information to absorb.

The next page was a drawing of some kind of ring, a finger ring this time, although it apparently came apart in three jeweled bands that could be rotated back together and locked. On the next pages he got to read an article about the history of wedding rings, which mentioned something called a gimmel, as illustrated by the drawing on the opposite page: three or more interlocking bands, and on each a line of fairly bad poetry that rhymed, more or less. Some of the examples were in English, some in Latin.

"Haven't I seen that before?" he wondered, then waved away the thought. No time for puzzles.

The crabbed, spiky handwriting went on some pages further, mostly in verse: the quatrains of a ballad, a sonnet of doubtful value, followed by another even worse. He could practically hear goblin giggles echoing off the stone walls of his hideaway. Some were totally vulgar, accompanied by crude drawings that were, oh god, animated. But what were the noises?

Noises? Thumps and bumps rattled the windows and something rustled in the thatch above the ceiling. His lordship's restrictions apparently held even against his own, but his "helpers" were surely playing around the eaves on the balmy summer night. That he could ignore.

Reading further, his eyes widened, breath came quick, like a child who wakes to hear the prancing and pawing of reindeer on the roof. If the hints meant what they had to mean, he could almost count this whole sorry business to have been worthwhile.

Ben never talked about it—it was just too hard to explain—but he had spent four college summers as a gentleman retainer at Farthingale Hall, a strictly governed Elizabethan manor and village in Somerset, open only rarely to the public. A bastion of experimental archeology, as some called it, where the best residents immersed themselves in study and practice, and were adjudged to be very Elizabethan indeed. It was a secret passion, of course. One of those things he left out of his reality show resume, along with the incomplete minor in Early Modern poetry and numerous seasons of a history-obsessed Renaissance faire back in California. Where he had, indeed, left his swords.

Oh, man, Shakespeare's England? Really? How did they know when he didn't know himself? And if they knew, why not… "Magic, Ben" seemed a cheap explanation, but probably the best he was going to get. And something about the nature of time.

Okay, focus.

The next diary page gate-folded out and out again to show a street map of London in the year 1590, or part of it anyway, with labels floating over certain streets, buildings and landmarks. Within the old City walls, the lines of the streets was not so different from the London he knew, though some of the names had altered over time.

The map maker had attempted to represent every steeple, every guild hall, every roof top, well, water pump, and mansion from the river to the Moor Gate, the Tower to Whitehall. When Ben looked at it with care, it focused like a magnifying glass on one area, perhaps Cheapside, until it moved and swung the view down to old London Bridge with its lugubrious burden of traitors' heads on the Southwark side. He took a deep pull on his beer and folded the map away so he could move on.

He sat back, aches and pains forgotten, to let the analytical mind, without irony, begin processing not just the words and images he had just read but tone and intention beneath. The first expedition had held more excitement than expected—rabid wolves and deadly ice. But the diary when it came to him had shown none of that. Now, when he looked past his own excitement toward the next goal, he saw the threats buried in the jokes and maps and Victorian scholarship. Titania's wolves had been a real danger; the next journey would doubtless be worse.

"You guys could be a little more helpful, you know," Ben said aloud. The rustling in the thatch abruptly ceased. "Maybe a warning sign? Something?"

No answers came. He shrugged and picked it up again, but the final written pages showed nothing explicit. Perhaps they did not, or could not, know. Perhaps it was part of his quest simply to face the unknown and deal with it.

The one note he had ignored—the one circled round and round with heavy pencil—had been leaping ahead again, drawing his attention then hiding, hopping from page to page too quick to read until he had finished everything else. And when he turned the last written page, it rested for a moment, then started blinking. Blinking?

Check Your Messages!!!

That made him sit up straight, but also twitched up a smile. He was stuffed with good food and good beer, and though he had slept awhile, his eyes were growing gravelly. But he let out a breath like a sigh, resigned to following the directions while he actually had the time.

"All right, all right!" he laughed, and spun in his chair to the desk, the laptop and the phone.

Phone first.

Peter, wondering in his clipped Northern accent where the hell Ben was. Didn't Ben know that people were waiting for decisions, design approval, scheduling? Projects were hanging fire? Millions of pounds were on the line? Didn't he want to be rich as, well, my god even richer than the Sultan of Dubai? Call me back tonight, any time, tomorrow latest.

Peter, of course, was the one who wanted to be richer than the Sultan of Dubai, so he could wait. It was all crap anyway. The program, the books, the guest appearances had done him well, yes, but nothing that was going to make anyone that kind of rich, unless Aubrey showered him with gold, or something.

Mellis, awake, bespelled, sometime during the afternoon, and in excessively happy tones, reporting on Prize Day. She didn't mind he wasn't there, and Sparrow was so, so happy even though he hadn't taken any prizes except one for a diorama of Fairyland that she didn't understand. Now poor Sparrow—she never ever called him that—wasn't feeling very well tonight, but that was all right, he was so, so happy, and Mellis was so, so happy to feed him Mrs Danvers's chicken soup—which Sparrow didn't care for, having kale in it.

Various Women's Institute ladies: "It's not all jam and Jerusalem, you know, Mr Harper!"

Dinah Shorland, two or three times, trying to confirm his sitting in with them at the Star on Saturday. And could he please bring the harp?

What day was it now? His hands felt like they would ache until September, so maybe not.

And on and on. It was all stomach turning. He skipped to the next one, and the next, and the next. The phone had been ringing and the e-mail backing up; everybody wanted something from him, even people he loved, and all he could think about was his little boy frightened and alone with strangers, his wife some kind of zombie, and oh my god the village phone circuits must have been besieged with gossiping neighbors all afternoon!

And now here he was, trapped in the only safe place within his home, separated from the rest by perilous magicks. He was also caught in a seriously dangerous domestic squabble between two people who shouldn't even exist. Not to mention, sailing through time and space without even the comforts of a transdimensional hazmat suit.

"Still think it's mad, I suppose," said the smooth, professional voice.

With its characteristic electronic sizzle, the laptop monitor had popped on, and there he was, the king of Faerie in wide screen digital splendor. The sapphire in his ear gleamed subtly.

Ben sat back with folded arms, shaking his head.

"Well, actually," he said, choosing his words. "Yes, I do. But I got myself into this. Worse, man, I got my wife and child into it. Did you hear that phone call from Mellis? She hasn't called him Sparrow since she signed him up for school."

The look on Aubrey's face might actually have been surprise, though he covered it swiftly.

"Isn't that his name?"

Ben yawned extravagantly. "You know, if you want me to get some sleep, you should..."

"Ben, stop— Isn't Sparrow his proper name?"

"No, it's..."

"Don't say it!" Aubrey snapped. "Don't say it at all." The long blue eyes narrowed in something like a considering frown. "That means my lady doesn't have his true name. Ben, listen. Whatever you do, don't speak it out loud until this is done. If you can manage, don't even think it."

"Mm, okay, sure. Oh right, the power of names." Ben yawned again but gave up the question he'd been holding on to. "Tell me how he is, please?"

Now Aubrey gave him the relaxed, languid smile. "That's why I called. On your keyboard, press Control G."

"But that's my macro for..."

Sigh. "Just do it, please."

So he did, and there he was, a fair haired little boy with eager eyes, sitting at a picnic table under a tree, surrounded by grownups who were singing or playing instruments. Out of habit, he spun up the volume on the keyboard controls, and yes, he could hear at least a little. This time Sparrow's teacher was a tall, very handsome man in a golden tunic and silver chain mail byrnie, something like the men of Alfred's mead hall, but taller and far more grand. His movements, like theirs, were those of a warrior, but modulated for the child. He sang a phrase for Sparrow in a mellow voice and waited, apparently for a response.

"Gwydion," said Aubrey from the picture-in-picture box in the lower corner of the screen, apparently pleased with himself. "He was happy to take on the boy's musical education."

"But, you know, the asthma," Ben said sadly. "Sparrow can't sing when he can't breathe."

"Where he is, that's not a problem."

Sparrow's father glared with sudden irritation. "And when he's home, and can't breathe again, and remembers what he's lost? What then?"

"He will have learned something, nevertheless."

Ben closed his mouth and stared, then gave all his attention to his son, just watching. "Does he ask where we are?"

"All the time, but he is content, mainly, that he'll see you soon. He knows something of the danger, but he's no longer frightened."

"What are they doing now?"

The boy and the warrior bard seemed to be holding or maybe braiding something between them while they sang: golden strings, or ropes, or serpents of light, two in each hand.

"I'm not sure, but I think Gwydion is doing a making. If he can accomplish this, Sparrow will really have learned something, and so young."

"It's past his bedtime." The picture faded and the tears that had been lying in wait now streamed down Ben's cheeks unchecked. "And mine," he croaked at last, but Aubrey had already vanished.

22
Verses

In the misty moisty morning, Ben got up from the sofa where he'd finally crashed to find clean clothes laid out for him: jeans, underwear and socks, and—and this was a surprise—a creamy linen shirt with ruffled collar and cuffs that he'd worn to the village fête the last couple of years, the last remnant of his Farthingale kit. When he tucked it into his jeans and threw on the leather jacket, shooting the cuffs so only the box-pleated ruffs showed at his wrists, Mellis called it his Tudor Rocker look, and sighed with extreme romance. There was even a fresh pair of soft leather boots waiting for him, cleaned and oiled. Unlike the diary, this clue at least was politely expressed and not covered with crumbs of cheese, and if Raven wasn't here to manage his costume needs, what else could he do?

The gorgeous smell of bacon and more of the Brownie's extraordinary bread, still warm from some faerie oven, lured him to breakfast which otherwise he would have forgone, so he dressed as ordered, neatly laying the clothes he'd slept in over the arm of the sofa. Then while eating, he flipped again through the diary, trying as best he could to separate the nonsense—of which there was a good deal—from the hints and clues and outright instructions, which were few.

There was something new: one small, printed triad at the bottom of the very last page, each item illustrated in miniature.

❧ AN OAK LEAFE

❧ AN IRON NAYL

❧ A SILVER HAYCORN

Haycorn? Oh, okay, acorn. Well, hmm. All right, he'd collected an oak leaf, even without being told. What was that about? He folded the corners of that page into a pocket, retrieved the leaf and slipped it in there for safety.

Something else had been tucked into the back of the book: a folded sheaf of papers, stitched with linen thread and tied securely in the middle, like a gift. On the cover:

Harpers Quips & Verses or
a Groats-vvorth of Songs
for Gentlemen.

Poetry? Some of his own poems, apparently: some excerpted and some whole, neatly written out in a good, moderately legible Secretary hand. It might even be extremely legible, he thought, if you happened to be an Elizabethan secretary. One was a complete free-standing sonnet: "I sent my love to you in all my letters," it began, written for Mellis during a brief period of awkwardness just before she'd agreed to marry him. He'd been meaning to set it to music, but other things kept getting in the way.

There were couplets taken from some other poems, some quatrains of what he called not-ballads, knocking off Sir Walter Raleigh, mostly. "It's okay," he'd tell Mellis when he wrote one and pinned it in a tree for her to find, like that guy in As You Like It. "It's not great but it's not-ballad." And she'd throw something at him, then read it and throw her arms around him. They were doggerel but she didn't care.

Scattered in among all the familiar and marginally decent efforts of his own were poesies, like the ones in the wedding rings article. Just a few short lines suitable for applying to marriage bands and gimmels like the ones he'd read about: MY HEART'S TREASURE, NEVER MEASURE. AS MY HEART YOU KNOW, SO SHALL LOVE GROW. Not wonderful but right in keeping with the custom. Presumably he'd need these at some point.

So all right, he was ready. The anxious itch in the corner of his mind that told him where lay the object of his desire, the tug at his chest that had been so clear in Faerie, was faint and ominously non-directional, even when he focused on it. The office, perhaps, was so well protected the golden thread that drew him through time and space couldn't find him.

And on top of that, no Raven. Was he supposed to wait?

"What's going on?" he said out loud, stuffing the cell phone into his jeans and the diary into his jacket. "I'm ready! Let's go!"

Was it safe to try to get out of doors by himself? Was it even possible? Did the barrier work both ways?

"Raven!" he called. No answer, nothing.

The phone in his pocket buzzed abruptly. A text from Aubrey just said, "Go."

Between two thoughts he was standing in his own rustic back garden with a golden artifact shouting at him through the mists of a Dartmoor morning when cloudy was the weather. The grass under his boots was wet with dew and rich with country odors.

"Ah!" he said, apparently to himself. "Okay, good. And?" he added expectantly. Nope, no further instructions, and still no Raven. Although there was someone, and she made Ben step back a bit before recovering himself.

A 10-inch-high someone of voluptuously female persuasion hovered at his eye level on silver wings, once dainty, now heavily outlined in black and slashed with runic graffiti. Her orange hair was chopped off at the ears—which were long and furred, like a moor pony's—and a grey patch was shaved down the top of her head from front to back. A leather bustier laced her in with yellow and black ribbons, and she sported a spiked dog collar at her throat, ripped black fishnet tights, and a string of studs like blood drops ranging up one ear. A tattoo on one shoulder kept changing, as if she hadn't made up her mind about it.

"You're kidding," said Ben dryly. "Really."

"Yeah, well," the phenomenon drawled in an accent and style that typography cannot reproduce. "It's Pauly, innit."

"Pauly.".

"Yeah, used to be Sweet Pea, but that was lame, like, so milady, she changed it. New wings too, innit."

So all right, a queen's minion. "And she sent you?"

"Nah! I just wanted ta give ya some advice, like, see?"

Was she chewing gum?

He rolled his eyes and tried not to think of anything, anything at all. And to remember that she might be the size of a Barbie doll, but she was still one of a dangerous company, possessed of unknown and unfriendly magicks.

"Look, lady, I gotta go."

He ducked around her, crunching toward the garden gate on the slatey gravel path Alan had installed. Not to be ignored, she fluttered up quite literally in his face, poking a blood-nailed finger at his nose.

"You look, big man," Pauly snapped. "She don't wanta hurt 'im, just make 'im happy. She wants ta give 'im more'n any human child even wants, 'at's what! Yeah, more'n any human master could give 'im. She can make it worth your while. Make you rich, innit! Give 'im up, yeah?"

"Sparrow doesn't want a master," Ben snarled, reaching to push her aside. "He wants his parents!"

Flitting back like a huge hummingbird, the little guttersnipe flipped him off and stuck out her tongue, then in a pop was gone, followed by a familiar harpy screech and a fading of raucous laughter.

Raven would just have to catch up.

Sunday

23
Southwark, Spring 1599

Ben was humming the baritone line of an old madrigal when he followed the thread of the dragon ring onto the bridge arching over the stream at the bottom of his picture-book garden. Another few steps took him through flower-scented Faerie woodland, and the next onto rain slick cobblestones, where he fell in with the jangling and wrangling market day crowd massing toward London Bridge on the Southwark side, just as the gates were opening. A far cry from the stillness of the medieval snow or the soft airs of Faerie, the sudden noise nearly knocked him down, but he was laughing as it did so.

The diary had nailed it. He was here, really here in Shakespeare's London! Yes! It smelled even worse than he had heard, but it was real, and oh my god he was here! It was better than Faerie. It was better than anything!

Still a few hundred feet or so out from the gate, where the paving stones gave way to the mud and ruts of the Sussex Road, he stood aside, just beaming with pleasure.

Across the bridge lay the great city itself. Here on his left hand was rowdy, ungovernable Southwark. If he ran like a 'prentice on holiday down this side street, he would pass St Saviour's Cathedral, skirt the bishop of Winchester's palace and gardens, and the wall-to-wall taverns and bawdy houses till he came to the Bear Garden—which he would avoid as nearly as the whores—and then at last to the theatre of legend, to the great Globe itself. And if the house flag flew high above it, there would be a play today. And who knows, Will Shakespeare himself might be there! And maybe…

And maybe he'd be beaten and robbed and left in an alley

before he ever got there. He pinched himself ruefully and tried to remember why he was here. Best to stick to the task at hand, but oh, the distractions were great.

Speaking of distractions, where was Raven? Just a little concerned, Ben scanned the faces in the crowd, expecting at any moment to spy a pretty youth in black doublet and hose. Or more likely to hear the worldly drawl of some sardonic quip, just over his shoulder.

The early breeze coming off the river smelled only of incoming tide and humanity. The reek from the refuse pile in front of the nearest houses made Ben cough, but no one else appeared to notice or mind. Church bells were ringing out all over London, and the hubbub of voices murmuring, shouting, laughing led him on.

The crowd streamed forward through the narrowing dog-leg approach to the bridge, packed in layers of wool and linen, hustling, jostling, women with baskets over their arms or on their backs, men in broad straw hats. Some came with mules or donkeys, panniers stuffed with apples or cloth, or herbs picked under the new moon; with goods to sell, and money to buy. If Ben got a few curious looks, he never noticed. Someone among them, soon, ought to be Raven.

The bridge itself was a marvel that rose overhead and across its expanse, a wonder of the world: not merely a bridge, but almost a village built end to end and edge to edge with fine shops and fabulous houses three and four stories high, even a church and a small green park, while the tidal waters of the Thames rushed twenty feet below between massive piers of oak and elm. Tradesmen and servants, dogs and geese, even a pair of bullocks clogged the path as it tunneled toward the metropolis.

Falling in with them and staring about like a country mouse, Ben's gaze traveled up the face of the massive stone gatehouse where, as the map had shown him, a cluster of pikes thrust out over the gate. Today only two were decorated with the half-rotted heads of traitors. At this distance, they might have been stage props, but he knew perfectly well they were not. At first glance, he thought they were moving, and his stomach churned slightly in response. Yes, there was movement, but it wasn't the dreadful heads themselves.

Birds, of course. London's kites and ravens, the ancient scavengers, cleansed the city of its garbage, delighting in rotting flesh. He grimaced, thinking of his missing companion, when one of those birds called from above and flung itself into the air, circling high over head. Then while he stared, a ragged gobbet of rotted, maggoty flesh fell, splat, in his face.

"Shit!"

Disgust crashed over him with slime and stench. He gagged, swore, frantically clawing the thing away, and staggered back, then turned and ran, or tried to, shoving through the crowd and setting all to cursing. Finding a pile of straw and offal to be sick over, then stumbling on, stricken.

Straighten up, he told himself when he fetched up at last against a lime-washed wall, some sort of shop or house, he didn't care so it was out of range of the horror.

Think. You know all this! Snap out of it!

Sure, he was familiar with the realities of the age. Re-enacting and living history acknowledged these things. He and his colleagues had discussed them more than once in and out of character, nodding sagely over a midnight beer about how accustomed people would have been to daily horrors. So why was he panicking?

Because the reality was far different, and he should have known that, too. Which only made it worse.

But gradually he felt his breathing start to steady and his thoughts to clear.

"This is childish," he muttered under his breath. "I have a job to do. The artifact is across that bridge, somewhere deep in the city, and my son is trapped in Faerie. I am not going to let severed heads, or a pile of shit, not even the chance of seeing Shakespeare on stage get in my way. It'll be fine. Just don't look up at the gate."

And where the hell was Raven?

Further from the gate the crowd was more diffuse, the roar of the street less muddled, more likely to break into individual sounds: the creak of a wicker basket, the clatter of cartwheels on cobblestones, iron-shod hooves, a woman's gentle exclamation, and curious voices asking questions. The crowd was thinner, too, which meant his muttered pep talk was just as audible, and collecting hard glances from passers by.

For the most part, like crowds anywhere, folk quickly glanced away, not wanting to deal with the fellow in the outlandish dress, doubtless mad or else a foreigner. Feeling a little bit faint and quite a bit foolish, he took a deep breath, squared his shoulders, and prepared to launch himself into his task once again. He even tried on a thin smile, hoping to convey a sense of healthy well-being, trying not to look like a tourist. So why were they staring at him? When he stared back bewildered or shook his head in mute incomprehension, they raised their voices or slowed down to speak each word very carefully as they might to a deaf man, or an idiot.

One woman with a basket of leather points over her arm pulled down the dust cloth from her mouth to say distinctly, "Whad oost ow ga tyay gan a bed lam."

Bedlam? Did traveling the worlds cause brain damage? "Nay, nay, goodwife, I..."

She looked from him to her daughter; they shrugged and moved along having work to do, while Ben shrank back, confused. The beefy man behind her took this as an opening for real abuse, and aimed a blow with a cudgel that clipped his shoulder before he spun aside. The fellow guffawed, jabbering something to his mates as they moved on leaving Ben facing a pack of children, most of them shoeless and all of them staring at him shamelessly. When one hooted some unfathomable but clearly gross vulgarity and lobbed a handful of filth at him and ran, laughing, back to his pals, Ben looked down in dismay at his beshitten clothes, and the world tilted even further.

His jeans and jacket, all his clothes in fact, had come unchanged with him into the past. Even with the linen shirt and soft boots, he must look as strange as if he had just come from far Cathay or dropped from the moon. Fear and confusion must have marked his face, because now they all, adults and children, had paused to point and laugh at him, jeering and calling out, saying... what?

The language—the actual language—of the people around him had begun at last to register.

Yes, it was English, certainly, any fool could hear that, but— But the diction was more peculiar, more foreign that he could comprehend. It wasn't the "Shakespearean" he knew. It wasn't the "OP", the Original Pronunciation he'd studied and even heard at the restored Globe. It might as well have been Chinese. No amount of reading, no language tapes, no re-enactors boot camp had set him up for the clip and drawl of individual idiom, the curious twists and turns on the vowels, the shifts in rhythm, the sheer number of variations that divide a living language from a summer exercise.

But one thing was clear. The individual idiom in that babbling, gabbling crowd was turning ugly. A woman was screaming at him and prodding his shoulder with the tip of an iron-shod walking staff. Sure, if he calmed down and listened properly, if he had some time, he would sort it out, eventually fit his mind to the idiosyncrasies, wrap his tongue around the local accent. Explain himself. Sure. But he had no time. No time!

Then the humming that underlay everything, voice of the artifact, winked out, and panic slammed over him like a wave until gasping, he was absolutely sure he was going to fail, that he had failed already, and it rocked him back. His life was over, his wife and child lost. And all he could do was crouch, heart pounding, in the flung shadows of traitors, and shiver against a scum-slick wall with his arms wrapped over his throbbing head, trying not to retch. The yammering voices beat him to the ground, while somewhere in the distance he thought he heard the scorn of faerie laughter.

"Master Harper!"

Some haughty fellow snapped out the name somewhere above Ben's head. Oh god, he was about to be arrested, probably locked up as a masterless man and a drooling idiot unable to make himself understood, with no money in his pockets and clothes he couldn't account for.

"Come now, fellow, look up at me, I say! Where has thou been, thou great lump!"

A few folk nearest them chuckled and the crowd cleared aside, dividing itself around the nobleman in his fine clothes and richly caparisoned mount. Oh good, a show! Most were just happy that his attention was directed at some other hapless fool and not themselves. They also collectively approved of someone taking the madman in hand before there was real trouble.

In that moment, already shocked till he could scarcely breathe, Ben couldn't for the world look up, but in front of him rose the legs and broad chest of a handsome black stallion and, when he raised his eyes a bit, the well turned leg of oh thank god, it's Aubrey. He looked up at last and started to swear, then stopped as deep blue eyes flashed in a dangerously angry face.

Slowly, he unfolded and stood up, shaking and filthy. A safety line had appeared in front of him at last. The deep instinct to perform took over; experience gave him a place to stand, and he grabbed it.

"My lord, forgive me!" Harper barked out of forgotten habit, and made a leg, snatching his flat woolen cap off his head.

His cap? More relief. No longer Tudor rock star, just plain sturdy Tudor: black trunk hose and nether stocks, deep green serge doublet trimmed in crisp black passmentarie, straight black sleeves. Small neat ruffs stood at his throat and wrists. Clearly, he wore the livery of the great man frowning at him from under the brim of a tall hat pinned up with a fabulous jewel. If anyone saw the change, they preferred not to notice and carried on.

"Drunk already, man?" yelled a voice from the crowd.

"Aye, his lordship'll have him now!" cried another.

And every word registered as plain and meaningful as if he'd been born to it. Ben nearly fainted with relief, the feeling of reprieve so great it was embarrassing.

"I rise at the Tiger," his lordship went on testily, "to find thee gone, wandered off about some business of thine own, and what should I think but some harm hath come to thee in the night."

Ben humbly held his peace along with his hat, knowing that for one thing he deserved the upbraiding but more, that everyone else knew it too. His master had a right, even an obligation to give him a hard time in public, so he would stand and take the lesson while the world stopped spinning and his nerves came under control. And about time, too.

"Well come up, man. Don't stand gadding in the lane. God's death, come up, I say, sirrah! Mount up and be about my business."

Without another word, Aubrey rode forward and there waiting just beyond him was a sturdy jennet, saddled for riding with bulging packs thrown over its broad haunches.

"Stand not upon the order of your going, young Benedict," said the faerie king, more gently. "Let's go!"

"Marry, and with a good will, my lord. Gramercy, my lord!" And in a trice, as they say, his cap was fitted to his head and Ben was in the saddle. And as they proceeded to ride, his lordship deigned to turn their path against the stream of the thoroughfare, back toward the Surrey countryside. When they had cleared the traffic beyond Bermondsey Green, bell-like chimes sounded and the soggy morning had transmuted to fragrant country afternoon. They were riding again in Faerie, where they stopped without dismounting. This would only take a minute.

24
The borderlands

Off-stage at last, Ben Harper gulped and took a sobbing breath, collapsing against the saddle horn. "Oh, my good lord!" he gasped. "Thank you."

"You were spoilt by the ease with which you fitted in among the Saxons, I can see that," said the king, amused.

"I thought I'd be fine, the second I knew where I was! I know that era! Know it well! Not just the music or who fought who, but the language too! But, oh my god!"

Aubrey smiled wanly, looking every inch the elven lord in a carved velvet doublet of soft grey-green, high-collared with small, pearl-set diamonds at each quilted lozenge. "You learned French in school, and learned it well, got good marks. And then you went to France. What happened?"

"I remember. Idiom shock. Hey, at least I didn't wind up in jail. But you know, I actually speak English, I didn't learn it from a book! Shit, okay, Shakespeare's English I did, but damn it, it's still English!"

Aubrey raised a hand and the babbling cut off at once. "Enough. You have work to do. Are you prepared to proceed?"

"I guess."

The glittering eyes rolled. "Are you ready?"

Ben shook the last cobwebs out of his head and the nausea crawled away at last. And there, as he listened for it, yes, just there, a thready sense of the artifact tugged at his mind. At least he had the direction.

Still dizzy but improving, he nodded. "Yes, sir. I'm good. But can I ask… where's Raven? He said he'd always be there. I still have to get all the way across the city without getting robbed and beaten or dragged off to Bedlam." He pushed the panic monster down again. "I'm not even wearing a sword!"

"Aren't you?"

When he looked, yes indeed, he was. "Oh, I see. Well, that's something."

And so it was: a proper rapier with a plain, serviceable but graceful swept hilt. He drew it out, sighing as the familiar sweet hiss of steel blade sliding through steel collar scraped the air. "A fine one, too, sir. Brilliant, actually!"

"You'll serve Sparrow better if you stop babbling, Ben. Are you ready or not? "

Ben gulped, then slammed the blade home and took in a deep breath.

"Yes," he nodded firmly. "I am. And if I run into any further trouble, I'll just ask myself how Sir Francis Browne would deal with this and I'll be fine."

"Sir Francis Browne?"

His spine straightened, his golden-bearded jaw firmed up in a particularly Elizabethan attitude, and a certain twinkle gleamed in his eye. With some care, he set his cap to a jaunty angle and smiled like he knew what he was doing. And in that moment, finally, he did.

"Four years of Farthingale Hall must be good for something!" he laughed, then waved away an old joke that had sprung at once to mind. They turned their mounts, both good horses now, back the way they'd come. "And Raven?"

"In London, waiting for you."

"Waiting for me? But..." Cold lurked just behind the bravado, but he could ignore it now. "Okay, but I really can't do this completely alone."

"You won't be. I have a place in this time, Ben, as Raven does, and things to do. I will come with you a little way. You, though, human child, are the one with the gift. Only you know exactly where we're going."

Riding together, the countryside around them lost some of its brilliance and most of its savory airs as the gangrenous odors of London reached tendrils out to meet them on the road. The crowds had thinned as the sun crept up on their right hand, burning away the morning damp.

"Stay a little ahead of me—Sir Francis Browne—and keep your eyes open. It's the greatest city in the world, and you may not get another chance to see it! Lead on, if you please."

25
The City of London, 1599

Being properly dressed and accoutered made all the difference, as did entering London by the king of Faerie's courtesy through a service alley between two of the more fashionable houses in the Strand—on the right side of the river this time. Now the way was so obvious, Ben could hardly keep from urging his horse to a gallop, as foolish as that would have been. But now all he had to do was find the thing, look and listen with some serenity, and go. There might be time for a play at the Globe after all. How hard could it be?

And what again, Ben thought, are the most famous last words ever?

So though they moved along urgently, he took the time to look about him as they went up one street and down another, pausing now and then to listen. The trouble was, the hum kept changing, the voice almost stammering. It was so completely unlike the previous experience, he hardly knew what to make of it. Aubrey frowned at the diversions, but Ben had no explanation; he could only follow.

When it faded out completely, he stopped and the king waited with him without comment. When it grabbed Ben by the ear again, they could carry on. Each time they turned into a new street, they were assaulted by mongers of every kind. Wet fish and stock fish down by the river, apples and raisins further along. Pepper and pins, lace and lambskins, broadsides and broadcloth, the musical calls followed them through the city.

White sands! Grey sands!
Who will buy my white sands?
Who will buy my grey sands?

Ben's heart pounded, his eyes shone at every new thing, all his earlier fears no more than an idle dream. At his beaming look and easy manner, and cloaked in Faerie glamourie besides, every face that met his broke into a smile.

Ripe Strawberries, they're ripe!
Penny a pottle, fine strawberries ripe!

At last they rode into Cheapside, then as always the haunt of jewelers. Goldsmiths' shops and tinsmiths', pewterers' and jewelers' work rooms kept modest place on the ground floors of three- and four-story buildings on every side between homes and hostelries and churches. Well, that was a good sign. They were in the right place, more or less.

Then, the link again sputtered out. No matter how deeply he listened, it was gone. Undeterred, he stopped here and there to ask if any of these craftsmen or their 'prentices had seen or heard lately of any old gothic gold, country folk might even call it faerie gold. None had, they begged his pardon, and hurried on their ways. One gave up an impatient moment to wave him further up the road.

Eventually they came to a halt, looking up to the wistful face of a young girl in a greasy cap, resting her smutty chin on her elbows in a window sill above a fripperer's shop.

"Marry, good sir, you want the Goldsmith's Hall."

She can't have been more than twelve, and her snubbed nose was smudged with soot and grime as much as the apron bound over her shift. Cleaning the fireplaces today, from the looks of her. She'd not be allowed down among the ribbons and laces in the shop without cleaning up and putting on a kirtle like a decent Christian.

One question down, Ben beamed his most dazzling TV smile at her, and asked the next, while his lordship pulled a passing cloud around himself.

"And which way is that, sweeting? I've not been in London for many a long day."

She leaned way out and pointed a plump pink arm up the leafy avenue, which made Ben grin appreciatively. So all right, she may have been a bit closer to a nubile sixteen.

"O'er there, sir, yonder. Someone there will know. Then come you back and buy a ribbon for your lady love." She grinned and leaned down precipitously at him, and shrieked with delight when he tipped his cap in thanks. No one tipped a cap to the likes of her. Blushing furiously but still giggling, she reached for both sides of the paned windows and drew them closed before he could do another outrageous thing.

They moved along in the direction the girl had pointed, man and master both grinning a bit themselves. Ben was getting used to the peculiar behavior of his gift on this stop. Where the Saxon fragment had made the whole mead hall hum without giving any clearer clues to its location, the Elizabethan one had quite a different feel. It either dodged about like a 'prentice on holiday or it sang out, a clear anchor point in the narrow, over-hung streets—but an anchor that was curiously drifting with some unknown tide. Like now.

"It's moving!" he yelped as it nearly spun him off his horse back the way they'd come. Then it vanished again.

Folk in the street looked up at him sharply, the smiles a little dulled. Four sour-faced Puritans boiled out of a house heatedly discussing detestable enormities, and nearly careened into the horses. Aubrey snarled at them like a gentleman and they grudgingly touched their hats, which shocked them all.

"What's that, Sir Francis?"

"It moved, my lord!" said Ben more quietly. "It was close, then I felt it remove away. And now it's gone at once. I wot not how that may be." How hard could it be, indeed.

"Someone must have it in his hands," said Aubrey. "Belike in search of some honest craftsman hereabouts." He made a subtle gesture as he tugged at his gloves, and three tiny lights rose out of the middle of the air above his hand, like sparks struck from his jewels. Almost invisible in a shaft of sunshine, they scattered.

"What are you doing!" Ben hissed, thinking of ducking stools and burnings and things.

"Gathering news, of course," said Aubrey carelessly.

"Are you nuts? What if someone notices?"

The king of Faerie tilted his most tolerantly skeptical look on his waiting gentleman, and raised an eyebrow. "What say'st thou?"

"What, I, my lord?" said Sir Francis Browne, reddening slightly. It had been so much easier working with Raven. "Why naught at all, but saving your lordship's grace…"

"Patience, man," said his lordship. "Folk see what they are wont to see and look past the rest." He did, as he had said, have a place in this time, and power. "You, *exemplum gratia*, seek the Worshipful Company of Goldsmiths. But what do you see? The forest, Sir Francis, or the tree?"

That meant it must be right in front of his nose. Ben swung his gaze from side to side, up and down the street so remarkably filled with smart, lime-washed, timber-framed or red brick buildings with their chimney pots gleaming in the sunshine. Then he gave up and stared, yes, right in front of him.

On the opposite corner, a stylish building with leaded windows was quite like its neighbors but twice the width and four stories high. Shifting in the saddle for a better view, Ben could also see that the same fair structure reached down the length of the leafy lane beside them, which the faerie map had marked Carey Street. It reminded him of an expensive office building in modern Plymouth. Was this it? Only one way to find out.

Nodding politely to a well-appointed carriage as it pulled away, and flipping a groat to the inevitable beggar, they picked their way across the road. At the top of a wide set of polished stone steps stood a massive pair of doors, gilded and carved with images of some saint doing saintly things: feeding the poor at his doorstep, giving away treasure, healing a peculiarly crippled horse. And tapping away at a tiny anvil.

More to the point, above the door was a coat of arms gleaming in gold and enamel work, quartered in red and blue. On the shield, gold lion faces counter-changed with some kind of golden salt shaker and a pair of, what, buckles? The whole thing was supported by prancing unicorns and topped with a noble lady holding a pair of golden scales.

26
Lost

❋

Ben made a face.

"The Goldsmiths Hall. Of course. Hey, I could have been a herald," he muttered wryly. "But Mother said music was more practical."

As if on cue, the doors swung back and two prosperous fellows emerged with expansive bellies and short gowns of cut velvet in sober brown and black, furred with handsome wolf skins in the collars. Jeweled gold rings glinted from almost every finger except, of course, the middle, for they were no fools.

"I pray you, my masters," Ben called as they reached the bottom step. "A word, by your leave."

They looked up at him, then at the splendid nobleman on the very fine horse beside him, and each did a creditable reverence, hat in hand, while automatically totting up the wholesale value of the jewelry. Their hats remained politely in their hands all the while thereafter.

"My lord? How may we serve you?" said the more slender of the two, though neither was a dainty fellow. Addressing the master, naturally, though addressed by the man.

Lord Aubrey sniffed a bit and patted his stallion's shoulder to still him. Two sparks of light flashed as if alighting on his glove rather than being cast by it, but no one noticed. One gleamed like a sunbeam in the gold and green livery badge stitched to Sir Francis's shoulder cape.

Ben went on as if they were looking at him. "So please you, masters, can you tell us what this place is and who bides here?"

The two men exchanged glances then looked back at

Aubrey, who ignored them. "Why it is the guild hall of the Worshipful Company of Goldsmiths, of course! And many do labor within it."

"Excellent!"

"Whom do you seek, my lord?"

"Marry, good sir, we seek a goldsmith of the name..." Ben caught it as it came into his head, and before it could slip away. "Tandy. Is Master Tandy within, or can you tell us where to find him? My Lord Aubrey here has been recommended to him but we—that is, I—seem to have lost the way."

"Ha! Marcus Tandy, mean you?" said the stockier, and so more prosperous, of the two with something like a sneer.

"My good lord, I pray you, go not to Marcus Tandy!" his friend most heartily agreed.

"Nay, sir?" said Ben in surprise. "And wherefore?"

The first fellow's face grew quite pink and he blustered, urgent with gossip.

"For that he is a knave, sir! A constant debtor, and a tradesman of little honesty, if belike he hath some skill, and albeit he is a master of our craft. And moreover that he hath owed me some ten pounds since Christmas last. Ten pounds, sir! I pray you, come to my shop if you have need, my lord. Thomas Garrard is my name, and I shall..."

"Or I, Andrew Penny!" inserted his friend. It's always time to advertise.

"My lord?" Ben queried, seeking instructions. Lord Aubrey remained aloof. "My masters both, I thank you for your news but it is a thing my lord is minded to judge for himself. And so please you, can you tell me whence this Tandy may be found or must I seek elsewhere?"

"He liveth but the street above us here, my lord," said Thomas Garrard. "In Mayden Close. A mean shop now, with a mouse over the door. Marry, a good trade it was to him, once, and thriving."

"Aye, and then the new wife came," Penny grumbled. "And her spending daughter."

"And Marcus the mouse to her cat. Well, you shall see it for yourself, my lord," Garrard added. "You shall see."

"My thanks, my good masters," Aubrey said, deigning to speak at last. For a moment Ben thought he was going to ruin the whole charade by offering them money for their pains, as if they were servants. But he only nodded genially to them both, turned his horse and proceeded as they had directed.

A few paces later Ben looked around, frowning, for the street was entirely empty, even the water and whatever else ran in the gutters had stopped. A bell had begun to ring, and its tone also halted. Aubrey relaxed in the saddle and turned to him. "Do you have enough to be going on with?"

Ignoring the lingering headache, Ben said "Yeah, I think so. But who's this Tandy guy? And why do I care? It just popped into my head from… Yes, yes, I'll be fine," he added when Aubrey looked particularly doubtful.

"You've needed a powerful lot of rescuing lately. I may not always be at your call, human child, so you must go with care. Follow your gift. And please, Ben, try to stay out of trouble."

At that Ben sat up straighter in the saddle and settled the reins in his gloved hands. "Good my lord, I shall."

The time stream lurched forward again.

"Then best be about it, man!" his lordship snapped as London came up to speed, but the lord of Faerie had already ridden out of it, leaving only the shimmer of crystal chimes and the smell of violets. Violets, forsooth.

Well, all right. He was armed with knowledge. He had money in his purse, sword and dagger at his side, as well as handsome livery identifying him as a man with prospects. He wanted only patience. Last time, his gift had led him to King Alfred's hall but the fragment had come to him. Perhaps he needed only to wait.

When his gift dropped out, Marcus Tandy was all the clue he had, so he ambled up the relatively quiet street to find him. And when he reached the place where Forster Lane met Mayden Alley, he halted at a modest tavern called the Blossom, and gave the ostler's boy sixpence to mind the horse. Not, he thought strolling away, that anyone was likely to steal it.

Now he was on foot, and ready. The dragon ring fragment

was on its way; just find the damned place and wait?

Mayden Alley proved to be little more than a grim, crooked passage connecting two fine avenues filled with folk. The day itself felt darker and shabbier there, and the eyes of rats, or something less wholesome glowed back at him as Ben ventured within. As it snaked away from Forster Lane, he spied a low gate between two slouching tenements, which opened into a mean little courtyard ringed with shops. Had it not been for Oberon's spying faerie lights (whatever they were), Ben might never have found it at all.

A foul feeling and a chill air radiated from it, or perhaps it was just his imagination. It was darker even than Mayden Alley, as if the sun never shown there at all. It was no place to wait, Ben decided quickly, unless he was in the mood to defend his purse and possibly his virtue. Now he had marked it, he shuddered and walked on by.

And as he did so, like a light switch, the pulse of direction, the golden voice he'd been waiting for snapped back into his head. It was out there, but south of him, nearer than before and moving towards him. As he emerged blinking into Aldersgate Street, Ben wondered if he should have kept his ride after all. But no, he needed to be both quick and flexible. Someone was wandering around with enchanted gold, and this street was deeply crowded. With Raven still somewhere about his own business, wit and subtlety would have to be his tools.

27
Appetites

❈

Follow your gift, the man had said.

And Ben's gift—having deigned to show up—told him to hold fast. He found a shaded corner suitable for lurking, courteously parked his sword point behind his heel, and took up a relaxed but gallant stance as he waited for the artifact to come to him. The half-timbered shop he leaned against in his Errol Flynn sort of way was a reasonably respectable tavern judging by the patronage. And the green yard between it and its neighbor was pocked with summer flowers.

Someone had thought to scythe the grassy undergrowth from time to time, and knocked together some benches and a low table. So when the landlord sold him a tupenny ale for the privilege of loitering there, Ben amiably bought a round for those loitering with him. The ale was cool from the cellar and not too new, a little sweet but tasty on a spring day, and he was glad of it.

Minutes ticked away. Clouds rolled in with the smell of rain; the sunlight flared and dimmed at intervals. Folk came and went, someone bought him another drink and told a rambling story, and Ben just listened to his gift. The familiar muttering flared and dimmed, too, as if the artifact were wandering aimlessly in the district. Now, as St Martin's church down the way stroked out another quarter hour, the dragon's voice retreated, faded, then returned, growing stronger, and stronger still. A proper smile crinkled into Ben's eyes for the first time all day.

"That's it!" he said softly. "Come to poppa."

It winked out again.

"Damn it! No! Why?"

He peered down the avenue, so straight on the map, so crooked in life, crammed with corners and edges. Thatched, tiled, and shingled shops and workshops crowded in with houses and taverns that elbowed each other out of the way, cantilevered out to block the sky, all filled with shouting, calling people. Ben willed the artifact to reveal itself, and got no response. It was coming towards him, he knew it was, but its voice was definitely gone. He listened, really listened into the spaces between the buying and selling, the flirting and arguing, beneath the singing, muttering and bustling. Nothing. Even watching closely, the only thing worthy of remark in the stream of humanity was a single swirling eddy apparently being created by one man, marked out from the rest by his height, and that of his hat.

Strolling up the street in fits and starts came a sturdy young man of about 22 with a shock of plain brown hair sticking out from under a sugar loaf hat somewhat the worse for use, and a country bumpkin look about his fresh, pleasant face. Ben smiled as the fellow approached, and envisioned success. That had to be the guy he was looking for.

He was a head taller than anyone else in the street, almost as tall as Ben's own six foot height. With massive shoulders and narrow waist, probably a champion wrestler in his district; a ploughman or a blacksmith, maybe. He looked as though he could carry a young bullock to market on his shoulders. That he was young showed in the merry sparkle of his unlined eyes. The small brown beard and meager mustache, too, were still getting used to being part of his face. That he was a countryman was clear in the moon-faced awe he brought to everything his eye lit upon.

Ben found him a joy to watch as the lad worked his way up the street, appearing and disappearing as he strolled back and forth, crossing and re-crossing the lane like a wide-eyed tourist, stopping at every doorway and stall to peer within. The lad would chat with the tradesman or craftsman or goodwife at the window. Ask a question, trying not to look foolish and failing, of course, with a goofy grin. And in between, he would throw back his head and carol out a song in a clear, true tenor.

The nearer he came, the more amusing, in a kindly way, Ben found him. Colin Clout's come home again, he thought.

The fellow walked with a wide-legged gait as if ill-accustomed to his fine new boots and wide trunk hose—neither too fine nor too new—bought second-hand no doubt in Birchin Street. The enormous linen ruff at his chin, nearly eight inches deep but sparsely pleated, wanted some time with a poking stick. Properly shaped and starched it could have been two inches tall, fashionably framing his baby face like the head of John the Baptist on a platter. Instead, the ruff collapsed across his shoulders like a wilting swan, but oh my, he was proud of it.

On a whim, Ben Harper shifted his weight to both feet, pushing away from the ale garden wall.

"Let's just see who you are, my lad, shall we?" he said to himself, and moved forward, nearly treading on a street seller who appeared almost exactly from nowhere.

"Wanting company, sweeting?"

Company of a girlish kind, she meant. She had stepped neatly in front of him, blocking the way and breaking his concentration. The ploughman disappeared, sucked again into the crowd.

Startled, Ben glowered at her, saying nothing. She was pretty enough under the pixie-pointed linen cap, he thought, and buxom, surely. Surprisingly clean, too, for a monger, though her skin was coarse and tanned as a gypsy's, and marred by an ugly line of keloidal scar in the hollow of her throat. Like a gypsy's too, long black hair escaped the cap to curl around her face and down her back. One scandalous tendril fell forward across the generous mounds of her bosom. She breathed in, and out, just for him.

So she was not quite as young as she looked, and sly. The features were sharp, the eyes hooded. Who did she remind him of?

She had a basket on her arm all woven and wrapped in brightly colored ribbons and holding in its round belly a few tragic oranges and a lemon. The expression she turned up into his face was meant to be sympathy, but looked more like appetite.

He waved her away. "Not for me, lass, nay, I thank thee."

Had he ignored her, she might have moved on. Addressing her directly opened a door which she was happy to sidle through. When he moved to go around her she stepped in his way again, then back when he moved back, the endless dance of polite misunderstanding. Too late he tumbled to his mistake.

The woman laughed, a throaty chuckle that couldn't be trusted. Ben just growled his annoyance and pushed past her. Some kind of scent rose from her hair, musty and stale.

"Tibbit, master," she teased, or tried to. "I'm called Tibbit." Two paces away, and he halted in mid stride. "Ah, now, let us mend thy sad heart, sweeting. Take an orange, two a penny! Or lift my skirt for sixpence?"

Against his will, his head turned and his body too, but this time he actually looked at her. In fact, she really was too clean, and all her neat, even teeth were white as dead men's bones. And there was something else, something more unwholesome than just paid sex, something foul as ditch water. Who was she really?

"I said no, wench. Leave off!"

"Nay, sir. How can I? Fine gentleman like yourself, you'll be wanting a lass to take your cares away, and why not. Everything's got a price, don't it?"

"No!"

"Oh, yer honor don't mean that."

"I'll mean it and prove it, too," he snarled, as one hand drifted to the swept steel rings of his sword hilt. "Be gone!"

She never even flinched, but reached a curiously well-manicured hand to his chest, the pressure urgent over his heart. A chill shot through him.

"Only a shilling if you hire the room above as well," she added with a nod to the windows over the alehouse. Inexorably, unless he meant to lay hands on her, she forced him to step back and step again until the back of his head touched against the shadowed wall. "If you wish."

"Stop it, damn you!"

It wasn't panic, this time, it was anger—at her, but mostly at himself. What would Sir Francis Brown do?

Gloved fingers started to curl into a fist.

"Ye may wish to take yer time, yer honor."

She was fingering the golden livery badge on his chest, stroking his sleeve, almost crawling into his arms and smiling, but her eyes were wolfish, sharp and hard. Her mouth with its sharp little teeth moved hot across his face, her breath like a poisoned fume.

"Mom?" he thought, "if she's not really a woman, I can hit her, right?" But all he could do was stand there.

"But why wait?" Then her fingers grabbed his sword hand, and thrust it between her legs.

"Jesus, no!" Ben bellowed and, snapping the spell, flung her back in a fury so that she tumbled over a form bench, petticoats over her head, her goods all on display now for free.

His dagger flew into his hand as Tibbit fought her way out of the tangle of linen and worsted. When she saw the knife, she shrank back feigning terror but her expression was vicious, red eyes blazing.

"I know you, witch!" he said hoarsely, more darkly sincere than he had ever been. "Come not near me or mine again, or I will surely kill thee."

No one else felt moved to challenge him. The idlers who had been watching grinned vulgar, gap-toothed, but gratifyingly human grins, and went back to their drinking.

"You'll never find the dragon ring, Ben Harper!" The shrill cackle of Tibbit's taunt followed him as he turned and ran from the stink of her magic. "Never in time!"

28
Found

He muscled his way across the street, letting the busy crowd swallow her up behind him. The last mocking screech still rang in his ears as he stumbled toward the church, longing for a place to sit down, catch his breath, get the smell of corruption out of his mouth and nose. Breathe. He knew, suddenly, who she had looked like, who she certainly was:

"Pauly!" He spat the name.

Titania's punked-out minion, tarted up and transformed for the times, still delivering the faerie queen's hate mail. He'd looked right at her. How had he not seen the glow of Faerie on her? Seen the wolf? The livid scar in her throat made sense now; he had put it there himself.

Light-headed and dizzy and still standing in the road, he kept thinking "This is wrong, so bloody wrong."

Which is why he was not entirely surprised when the earth went out from under his feet, and he was suddenly slammed up against a wall with his hat shoved down over his eyes and his collar climbing over his ears. The surprise was that the huge hand which held him pinned did it so gently that he was able to squirm about in time to see what he'd failed to hear coming: a cantering double handful of matched riders escorting a smartly dressed gentleman and a lady glittering with jewels.

The lady nodded graciously as he dragged off his hat with his one free hand. For a moment their eyes met across the crowd. Did she smile at him? Did he for godssake know her too?

"Probably," he thought with a weary sigh. "Huzzah."

Other folk had calmly stopped what they were doing to stand aside, give courtesy, or pull a child into a doorway as the gentry passed. They returned to their business as if nothing extraordinary had happened. Ben had been rescued—again. Could the day get any weirder?

The massive hand let him go. Ben tugged his doublet in place to where he could breathe properly again, and looked for his rescuer. Who he saw was the ploughman with the comical ruff, now down in the lane watching the noble entourage disappear towards Westminster in a cloud of dust.

"How now, friend!" Ben shouted with more kinds of relief than he could name, and he thrust out his hand when the man spun around. "You have saved my life! We are well met, well met upon this excellent morning!"

"Well met indeed, master," the lad said in a familiar accent, and strode forward eagerly, doffing his cap and grabbing Ben's hand to shake it with cheer and no doubts at all.

And as their hands touched, Ben's gift snapped on at full volume and rocked him back. For the song was muddled but the chant he'd been waiting for was clearly, absolutely right here, somewhere on this excellent young man's person. Grinning hugely, he gripped the man's hand like a life line.

"Jack Greengage is my name, though at home some call me Jack Plough. And I'm from Devon come to make..."

Laughing, Ben finished for him: "Thy fortune, lad, of course you are!"

"Nay! Nay, sir, not so!" said Jack, looking a little puzzled. "I have come because my fortune is made, and I must make a way in the world with it. And the best way to make a man's way is to get him a wife, en't that so? But stay, I have saved thy life, yet I know not thy name! Pray tell it me, and I shall buy thy dinner!"

"I am called Sir Francis Browne," said Ben, embracing his persona. Ben Harper might be awkward and out of his time. Francis Browne never was. "And by God's beard, I too am a Devon man!" They both exclaimed about the coincidence and named their respective villages and relations and nearly proved they must be some kind of distant cousin—which sounded shifty, even to Ben. But perhaps no one had warned the kid about the dangers of the big city, and the coney catchers and upright men who preyed on the unwitting, and especially upon country boys new come to town. So they clapped hands once again and set forth to dine.

Clearly, they had to talk and, as it happened, Jack had already spied out a decent looking ordinary in his meanderings, where the rushes on the floor had been lately turned, and a plate of stew with actual meat in it could be had with bread and ale for a hugely inflationary fee. He talked Ben into dining with him, if only to get out of the street. London in springtime has always been a chancy thing for rain, and the bright intervals were losing ground to the shadowed ones. If the threatening storm broke, it would surely be better to be indoors with ale and a good fire.

If Ben had doubts about the wisdom of eating anything in Queen Elizabeth's un-pasteurized England, he sat on them. He was starving, having lost his breakfast hours ago, and a hungry man makes bad decisions—as the day so far had shown.

The ordinary, a cook shop, in blessedly cobbled Cheapside—not a restaurant, for there were none, but not yet an inn—was called The Raven's Nest. An omen? Raven wasn't there either.

First, he had to sort out the supposedly fixed price with the landlord. Jack appeared to have cash to spend, but that was no reason to squander it. Ben the negotiator compounded with Sir Francis the gentleman, and ganged up on the management until suitable terms were settled. The food, when it came, wasn't even too bad, although the flavors were odd. Ben's only regret was that he wouldn't be able to tell anyone about it later. And so to business.

Start small, he thought, and build.

"I heard you singing, Jack, before we met. What song was that?"

"The words are called Sweet Bess She Is Myne Own True Love," said Jack. "And the tune springs straight from mine own heart."

"Then th'art a poet, by God! But tell me how should'st

thou betake thee a wife in London town when Bess is already thine own true love at home?"

"Why good, Sir Francis," Jack laughed. "It is my Bess I do mean to wed, just as soon as I have had a golden ring made to put upon her finger. 'Tis why I've come to London, as I shall tell you."

And so began the tale that waggled all the way through the mutton from shank to shoulder. The ploughman, to condense his streams of country talk somewhat, had turned up not merely a few coins under his plow, as one sometimes did, but a hoard of gold, seemingly from medieval times. True gold coins, stamped with the crude image of King Alfred himself.

"Him that burnt the cakes!" the boy laughed with irresistible excitement.

Among the treasure, too, had been silver coins as well as gold, a broken crucifix, and the most curious bit of all, an odd twist of broken gold with some old words on it, magic words no doubt.

Ben's heart pounded, aching for the young man to bring out just one piece to show him, just the one odd piece that was nattering at him, so he could read it and go home. But Jack was wisely keeping it all stuffed up snug in his doublet.

"Now, Jack, my friend." Ben wagged an admonitory finger, stern as an elder brother. "When treasures are turned up in thy master's field—surely such things belong to him, no matter who speed the plough."

"Aye," Jack said, his merry face alight. "Certes, that is so. And certes, so I did."

"I took you at once for an honest man. What then? Say on, so please you, say on." But wait, the American thought, there's more.

And so there was. He had taken the treasure, had Jack, to his master, old Jacob Blackhurst, and he was as cranky an old Puritan as ever there was on the Dartmoor. But he, for all he was a pinchpenny of the worst sort, had recoiled in horror. "Faerie gold, he said it was. Unlucky! Cursed! Pitch it in the mill pond, he said, but take it from his sight."

"Many would agree with your old master, my lad."

"Nay, that's naught but foolish superstition, that," said Jack stoutly. "For I've spoken with the little folk. They said it were not their gold nor never was, and they cannot lie."

Ben grinned, cheerfully wide-eyed. True, the fae never lied, outright. And after all, though the dragon ring was made in Faerie, Odin had gifted it to a Dane.

So Jack, who was a simple man but no fool, had taken the gold to the mill stream and washed it in the upstream waters, saying his prayers all the while, in the fair expectation that any faerie magic would be bound up in Christian prayer and broken in the mill wheel foam and washed away. Then, having done both as he was told and as his own wit informed him, and leaving a gold coin at the bottom of the mill pond for luck, he had left his plough at his mother's house, kissed his dairy maid sweetheart, and set out for London, his fortune, as he had said, already made. To be sure, he had not brought all with him. Only the silver coins for his traveling, and the twisted bit of gold.

"And so am I come to find a master goldsmith who will take that piece and make it into a wedding ring for my sweet dear. With the rest he shall make her combs and carcanets, whatever he may. And then," he said proudly, sopping up the last of the gravy with the last of the landlord's best white manchet. "I'll have the banns cried at Saint Rumon's church and three Sundays thence, I'll take her to my wedded wife."

The unwitting poetry in him was almost too cute for words.

"A goldsmith? Jack, how long and wherefore hast thou wandered the city all day? Why did you not go at once to the Goldsmith's Hall?"

That at least was honest concern, Ben felt no shame in asking. He knew they were going to end up at Tandy's, but not why or how. There would be no way to read the artifact until they found a goldsmith. Until, in fact, they found Marcus Tandy. Jack was not so innocent that he would display a treasure in public, even for his new best friend.

"That were my quest when we met, Sir Francis. So early this morning, I went into the great church of St Paul's, and some good folk there gave me directions, but I have yet to find the way."

"St Paul's!" Oh dear. Not good. Cathedral it might be, but its precincts were notoriously secular. "What folk?" Ben asked cautiously.

"I met any number of fine fellows as I strolled about. A fair building, is St Paul's. I never saw a tower so high!"

"And these friends?"

"Two fellows who took me to buy me these fine clothes when they heard of my new fortune. They said I must, so as to be taken for a man of means! And bought me excellent ale besides, though I must needs lend them an angel till tomorrow."

Ten shillings, that would be and, as Ben knew well, far more than the price of ale for three men even if they sat in the ale house all day. Poor babe in the woods.

"I'm sure they did. Friend Jack, that place is infamous! Look you, I have somewhat here ..."

Ben reached into his doublet and brought out the diary, new covered in green sueded leather with a title picked out in fresh gilt on its face. (Faerie magic never ceased to delight.) Tucked into the back, as he had hoped, was a pamphlet of a few printed pages, called the *Ground-werk of Coney-catching, set forth by a Justice of the Peace of Great Authority.*

"This great city is infested with every manner of thief, my friend, and many haunt the precincts of St Paul's. Aye, as many thieves as booksellers, and more than clerics. Now I have this pamphlet—"

"I cry your pardon, Sir Francis," Jack said, digging into his purse. "Is it better than these?"

He spread out four or five of Robert Green's handy guides to knowing the ways and means of the London underworld.

"Sooth, Jack! Whence came these, then?"

"Seeing I were new come to town, though how he knew that I cannot tell, a man pressed these on me. Some sort of lay preacher, belike. I gave him a silver shilling for the favor."

"Mine is no better, I fear," said Ben. "And have you read ought of those?"

The ploughman hung his head.

"I have not. For while I learned my letters well, and can read my Testament," he said with some pride. "Yet I have had no time. Instead I have marched up and down this street here from the great gate yonder to the broad river below, and met many a fine neighbor and learned all manner of thing, and ne'er yet seen the street they sent me to. Mayden Alley 'tis cry'd, unless I mistake me."

Oh fine. Ben was beginning to sense a horrible pattern.

"Sweet Jack, did they tell you the Goldsmith's Hall was in Mayden Alley?"

"Aye, they did, unless my poor brain hath clean forgot."

"And who are these great new friends of yours, of what sort?"

"Why, two brothers, sir, of the name Quiney. The one is called Merwin, t'other is Ned. And they have a sister besides, a young and virtuous widow. She is called Bess, same as my beloved." His face went all moony again.

"Oh, my innocent friend, many kinds of business do traffic in Paul's Walk, but virtuous widows are not found there, with or without their brothers."

"Are they not?"

"Nay, they are not. And nor is the Goldsmiths Hall in Mayden Alley, though it will take you there, nor in St Martin's Lane nor Aldersgate Street, as you've proved already."

Honest Jack couldn't help but look doubtful. He had been taken up and made much of by a pair of city slickers, and of course he had been flattered. But now, it had to be said, his eyes narrowed a little.

"If you will forgive me, Sir Francis. You have been my friend no longer than the Quineys, and your talk to me is no less comfortable than theirs. Can you tell me why I, taking care in the great city, should put your word above theirs?"

Of all the times for the boy to prove he was shrewder than he looked.

"God's Blood, Jack!" said Ben cried with some passion, which vulgarity shocked the countryman to raised eyebrows, and some in the room besides. "I am entirely in debt to you for my life! I seek only to return that favor. And besides," he added more quietly. "I want nothing from you, but to be the sword in your hand."

Evidently, that was the right argument. Saving a life creates a bond. And really there was no way he could have been cozened into friendship. The noble entourage had simply pounded through the Aldersgate and erupted into St Martin's Lane without warning. Ben watched the guileless face hopefully.

Now Jack was nodding and looking almost grim.

"I fear I have been taken for a fool by those brothers, if brothers they be. But what did they want of me, I wonder?" He paused and Ben let him. "No doubt to lure me to some dark place and rob me, for I did tell them of my fortune. Well, I have been saved from my own foolishness, methinks."

For a moment, Ben could almost see a shadow of the Saxon fyrdsman about him, blurred through the centuries, and it made him smile.

"Come along then, we're done here. Let me show thee a thing, and we'll lay a trap of our own. Poor felons, they must be half mad waiting for thee to find their wretched alley!"

He wondered suddenly if being accosted by Tibbit had been part of a larger plan, or merely opportunity. No, Titania had been meddling from the start. This whole scam would be her doing, somehow.

From the leafy courtyard behind St Martin's church they could peer between houses towards Forster Lane and the grand building with its fabulous door that was home to the Worshipful Company of Goldsmiths. Satisfied that he had found it, Jack wanted to go in at once and find him a jeweler, but Ben cautioned him back. It was doubtless being watched. But more than that, the so-called brothers must be dealt with lest they prey on any others.

"They have constables in the city, aye? Should we send for the watch?"

How to say no, Ben wondered.

"They are weakly manned, my friend, and easily corrupted, and moreover subject to the law. A good thing, aye, indeed!" he hastened to add. "But so far the Quineys have done nothing to you. How should they be charged?"

Most probably, the villains meant either to rob Jack in the dingy side street, or possibly—and this was scary—to take him to Marcus Tandy to be fleeced and shorn in private.

And we're going there, why, exactly? Because the faerie king's intelligence said so, that's why. Best to just use the information, not over-think it. For all his good heart and sensible wit, the ploughman was too kind by nature to be truly devious, but Ben sensed a healthy feeling of outrage and betrayal, and bit of chagrin. It fell to him to focus all that and turn it to good use.

"Will you be ruled by me in this?"

Jack nodded, and Ben explained as simply and quickly as he could what Jack was to do. He described the entrance to Mayden Alley in detail, and cautioned him to notice what he saw in the tail of his eye or risk missing it once again. Fore-warned, fore-armed, and in good company, Ben the organizer considered the problem.

Imprimis, Jack's size alone should discourage any violence, at least to start with.

Point the second, they were aware of the con.

Point the third, the bad guys didn't know the mark was aware of it.

Conclusion, tables would be turned.

A simple plan had assembled in his mind by the time they stepped over the whining beggars clustered about the saints in St Martin's medieval porch. And Ben was actually beginning to enjoy himself.

29
Mayden Alley

He watched young Goodman Greengage, whose friends called him Jack Plough, stroll up the street one more time, trying to "act natural". For Jack, of course, acting natural meant stopping again in every shop or doorway he had looked into before, and salute, nod, or chat as the occasion suited. If anyone noticed him a bit more nervous than earlier, he moved along before they could mention it.

When the ploughman had a decent lead, Ben stepped off, shadowing his new friend from the opposite side of the street. The crowds had thinned somewhat at the middle of the day, so keeping him in sight was no problem, though remaining unseen himself was more of a challenge. Even idle apprentices were hiding from the threatening skies by actually reporting to their masters. The morning's marketing done, good housewives retired to their houses as craftsmen to their tools. Still, enough remained to provide some cover. Anyone looking for Jack would see him first and never notice he had a tail.

"Weird," Ben thought. "Last time, chased by wolves, this time chasing them." Then he danced away from a tavern door just as a drunk came sailing out of it to land swearing in a dung heap.

He looked up again and caught sight of Jack at once. Good. Almost there, and not before time. Another house, a couple of shops, then Mayden Alley's almost invisible opening and the dismal close within it. Wasn't this street shorter the first time he'd walked it? Maybe it had been, and maybe it was just rolling grade from the river to the gate that was working against him. If he'd had a watch, Ben would have been checking it impatiently; as it was he kept fighting the impulse to look at his wrist. Around him, he noticed, shopkeepers scurried to bring in their goods, sensing rain and maybe something else.

A sharp bit of breeze smelling of green meadows came tumbling down from the Aldersgate, spinning up trash and coaxing leaves from trees. He stood back into a doorway to let the little whirlwind pass him by before it smacked and broke up across the knees of a cordwainer's apprentice, trudging past with strings of shoes on a pole slung over his shoulder. Ben barely caught his own cap as the breeze nipped it away, so he almost missed the snarling oath and the flash of red in the 'prentice's eye. All right, so something was definitely following Jack.

When he looked quickly back up the way, Jack had gone! No wait, not gone. He was right there after all, standing at the corner with his hat in his hand, scratching his head and looking a bit dazed. He had simply been caught up inside a kind of aura that made the glance slide away from the dismal street, which might be no more than distaste, and might actually be a spell. In a moment, Jack was giving an awkward reverence to someone out of sight, and smiling like an idiot. Then a dainty hand cuffed in lace appeared out of the shadows and touched the boy's sleeve.

Quickly, Ben crossed the street and closed the distance between them. With a hand to his sword to keep it from rattling, he listened; marked too how the cordwainer's apprentice passed him, shoeless now, then put all thought of the fellow aside.

A genteel voice with just a bit of an edge to it was simpering.

"Fie, you say that as shouldn't, Master Greengage!"

"Nay, Mistress Pennyfeather. 'Tis no harm. You are a pretty thing, in soothe."

Oh dear. This didn't sound good.

"Beauty is naught but vain show," she replied fervently. With a tight grimace Ben pictured her in sober Puritan black, a white collar and tight cuffs like a Thanksgiving pilgrim. Then she sighed, "What good is beauty? My dear husband is with God, and I have none to protect me from these grasping lawyers!"

"Lawyers, mistress?"

"Aye, indeed. My husband's will must be proved but there are no witnesses. I fear I shall be trapped in London forever at the mercy of the Court of Chancery. Lawyers want gold, though they will be paid out of the estate in time. Gold for their expenses, they say," she wailed. "And I have so little, barely enough to keep my poor little son, poor sickly little child!"

Jack's heart must surely be breaking.

"I have gold, mistress. Did your brothers not tell you, I have come to London to ..."

No!

"To seek your fortune, I know, Master Greengage, and they say also..." She paused to sob a little into a handkerchief.

Oh thank god, he hadn't interrupted to tell his tale once again. He was learning. Now the voices faded a little, moving away from the corner. In a moment he would have to act, unless, ah yes, here they came again. A few more words of her long sad tale, then away, advance and retreat up and down the alley in the growing chill, keeping the mark unbalanced.

"And thus I cannot take your money, good Master Greengage. Though I am desperate to secure my son's inheritance, and continue to live in my house, for which I needs must have gold, as much as possible—for the lawyers! Still I could not so disgrace myself by accepting such a gift!" The sound of gentle weeping followed.

Jack was now supposed to say "But you must" and hand over everything, of course. And yet to Ben's relief, he kept his wits about him and said instead, "Very well then, mistress." He did, to do him credit, sound just a bit sad. "I shall not press it upon you."

There was a long pause. A sniffle. Ben imagined the wide-eyed blink.

"What?" the girl snapped.

He smothered a snicker, still out of their sight.

"What?" she demanded again, more shrill this time. "Why, you would have me reduced to beggary? Live in the streets?

My sick little son will die! My..."

A tremulous catch in her voice as she recalled her task and sniffed a bit. Surely, there would be tears at this point.

Better than BBC Radio Theatre, Ben thought. Jack might not even need him to get out of this. If she stayed angry and lost herself, he could just walk away. Except for one thing. This tragic doxy and her brothers weren't human.

Instead of tears, he heard a crooning, a low voice humming then singing: "Follow me, follow me to the bower, sweet.

> *There we shall together*
> *sweetly kiss each other,*
> *and like two wantons*
> *dally dally dally,*
> *we shall dally."*

For a moment, though he was not her target and knew better besides, Ben started to slide under the binding spell of her voice.

Then a rattling cart rolled across his path, and he caught the acrid stink of a dog squatting to shit at his feet. And then a stray rain drop fell out of the lowering sky and spat in his eye. He blinked it away, muttering a curse, drew sword and dagger and rolled silently around the building into Mayden Alley.

She did not, as it turned out, look like a pilgrim. A fine gown of rose pink trimmed with pale blue displayed a delicately heaving bosom edged with point lace, which just now was being cradled in the arm of the moon-faced ploughman in the dreadful ruff. Ben couldn't see the boy's face, but he suspected an even more foolish expression than usual. The girl—Tibbit or Pauly or Bessie Pennyfeather, whatever— still hummed her song while one by one picking open the buttons of his jerkin. And under it all, the voice of the dragon ring was chanting its story.

She didn't see Ben at once, altogether focused on the task at hand, and the watchdogs she must have set had missed their cues.

"Ah-ah-ah" Ben tutted, tapping her dainty fingers one, two, three with the flat of the rapier. Each time she snatched the fingers away but returned, as determined as a cat to have her way. "I said, no!" And smacked them. What a pity, the barest hint of the razor sharp edge whipped a bright red line across the knuckles.

Her head snapped up, the eyes red flames, sharp white teeth bared in fury.

"You!" she growled. The ragged scar at her throat was glossy in the bale light.

"You knew it would be, sweeting," he said, and with the blade, gestured at the scar. "I thought I'd killed you already, oh, centuries ago."

He'd been terrified, tormented, misled, and harassed in this town, and he was just bloody tired of it, which made him cranky and sarcastic besides..

"We do not kill so easily," she whispered, watching him.

"I see that. Now let him go."

"Not without what I was sent for. It's here, I can taste it!"

"Aye, it's there, and you, minion, will let him go—now! Jack! Snap out of it!"

The song had stopped and a glimmer of fitful sunlight shafted briefly through the gloom, glinting off the bright steel and into Jack Plough's eyes. The boy winced, and blinked and pushed her away. "What's this!"

"Marry, Jack, it's a faerie of my acquaintance, who has nearly cozened you out of your fortune, your future, and God knoweth what else."

Pauly stomped her dainty foot and glared, arms crossed over her chest. "Jerk."

"Faith, Sir Francis, art mad?" Jack objected, nervously buttoning up his jerkin. "She's just a lass!"

She smirked, tossing her long silver hair. "Arse-hole," she sneered.

Ben's laugh was not a merry one. "Bitch"

"Idiot."

"Goblin."

"Bastard!"

"You bead, you acorn, be quiet! I'm afraid she is not, my friend. Just a bog-common marsh faerie, promoted above her pay grade, aren't you, darling?" He flipped the deadly point of the sword through her hair. "Tsk," he added, amused as hell. "You really need to take more care in costume. Hair on a modest widow should be put up, y'know. You look like a Ren Fest refugee."

But Jack, who hadn't understood a word, objected. "Nay, mark you, Francis, I've seen them, the faeries, and they're wee, little things." He shaped the size in the air with his hands, more or less. "Like so, or... Not like this!"

"Fool!" she snapped, and with a wink shrank down into a brief mist, a shift, a shadow, and was again the huge black wolf of the Saxon wood.

Jack took a step back, appalled, while the tip of Ben's blade followed her steadily to the ground.

"As you see. Not one of your piskies, no, but a full-featured, shape-shifting fae from Titania's court. But she does have brothers, in sooth—like the one behind you! Watch yourself!"

Two thick-set brutes, the Quiney brothers he had no doubt, resolved out of the shadows, armed and snarling, and launched themselves at Jack. The black wolf that had been a girl threw back its head and let loose a gleeful howl, and Ben slammed his blade right through it, letting it choke on the blood that gouted like quicksilver into the gloom. It yelped and twisted, nearly disarming him, but not quite. The smug look, however, died only as the creature crumpled to the ground, and vanished in an oily fog. Ben never noticed because he was turning his rapier—oh, so beautifully balanced—to Jack's relief. He had run from them across the Wessex snow, but not this time.

At his back Jack, huge in his anger, wrenched the massive cudgel out of the other fae's hand and smashed it into the ginger beard. The jaw cracked and it spun around, then recovered, so Jack hit it again, laying on with a good will, and pursued the creature yelping all the way down the alley.

Ben's was the larger of the two, with a short, thick neck and a sharp nose like a wolf's muzzle. Spiky colorless hair stuck out under a steel cap. It had armed itself with a thick short sword and the round steel buckler that could punch as well as block a blow. Cannier than its fellow, this one circled, snarling and displaying pointed teeth, looking for a fight. Ben tried feinting left, tried again, but couldn't draw it. It was circling, trying to get behind him, or to force him into a dizzy spin.

Bellowing his anger and frustration, Ben charged, throwing a flurry of blows that should have landed but he had been too long away from the discipline. Time and again, the creature threw him back, bouncing him off the buckler with a brazen clang, laughing with scarlet tongue and fiery eyes. Ben was gasping, out of practice, regretting every year since giving up sword play for a real life.

When the broad sword whistled past his ear, Ben twisted to catch it on the crossed hilts of sword and dagger, but was driven down, his strength no good at all to stop it. Then the buckler slammed into his shoulder, pounding him into the back side of a shop. His dagger hand came up, stung but still useful, leapt out to score across Quiney's chest, only to scrape the links of a mail shirt hidden beneath the jerkin.

Then suddenly, the thing halted, backed up and dropped into a crouch above the muck of the alley, and it was a wolf gathering to spring. Ben braced himself, bringing up his sword hand and hoping it would respond, wondering where the hell Jack was. But the attack never came.

Instead, a silvery voice he recognized now came weirdly out of the wolf's mouth and rang in Ben's head, blocking everything else.

"You have lost already, human child! Why should you die, so far from home? Why, when we could be friends. You will not…"

With a grunt, the ploughman brought down the knotted root-ball end of his cudgel once across the massive neck and once again, as it fell, into the side of the thing's head. A boot to the shoulder rocked the body, fae or wolf or whatever it was, over into the mud. Again the silvery hiss, and again, the evidence sparkled away.

"Master, what was it?" Jack asked, peeling Ben off the wall and handing him his hat.

"A lesson in applied geometry, my friend" Ben said. "And

temporal mechanics... among other things."

Looking up and all around the alley, he was gratified to note that not a single window had opened, and one or two may even have been slammed shut during the scuffle. Probably too common to notice, he thought.

"But, who or mayhap what were they? And what sort of speech were that you had with her? Was it French?"

Like Ben at the bridge this morning, Jack hadn't understood a word.

The American shook off the question and said, "I fear your ruff's taken the worst of it, my lad. And mark you, no one has called for the watch! Art well, no hurts?"

The countryman patted the lumpy bulge in his breast and nodded, though Ben knew perfectly well what was still there.

"Excellent well. So— now that we've done our manly best by the metropolis!" Ben Harper gulped his breath and sheathed his sword with a silver hiss. "Let us go and find ourselves a goldsmith."

30
The Sign of the Mouse

Staring into the squalid cul-de-sac, Jack and Ben together surveyed Mayden Court with serious distaste. It smelled foul, and looked worse. But there it was, the object of the exercise. Wedged in between two sagging tenements and about half way round one side of the trash-tumbled courtyard there was indeed a door bearing a sign in the form of a crudely carved mouse, with the time-stained arms of the Goldsmith Company fading from its rump. A pair of rats the size of terriers were humping on the doorstep. That didn't help.

The two men exchanged doubtful looks, honest country men bonded in the treacherous city.

"This vile hole?" Jack said doubtfully. "You're sure?"

"The place does look in want of custom, aye," said Ben. It looked worse than that, far worse, but he was trying to be positive. "Belike the work comes not too dear."

So here they were leaning against each other, exhausted, in a misty drizzle and all out of whichever natural humor it was that supplied a man's vital spark. A proper spring downpour was only minutes away, and Ben wished he had a clue what exactly he was facing. And where the bloody hell was Raven?

Well, never mind. He took a deep breath and straightened, shifted the sword belt a little on his hip, adjusted the bedraggled cap. The handsome green livery had lost its charm and some of its integrity, the sweat-soaked wool sitting on him like an old Army blanket.

"How easy is a bush supposed a bear, eh?" he quipped, giving Jack a friendly punch in the arm. "But is it just a bear, or the devil in a bear's array?"

Jack frowned, trying to work that out. "What's that?"

It had meant something, Ben thought ruefully, when it came out of his mouth. Rather than try to make sense of it, he pulled a carefree smile from somewhere and waved a weary hand. "A foolish thought, no more. The rain it raineth every day, eh?" he quipped, reaching for a more apt quotation. "We should at least look in, if only to get out of the damned rain!" He hoped he sounded more confident than he felt.

Minding where they put their feet, and watching the shadows, they crossed the courtyard and stepped into the shop.

The door was small and the windows shuttered, but the narrow room within was long and flooded with clear white light. Wax tapers to a ruinous expense stood in every corner, in sconces on the walls, and lamps on the sideboard where jewels and cups and other things should have caught the light in their framed displays and thrown it back. But few did.

On one side, a boxy staircase descended from the private rooms to a landing before continuing into the showroom. In the space beneath, a few open shelves displayed chamois-covered cards half-empty of rings, and a finger-marked crystal jar with a dome like a Moorish tower on a silver base blackened with time and lack of care. Some sample materials were set out on a case: a thin slab of malachite, a branch of coral, some cheap river pearls.

On a scrap of black velvet lay a pile of silk laces tipped with aiglets or strung with beads of enamel, a Venice gilt tortoise with a mesh of pearls in its back, and six more like it, not quite enough buttons for a pair of sleeves. Another cupboard displayed a few mean goblets and christening cups, let to stand unpolished till they had turned almost golden. Some pewter plates ranged in a sideboard for display, but pewter was not the goldsmith's trade, so those must be for some other use. Pinned to a shelf, a beaded purse for coins or keepsakes, and lots of empty space.

And that was all. Not a finished jewel of any quality glimmered behind the counter. Master Garrard was right. There was little here but leftovers and cheap trinkets. This shop had fallen on hard times if there was so little to draw paying customers in, and yet money burned promiscuously in the beeswax that gave so much pure light.

A dividing curtain was drawn back to show a broad workroom that must once have hummed with activity, crowded with workbenches and busy with the journeymen and apprentices who came to a Master to learn and live their mystery. Now only a low glint at about waist height was visible in the dim workshop to hint that the furnace was stoked at all. A brazier in each corner glowed red as well, though the annealing furnace stood cold. Ben knew his purpose was dire and his time short, but he couldn't help staring at the reality of the place, picking out the details.

The walls were neatly hung with tools and storage for more: crucibles for melting, cones for shaping, tongs for pinching, hammers of graded sizes from mallets to tiny watchmaker's tools and the anvils to bang them on. At the very back, a wide mullioned window looked into another dim alley. Another window, Ben noted, seemed to indicate a back door. Even on sunny days, working light must be scarce in there.

On the central table, gathering dust, sat a massive device with a turn-wheel for, he guessed, drawing metal into wire. And near it, bent over a palm-sized anvil set on a tree stump, one teenaged boy in a stained leather apron and cap was singing to the tink-tink-pause of a tiny hammer.

> *"Fine knacks for ladies!*
> *Cheap, choice, brave and new!"*

Even to Ben, his friend was practically invisible in the gloom but for the barest hint of a faerie glow, almost lost in the spinning dust motes of grey light.

The boy looked up for a moment, and winked.

"Rafe!" Marcus Tandy, stout and red-faced in a stained buff leather apron over his second best suit, bustled down the stairs like a man consumed with great affairs, great matters, more business than he could handle, maybe he could fit your commission in next October, but all the same affable and anxious to please.

"Rafe, thou idle rascal!" he blustered into the workshop. "Is my lord of Essex's commission complete? And my lady Bedford's?"

So they were all play-acting a little today, that was certain. In truth, the man looked more like a clerk caught napping than a master of one of the great livery companies. Pink creases from an open book marked one cheek where he'd fallen asleep at his desk. Sharklike, the toothy smile he wore came nowhere near his eyes. Yet he buzzed enthusiastically.

"Work to do, sir, aye, much work to do. Christ save you, boy, dost work in the dark? Get more candles in there! And shut that window! Rain threatens and winds melt down good wax. Build up the furnace, too."

It was like a set speech from a play, or—who was that guy? Hollyband? English for Emigrants. Not important now, Ben, pay attention!

His professional smile was getting cold, so he licked his lips a bit and set it again, taking up a slightly less patient pose.

"Marry, I shall have to beat that boy! Oh, we are busy, here, good sir," the Master added as he hustled past Jack to pump Ben's hand in a hearty greeting. "Busy as bees, I say! Good day, good day, good sir!"

Jack had to step back rather than be bowled over as, the stream of talk unceasing, Tandy hurried to poke up the show-room fire.

Raven looked up from his work.

"Master, I will!" he called back.

The black hair was cropped much shorter than usual, but the pale gold streak still gleamed its reminder of their purpose. Though he never moved from his stool, fires leapt up, and the level of light increased perceptibly, like sliding a dimmer switch. Tandy was too frantic to notice.

"Now tell me, good sir! Say how can we serve you, you and your, ah…" He quickly looked Jack Greengage up and down, assessing and dismissing him in one go. "Your trusty pleasant servant."

"How now?" Jack barked, for that touched his pride.

Tandy just rolled along.

"A ring for a lady, perhaps? Matched goblets for a wedding? A fine carcanet in the name of your honor's patron? What mark is this I see upon your honor's shoulder?" He flicked a knowing finger at the bouillon-stitched livery badge.

Oddly, it showed rather less wear than Ben expected, given the recent brawling. In fact, his whole kit had freshened up considerably. Ah, that would be Raven's well-known touch.

"Fine tailoring for such a brave fellow, i'faith," Tandy went on, still gushing. "Perhaps your honor brings a commission for…"

He paused to let the question hang in the air.

"I am honored to wear Lord Aubrey's livery," said Ben, picking up the cue. "But I fear I come not on his honorable charge but on mine own. Which is," he added momentously, "this modest pamphlet of verse writ by myself."

Tandy stepped back, non-plussed and frowning.

Pleased that someone among the small and fae had read him so well, Ben saw the booklet now was printed at the Sign of the Bull outside St Paul's, not written out by hand, and the byline read as he had hoped: Francis Browne, Kt.

He held it up proudly. "Which containeth within it many fine lines of verse for diverse occasions, both in Latin and good English. Lines of poesy that might be put to use by your clever craftsman in a wedding band, new and unique sentiments for lovers to engrave upon a jewel or locket. Sonnets for lovers and songs for the heartsick. Thus:

"O fairer than ought else the world can show," he declaimed. "Love only breeds thy beauty's overflow."

Ben launched into the pitch as it came to him, with samples, embroidering at length like a used car salesman till he ran out of breath, and even Jack looked ready to buy a copy.

Master Tandy, however, did not. His face drew down and further down, in fact, until Ben stopped. The man stared for two long seconds, and abruptly turned to Jack.

"And you, my fine, eh, fine fellow! You are new to the great city of London, I can tell, for I have an eye for such things. How am I, humble craftsman that I am, to serve you this fine, uhm, day?"

It was Jack's turn to be startled, and it showed in his face. How could anyone not want to buy such wonderful verses? And all so conveniently in one tidy package, printed for all time? Why would anyone choose to address a ploughman over a knight and a gentleman?

But so it was, and after two beats of stunned silence, he launched into his set piece.

"Jack Greengage is my name," he said, as he had said it over and over through the day. "Though at home some call me Jack Plough. And I'm from Devon come to make…"

"Thy fortune," said Tandy, shifting at once to the patronizing diction he used with his servants. It was tragic, surely. Disappointed now twice in ten minutes. "Yes of course. I fear I have as many servants now as ever a man might need withal." And now he looked a little sly, shifting a quick glance back to the boy in the workroom. "Belike I might have an apprenticeship to sell, if th'art willing to learn."

"Nay, nay!" Jack cried, more and more put out. Could the man not see how finely he was dressed, that he was a man with money in his pocket? "I have come because my fortune is made, and I must make my way in the world. And the best way to make a man's way is…" In blank frustration, he turned to Ben. "Sir Francis, prithee tell him for me! Thy wit is greater than mine."

Having diverted the goldsmith exactly as intended, Ben had stood to the side, content to watch Raven intent on some piece of work. All was in motion. Any second, Jack would have the artifact on the counter, and the golden voice that kept muttering just below his understanding, like a conversation in another room, would sing out and he could go home. But again, like it or not, he was part of the story.

"Sir Francis, art well?" Jack said, touching Ben's shoulder.

"Well, enough, Master Greengage, I cry your pardon. Say on."

Swiftly he told the plain tale. And when the faerie gold was mentioned, gold Tandy would not have to buy himself—gold he would be paid to take into his hands, in sooth—those sharp eyes narrowed greedily.

"Gold, say'st thou?" Tandy's attention was at last all on the simple countryman, with something disturbingly crablike in his manner.

"Show him what it is, then, friend Jack," Ben said, and gestured the boy forward. As in Alfred's court, that sense of the suspended moment stopped his breath in anticipation. Thunder hovered in the air, and the taste of rain, waiting for the storm to break.

The music of a goldsmith's shop should be in the velvet-soft *tink* of the jeweler's hammer, the minor-chord chime of gold medallions as they fall, the chorale of the colors and lights of precious gems settling into their frames. Yet all here was black discord, a jangling of needs and sense. Even Raven's silver hammer had fallen silent. The only clear note was the dragon fragment in the ploughman's care.

With a glance at Ben for confirmation, Jack reluctantly opened the middle buttons of his ill-fitting jerkin and pulled out a worn ploughman's wallet, and reached in.

31
All that glisters

By some delight of fate and time, the first piece that came to Jack's hand was the most precious. Ben's heart lifted even before he could see it. As soon as all that expensive wax light flared across the gold, the story tumbled forth for Ben to read and feel, and as he did, he resisted releasing an audible sigh of relief. Somewhere in it was the word 'me', though not quite in English, and with it an incomplete promise of peace.

Even flattened and battered, it shone with a light of its own, though Ben thought perhaps only he could see it. And Raven, who had come in from the workshop. And maybe, just maybe, Jack could too. Oh thank god, they could go home!

"Tan-*dy*!" came a screech from over head.

Or not.

"What are you doing, Tandy? What are you thinking of!"

A vision of late Elizabethan vanity stood on the stair pushing the sumptuary statutes to their breaking point, crusted with the jewels the merchant no longer had for sale.

"Now, Averil, the courtesies," said the Master without turning around. "We have a patron!"

"Patron! A patron?"

Averil Tandy minced delicately, as she hoped, down the stair holding up a mauve gown of watered silk that already cleared her ankles as much as fashion decreed, showing off her red-heeled shoes. The skirt was draped and pinned over an enormous French farthingale round as a regimental drum.

You could have laid a dinner for six on it, Ben thought in awe.

The hair, which she had washed in some noxious potion in

a misguided attempt to achieve the pure Saxon yellow of her fore-mothers, was pinned up over a framework with springing curls bought at the wig-maker and dyed (but failing) to match.

"Is this a patron?"

In the space between skirt and hair, as they could see all too well when she turned, her middle aged bosom was deeply on display, with blue veins drawn in and powdered over white as milk to mimic the pure translucent skin of a young girl— not very successfully, all in all.

In certain lights, she might not look entirely comical to her more gentrified friends or at least to other merchants' wives with fancies of youth. But for the honest ploughman and the BBC front man, tired and stressed out at the end of a taxing day, that much sophistication was beyond their scope.

Flat out surprise drove courtesy from the room with a whip. Ben snorted into his hand and turned away, but Jack's laughter bubbled up and his guffaw was right out loud.

In seconds he caught the looks on Mistress Tandy's face (outrage), and Master Tandy's as well (horror), and swiftly apologized as soon as he could catch his breath. Ben was simply trying to move away from the scene. Really, his work here was done—except for finding either a silver acorn or an iron nail somewhere. He could go! But how could he leave poor Jack with these comic book characters?

"Tandy!" said the mistress of the house once restored to a tenuous graciousness. In that corset, it was her only option.

"What mean you spending time with this fellow? Can you not see a proper patron awaits you here?" She directed a wobbly curtsey at Ben, assuming as Tandy had done that his livery bespoke noble custom.

"Averil, my dear!" Tandy exclaimed, stricken, adding to Jack. "Pay her no mind, your— your worship, no mind at all. What do women know, eh? Eh? Nay, poppet, that fellow there is a player, a poet of some sort, and was only kind enough to bring this fine, big gentleman here to see me. The poet is of no matter, no matter in the world! While this good fellow here, Master, uhm... nay, nay tell me not! I have the greatest eye for names. Come poppet, sweetest love, he hath brought his own gold to use, and hath more besides. Pray fetch us some wine for our guests, eh my dear? Oh the best wine, aye, the best!"

Then to her continued confusion, he added, "Faith, dear one, I will show thee." And he hustled her quickly into a side room.

Jack looked simply bewildered as Ben threw himself at Raven who was waiting, glittering with mischief.

"What the hell are you doing here?" he demanded. "Working? And where were you this morning?"

"You have to go," said Raven.

"What?"

He turned to Jack and placed an earnest, long-fingered hand on the lad's shoulder.

"The woman was on the stair while you talked. She mistook you for each other, but you have shown her which is which. Now she knows all, and wants all besides."

"What mean'st thou?" Jack exclaimed in what he thought was a whisper. "Who art thou, fellow, to know my business?"

"I mean she is a greedy sow," said Raven. "Who will tease from you where you are lodging, and if you have hid your gold, take what you have brought with you and all besides, and your life as well, if needs must. Human child," he said looking into Jack's eyes, "You must be gone from here."

And for a moment, Jack appeared to see in the apprentice something like Raven's true nature. The blood rushed away from his face, and he might have fainted right there had Ben not stopped him with his human touch.

"She's not..." Ben asked.

"The Queen?" The fae youth shook his head with a disgusted look. "No. But I feel her coming in the rain and wind. Listen." A proper rain indeed had started tapping at the workshop windows. "And Averil Tandy is open to her, calling her to you, though she knows it not. Do you have what you need?"

Ben lifted his hands. It was as good as he was going to get. He bundled the gold shard back up, grateful for a chance to actually touch it, however briefly, and thrust it into Jack's hands.

"Put this away at once, we have to go!"

"But I need a ring for my Bess!" Jack protested.

"You'll find a proper jeweler," said Raven. "The back door is unlocked. Now bring thy gold and come along—hasten!"

But it was already too late to leave unnoticed. The door from the parlor burst open with a bang, and the roaring blast of a wide-mouthed pistol. A cupboard full of tarnished silver exploded next to them.

"Thieves!" Tandy shouted. "There are thieves in my shop! Help ho, my neighbors! Help!"

The couple came screaming into the room, one with yet another pistol primed and the other waving a kitchen knife in one hand, her fabulous skirts snatched up to her knees with the other. In a moment the neighborhood would be roused, or so the Tandys hoped, and no way to say the gold had been the ploughman's when he came in. And who would believe a mere player and his bumpkin accomplice had come by such a treasure by any honest means?

"Go, go, go!" Ben shouted, shoving Jack around the counter and towards the back door.

The young men had the advantage of youth and good will, Tandy had nothing but a spent pistol. They had candle stands and a wall full of brass scales and hammers and tongs which they were perfectly willing to drag down and throw behind them without looking. The air fairly buzzed with ironmongery and violent oaths.

Ben tried to shove the massive wire drawing machine to the floor but found it bolted down and the table too heavy to turn. Recovering in the lull, Tandy was almost within reach when Raven lent his slender elven shoulder to the task.

"You dare not, boy!" the Master shouted. "You cannot do it without you break our contract." And over it went, and Tandy under it, howling.

Raven grinned down at the man where he squirmed, and said gleefully, "Out upon that contract, Marcus Tandy, for you are a whoreson thief and a rogue, and I'll no more of you!"

He stopped to catch up the jewel he'd just finished, tossed it in the air and caught it again, hugely pleased with himself.

For he'd made it himself by the skill of his hands, and made a creditable job of it indeed. He'd earned it, he thought; and besides, it wasn't safe to leave fae-wrought things lying about. Made with tools or sung into being, part of himself would always be part of it.

Then he followed the two mortal men stumbling out into St Alban's Row just as the sky opened up. Mayden Alley was black with rain, and a chill wind dragging it across the city like a cloak.

On a whim, he turned back and unlatched the door again. He gave a shrill whistle. Every candle, lamp, brazier, and furnace went out, plunging the place into darkness and sudden cold. Even as the rain swirled around him, Raven's sharp face lit up with delight. He slammed the door with a gesture and sealed it with a word.

32
For want of a nail

"Witchcraft!" Averil screeched, as her fashionable red heel caught on the drawing machine and she sat down suddenly among the mess.

"Devils!" shouted Tandy, desperately trying to push away the fallen tool and wishing to God he had sold the damn thing when Averil told him to. "Thieves and witches in my house!"

"Oh, shut up, Tandy," snapped his wife slipping on her cheap satin.

Out in the street, Ben Harper shouted, "What are you playing at?"

The Raven boy was listening at the door, then he laughed and cried, "Come on! Run!"

They ran. The district must soon be in full cry, rain or no. But the streets were sticky already as the gutters filled, and Jack's fancy second-hand boots were never meant for cross-country exercise.

They pelted around a corner, ducked across the lane and into another alley, this one already an oozy kennel of sucking mud and noisome muck. Running blind, Ben tripped over a slop bucket which set it spinning into the ploughman's path. Heedless, Jack punted it aside, bounced it off a cringing beggar, then stumbled through the thin edge of a rubbish heap to emerge stinking with his cheap boot soles dissolving under his feet.

At the next corner, his long stride had overtaken Ben, then one disintegrating heel spun out, throwing him across a slick patch of paving stone; the other slipped a nail completely, and both feet left the ground. The leather wallet flew from Jack's fingers and disappeared into shadow. His hands grabbed air, then mud, and the gutter came up in his face.

With a gleeful halloo, Raven flew after the gold as swift as thought.

"Up, man, come on!" Ben yelled, expecting any moment to hear the harpy screech of Titania's entrance.

Lightning sheeted the sky, thunder crashed directly over their heads. Raven was back almost before he'd left, the wallet clutched in one hand. Between one moment and the next, the air around them was still and silent, and oddly sweet-smelling. Raindrops hovered quivering in the air, each a tiny prism of light, though three yards away, the street was invisible behind a wall of rain.

"Timing is everything, kid," Ben said, gasping but relieved to be caught out of time for the second time in one day.

"Marry!" Jack croaked in a small voice from where he still sat in the mud, quite dismayed. "Is this the Faerieland, in sooth?"

With a slightly mad laugh, the fae apprentice tossed the wallet at Jack where he sat blinking in the mire, and bowed with wild grace. "Thy fortune, fortunate mortal! Keep it well!"

"Raven!"

"Timing, sir? What, this?" the boy said, swatting away a raindrop with a wicked grin. "This sort of 'timing' is not within my gift! This is my lord's doing, sure."

Ben nodded at the whey-faced ploughman, miserably clutching his precious parcel to his breast while the rain hovered.

"You want to answer Jack's question?"

Birdlike, Raven cocked his head and thought about that, made a face or two, then blinked, wide-eyed. "No, don't think so." Though he did add with vague sympathy, "Pity about the clothes, friend."

But Jack was determined to know more, clambering up out of the muck through the suspended rain. "I wot not what you say," he gasped. "Neither of you, nor what manner of speech this is. Be ye devils then, or witches? Or have I run mad, i' faith?"

No one answered that right away, either.

Still resting hands on knees while his breath caught up to him, Ben said only, "How long do we have, I wonder."

Then his head came up, focusing back the way they'd come. Batting away a handful of raindrops, he felt his sight clear, and... what?

Pale against the empty lane before him, ghosts, or something—shadows of themselves—ran along the path they had just run, around that corner there and into this empty side street. He saw himself, then Jack, knees up, almost clownish, painfully slowed by the sticking muck of hard-packed earth dissolved in rain. There, Ben stumbled, there Jack's boot broke, and there a boot nail snagged on a stone and the ploughman went down.

The ghostly figures dissolved into the present moment, the rain began again, though less fiercely. And what remained, jammed next to a stone half upturned in the middle of the path was an iron nail sticking out of the earth. With a sigh, Ben Harper straightened and walked back to it, the rain tapping at the back of his neck.

"So there you are," he said quietly, and pinched the squat, hand-wrought bit of iron between two fingers. At once, he felt a dull little vibration, and he thought: B-flat.

He slipped it in behind the buckle of his sword belt, and he returned to his companions.

"Nay, my honest friend," Ben said, putting out his hand to Jack. "We be not witches nor demons nor no other kind of wickedness. I am a man as thou art, and an honest one too. I give you my oath on't."

Jack Greengage blinked as rain beat him mercilessly about the head and shoulders. He looked more like a weary river otter than a man of means, but he met Ben's eyes and apparently still liked what he found there. He took the offered hand in a firm, comradely grip, then embraced him like a brother, not minding the muck running down hands and faces and everything else.

"You have saved my life this day, twice over!" he said, voice breaking with emotion. "I am in your debt, me and mine, a great debt that shall never be forgot."

"And thou hast spared me a great folly," said Ben. "Think of such a fellow as that Tandy using my verses in his misbegotten jewels! Live well, lad, and we'll be square."

"And the gold?"

"Ben," Raven said. "The time."

"Marry, Jack, as we spoke of. Go down to the Goldsmiths' Hall in the morning, and ask..." A merry thought tripped across his mind; Raven's madness must be catching. "Nay, tell them Lord Aubrey's man sent thee to find Master Garrard or Master Penny. Let them fight over your custom, if they will."

"I shall do it, Sir Francis Browne, though I think there is more here than you have said."

"God's death!" Raven snorted with impatience. "Any time, Ben."

"Go home and marry your Bess, Jack, and remember..."

Raven's hand came down on his charge's shoulder, walking him backwards over a curiously un-muddy track.

The harper threw up a hand in last farewell. "And have a dozen fine fat children! Rest you merry!"

Then they turned the next corner and Raven let him go rather than make him trip over a paving stone as they stumbled out of the sixteenth century altogether.

"Wow!" Ben was shouting at a cluster of dancing dryads, somewhere in Faerie. "Did you catch all that? That was so cool" He was all but bouncing.

"You were brilliant," Raven said dryly. "You'll be doing Hamlet next."

"Yeah, yeah, I still got it. I mean, once I got over the initial... But I still got it! Life is improv, man!"

"Could you have dragged out that exit any longer?"

"Shut up, I was having a good time."

33
What Jack did next

Still amazed and trembling, Jack Greengage, whom the parish called Jack Plough, blinked twice, walked to the end of the street and looked every way, but there was no sign of the gentleman or the strange wild boy. He knew not where he was nor what had truly happened this long day, but no one was pursuing him in the pouring rain at all. His fine new clothes were in rags and the brave hat was long gone, the soggy dish clout at his throat all that remained of a vast and stately ruff. He was ten wet streets away at least from his lodgings at the Blossom, if he could even find it again. But his faerie gold, his future, was safe inside his ruined doublet.

And perhaps the faeries—for if Francis Browne was not, still his mad friend surely was—perhaps they had done him one last service. Right in front of him was a shop where he was known. The window was closed and the goods taken in out of the weather, but there was warm light behind the thick glass roundels, and the Master was a Devon man. Early this morning the mistress of the house had offered warm cider to a stranger. Perhaps she would again. And then oh, what a tale he had to tell!

34
Diamond Cottage

"So what were you doing there?" Ben asked as they emerged from Faerie more or less where he had entered it that morning. It appeared to be about tea time in England.

Raven thrust his hands in his pockets and said, "Checking my email."

When that got no response, he added, "Learning to work with gold, of course. The hard way."

Ben sighed, but he had to ask. "Okay, I'll bite. Why?"

"Immortality is a very long time, Ben. What's time for if not for learning? But waiting for you, mostly."

Their boots thudded on the footbridge over the stream that divided Iveston grazing common from his own flower-filled back garden, and staggered wearily up the rise to the cottage.

"His grace said you have a place in that time. That was it?"

The boy wagged his head in that abstracted faerie way, as if there were simply too many answers to choose from. "Sometimes I'm one of the ravens at the Tower, keeping England safe from the conqueror's heel."

Was he kidding? "I suppose you know I freaked out at London Bridge and cried like a little girl."

"Did you?" And that was the end of that. "So what's next?"

"As soon as we're back," Ben began, then pushed aside the garden gate and walked immediately into the office. "Right. Now that we're back, I have some extremely mundane things to deal with."

"Oh?"

"Yeah. I'm sick of hiding from … Oh thank god, I'm

starving!" A platter of sandwiches waited on the side table, and two mugs of excellent local cider. "This'll do for me, what're you having?"

"What, nobody fed you in Great Bess's England? Shocking. Those people are always eating, they're like hobbits!"

"Mutton stew, precious, and good manchet bread. But no taters. And that's after taking the four-pence-ha'penny-farthing tour of the city whilst engaging in extended improvisational theatre with the king of Faerie."

"Life is improv, Ben."

"Life is also getting hit with a cheesy glamour, almost getting run over by the armed and mounted entourage of a certified Great Lady, and being rescued from said dire fate by a talkative boy from the country. Then after lunch? Let's see, broke a minor binding spell for said country boy, fought off shape-changing thugs in the street, and had to kill that frickin' wolf again!"

"What?" A raven black brow shot up, to Ben's entire delight. "Busy child."

"Just another day at Hero Central."

With that, Ben threw himself onto the sofa, grabbed the first sandwich and picked up the phone.

"It's a good job, isn't it?" said Raven.

"It does get the blood moving," Ben said around a mouthful of roast beef and mustard. "And now, for a few well chosen words."

It took more than an hour, but he did it. Heroically. First he attacked the waiting phone messages.

"Peter? Hi, it's me. Sorry I've been a pain, but I've given it some thought and the answer is no, no misbegotten search for the Most Disorganized Home in Britain, no Halloween special, and my personal favorite, no musical comedy. No, I don't need more time. No, I don't want to be richer than the sultan of Dubai, and frankly, I don't want you to be either. I know I have a commitment for the new series and… Yes, of course I'll honor it. But no more books, at least no new "Now or Never" books. In fact, as soon as I get these galleys done…" He

　　　　　The Dragon Ring

glanced at Raven who stared back over his cider, bemused. "That's it. I'm taking a year off. Maybe more. Well, I don't know yet, that's why I need a year off."

"Mrs Dawlish/Miss Jones/Ms Whinger? I'm so sorry, the Women's Institute of Giddy-under-Moonshine/Lower Penhermione/Storping on the Swuff/London SW1 is going to have to do without me this year, I'm afraid. No, I don't need to reschedule. No, Thursdays are no better. Yes, next year, too. You can order as many books as you like. Thank you, yes, good afternoon!"

"Iveston School? Yes, this is Ben Harper, Sparrow's father. Is everything all right? Yes, I know, he wasn't feeling very well, and I think his mother may have... Yes, quite. No, no need to send anyone by. I've sent them both off to his grandmother in Exeter. Yes, everyone's fine, no worries. Thanks so much."

He knew they really were fine, more or less, or would be soon. He only hoped that the changeling would just wither away without witnesses, and that Mellis's treacle-by-enchantment attitude would hold until he could fix everything.

Everything! My god!

The important thing was that he was finally taking his own advice, and tidying up. With each call, he packed up a part of his life that was dying, perhaps already dead. Like getting rid of trashy mementos and outworn clothes, and gifts you'd never used, it had to be done. And he could feel it working! He felt lighter already.

Duty done, apologies tendered, there was one call left to make, this one with pure joy. Dinah and Tom had been Mellis's friends since their school days, long before Ben and his team had come in and sorted them out on television. He loved sitting in with their eclectic little trad/rock pub band any time he was free. Now while waiting through their rambling, slightly goofy leave-us-a-message message, he thought something could be done to keep that music going, maybe even make something more of it. Mellis was right. As she always was. It's all about the music.

He got sent to voice mail.

"Dinah! Hi, it's Ben. I'm so disorganized right now—yeah, stop laughing—I don't even know what day it is. I'm going out of town for a few days, but give me a call and leave the exact date you need me. I'll be there. In fact, I'd like to, well... We'll talk about it. But whatever, I'm in, okay? Brilliant! Love you both! Bye."

By the time he put down the phone, he'd finished every crumb of sandwich and drop of cider, and dealt with every issue he'd left in limbo through months of growing dread. Something about facing deadly magic, cosmic curses, and the potential loss of the world as he knew it had thrown things wonderfully into perspective. He ached down to the bone, his Faerie issues weren't over, but his stomach didn't hurt any more.

The phone clicked shut with a satisfied snap.

Raven had the head phones on, right hand on the mouse, the other stabbing the keyboard, and was merrily clicking, ducking and dodging and blasting crowds of super villains. He'd changed his greasy apprentice's gear for the dashing look he favored: tight black jeans, ruffed black silk shirt open at the throat. The open leather jerkin sported a row of silver buttons, but the sleeves had vanished. He had caught back his long black hair under an elastic looped through a brand new, 400-year-old jewel: a stylized raven carved in jet, mounted in a circle of gold, with a sapphire spark in its eye.

"Better now?" Raven asked without turning around from the computer desk.

"Much better, thanks!" said Ben with a happy sigh. "I just hope Mellis doesn't mind when I tell her I'm giving up show business. Well, some of it."

"You need to bathe," said Raven.

"I do."

He was wearing the clothes he had left the house in, which felt as if he had crawled through a sewer in the rain in them, which he more or less had. Replacements, clean and pressed, waited on a chair.

"I see you've acquired a Brownie," Raven added, then exclaimed suddenly in a language Ben didn't recognize and began typing furiously. Hundreds of costumed villains died spectacular deaths on the streets of Hero City while Ben was in the shower.

35
Ten-minute warning

The diary had remarkably little new to say, which Ben found mildly troubling when he turned to it again. For all its nonsense, he'd actually used quite a bit of it so far, even the terrible jokes. If he had read it, he could use it. With the antique London map in his head, he had known where he was, and where things were, even alleys and back passageways that were no more than a speculative line of ink on the page.

Now, cleaned up and comfortable on the beat up old sofa in the office, that elaborate fold-out map was just a two-page spread like a page in a tourist guide, with the URL for the Canadian university that had put it online. The poesy ring was only one of many examples. Which ring was Bessie's, then? What had become of it? Hell, there had been way more gold in that piece than even one of those fancy gimmel rings needed. Well, Jack had wanted to shower her with golden goodies. Perhaps he had. Good lad.

As before, the adventure had been written up with irreverent hilarity and devastating accuracy. Ben skipped over all that. He was pretty clear on what had happened, and was unlikely to forget the worst bits at the beginning. Humiliation is a great teacher.

But where was the new stuff?

Maybe he was being overly anxious. Maybe the little folk had had too much fun with the recap and had tired out their poor wee hands. Ben laid the book down and put his head back, closing his eyes for just a minute. Ten minutes. He put his feet up and his head down on the over-stuffed arm of the sofa. Maybe an hour. Just an hour is all.

And in a good hour or maybe two, the afternoon light had softened into evening and Raven was shaking him.

"Wake up, sir. Something's wrong. Wake up!"

"What?" Ben came awake at once, if not well. "What's going on? I'm not ready!"

Raven's face so close to his own was a picture of anxiety. "Ben, I can give you about 10 minutes, maybe less, then something's going to blow that I won't be able to hold."

"What do you mean? What is it?" But he was awake and scrambling to get shoes on.

Raven kept looking over his shoulder as if at people or events in another plane, as if looking into Faerie.

"Coming toward this house, kind of quick."

"What!"

"Can't tell, but it's not good. Seriously not good. Whatever's in the diary, you need to get it out now."

He tossed the little book at Ben and stood back, senses on alert. When Ben caught it, it lurched open on its own to the last written page. And… nothing. Well almost nothing. A few pages filled with tiny type—song lyrics, some old and some very old indeed, and some still in copyright, not that Faerie cared. He scanned each one as quickly as he could, but it took too much time. How could he possibly need this now!

Was that all? Almost as he asked for it, a single page flipped over and sketched itself out like a blue print or a schematic. Then names filled in, starting at the top with Jack Greengage alias Plough and Bess Leere, both good Dartmoor names. A genealogy, well that was nice. They'd had four boys and six girls, and of them only five lived to adulthood, married and had children of their own. There was no leisure now for grief over sorrows some 400 years gone.

The chart trailed off at the bottom with flashing arrows MORE! MORE! MORE! urging him to fold out another leaf which, like the first, animated its way across the pages with a few handfuls of familiar surnames, some odd foreign intrusions, until ending with Hestons and Powells, who were Mellis's people. And when he folded it open this time, the next page showed Benedict Harper and Mellisande Powell, one child, Dominic Anthony Harper-Powell.

Sparrow. But Oberon had said that Faerie didn't know Sparrow's true name! Yet there it was, lettered in by invisible faerie hands taking their god-damned time to show him.

"Son of a bitch!"

"What?"

"She has his name. Your bloody queen has Sparrow's true name! How?"

Raven shook his head, face stricken. "The shields are falling, Ben. We need to get out of here, now."

"But Mellis, she's upstairs."

"No, Ben, she's not."

"But..."

"Hush! Listen!"

From the landing behind the office door came low and faint the sound of a woman softly crying. Then not so softly, rising into a despairing sob.

"Mellis!" Ben had his hand on the door almost before Raven could stop him, but not quite. "Get out of the way!"

"No, Ben! It's a trick. Can't you hear it? Come on, we have to go now!" The desperation in the young man's voice almost matched the one behind the door.

"No, man, that's my wife!"

But his friend was shaking his head, while the door rattled. Someone was shaking the handle and thumping a fist on the frosted glass. But it wasn't locked, only enchanted. And the shields were falling.

"Listen, damn it!" Raven had him by the arm, across the room, a heartbeat from the path to Faerie.

Then something slammed against the door with way too much power. The voice was sobbing and howling his name.

"Get off me, she's..."

Like a bomb, the door exploded off its hinges, and there Mellis stood in a long yellow dress, fists clenched, face contorted with rage and red-eyed with weeping.

"I'm right here, you fatherless bastard!" she roared, but the voice was not her own. "What have you done with my child?

Where is Dominic!"

Teeth bared, deaf to his cries, she launched herself into the crowded room, flinging aside books, instruments, electronics to get at him, and when she did, slapping and punching at his face and shoulders with all her strength, and howling hysterically. An awful red light glowed baleful from her eyes, and the harper knew even while fending her off that Titania was looking out at him and laughing. Torturing Mellis, and laughing at him.

But knowing that Mellis wasn't in control didn't help. He tried to catch her wrists, but she moved with a frantic speed he couldn't match. Then with impossible strength she slapped his face, and while he was still reeling from that, grabbed him and lifted him off the floor, still screaming. "Where is my son?"

"Titania, let her go!" he shouted back, struggling and straining to break her grip. "Please, don't do this!"

Then he was airborne, limbs flailing to cover his face as he crashed through the big paned window. He landed half on the grass, half skidding across the paving stones, his hands and arms cut and bleeding, trailing thick chunks of laminated glass. Safety glass.

Still bent on destruction, she ripped books from the shelves, tore them apart, smashed the mandolin over the Gibson, the Martin over the desk, one by one heaving them all in wire-sprung jangling pieces after him in a cacophony of demolition. Sweet Moytura, the golden harp, was harder to break, bound together with the extraordinary tension of the strings, but Mellis tried. The sound box cracked, partly shattering as Ben threw up an arm to catch her as she soared toward his head. A CableACE award would have speared him if he hadn't flinched away in time; it buried its sleek point in the earth instead.

Weeping for Mellis, he struggled to get up, and fell, swearing at the queen.

"Titania, stop this!" he called out through bleeding lips, and put up his hand to bat away a first edition *Tom Sawyer*. "Honey, you have to fight her! He's safe, I swear!"

"You lying bastard!" she screamed as she hurled books at

him with both hands. "What have you done with Dominic?"

All he could do was duck and crawl for cover in the lee of the shattered window with its millions of little shards hanging out of bent and twisted frames, piled like hoards of diamonds where they fell.

"Oh god, Raven, can't you do something?"

Frantically, he looked around but again the boy was gone when he needed him. All he could do was keep trying to talk to his wife, to find Mellis in all this insanity.

"Look, Sparrow is upstairs, isn't he? Honey, he's in the nursery!"

"That's not Dominic, you lying shit," she moaned, collapsing to her knees in the ruin, and that voice was her own, but just as angry, just as grief-stricken. "That's some mewling thing with my Dominic's face. It wouldn't eat, now it won't talk, it can't even walk any more. And its eyes, Ben! It has no eyes!"

And that was how the queen had gotten Sparrow's real name. From the one person who had been left out because she hadn't believed him. The one person who never called her son, or thought of him, by any other name but the one she had given him, her father's name. Titania had come calling, she had found the weakest link, and broken it.

Somehow he got up, and staggered to the garden door managing to push it open against the broken glass and books, shells, stones, mementos she'd flung against it. But the bale fire of possession smoldered again as he approached.

"Tell me," she growled, reaching for the nearest thing to hand—a paper knife, a letter opener shaped like a Renaissance dagger, not especially sharp-edged but wickedly pointed.

Teeth bared, eyes red with weeping and madness, slowly she laid the point to the soft hollow of her throat where he had placed so many kisses.

"No!"

Titania growled with Mellis's ravaged voice. "Tell me where the brat is, you tone-deaf, death-ridden swine, or she dies by her own hand!"

A single dot of red blossomed, beaded up beneath the knife

tip.

Her free hand flung out and a ball of power blasted from her fingers point blank, missing him only because she meant to.

"I don't know," he cried, more frantic than ever. "He's in Faerie, but I don't know where. How would I know? Please, don't hurt her!"

Gasping for breath, leaning on one aching arm, Ben reached for his stage voice and bellowed, "Oberon, for godssake, I've done everything you asked. End this!"

And there was one-eyed Odin, tall and massive behind her, and she froze. With a swift gesture his travel stained cloak swept around her, covered them both, and with a blast of thunder, they were gone. Ben collapsed and this time, he fainted.

36
Snow White

Mercifully, a faint is a fleeting thing. Again Raven was shaking him awake, but now Ben was in the comfy chair upstairs in his own parlor. When he came to, he snarled and pulled away.

"Get away from me," he snapped. "You little shit, you left me again. You left her! What the hell are we supposed to do by ourselves against the queen of air and god-damned darkness?" He flung himself from the chair, swearing and pacing the room, the tears banished under the onslaught of his anger.

Raven waited, hands thrust into his pockets, and waited some more as Ben finally marched up to him shouting into his face till the pale streak in his hair stirred in the breeze of it.

"And where is she now, okay? Do you even know? Is she lost in Faerie too, you poncy freak?"

Raven put two fingers out and, without touching him, pushed Ben back a few inches. The urge to form a fist and knock some sense into him may have been strong, but the fae resisted, possessed of more interesting powers. Instead, he made the man stand away, and with a twist of his hand directed Ben's gaze across the room to where Mellis lay on the sofa, propped up on pillows, and glowing faintly in the twilight.

"She's dead!"

"No, Ben," Raven said quietly. "It might be easiest to think of her as Snow White."

Mellis's husband, on his knees next to her, caressing her hand, a very cool hand, turned a ravaged face again to the fae. "Snow White?"

"You know the story. It's a kind of trance, like before, only better. She's fine, and she's protected. This will allow her mind to heal, and keep her out of harm's way in the mean time."

"You did this?"

"It is my lord's doing, at Odin's hands. You saw him."

"No."

"You missed a number of things, it seems."

"I was... preoccupied."

The young man paused, frowning slightly as he sorted out foreign passions and reactions. "You're angry with me, I understand."

"You left."

"I did not leave you, Ben Harper. I caught you when you went through the window and softened the fall. Pity I couldn't save the guitars, but I was somewhat... preoccupied. The harp and the Gibson can be repaired. The Martin I fear is lost. My lord's harp, of course, has its own safeguards—she seems to have overlooked it. Anyway, after the power blast—and that was a surprise, coming from your wife's hand, I can tell you. After that I... retreated to Faerie, rather than be blasted out of time—again—where I would be of no help to you at all. As for the mess in the office, your Brownie has her work cut out for her, but all will all be restored by the time we return. Eventually, your family will be too."

Then he added with a note of finality. "For now, you have a job to do, and we must get to it."

"Are you nuts? I can't leave her!"

"You can't help her, either, human child," the raven boy said sternly. "You must finish your task. Or everything will change, remember? Everything."

"I don't care about Oberon's England!"

"Ben Harper, it is not Oberon's England at risk, it is yours. You know this."

"I know, I know! Damn it, can't I have a minute?"

"You've had it." Raven's long eyes glittered like chips of flint, inhuman and remote, and his jaw was set. "You want to save her. To save Sparrow. Let's go."

"Wait." His wedding ring came off Ben's finger with one, two, three twists leaving a band of pale naked skin behind. Then gently he drew Mellis's ring from her left hand and immediately replaced it with his own. If anything were to happen, if she woke when he wasn't there, she would know he had been there, know that he loved her and had gone into battle wearing her charge. Her ring slipped with surprising ease onto the little finger of his left hand.

For another long moment he knelt at her side. He wanted to save her, yes. He wanted her awake and making music with him. And he wanted Sparrow a normal, laughing boy poking at bugs in his own garden, not in fantasy land. And he wanted his life back. He was tired of being used as a football between two self righteous...

"Are you done?" Raven snapped. "You're angry, good, but there is no time. I would take care of this part for you, if I could but I cannot! And you're the only one who knows where the last piece is. There is little time left in the pattern. You've got to focus!"

At the moment, Ben's ears were ringing with the clashing discords of his own needs and his wife's, and the world's. With a will, he dialed down the volume and did as he was told.

So he rested her hand lightly at her side as she lay fraught with dreaming. Then he got to his feet and stepped back, and finally walked away.

One thing was clear, he thought, gazing out the back window into the hazy moorland beyond. If he was going to do this, he had to shut all this emotion away, box it up, dump it, or the gifts he had would be lost in the jumble. Having done that, another clear thing surfaced; there were no new diary pages for the last piece of the dragon ring, because it was really and truly lost. No one had a clue where it was.

So Ben turned his senses inward and listened under everything else, until he felt more than heard what he was looking for. It was closer than the others had been, and the feeling was curiously layered, like a place and time he'd been before, and a little like... With a grim certainty, he knew.

"Look, mate" he said soberly, meeting Raven's eyes at last. "Sorry about, y'know, what I said back there."

"Hmm," said the boy with the ageless face. "I seem to have missed it, sir. If you're ready?" One by one he handed Ben his jacket, his glasses, the diary.

Ben Harper took a deep breath, summoning his courage, and shrugged into the jacket. Dry-eyed, he threw his fair haired lady a farewell glance. Unlike the last occasion, he had the will to say, "I'll be right back. I love you." Then he grinned a little wildly and added, "Don't go anywhere."

Then they walked out the front door with the slim elven hand resting lightly on the sturdy human shoulder.

Monday

q

37
Ivestone on Moor, Summer, 1763

The third step put them on the grazing common on a warm summer morning with the fog burning away, the same as home but different. Well, not entirely different: Ben swore, skidding in a pile of sheep shit.

"Propitious start, Ben," said Raven from a safe distance.

"You're magic, can't you do something about this crap?" Ben was trying to clean his boot by dragging it through the close-cropped grass,

"Sheep crap on the common, Ben. Not for me to meddle with Nature. She hates that."

But before Ben could retort, the mess had disappeared. "Thanks. So, okay, where are we?"

Raven raised a long elvish brow and smirked. "A little sheep poo scrambles your brain as well as your good humor? My, my." He drew in a deep, appreciative breath and threw out his arms. "Smell that, sir! Clean air on a summer's day, probably for the last time on this planet, ever. Mr Watt's steam engine is developing daily. Any day now it will be locomotives, factories, automobiles, smog, the breakdown of the nuclear family, urban blight..."

"Still smells like sheep shit." Tiny voices in the landscape were laughing at him. Naturally. "Yeah, okay, it's Iveston, sort of, I get that. But there's been a settlement here for 900 years. When are we?"

"Look around, Sherlock. Can't you tell?"

So he looked around. The dips and folds of the land were more or less the same, but woods, roads, drinking establishments? These things are subject to change. Or not.

Behind them, a low stone building with a sign swinging over the door: a night-blue background and a gleaming yellow eight-pointed compass star. The Day's Star, indeed, with the brew house behind and a plow horse grazing in the yard, and the beer wagon parked off to one side in an open structure, probably a barn. It was also neighbored on one side by two rows of low, sad dwellings: miners' homes. A busier village than his own, when the local tin and copper mines still ran as they had since Tudor times. That narrowed it down.

Behind the church, only a windbreak row of elms stood where Sparrow's school would one day line the road. And over there, beneath Raven Tor the hillside was white with sheep, far more than Ben was used to seeing, with their shepherd and his dogs and a boy.

They strolled away from the pub, wandering past the churchyard and into the village proper for further examination.

Iveston was clearly prospering, larger than its twenty-first century incarnation, with more dwellings and shops around a post-card green. Its children must for the most part stay, work, and marry here instead of going off to university and migrating to the cities, or to other countries.

A tea room and greengrocer, a butcher, and a blacksmith under the obligatory chestnut tree marked three corners of the green where the post office and village hall would rise eventually. Women in long dresses and white frilled caps were doing their marketing with baskets over their arms, their maids, their daughters, and their smallest children in tow—no different from their counterparts in the villages of colonial New York or Maryland. Clothing is always a good clue.

At the fourth corner where Ben and Raven stood was St Michael's church, the same old Norman pile he knew, though in need of a good scouring and some repair work. They had already noticed that the churchyard was smaller. The vicarage by it was a sturdy house built like the church in the local granite, only it was freshly painted. A long, covered passage led from its second story to the choir, and a narrow staircase cut a space between. No, it was more than a passage: a good-sized timber-framed room, with ample windows, and roofed in blue-grey slates. It jettied over the passage of a double gate into the churchyard.

From above came the sound of boys' voices chanting in Latin.

> *Qui quae*
> *quorum quarum quorum*
> *quibus quibus quibus*
> *quos qua quae*

"Fee fi fo fum," Ben said cheerfully. "Pronouns! That must be the old schoolroom, then. Collapsed, what, a couple of hundred years ago. There's a story."

"Of divine deliverance, yes, I know. I've taken the tour."

"Well. So that's where the boys are. Where is everybody else?"

Raven shrugged. "Be busier come market day." He was already falling into the local accent, which meant that yet again, this was a place and time the raven boy belonged to. "Some people have to work for a living, Mr TV Presenter. And speaking of efficiency, why are we dawdling?"

"Oh, ah..." Ben stammered a bit, trying not to sound as disoriented as he felt. "I mean: we're in the right place, I'm sure of that. Thing is, ah, it's not exactly here yet."

Raven seldom registered surprise, but he'd had a rough day. "Not here yet?"

"We're close, yeah."

"And in the mean time?"

"Check your email?"

Don't be embarrassed. Nothing to see here, move along. "The little folk have been able to prep me before, along with the bad jokes. But it was different both times. Turns out, like you said, no one knows where it is, literally no one! I'm only at the edge of figuring it out. I don't always know where something is; sometimes I just find it. It's here. Or it will be."

"And here is?" said Raven, mischievously.

"Uhm..."

"Okay, look at your shoes."

"Why?" But he looked down, because that's what you do,

and saw square-toed, square-buckled brown leather brogues and, incidentally, stout woolen stockings gartered at the knee, disappearing up into plain brown knee britches. Above that, a shirt with plain cuffs and a neck cloth under a many-buttoned waistcoat that lay like an apron over his thighs. "I see. "

He looked up again. "I'm a pirate?"

"You do look a bit like Paul Revere," said Raven who, come to think of it, looked a bit like, well, like someone who knew Paul Revere. Or the servant of someone who did. For a change, they were both dressed without flash or dazzle. Each wore a plain frock coat with buttoned back cuffs, and each had his hair tied back in a short pony tail.

"I'm getting used to fancy dress," said Ben, admiring the coat. "How will I ever put on a tie again? All right, it's 17-something, and… oh!"

He stopped, and stared up between the shops, eyes lifting to the gables of the stately Georgian home that peeped out of the trees beyond the village green. "We have been here before! That's Diamond Hall."

"I can see your house from here," Raven said with a straight face. "Well, parts of it anyway. And it's seventeen sixty-three."

A light carriage was rattling up the Plymouth road. They turned at the sound and followed its progress as it slowed slightly in front of the Star, then picked up the pace again hurrying toward the Hall.

"But it… it can't be." It was Ben's turn to shrug. "Well, I guess it can. I know I'm in the right place, I just can't feel the, y'know, the voice of the thing. But it must be here, or rather…" He lifted a nod towards the gables. "Up there. How can it be up there? I saw it shoot out of there! Are we up there? Right now?"

"Don't be ridiculous, Ben Harper."

"Time travel, Hrafn Alfsigr."

"You know perfectly well you don't want me to explain it, sir. However, it is a year later. The lady in the carriage just driving by is…"

38
Where the wild things are

Bang! The double gate under the schoolroom slammed and bounced heavily behind a stout matron in a gown and silk mantua, right out of Tom Jones. Her aggressive bosom was swathed in a lacy fichu, her fair Saxon hair was strangled into complacency under a straw bonnet pinned up in the back. Furthermore, she was surrounded by a crowd of yapping spaniels—the bounciest pair of which, Ben noted, had a somewhat fae look about them. One was already eyeing his buckled shoe.

"You!" she shouted, halting in the shade of the building and pointing an accusing finger. Having got their attention, she then launched herself towards them at a march. "Rawley!" The dogs gamboled along, yipping merrily.

Ben edged back, wary by now of anything canine, and almost tripped over Raven who had stepped behind him.

"What are you doing?" he hissed.

"Hiding, of course."

"Man, you are such a coward!"

"Just— just stand your ground."

"You stand your ground, dammit!" Ben snapped and stepped aside, exposing the boy. "Don't tell me—your 'place' in this time is village idiot."

"Oh, shut up and make a leg, man, for pity's sake."

Ben felt like he'd stumbled into a panto play with the falling over each other and pretending she couldn't hear them. In fact, she hardly noticed Ben at all as she thrust her waggling finger into Raven's face.

"Mr Rawley! Why are you not in the school with Mr

Corbin? Well? Bad enough half the boys are truant, but you! Idling with riff-raff and... Do not stand like a jackanapes when addressed by your betters. You have work to do, have you not? And yet I know you have been drinking in a public house! You were seen there! Make me an answer this instant, and mind your tongue or I shall see the cane across your own back, you young rogue, be sure that I shall!"

When she paused to draw breath, Raven assayed some sort of courtesy and jumped in, three-cornered hat in hand, to frame a reply.

"Mrs Corbin, honored lady, it is nearly dinner time, our young scholars are about to be released, thus Mr Corbin has no need of my assistance at this time. But even so, you must know that I was at the Star last week because when the post arrived I learned there was a letter from Miss Day."

Eyes widened, lace fluttered. "Miss Day is returning?"

He nodded humbly. "Indeed. And it is on her instruction that I came to the Star today to collect this man from the post coach."

Ben nodded when Raven indicated him, mute for safety.

"I am to take him up to the Hall to begin some work. As you recall, I remain in the employ of the estate, and shall return to my post with the parish in the event that she departs these shores once again except on the happy occasion of her much-hoped-for marriage."

Ben could only stare in awe. In all their hours together, the boy had never been so talkative, and had never once explained anything to Ben's satisfaction.

A glance from the schoolmaster's wife dismissed Ben at once as some sort of tradesman or laborer. She was obviously simmering with questions about the mysterious Miss Day, when the first boy to be released from pedagogical bondage, an infant of about 9 years, rocketed from a door at the top of the narrow stairs, slamming it soundly behind him. He hopped the steps two at a time to about the half way point, then remembering something turned about, hopped up the steps again and disappeared through the door. It closed with a decided bang. The muffled sound of a schoolmaster's angry correction, then the latch opened and the door slammed behind the child again. Plump Mrs Corbin beamed, admiring the agility of her youngest offspring.

The darkness that was collecting at the outward corners of the building did not in the least claim her attention.

"If you please, Mr Rawley," Ben said, adapting as usual to the mode of the day. "Pray look upon the corners of the wall up there. What do you see?"

When Raven turned his gaze, he frowned. "Shadowlings!" he breathed. "Mark them, Mr Harper. The day is about to get interesting."

At the corners, the shadows stretched and thickened, giving a curious impression of fingers binding the little building in a hand's grip. Some sort of pressure drove a slithering darkness along the lines of timber and brace, while death-pale creatures, all splayed fingers and toes, clambered lizard-like under the eaves trailing wisps of shadow behind them. Then the clock in the belfry ticked over to 11:00, and a single bronze bell began to toll the hour.

"There you see, madam?" Raven had to raise his voice. "Dinner time."

"Is there no end to your impudence, ye rogue!"

"Mam!" shouted young master Corbin from the bottom of the stair. The last stroke of eleven was just fading as he hollered again. "Mam! The schoolroom wall hath a crack in it over the door. It's as long as me, and growing greater!"

But they hardly heard him over the wheezing whine and crack of plaster and clay, and the groan of timber abandoning its load with a huge sigh. A wrenching shriek and a massive crack broke around the corner from the door and tore along the shadowed line of the nearest beam.

Shingles began to slide in a rush like a clatter of little hooves from the roof roaring upon the gravel path below, kicking up an enormous cloud of dust and the smell of old horse glue and tar. Shouts and screams like the noise from a roller coaster rent the air along with the masonry, and the supporting timber exploded outward and collapsed.

"Thomas!" Mrs Corbin screamed, then turned a doughy,

pink-cheeked face to Raven.

This time a familiar, terrible light shone in the woman's face, and Ben hissed.

"Bugger! Not again!"

The woman's head nodded with recognition and a peculiar expression. But then the faerie queen shocked him down to his socks, and Raven too.

"Help them!" she ordered, the steely voice issuing from Mrs Corbin mouth.

"What?" said Ben.

Shaking his head in disbelief, Raven echoed, "What?"

"I sought to distract you, boy, no more. Not this! I do not harm children."

"Point of order!" Ben objected.

The hot gaze turned on him in fury, then dismissed him. "Don't argue," she snapped at Raven. "Help them!" Then she was gone.

The north wall, the mate to the one they faced, had obviously been crumbling as well and from the same source, for the whole east end of the room shuddered and caved in, timbers and beams crashing to the floor in boiling clouds of white dust. Four boys who must have been standing against the wall slipped screaming under the slithering framework—scrambled to keep hold of the shattered floor, with little hope of hanging on.

"Come with me!" Raven said to Ben, then yelled to Mrs Corbin's spaniels. "And you that know me, follow after, by the Queen's command!"

In seconds, Ben had closed the distance and was scrambling up under the gaping wall, dodging the falling slates though somehow only a few bounced off his shoulders, and none off his head. Balanced precariously on the mound of shattered schoolroom, he reached up to the smallest child who dangled whimpering from the edge, his little hands clutching a splintered bench that had lodged in the gap.

"It's okay, son," said Ben. "I gotcha. Let go."

"Sir?"

"Just let go, Satterly!" Raven shouted, as he grabbed the

next one's ankle. "He will catch you. It is all right, he's an American. Come on, Cruise, I have thee, let go."

Johnny Cruise fell into his arms with no more than scratched hands and face, and ran to where Mrs Corbin already had her own son in protective embrace, searching his face and head for wounds.

The last two were older boys, hanging on tight-lipped. They needed only to be lightly guided down through the obscuring dust to avoid the broken rubble invisible beneath their feet.

One sturdy fellow had a familiar look, and Ben just had to ask: "Which one are you, lad?"

"David Powell, sir."

Ben laughed grimly. "Of course you are. Unhurt? Go on then."

Jack Greengage's descendant, his wife's ancestor, or cousin, or something. An image of Mellis's pained face laid itself over the boy's, but he set it aside.

"Tom Ford, wait!" Raven halted the last one to ask, "There might be as many as thirty of you. How many today?"

"Please, sir," Ford, perhaps 15 years old, coughed over a cut lip. "Only seventeen today, sir, because of the cider pressing, you see. Sir, the Leere brothers were all at the bench hard by the north wall. It was falling away as this one did, sir, and the ceiling on their heads. Oh, I know not what's become of them, if they're crushed or fallen, but the very ceiling is in the room, Mr Rawley. Beams and all. It's like the end of the world, sir!" Then he too broke and ran to join the others.

Quickly the two men found their rhythm, working in counterpoint almost without thought. Raven had only to glance toward the staircase to see that Ben had anticipated him. Using feet and hands, the American was already carefully exploring the steep passageway.

"Can you get up there?" Raven shouted.

"It's all collapsed on this side," Ben answered.

The roof slates that should have directed rain to the ground now did the same service for Ben. Slithering under foot, they spilled him onto his backside and send him back down.

"No good," he went on, slapping away the white dust caking on his hands and hair. "The stair is completely filled in, and there's nowhere to go once you get there. The ceiling appears to be on the floor."

"And the floor is down here."

"We could lay a ladder across all this, maybe, but…" Ben shrugged. "We should start from the other side, if we can."

The village was gathering at a run, and was already diving in. The blacksmith and some men from the Star started in trying to clear the stair only to be driven back by further trembling in the structure. Raven shouted for them to stop and get back.

Childish screams and one panicky adult bellow were crying out from above. Women screamed for their children, hardly pausing to listen for replies, and some took charge of the few already rescued. And a twin pair of sturdy young fellows with bright guinea-gold eyes and silky hair patched blond and brown, attached themselves to Raven looking eagerly for directions but not saying much.

"We'll have to get in through the church," he said.

"The church? Can you do that?"

"Oh sir, you're so gullible. Come on."

Then he turned to the blacksmith and snapped an order. "Mr French, keep everyone away!" To the twins who had been King Charles spaniels: "Come."

Plaster and other dust still hung in the air, thick as a pea soup fog. Through the roiling haze Ben glanced up at the broken window and thought he saw a flash of that might be silver-pale hair, and a pair of worried eyes peered back at him out of the cloud, then vanished. Three children who must have been the Leere brothers, still as three small corpses, floated through the masking haze with unbelievable slowness to the ground, as if in a dream. Were they asleep? There was no time to worry about it; if the faerie queen had meant what she said, they were fine. If not, there was nothing he could do.

A groan of wood under too much strain and, hissing, the other side of the roof tilted, and the rest of the tiles spilled into the churchyard beyond the gate with a sound like the roar of the sea.

39
In the classroom

The floating super-fine dust had already insinuated itself into the dim and stuffy recesses of St Michael's transept and floated now like clouds of incense in the sudden silence of the nave. The aged vicar, Mr Fordham, roused from his mid-morning nap, was just adjusting his wig and doddering into the vestibule when the big front doors blew open ahead of Ben and Raven—without, it must be noted, anyone having touched them. Without pause for explanation, they ran for the carved stone staircase with its polished oak rails, heading for the choir loft, followed by the twins.

"You, sir!" said Mr Fordham. "What is all this noise? Mr Rawley, who are these men? And where do you think you are going?"

"Choir practice, sir!" Ben shouted back, just slightly hilarious.

"Ben, stop it," Raven snapped, then leaned over the rail. 'Mr Fordham, sir, there's been an accident. We need the key to the schoolroom, if you please."

"What sort of accident? Mr Corbin is in the schoolroom, of course. You must go around next the vicarage, as you well know."

"That way is blocked, sir. No one can come out or go in by that way."

"Nonsense" said the vicar without sounding convinced. "You cannot go this way. This door is always locked. Been locked for years, you see. Can't have the boys led into temptation, you know, the little beasts. That is, the *erm*, the dear, ah, cherubs."

"Indeed, sir, but there is no other way!" The desperation in Raven's voice was unmistakable.

"But I have not the key, you see. The little heathens stole it. Years ago. Hidden it utterly away and it cannot be found! It is not my fault!"

"Damn it!" Raven touched his head to the rail in frustration, then disappeared, then reappeared. "Sorry, vicar." And disappeared again, and returned once more. "Vicar, there are people out on the green who need your comfort and guidance. Perhaps it would be best if you…"

"What-ho?" The silly man was still staring straight up at Raven, while his wig slid further back on his bald pate. "Oh! Oh my goodness, yes, of course!" And he scuttled off, relieved to be tasked with something he understood.

Then the boys stood in front of the locked door, staring and stupid.

"What's the matter?" said Ben. "Can't you just, you know…?" He twaddled his fingers to indicate casting a spell, or something.

"I was trying to avoid anything quite so rude. It is a church, you know."

"Well, can we break it in?"

Each took a step back, surveying the solid oak door that matched the solid oak frame of the choir. In the preceding five hundred years it had survived neglect, a bout of restoration, and a brush with Puritanism; it was not going to give way now.

"Uhm, no," they decided. In the mean time, frantic pounding had begun from the other side. Dust puffed through the chinks of the doorframe with each blow. The muffled voice beyond was too deep to be any of the boys.

"Mr Corbin!" Raven called, and this time a subtle resonance told Ben that magic was involved. They could barely hear the schoolmaster at first, but he could surely hear his erstwhile assistant. "Mr Corbin, please!"

"God be praised. Mr Rawley has come, boys. Help us! O help us, almighty God!" Mr Corbin's Baccalaureate was in divinity, but as he could not deliver a sermon to save his, or indeed, anyone's soul of course he had become a country schoolmaster.

"Mr Corbin," Raven went on, speaking slowly and with care. "You must stop hammering at the door now. You must stop, sir, or you'll bring down the rest of the roof."

"What? Oh! Yes, indeed. But what shall I do?"

"It opens inward, sir. Stand away if you can and give room."

"Yes, yes I've done that."

Now with a look of intensity Raven gathered himself, and put his shoulder to the door and his fingers around the handle as if to set all his slender weight against it. "Ben, give me an A."

Without thinking, Ben opened his mouth and gave out a clear note in the middle of his range.

"I think that was an A," he said somewhat sheepishly. "I may have left my perfect pitch at home."

Raven smiled. "That's my lad. Now do it again, and this time, hold it." Then he added his own warm voice to the C-sharp above it. His free hand gathered the magic and spun it out—*click*—the door opened and started to swing inward gently. It caught almost at once against something on the floor, which moved aside as if on command. And perhaps it had. He had stopped singing, so Ben did too.

"'Pon my soul," he said, a touch theatrically. "The wood must only have been swollen shut, not locked at all."

The raven boy looked pleased with himself and added, "I'm sure that's it. Mr Corbin, sir, are you there?"

As soon as the opening was wide enough for a man, Raven stepped forward, but was bowled over at once by the tall, pot-bellied figure of the schoolmaster, periwig askew and littered with bits and pieces of everything that had fallen and swirled up around him.

"Yes, yes I am, thank you, a' God's mercy. Thank you. Now run away all!"

While he sped, almost tumbled, down the stairs in his haste, modern man and ageless fae leaned against the linen fold paneling and sighed out a laugh.

"What a hero," said Ben.

"Very well, now. Let's see what we have."

Raven pushed the door a little further, until it jammed on a pile of splintered wood and who knows what else, all piled in what remained of the corner. "It's like a war zone!"

"Or an earthquake. Can there have been a bomb of some kind?"

"No," Raven sighed, as much annoyed as troubled. "It's just what shadowlings do: speeding up natural aging, peeling open cracks, providing some incidental stress. If she didn't want this to happen, perhaps she should have made that clear."

Ben knew a little about earthquakes, though he'd never experienced the worst bits of a really bad one directly. The news stories, footage, and drills were familiar to anyone growing up in California. He'd never been trapped in a room like this one, but he knew that big beams in such a collapse often left pockets of safety and hope that might with care allow a rescue. And indeed, great beams that had split and sagged were precariously propped up on iron desks and each other. Slate shingles and broken glass, loose papers and books that hadn't found the ground outside filled in the spaces between. The ceiling was indeed in the room, or the half of it opposite. This side seemed to be holding firm, although being nibbled away by gravity at the now raw edges. And some of it had already broken through the floor. Ben thought he saw a shadowling reach out to give gravity a splay-fingered hand.

Both side walls had collapsed and fallen away on the far end. Lacking support, the plaster ceiling had crumbled entirely. Not a boy was to be seen, though their sighs and whimpers could be heard, and one might have been crying.

"Gentlemen," Raven called gently. "It is I, Mr Rawley. Are you all well?"

A range of youthful voices cried out.

"Be calm, gentlemen." The image of unflappable British stolidity, he raised his voice only a little, using the magical enhancements at his command to steady it. Behind him, the two fae boys were already on their hands and knees, eager to begin digging through the mess.

"Midgen! Wiggens!" he hissed. "You will wait!" Both sat

back meekly, looking up at him with huge eyes that almost made Ben laugh in spite of himself. They might look human now, but the dogginess was undeniable.

To keep them occupied, Ben sent them back down to fetch some clean rags and a jug of clear water, or failing that, wine. He had no magic, but his Red Cross first-aid card was only a little out of date.

Then Raven went on to still the voices that were rising again. "Be calm, I say. All will be well, I assure you. Pray be silent, everyone." The voices ceased at once. With his firm, light tone and patient certainty, a sense of calm filled the room, interrupted only by the creaking of wood and occasional rattle of falling litter.

"Now, is anyone hurt? Speak slowly." he admonished before the clamor could set up again. "If you are hurt, say your name and what is wrong."

"Blackhurst, sir. My hand is twisted, sir, but it ain't broke. And my head hurts!"

"Very well, Blackhurst. Who else?"

"My brother Humphrey, sir! Humphrey Dymock!" came a worried young voice from all the way across the room where sunshine swirling with dust motes like fairies was pouring across the blown-in door and the edge of a gaping hole at their feet.

"Go on, John Dymock. Is he breathing?"

"Yes, sir, but his skull is cracked and I think his leg is broke. There's a lot of blood. And he's unconscious, sir. Pinned under the door." The boy's panic began to get the better of him. "It fell on him, sir! And I cannot shift it! And the floor, sir!"

"That will do, Dymock. Can you raise your hand, please?"

A small, pale hand slowly floated like a white flag out of the rubble.

"Very well. Anyone else?"

Questions, locations, assurances proceeded as Raven calmly collected names and status. Most had been struck on the head to greater or less harm, and most had scrapes and bruises, one had a splinter and another a cut on his cheek. Some sounded groggy and others particularly bright. And there seemed to be only seven where there should be eight. They would have to hope young Ford had counted wrong.

When he was satisfied, Raven called again for silence, and got it. Ben watched as the young man gradually withdrew into himself, hardly breathing. Then standing quite still in the tiny clearing, blocked from the sight of the crowd below, he began applying his particular magic, to raise or lighten or shift the Chinese puzzle the room had become. Gesturing easily, he manipulated the air as well, clearing and settling the dust and keeping it down. But before he could get very far, he stopped with a look of alarm and a half ton of building materials suspended in mid air.

"Mr Harper," Raven whispered. "Is that a flame?" He nodded toward the remains of the far corner. "Over there."

Harsh giggling troubled the air as black shadowling shapes filtered through the wreckage, slithering like ferrets over paneling and broken equipment. Only as he watched, Ben noted each shadow slipped its darkness with a pop of flame, like throwing off a chrysalis, to hover flickering just above the most combustible wreckage, teasing. His brow creased with concern. *Firelings?*

They danced over open books and broken, splintered edges, sucking on the air, brightening as the dust cleared, waiting for the moment to catch tarred wood and brittle foolscap.

"Be gone," Raven commanded harshly. "In the King's Name!" The chorus of chittering giggles and catcalls grew louder and the flames brighter.

"The white queen called us," they cried. "It is not for you to dismiss us, bird boy!"

The first page of Lilly's *Latin Grammar* was starting to smoke.

He let out a sigh and lowered his hands gently, returning everything to place with a hint of annoyance. To Ben he said, "If I might have that A again, please, Mr Harper, but one octave up. And hold it? Thank you."

And gently, one eye ever monitoring the taunting sprites, Raven moved his hands again apparently at random, gathering in the air a silver candlestick and three pieces of glass, no, four counting the little one; a bit of slate, a brass lantern, and the master's favorite birch rod. And while Ben provided an anchor, Raven sang a strange formless tune that wove among the objects and set them vibrating, until he had summoned a chord that resonated with each piece and with the two male voices. He let it build, and the firelings hovered in place, crackling.

The music, if it was music, wasn't pretty to Ben's ears, but he held his note steady. Then, with enchantment shimmering around him like a jewel, Raven spoke a single word of power, and let all the pieces drop just as the first Latin page began to darken and curl.

For an instant, Ben gasped, as if the air really had gone out of the ruined room, and maybe it had, and in that instant, the firelings winked out, banished. Several boyish voices cried out,

"Gentlemen, again, your silence is essential." But Raven looked spent.

"Are you all right?" Ben said.

"Every day a new adventure," said the boy on a breath. And squaring his shoulders recommenced his levitation exercise, applying the magic with focused delicacy.

Like a giant game of pickup-sticks, he had to sort, slide, lift, balance and in some cases suspend half a dozen things including a downed ceiling beam so the puppy boys could go to work without bringing everything down on the mortal children his queen had not meant to harm.

Ben edged closer to one battered window frame and looked down where the first four boys had dropped.

"You do know the walls are down," he hissed. "Except for right here at this point. The whole village is in the street, aren't they? Watching you. And what about the kids?"

No reply. Perhaps it would be just another Dartmoor wonder.

When he had the arrangement he wanted, Raven spoke in his calmest, most modulated voice.

"Now, gentlemen, my friends are going to come after you. Midgen and Wiggens here will find the best ways to free you.

When you see them, you will also see a safe passage. Follow them out carefully. Mr Harper will tell you what to do next. Be good and patient, and do as they say, and all will be well, you have my word. Do you understand?"

A soft chorus of "Yes, sir!" returned with only one tearful whimper. If any of the boys were aware of enchantments, they gave no sign. Perhaps they were not surprised at all. Perhaps they simply had faith in miracles. No matter.

"Midgen, Wiggins," Raven said at last. "Find! Take care how you go! And leave the Dymock boys till last, they'll need more help and fewer witnesses."

He raised his magically enhanced voice one last time. "All of you quiet as mice, now. No one will be left behind."

The puppies dove into the remaining mess and with digging, piling, stacking, and pushing carefully but enthusiastically, made tunnels of crawl space to each trapped boy, and the two who were trapped behind a bunker of tumbled desks in the sagging center of the room.

Blackhurst, who was closest, emerged first, gasping and covered with dust and holding his head with a blood-streaked hand and a testy attitude, quite like his multiple-great-grandson Teddy. The wrist was sprained, but no worse. Ben looked into his eyes and thought the boy might be concussed, and gave him the usual first aid advice: see the doctor before trying to get home, don't fall asleep for a few hours, at least.

"Understood?"

The boy nodded, then winced.

"And avoid any operating heavy machinery, aye?" Ben added.

"Sir?"

"Never mind, mate, just go."

Tyler and Potter Major, both 11, scrambled out from under a table on their knees all the way to the door. Ben picked Tyler up easily under the arms and set him on his feet with a smile and a damp cloth to the face.

Potter Minor, no older than Sparrow, had been caught in the middle of the room with his arch nemesis Stinky Stancombe who, by the streaking down his dusty cheeks had been the source of the tears. Young Potter assisted the slightly older boy, looking smug, and bravely tolerated Mr Harper's prodding and cleaning the gash above his eye. Then he thanked Mr Rawley in a heroic whisper, bowed gravely, and marched out the door. Stancombe followed, still sniveling, with a cloth wrapped around his grazed knuckles.

That left only the Dymock boys, aged 9 and 14, of whom the elder was broken, bleeding and mostly unconscious, struck down while shielding his brother. Raven dismissed the puppies with thanks and reminded them to transform again before shocking the neighbors, then crouched to peer through the tunnel they had left,

"John, can you come forth by yourself?"

"I can, sir, but I don't like to leave him. He's so pale."

"Stand aside," commanded a musical voice above them, far more gentle than they were used to.

"Ma'am, if I stand aside…"

"Do as you're told."

Now that was the Titania they knew. And what could he do? The boy flung everything still in the air with a wave into the already cluttered churchyard where none would mark how it got there. Then he stepped back to join Ben while she, as she had before, hovered on airs of her own, draped in white and gold, crowned in diamond, and suffused with a glow like a minor star.

Seeing her in glory for the first time with his waking eyes, Ben could only stare, without fear but utterly in awe.

40
Angels

Down in the village, cheers went up as each boy emerged from the church and ran or stumbled or jumped into the arms of waiting relatives. Those whose parents were further afield were hugged anyway by Mrs Corbin and kept mindful of their dignity by her husband who, having recovered his own, was back in his usual form as a pompous ass.

Now, as the youngest Potter marched forth and Stinky Stancombe lurched hiccupping down the steps, the vicar, who had been praying mightily throughout the adventure, looked up again toward heaven and, coincidentally, the blasted shell of the schoolroom, and gasped.

"Oh my soul!" he cried, struggling to his feet and pointing up. "Angels! Behold, the Lord has sent his angels to deliver them!"

For an instant, he had seen not only Titania's blue-white beacon but the last hint of the intense ruby glow of Raven's power extended, which could not fail to be seen by any eye. But just as the neighbors looked up to see where he pointed, the light disappeared as thoroughly as if a Dartmoor fog had sprung up and swallowed it. Opalescent shapes could be discerned moving within a haze but all else was hidden from mortal eyes. Mr Fordham urged everyone to their knees and led them in prayer.

"Did you not think to veil those people from things they cannot know?" the queen snapped.

"There was some urgency, ma'am."

"Careless child."

All at once, the air was still and the room dim, as if night had fallen. All Ben could do was stay out of the way. She could ignore him all she wanted. Raven at least had already been relieved of his burdens.

"There are two children left, my lady."

"Do you imagine I am likely to forget?"

She went quiet, as if listening, though long strands of pearl-shadowed hair lifted and curled about her like strands of smoke. Then she smiled and, almost dancing through the air and curiously smaller than before, she wafted into the middle of the room,

Wings? Just in the corner of his eye, Ben thought he saw transparent wings at her back, limned in scrolling silver, that couldn't possibly be there. Surely he had dreamed that part!

Under her subtlest gestures, the carefully stacked, piled, re-arranged bits and pieces broke up and flew aside from her path as lightly as bits of straw, until the only thing left was a clear if broken floor and a young boy watching over the still form of the brother who might have died to protect him. Young John never noticed that the beautiful lady descended from the air above him. She was simply there, crooning and whispering comfort, which Ben found disturbingly out of character.

Humphrey's hair was matted with blood, and his breathing was shallow, but she soothed the younger boy's sorrows first. Passing a gentle hand over his face and touching his eyes and mouth with a mother's care, she sent him to sleep. For the other, she gestured to Raven to join her; he blinked and looked at Ben in dismay.

The queen hissed with impatience. "Come along, boy."

"Bugger," he breathed.

It was not a command he could ignore, so he came and knelt by her, careful to keep the mortal boy between them. Fine, that's where she wanted him.

"The leg is broken as the little boy said. Place one hand on it, aye, just so. You know the tune, I hope."

Raven nodded tightly, and as she took his other hand, his face began to change, soften, smooth away the lines of tension that had formed between his eyes, as he slid into a kind of trance. The queen shot a glance at Ben and said softly, "Make no sound, human child, on your peril."

He nodded, and held his breath.

Faerie magic sparkled the air. An unseen flute somewhere picked out a silvery, heartbreaking air in unexpected proportions. Had Raven disappeared? Or was he somewhere within the swirl of color and sound that moved around the children.

Ben shut his eyes against it and tightened his jaw, willing himself not to weep over a 14-year old boy who must be dead these two hundred and fifty years.

Hours passed, or only seconds, or none at all; the reality of the healing overwhelmed everything else. Then it was done. Light returned. Raven blinked, jumped to his feet, and stepped away gingerly, apparently unharmed but eager to remove himself from her presence.

"We're done. Let's go," he said, and grabbed Ben's arm.

The brothers Dymock sat up, stared first at the Lady shimmering beside them, and then at each other. "Please, sir," they said to Raven, a bit unsteadily.

Raven dropped his head, then went back and crouched by them. "You will pardon me, I hope, gentlemen, for taking so long to clear the path to you. You fell asleep waiting, did you not." He softened the stern schoolmasterly expression with a pale smile. "And sleep as we know knits up the raveled sleeve of care. I find you, Humphrey, are not so hurt as John imagined. Mr Harper?"

Ben nodded, feeling awkward. Even being on the edge of such power had left him dazzled and unsteady.

"You'll want some cleaning up. You may both go downstairs, if my lady..." The queen had gone, fading already from the brothers' recollection.

"Never mind then. Quickly, now!"

Ben hurried them, though it pained him to do so. Ominous creaks and groans had returned almost the moment the children crossed the threshold, and the floor was shifting under their feet. Oberon's pets had served their purpose. The truce was done.

"Run!" said Raven.

They ran.

The crash began in earnest as the rest of the ceiling crumbled to the floor and kept going, forced through the weakened underpinnings, carrying all to the ground and crushing the gate beneath. They stood, thank goodness, on solid stone with the great oak door at their backs, so they felt more than heard the final crash like artillery fire, a long roll of thunder, a hiss.

Then silence.

Perhaps there was still magic lingering in the lock, or perhaps the local wee folk were simply exercising their peculiar sense of humor. The heavy door swung lightly open. Little Arthur Leate, youngest of all the parish scholars, stood like Wee Willie Winkie all smudged and teary-eyed in the last square foot of tile that had not collapsed through to the ground.

Raven folded his hands in front of him—as if about to deliver a lecture, Ben thought—but what he said was. "And where were you, young Arthur?"

"Please, sir!" the boy gasped. "Mr Corbin was about to give me three strokes in front of the room, for falling asleep during the lesson. Then everything started to shake, and I ran and I hid in the fireplace. It wants cleaning, sir," the boy added sulkily, wiping his face with a sooty handkerchief.

"I suppose you fell asleep there, too."

"I did, sir."

"Clever boy!"

"Sir, is it over?"

"It is, yes," Raven said, ushering him through to the staircase, relieved to have identified the last child of young Ford's count. "Come along, now."

But the boy, true to his age and condition, had one more question. "Sir," said Arthur Leate. "Are you angels?"

Well, there's no answer to that. So they walked him downstairs and sent him out the door, to be cheered, examined and prayed over by the village. For themselves, it was time to get up to the Hall.

"Well done, both of you," said Titania. Ben jumped and

turned, caught off-guard as always, not knowing what to say.

Apparently nothing was required, so he gave her a courtesy—she was a queen, after all, and not to be trifled with—which she ignored. Instead, she laid a hand on Raven's dusty shoulder and leaned forward to place a tender kiss on his forehead. He reddened, bowed, and stepped away. Then she turned to Ben, and slapped his face.

The tears he had avoided earlier now started into his eyes, but he only glared back at her. Nothing had changed. Well, he knew it hadn't. Then she faded away, leaving just her beautiful voice and the trace of a sparkly cloud.

"You're better than most, Ben Harper, intelligent and full of song. Which is why I will honor you by taking Dominic to be my esquire."

Would she never stop?

"There are other boys, ma'am."

"Tell me, human child, is Sparrow like any other boy?" With a snap like a door closing, she was gone with a hint of expensive perfume.

"Too fucking precious," said Ben.

41
Diamond Hall, Summer 1763

"Seriously, what is up with her?" Ben said as they ducked out the back of the church, cutting through the graves. "Blasts you out of time, kisses your forehead? I mean, I know why she smacked me, but…"

But Raven wasn't listening. More weary than a lord of the fae should be, he stood swaying slightly between two mossy headstones, and said softly, "I know a bank whereon the wild thyme blows."

It was clear he required something more restorative than a brisk hike up the hill on a summer day. So Ben made an executive decision and found a tune in his head that ought to do. Hopefully a few minutes rest against a flowering tree, a gulp of water from a clear stream, breathing the wholesome airs of Faerie would be enough.

"Her who?" Raven said at last. Sitting by the shady river bank, his sense of humor—fae as it was—began to return along with his color.

"Fine, don't tell me."

"Okay."

A minute passed, then the boy knelt by the stream and came up with a dripping goblet filled with the sweet water. He drank deeply, then passed it refilled to Ben who admired the occasionally simple, mundane practicality of faerie magic. The water itself was like a tonic, as chill as ice in the blood, as warm as deep affection, and it calmed his spirit.

"And you're sure our saving all those kids didn't change history, right?"

Raven sat back again for a moment and closed his eyes, meditating perhaps.

"If you had read," he said, *"A Concise History of Ivarstanehaugh and the Parish of Ivestone-on-Moor,* by Dr Josiah Powell, J.P. (printed in 1888) you would know that the Iveston Deliverance was already famed in song and story long before you were born."

"And this famous volume says what?"

One lapis eye winked open.

"You heard the vicar, sir! Angels! In his memoir he records that by the special grace of angelic visitation, no serious damage came to a single child. You and I remain otherwise uncredited."

Good, he was recovered enough for sarcasm. Next question, while they had a minute.

"That last boy, there at the end. That was a lot of magic, wasn't it?"

"Aye, sir, it was. A powerful lot of magic. I dearly hope you won't be needing any for this next exercise."

"More than just a concussion, then, I guess?"

"Internal bleeding," said Raven, happy to have a question he could answer. "Skull fracture. And some congenital stuff that made it all more complicated."

"She couldn't have fixed him by herself?"

"Probably, but it suited her to use me." And now they were getting to their feet, meeting over. "Ready to go?"

"If you are."

In three steps they strolled into the stuffy, leather-booked library of a very fine house indeed, to the whistled tune of *Yankee Doodle.* Ben enjoyed the irony, and Raven was content that he should do so.

As before, the noon sun was baking the room's neglected contents though the draperies had been closed again, and the air was somewhat less redolent of old cigars and dead flowers. Ben gasped, then coughed on the dust as he had done the last time, but didn't mind as much, being prepared for it.

The wallpaper had peeled a little further and begun to

detach in one high corner, taking the cobwebs with it. Mice had pissed on the rug. Only the bloom of tobacco stains on the medallioned ceiling was completely unchanged. The house was empty, and this time it felt like it. No enchanted harp made soothing background music. No one was offering potent lemonade, which after the waters of Faerie might have been a disappointment. At least this time he knew why he was here.

Back to back, man and fae scanned the room looking for a glint of antique gold, a dragon's head like the prow of a Viking long ship with a double twist of plaited gold broken off behind it.

Ben frowned. His finding gift, his bump of direction, or whatever was working, and still there was no anchoring mutter, unless.... Did a headache count? The one thing he was certainly aware of besides the oppressive warmth was a kind of vibrating, directionless tension, a hovering moment as if between two heartbeats, waiting. A familiar feeling, but so what?

And who knows, he thought. The other pieces had been revealed in different ways, this would just be another.

His first visit had been cluttered with surprises exploding like little grenades that had taxed his credulity and his temper. And though he'd scanned the extraordinary contents of the room, he'd been in no mood to appreciate it. He was dazzled by the collection even as he peered into the shadows, thinking what treasures must going to ruin, but no golden thread or muttering voice drew him.

"I got nothing," he said at last.

"No harm in looking closer, then."

So they separated.

Glass-topped cases stood between each pair of book shelves closed behind beveled glass, and even more were arrayed to fill the room in long straight rows, each filled with curiosities he had not seen before: a flint axe, a portrait of Sir Francis Drake stippled on an ostrich egg; a Saxon chess piece stained by fire, a crumbling parchment map, an array of faded butterflies. And everything, even protected in glass, everything was smothering in dust. Gold and bronze, coral and

The Dragon Ring

carnelian, all had become uniformly grey with little tufts and tails and drifts of dust floating like seaweed on unseen tides.

Wonderful things, utterly without context or order. As he had before, Ben felt a deep desire to get it all cataloged.

Squinting at case after case, standing on tip-toe for the ones over his head, Ben chuckled when he realized what was missing: display lighting. There had been lighting before, when Oberon entertained him here. Now, it was just a forgotten room in a neglected museum with everything switched off. He shrugged and moved to the next table, listening as much as looking.

"Miss Scarlet. In the library," he said, drawing a finger through the grime on one of the iron pieces nearest to hand. "With the, uh, Roman thing. What is this?"

Raven glanced over from the case of butterflies. "Medical instruments," he said idly. "The crusty bit there is probably blood."

Ben snatched his hand away, while Raven's face creased in a curiously open grin. He was looking a good deal more like himself; if anything, a touch less reserved.

The dragon ring had to be here somewhere singing its story, Ben thought, but hidden somehow. He had been able to go arrow straight to the others, once he was near enough; but every piece here was old and each had a story to tell: every hand that had held it, every place it had been. Most of them, not being magic of themselves, were faint; many were brief—especially the fakes. But some were as complex as a novel. He needed to push all their voices aside and read just the one tale. Just one. Then he could go home and wake Mellis.

Tired of straining his eyes in the breathless gloom, he went to the windows and thrust aside the velvet draperies, half disappointed to find a quite ordinarily expansive Devonshire estate spread out before him. A broad lawn and gardens rolled down to a rustic gate, the tell-tale tree line marking the path of the brook; to the high moor and, he knew, Raven Tor just beyond. It was almost the same view as the one from his own parlor, two hundred and fifty years from now.

"So now what?" Ben asked, blinking at the midday glare.

Curious how the boy's stance and carriage changed again. "Will you give me leave for a moment, sir?" said Raven with a new and curious sort of deference.

When Ben faced him, the fae looked almost apologetic. "What's going on?"

"As you said, I have a place in this time, and things to do. Somewhat in the village, and also in this house. I'm needed."

"Okay," Ben said, then cocked his head and considered, and realized it was okay. He was fine. No, really, he knew how to come and go on his own. And so far nothing here wanted to kill him.

There were summer fairies scrolling floral traceries in the glinting dust motes and skiing in the grimy cabinets leaving trails of pixie dust spinning in their wake. The pixies themselves had gone, perhaps to find other more rustic places to play. Like ghosts, the creatures he could see hardly knew he was there.

The only musics were the natural harmonies of the faerie world where it resonates with ours, and the stories of each of the pieces in their glass cases. It was, all in all, remarkably peaceful, as if everything were dreaming and only humming in its sleep. As Mellis would be, until he got back.

That thought quirked up a small smile that reached all the way to his eyes, and he nodded with confidence. "Sure. Need any help?"

Raven started to wave aside the suggestion, then halted, considering. Eventually he said, "No, I think not. Although the pattern here is curious."

With another moment's consideration he spoke hurriedly: "Ben, listen to me. When you see me next, I shall be with Miss Priscilla Day, the heiress that my lord bade me tell you of." His language was wrapped again in this century's idiom, as he surveyed the room with a calculating eye. "This place is full of shadows. I pray you stand hidden in them as best you may. Say nothing, and on no account may you interfere. Any interference unless I particularly ask it of you will recoil, and events will spiral into..." Catching himself, the boy waved away the explanation. "Never mind, sir. Simply do not speak unless I call on you by name. Do you understand?"

Ben nodded soberly and stepped back, careful to avoid raising too much dust. Then Raven bowed, turned and left, walking out of the air before he even reached the double doors at the far end of the room.

42
Career change

Wait in the shadows. Fine. It was curious, though, now that Ben thought about it. Of the three shards of the dragon ring, the most complex one, having the longest story, had sailed off to its intended temporal destination, a world where the music was simple and declamatory. Another, whose song was fragmented like the intersecting twists and spirals of the gold, had landed in a time where even popular vocal music reveled in polyphony and elaboration. The last had hardly moved at all, apparently, and its story was lost in this busy, jangling room, where he stood holding a three-cornered hat under his arm.

Harper errant, he thought wryly. That's me.

Maybe what was really weird was that the one of them had gone to the one place in time that Ben might have chosen himself, if he'd been asked. And then gotten him lost. Was that lucky, or was there some meaning in it?

And if he were going to follow directions—and how crazy would he have to be at this point not to—he still needed to find and bring home a silver acorn. He had no idea why it was going to be important, he just knew that it was. Finding both his gold dragon and a silver do-dad was going to take a while.

So here he was, up to his ankles in dust badgers, reduced to checking places where his dragon could not possibly be: under a table, behind a chair. Though he stopped again every few minutes and listened very particularly, he couldn't get any better a fix on the damned thing. What if, as in London, his gift had brought him to the right general location but not the precise place. What if it were in the house just not in this room?

Okay, he thought, completing a final circuit of the tall cases. But if it's in the house, where's the thread? Why can't I feel it. And where the hell is Raven?

Then two things happened not quite simultaneously.

First, a whiz of air rushed past his head, almost clipping his ear, followed by a crash and a tinkle of breaking glass. And with all that came the sudden and utter certainty that he was standing in the exact moment of the second finial's arrival in this time and place. Broken glass from the last cabinet next to the window covered the floor, and underneath it glinted, unmistakable, a smallish piece of antique gold with just the slightest glow of enchantment flickering and snapping around it.

And there, too, was the low muttering, the hum of the artifact's story, a fresh note in the chorus of the room. Relieved and so ready to go home now, Ben almost laughed out loud, then froze. Footsteps, voices in the hall. Wait.

At the far end of the room the double doors clicked open to admit Raven, liveried in sober black, with his hair hidden by a plain white periwig, its pigtail tied with a crisp blue ribbon. He scanned the room and, hesitating, noted Ben's position, then spoke over his shoulder in a refined version of the local accent. "It is dreadful dirty in here, Miss Day. Old Mr Day said no one was to touch it, and no one has. Are you sure you want to come in?"

Behind him, a man's nasal whine drawled, "Of course it's filthy, man, just open the door, damn you!"

From stock still in the center of the room, Ben dove for the deep shadows. Raven bought him a little more time with some further words of concern. Then he pushed the doors open the rest of the way and stood aside for a woman in her late twenties, Ben thought, chinless and quite plain, dressed in a simple grey gown with a pointed bodice. Her hair was pulled tightly away from her face with a few sad tendrils dripping over her ears, all under a flat straw hat.

This would be the heiress, though she looked as poor as a church mouse. The feckless fellow who barged in as if he owned the place wore an officer's regimental scarlet and a sour expression. That would be the cad Raven had mentioned before. They looked as if they'd dressed for some Revolutionary War costume drama. And though they were clearly the love interest in this picture, they didn't seem to be enjoying each other's company.

"Good Gad, Polly!" the cad exclaimed in tipsy annoyance. "One room is worse than the last! Furnishings decrepit. Draperies rotting away. Damned glass broken!" He sniffed and sneezed and frowned, carving even more deeply the crevasses in his narrow face. "I smell mice."

A goblin they couldn't see popped in with a raucous cackle and blew dust up the fellow's nose, screamed with laughter, and vanished with a pop they couldn't hear. Sneezing fits ensued, accompanied by fitful swearing.

The heiress simply nodded blandly, slowly pacing through the slanting sunbeams. "Another room full of Grandpapa's foolishness," she agreed, staring without interest or care at all the bits and bobs of antiquity. "You're quite right, of course. Oh my goodness!" She realized he was sneezing and carrying on, and offered a half-hearted blessing. "But perhaps it could be improved. I used to love it here, when I was young and Grandfather Day was in his health."

"The only thing that's going to improve this place is the selling of it. Or a bang up fire!"

But he wasn't really listening. He strolled among the displays, murmuring a drinking song.

> "Here's to the maiden of bashful fifteen;
> Here's to the widow of fifty;
> Here's to the flaunting extravagant quean,
> And here's to the housewife that's thrifty.
> Oh!"

"Now Jasper, you know I cannot sell it. Nor even take possession until I marry, and even then I am not to sell it out of the family."

At that Jasper recalled, briefly, why he was here, and made to exercise his courting muscle just slightly. He took her hand and kissed it, gazing soulfully into her eyes. "Of course, dearest

Polly, of course. And when we're married…"

"When we're married," she said sourly. "I hope you will call me Priscilla as I have asked you, repeatedly. 'Polly' is vulgar, as if I were your chambermaid!"

"Don't be a prude, dearest. You shall be mistress of my bedchamber, eh, as you are of my heart, eh? You know you love bein' called Polly, y'know you do! And when we're married." He grabbed her by the waist and pressed her to him, stroking her cheek, the pallid skin of her throat, the corner of her mouth. "And when you know me better, you'll like it well enough. Eh? Ha-ha!"

He snugged her up more tightly in his coarse embrace and laughing, chanted the next verse to his song:

"Here's to the maid with a bosom of snow;
Now to her that's as brown as a berry:
Here's to the wife with her face full of uh, la di dah,
And now to the damsel that's merry!"

With that he thrust his pelvis into her petticoats in a way that made Ben twitch to step out and do something. Raven only stood by, expressionless, like a statue of the perfect servant. When Ben caught his eye, the boy permitted himself a small frown and slight shake of the head.

"Jasper! Jasper, stop it!" the heiress squeaked. She tried to slap him but was too close to get a good swing, so she pounded feebly at his shoulder. He grappled and growled and laughed at her distress, grinding away. The hand at her waist had wandered down, frustrated with padding and petticoats.

"Come on, kiss me, Polly, me heart! We'll be married soon enough, then this and you shall all be mine."

"Jasper, no! Rawley, help me!"

Freed to act at last, Raven moved, taking only the few steps to where the cad was doing his best to maul his hoped-for bride.

"Stop, sir!" he said. He tapped the man once on the shoulder, then again with more conviction, and finally grabbed his arm, and still the fellow snarled and warned him away.

"Lay hands on me, will you!" Jasper barked. "Be gone,

damn you!" But momentarily he cut his losses and stood down, straightening his coat and scowling. "You'll stay out of the affairs of your betters, boy, if ye know what's good for ye. If y'want to keep your position, you'll learn your place!"

"I beg your pardon, Captain Jarvis," said Raven in a repulsively subservient manner which he countered by continuing. "But I take my orders from Miss Day."

"Polly," Jarvis said thickly, still staring at Raven. "When we are married we shall indeed sell this filthy old pile. Or if my solicitors can't break the will, we'll shut it up tight and turn the idle staff out upon the road. That's good household management, I say! Besides," he cried, jovial once again. "Who the devil lives in this wilderness, so far from London? Nobody, that's who. County society? Country bumpkins, I say! Good gad, woman, are you crying? Why the devil are you crying?"

She was staring at him, red faced and appalled, fingers poking at the bruised mouth he had left her with, but saying nothing. She had to marry if she wanted her inheritance, this house and a small fortune. And she had to marry this monster because he was the only one who'd asked. He had debts which her grandfather's money would settle, he had a reputation as a rake that marriage was unlikely to stint, and he had the manners of his class, which she loathed. How could she marry such a boor and a bully?

"Nobody lives here, m'dear," Jarvis rattled on. As if nothing had happened, he was striding about staring at the display cases, scratching the shiniest bits to test for gold and silver, hoping for hidden treasures.

And pocketing a few, Ben noted with alarm.

"Nobody of appearance, nobody of consequence. Nobody at all, as far as I know of, except madmen and peasants. Might as well be Mesopotamia! Nay, m'dear, we'll build us a grand house in town, and should you ever get, oh, sentimental—" he made it sound so nasty— "about the countryside, you can take a carriage and go gadding about on Hampstead Heath, or in the Windsor Great Park, or some such."

"I have no carriage. I had to hire the one that brought us here."

"Oh, but you will, chick! Scads of 'em! A carriage for every day of the week!" He sauntered back, having dismissed most of the collection as trash, and chucked her under the chin. "And as many pretty gowns as you want, too, eh? I'll see to it, won't I. And perhaps…" He flipped one of her lank curls. "A hair dresser. Yes, when you are Lady Jasper Jarvis—and when I have had some hard words with those bankers—you'll see. Every luxury will be yours to command."

"Yes. When you have your hands on the money," she said slowly.

"Or if the park is boring, when the season moves out of town, we can visit my great friend Lord Farquhar. You know Freddy Farquhar? Farquhar," he said again at her uncomprehending look, then giggled like a nasty schoolboy. "It's like a duck, d'ye see? Qua qua qua! Farquhar! Amusing, yes? Like a Latin lesson, see. Qui Quae Qua-qua-qua! Haw haw!" Then he frowned a bit. "Farquhar says it all the time. No idea what it means."

"Jasper?"

But he was singing again.

> *"Here's to the charmer whose dimples we prize;*
> *Now to the maid who has none, sir:*
> *Here's to the girl with a pair of blue eyes,*
> *And here's to the nymph with but one, sir."*

> *"Oh! Let the toast pass,--*
> *Drink to the lass,*
> *I'll warrant she'll prove an excuse for the glass."*

"Well never mind. Freddy has a place in Surry or Sussex or somewhere, much closer than—where are we? Devon? Good Gad!"

It was like some interminable Masterpiece Theatre, and Ben just wanted to gag, watching them. The asshole not only wouldn't shut up, he was utterly oblivious to how much ground he was losing—had lost—with the sad, homely Miss Day as each greedily fatuous second passed. She was plain, not stupid.

"Jasper!"

What both Ben and Raven noticed, which the lecherous bounder had missed, was the effort Miss Day was putting into dragging a ring off the fourth finger of her right hand, but not to move it to the opposite hand as she should on her wedding day. Tears had sprung into her eyes, though with despair or frustration or some other unfamiliar emotion was not clear.

"Yes, my duckling?" he said at last, turning to face her. Mistaking her effort for some kind of invitation, he rushed to throw himself upon her once more.

But this time she was ready. With one straight arm to his chest she stopped him in his tracks. "I cannot do this!" she cried, looking a little afraid of her passion. "I will not marry you, Captain Jarvis. No, I will not. I— I don't give a— a damn about this house if you are the price I must pay for it."

And with her free hand she flung the ring to the floor where it bounced and rolled in the dust leaving a misty trail across the parquet. Then it spun twice under a cabinet, where it crackled in broken glass and stopped.

From all about the room, faeries of all sorts looked up with tiny round mouths in their tiny surprised faces, then raised a cheer she couldn't hear. Ben nearly broke into applause himself, and Raven sighed with relief.

The captain, however, cried out in alarm and dived under the furniture, reaching for the ring in spite of being attacked on all sides by dust bunnies—some apparently with teeth. He might have bought that ring with her money, but he could certainly sell it as his own.

Ben was still shaking with suppressed laughter when the sound of crunching glass told him all too clearly where the ring had landed, and where the acquisitive Jarvis had followed, which sobered him up at once. Under that cabinet, among the broken glass, was not only a relatively expensive engagement ring, but a priceless three-inch piece of twisted gold with a dragon's head finial. And sure enough, the next thing he heard was the pirate's bark of discovery.

"Ah ha!"

Jasper rolled to his booted feet with a grunt and a bounce, not minding at all his deep glaze of dust, cobwebs, and clinging house gremlins. Triumphant, he clutched in one hand the gold and ruby ring, in the other, the dragon fragment with its chanting story growing louder and clearer till Ben wondered how these two stupid people could hear each other over it.

"This will assuage a broken heart. Mine, I mean, Polly Puritan," the cad sneered. "What you do with this house, this land, your frigid heart and your old maid's thighs means nothing to me. Less than nothing. In fact, I'm glad to be rid of you. But at least I shall have had this for my trouble."

He was waving the jewels practically in her face, which she turned away in shame. Raven moved to comfort her, but as Jasper marched toward the door a floor board somehow sprang up in front of him, and a bust of Caligula fell from a shelf on top of him, and Raven's foot went out and Jasper went down, flinging out his treasures. Raven snatched the wedding ring out of the air, but the artifact sailed out and across the room.

"Ben Harper! Now!" he cried.

Right on cue, Ben reached from the darkness and snatched the fragment out of the air, whence it came into his hands crooning like a lover. The rest of the story was there, the simplest part of it with the fewest changes, with the thrum of the music of that singular jewel imprinting itself on his mind along with the scroll work, the rune, and the Old English words for 'he made'.

While in the meantime, Raven was exerting his own special talents in booting the red-coated idiot back to his regiment by fair means and foul. When he returned, he held the jeweled ring lightly between two fingers.

"Miss Day," he said, bowing to present it.

She looked at him, cheeks carmine with shame and shock. "Rawley, what have you done?"

"Found your ring, Miss,"

Trembling, she plucked the very last piece of her fortune from his fingers, then hurriedly thrust it into a slit pocket in her petticoat and left it there.

"Well, my goodness!" she said. "You appear to have saved me from a terrible fortune, although I have lost a fortune of another kind."

She sighed a little, and sniffed; Raven, the perfect servant, conjured a frilly handkerchief from somewhere with which she dabbed at her not very swollen eyes and very pink nose.

"And who, sir, are you?" She turned, frowning into the corner. Raven nodded, and Ben stepped forward into the light, giving an antique sort of bow, hoping to get it right. "Are you a thief? Have you come to steal all this trash, like that pathetic bounder."

"No, Miss Day," Ben said, searching for a true but safe answer. "Just a traveler."

"Well, you may steal it if you like. It isn't mine," she said bitterly. "And now it never shall be. It may never be anyone's. Do what you will with it, it is not for me to care."

"You may still find someone to love," Ben said with the sympathy of the happily married. "And to love you."

"No!" she said, and actually stamped her foot, her little fledgling anger returning in a rush. "No, I shall not, and that is enough of that. I have been considering of another life completely. I have a friend in Fort Albany, that's in the New York colony, you see, where I live. She teaches the officer's children there to read and do sums," she added earnestly. You could see the possibilities already building in her imagination. "And the savages might be taught as well, so... so that they may come to God."

"Well, Miss," Ben began, but his friend stopped him with a look.

"Nay, I shall never marry," she said firmly. "And I shall be a happier woman for it."

And that was that. Miss Priscilla Day spun on her heel and marched—daintily but with determination—toward the doors. "I shall need an escort on the journey, Rawley. Perhaps you would like to come as well."

Raven gave a deep bow as she passed him, and then fell in behind her. When the doors clicked shut, Ben was left holding the dragon alone, but for a couple of pixies still fascinated, still wide-eyed as teenage girls over the incomprehensible human melodrama.

"What do you do with it now?" said a sultry voice behind

him. "That's the question."

43

La Sylphide

Ben had come to the conclusion that this was the height of Faerie humor, starting the conversation from a shadow or behind a man's back. Or both, whenever possible. So when he had made up his mind to respond, he put the dragon fragment on the floor where it had landed, and stopped listening to it. He had what he needed. Miss Day had forfeited her inheritance—the thing he was above all things not to prevent. It would be sold off with the rest now, and move on. That was the reason he had come, not to play games with the fae. On the other hand...

He turned around. "Oh good," he sighed, shaking his head. "Very good. Nice."

Goodness had nothing to do with it. She was built like a very young Mae West and filled out the dress just as provocatively, but the ears that separated the golden hair on either side of her oddly long face were those of a deer.

Not Titania, no question, and probably not Pauly either, but,

"Do you have a name, miss?" he asked politely. "And would you happen to have a silver acorn about you?"

"Can't you tell, sir?" said Raven coming in out of the 18th century at his side and striking a pose. "Gaezel always has exactly what you want."

And it was true. Around her long, slender neck sat a gleaming silvery choker of acorns and oak leaves, and on a long silver chain that swung from a girdle of green leaves, a fat silver pendant shaped like an acorn. When she shifted her weight from one hip to the other, it rang like a bell.

"Is that for me?"

"But it's not safe to want anything she has. She's the sort of girl who generally takes more than she gives."

Both men standing with arms crossed and one hip cocked, mirror images dark and fair, exchanged a look and turned back to the girl, both just the tiniest bit skeptical. She was standing in a pool of silver light, as if wherever she was, a full moon shone. And perhaps it did. The long golden hair shimmered over her shoulder, the doe-eyed face on the verge of a pout.

"Is that so?" said Ben.

"Oh aye, sir," Raven said. "She's a kind of sylph, but it's best if you think of her as a sort of vampire. Isn't that so, Gaezel?"

Her head came up, rebellious. "Are you going to while away the time insulting me, or listen to why I've come?"

"Is that a trick question?" said Ben, grinning. Mellis had a student like this almost every year, and he was still marginally flattered the first time they tried to seduce him at a college event, before they knew whose husband he was.

"I am sent," she said in a very silky voice indeed, "to bid you come into the garden."

The boys exchanged glances once again, this time less amused.

"But I'm done here," said Ben. "If you'll give me the acorn. Raven, is she one of the queen's? Why should I take orders from her?"

"It is usually recommended to answer such a summons politely at least, better still to confirm the source. Gaezel, is this Her Majesty's invitation?"

"I cannot answer, for I do not know. But I think not."

"It cannot come from the king, surely." Again she shook her pretty head, almost achieving a look of childlike innocence.

"How come you here then?" Raven demanded, his restored power glimmering about him. "Who sent you?"

"I know not, my lord!" she cried angrily, and addressed herself only to Ben. "Ben Harper, you are asked to go into the garden and enter the maze. When you solve the maze, the help you need is there."

"What's that supposed to mean?"

Raven frowned, then touched a soothing hand to Ben's shoulder and said thoughtfully, "I think... You know, I think perhaps she comes from the moor, from Dartmoor itself and its folk. Isn't that so, sweeting?"

The beauty of Faerie said nothing but stared with moist eyes and inviting lips.

What does that mean, 'from the moor'? Ben wondered. He was about to ask how the moor could be alive or sending messages, but mentally slapped himself so Raven wouldn't have to. Stupid question.

"Hang on," he muttered. "Maybe I missed something."

He patted the pockets of his jacket for the familiar angles of the diary and pulled it out. The book had been part of the process every step of the way, so far. He might never understand how it worked, but certainly at each test there had been something he needed to know, and some knowledge to carry forward.

He dragged—no, lightly lifted—a spindle-legged chair out of the dust and took it over to the window where the long summer afternoon was gently passing. Then he sat down and flipped to the last written pages, expecting nothing more than the lyrics he had seen before and still didn't need. Raven watched quietly, keeping an eye on the sensuous sylph in the moonlight.

There was the usual goblin graffiti and goofy scrawls, and now lewd drawings appeared of Gaezel and a man who, he supposed, was meant to be himself, grappling in unlikely poses. Very funny, he thought, turning pages with impatience. It did no good to flip to the back, because there was never anything there until he had turned the page before it.

Another page, and Ben almost gasped. Now the lyrics were marked with musical notation, chord progressions, key signatures. And not just songs but dance tunes, lullabies, and marching songs, work songs, folk tunes and old chants, love songs and rock ballads, and melodies he'd never seen before, most of them tuned apparently for the harp. It was all remarkably small but as he touched a finger to any one thing, it

The Dragon Ring

popped out and the rest faded back, just as the London map had highlighted whatever he needed to see.

Whoever was keeping this diary for him, by whatever magic, was pleased enough with his efforts. In all the nonsense, there was always something he could use.

"What's the first thing she said to me? Never mind, you weren't here."

"She said: What do you do with it now? That's the question."

"Right. Rhetorical question. Practical answer: we leave it where we found it, just as his grace said to begin with."

Raven nodded. "Good. And then?"

"Well, it's just the usual scribbles, isn't it? A bunch of jokes and cartoons, same as always. It goes on, and then all this music, tons of it! These here are single-line melodies like an O'Carolan tune. In fact, this one is an O'Carolan tune. You put in the variations as— you— go."

Ben flipped another page, then back, then forward. Then he read aloud: "If you can name all the tunes you know, you don't know enough tunes."

"What?" said Raven with a laugh.

Grinning, Ben repeated it and added, "It's something Tom Shorland says, Dinah's Tom."

He turned the last page, and the diary just stopped with a single stark imperative, dotted with a tiny flower. He looked up at Raven, at the lovely Gaezel, then Raven again and shrugged.

"It says: Go into the maze."

44

"In my end is my beginning"

❋

It occurred to Ben that, unlike the previous adventures with their various scenic wanderings, this third task had been particularly claustrophobic. Even if he didn't get to see much of a real eighteenth century house, a stroll through its garden maze on the way home might not be so bad.

"Let's go then."

Raven gestured at the girl as if shooing away a puppy. She turned with a sniff and began to walk away from them. And as they followed the hypnotic swing of her admittedly sexy backside, the midnight garden of Diamond Hall in summer washed around them in airs rich with roses, silent under a blue-black sky lit with more stars than Ben had ever seen, anywhere. Overhead washed the great banner of the Milky Way and all the billion suns pricked out in their constellations spinning on the axis of the North Star. And nowhere, even on the edges, was there any sense of the great cities of the world staining the air and sky.

"So," he said, stopped dead between two rows of rose bushes. "Is this the sky in 1763, or..." He noted that his eighteenth century guise had fallen away, leaving him in the familiar jeans and jacket. "Or at home, or somewhere else?"

Raven paused to look up, considered, and said "Just here, just now it is 1763 with Diamond Hall behind us and its maze before us. Why?"

They had come to a low stone wall topped with a box hedge that Ben had seen from the window. It had an elaborately wrought iron gate in the middle, overgrown with ivy and sweet night-blooming vines. Through the gate they could see the dark, leafy face of another, taller hedge looming within, with a break in the middle. That would be the maze.

Gaezel gave them a luminous smile and gestured at the gate. "It is your path, human child. Find the answers you seek."

Cautiously, Ben put his hand to the cold iron and pushed, just slightly. The catch released at once, the gate swung open. Silence fell, but the hedge maze in all its parts lit up with fairy lights provided by real faeries. Feeling the grass spring stiffly under his soft boots, the scent of jasmine clinging to the air, he walked down the ten or so sloping feet to the entrance, marked now by candle lanterns made of beaten copper glowing red gold in the night.

"Is there a password or something?"

When there was no answer, he looked back to where Raven stood just beyond the iron barrier, watching with interest.

"I'll find my own way in, Ben Harper," the boy called softly. "Don't get lost."

Ben twisted up a slightly nervous smile and waved a quick salute. "You know I never do."

Besides, he thought as he faced the sparkling, leafy dark. Everyone knows how to get through a maze. Put your left hand on the left wall and just keep... He straightened his leather jacket, hitched up his jeans, and took the next step.

And we're walking.

Almost at once, of course, the flaws in the plan appeared. When he turned to look back one more time, the gate was gone and the dense black shadow that had been many-gabled Diamond Hall was gone as well—in which case, anything could happen.

"Okay," he said aloud. "Maybe it's not that kind of maze."

Out of habit, he started left, took a turning that felt correct, and another, walked a little further then stopped as rustling leaves closed rapidly in front of him. When he turned back, the hedge closed the gap behind him. Feeling for a direction had become second nature in the last few days. He knew he could find the center of the maze and the way out again, but it was no good if he couldn't move out of a closed box. The tinkle of faerie giggling didn't help.

Then he saw that at his feet, almost camouflaged in the foliage, stood a wee small man dressed in rags of brown and green, with a hat that was partly leather and partly leaves, and a red heron's feather. His nose was so long and so curved down that it came almost to his chin, which was so long and so curved up that it came almost to his nose. One bright black eye seemed to be trying to look behind him but swung round to match the other. When both eyes focused on Ben, the little man jumped, startled.

"Too tall!" he croaked.

So Ben crouched down amiably to be a little less too-tall, and endeavored not to be so rude as to say what was on his mind, which was that the little man looked like an understudy in a Punch and Judy show.

"And who are you, please?" he asked instead.

"Say me a riddle-diddle!" demanded the little man.

"A riddle?"

"A riddle-diddle. You know."

Ben frowned, thinking. It sounded like a clue to a kind of word game he sometimes played with Sparrow. You knew how many syllables were in the answer by the number of syllables in the pattern, and like the pattern, it had to rhyme. It also sounded vaguely like some of the silliness in the latest diary pages. Worth a try.

"Let me see if I understand you. I say the riddle-diddle and you have to answer it?"

"Yes! Yes! That's it!"

"Cool, okay, well. Let me see. What is a … a Norseman on a motorcycle?"

"Easy-peasy. A biking Viking!" And he burst into a merry cackle echoed by tinkling faerie laughter. "Now, I ask one!"

"I see. Okay, go."

"What is a rabbit what tells a joke?" the little man croaked.

It was exactly like playing with Sparrow, but weirder. "A funny bunny?"

"Yes, yes! That's it!" cried the little man, and a barrier vanished with chiming music. "Follow your gift, Ben Harper."

That's it, Ben thought. I am now, officially, part of a faerie tale. A faerie tale for loonies, I admit, but there it is.

The path was fairly broad now, and curved away to both left and right as if he stood at the bottom of a circle. Something was wrong.

He sniffed the air with a frown. Was that smoke? He could smell smoke. And hear the cries of children, and women calling for their husbands. In front of him a vision opened up of red flames and smoke. The village on fire! His home in red flames! He could smell the billowing smoke and hear the roar.

Of nothing. Remembering where he was, he stopped on the ragged edge of crying out. "Now wait a minute," he said sourly. The vision had edges, like a drive-in movie—wide screen and high def, okay, but fake. "Nice try, 'Galadriel'," he sneered, not even bothering to raise his voice. "But I saw that scene. The book was better."

Noise and picture vanished with a *whomp* like a special effects fire going out. It was good to be reminded, perhaps, that the magic of Dartmoor had its own moral compass, which was as changeable as the magnetic one out on the moor. Back to the business at hand.

45
Riddling news

Ben examined his options again to be sure they hadn't changed. Nope, still standing at six o'clock on the dial. He could bear right and curve left or bear left and curve right. Typical. So he took the right-hand passage with hardly a thought, knowing that his goal was right where he'd left it. But in five minutes walking, the path didn't seem to get him any nearer to it. Briefly, he thought it might be spiraling; seven-foot curved walls continued curving to the left but the goal position didn't change. Was it simply a circle? That hardly made sense, not if they actually wanted him to reach the middle.

Then abruptly, with that disconcerting feeling of being in direct response to his thought, the curve broke on the right hand wall. He could go on, or take this break. It felt like the wrong direction, but tracing a circle wasn't doing the job either. So he took the break.

And stepped at once into a foggy twilight at the mouth of a broad tidal creek where Vikings had drawn up three dragon-prowed long boats and headed inland to hunt. But whether they would return with plunder or supper on the end of their bitter spears, there was no way to know. A single man had been left on watch, tall and cloaked and masked in his plain iron helm, leaning on his spear.

Ben blinked, unprepared for the abrupt change from moonlit garden to misty shore. Great maze, he thought, and stepped forward, crackling a slender branch beneath his heel.

The man on guard turned to face him, ready to bark a challenge, then halted and boomed out a laugh instead. Odin strode to meet him through the beech trees.

"So it is time already, is it?" he said in his genial mead hall voice. "You have done very well, Ben Harper!" And he slapped the harper on the back in that hearty Viking way Ben loved so much. Sort of.

"All Father?" said Ben, puzzled but pleased to see him. "Do you know what this is all about?"

"Boy, I only know what I've been told, which is this."

The god of war and poetry put off his helmet and laid it on the ground, and his spear beside it. Then he stood on a little tussocky hillock covered in fallen beech leaves that lay like runes about his feet, and began to recite:

> Ic eom wunderlicu wiht wifum on hyhte
> neahbuendum nyt, nægum sceþþe...
> *I am a wonderful thing, a woman's joy*
> *Useful to all, I injure none*
> *Save her who harms me*
> *I stand in bed with hair beneath*
> *Where the shameless maid grabs me—*
> *She ravages my head, holding me still,*
> *She soon feels me who forced me in.*
> *Wet be her eye.*
> ...wif wundenloc. Wæt bið þæt eage.

"Ha! Ben Harper, are you blushing? Come now, tell me what is!"

He wasn't blushing, exactly, but he was nearly doubled over, red-faced and laughing till he lost his footing on the leafy verge and slid down the bank.

"I get it!" he gasped when he could breathe again, still flat on his back with his house-dusty woods-dirty boots getting a light rinse in the stream. "I get it, I do. It's an onion! An onion!"

Odin frowned. "Is it?"

"You old fraud, of course it is," said Ben as he clambered up from the water. "I'll parse it for you, shall I? An onion grows straight up with its hairy roots in a vegetable bed. And its head is the green shoots, sticking out of the earth for the maid to grab it out, and take it off to the kitchen. It only harms the one who cuts it away from the root: that's the woman—it makes her cry. All that salacious, tortured metaphor, and then 'wet is her eye' just means what it says! Man, I hate those things, those old riddles of yours. Even if you did leave out about half of it, for which I thank you, lord."

Now the High One was laughing with him, roaring his approval.

"But you saw through it, clever fellow that you are, as the king said you would. Now go on, human child," he said at last as Ben was wiping hot tears from his eyes. "You have a few more stops to make. Follow your gift."

"Thank you, sir," Ben said. He dusted himself off and assayed a bow. "And thank you, y'know, for rescuing Mellis."

The old warrior nodded and shooed him away, so he turned and trudged up from the riverbank, which became, of course, part of the hedge again. Where a little blond girl in a blue pinafore skipped up to him and said, "If you please sir, I know the way," and pointed at a cave opening just visible between some fallen stones. It looked a little like a rabbit hole and a little too much like the Raven's Eye on the tor.

"Be serious," Ben said and looked for a new direction in the twinkling midnight lanes. And he found one.

From here there was no more endless circling. The turnings and changes became more ordinary, like a proper maze, no more peculiar than the one at Hampton Court. Except that every few feet a tiny winged faerie buzzed his nose and asked for a riddle, so he dutifully tickled them with all the simple ones that Sparrow loved.

What do sea monsters eat?
Fish and ships!

What did one duck say to the other duck?
"You quack me up!"

What gets wetter the more it dries?
A towel, of course.

Why do birds fly south in the winter?
Because it's too far to walk!

The little ones with their flower hats and fluttery wings giggled and shrieked and flung themselves all over the hedges, as if the answers were always a surprise.

And by and by the walls of the maze got shorter and shorter until Ben could see over them, and then reach across them, and finally, step right over into the center. Which, when he did, faded in a swirl of color and strange music to be replaced by a low stone wall, supporting a box hedge, with an arched gate in the middle. Only this time, the gate with its swirling flowers and night-blooming vines, was wrought of shimmering crystal and etched with silver.

Gaezel had not said to find the center of the maze, but the heart. Was this it? At the foot of the gate, a bubbling spring leapt up from the earth and chuckled down and away into the dark and out of sight.

The gatekeeper stood or rather leaned against the arch, with one foot cocked behind him, looking remarkably as he had when they had parted: Raven, arms folded and waiting in his all-purpose black doublet and hose. Humor danced in the long, inhuman eyes, and his black hair with its one pale lock of gold curled over his ears.

"Why," he said coolly before Ben could greet him, "is a raven like a writing desk?"

"What?"

"It's a classic, I know, sir, but the others have all been easy, haven't they? Why is a raven like a writing desk?"

Ben frowned, puzzled. "But there's no answer to that. Lewis Carroll said so—more than once, I might add."

"But this is Faerie," said Raven. "Find an answer, human child."

Ben thought, staring at the young man he had come to think of as a friend, finding him again as remote as the moon. Since there was no real answer, what would serve? Think, Ben, think. Odin's riddle was about resemblances and assumptions. Riddles always are, he thought. So...

The efficiency expert cleared away the clutter, and flicked the last cobweb off his imagination. Ben pointedly fixed his gaze on the single golden lock in the fae's black hair, and smiled.

"Because, Raven Boy, it has but one feather in the ink."

Raven considered, his head cocked bird-like to one side, then nodded.

"Good one, sir," he said, and the two sides of the gate opened and swung aside. Spring water burbled up at his feet and rushed down to a tiny cataract, then a few yards later another, stepping down through the distance to a tree-lined glade.

46
Borderlands

"So am I done yet?" Ben wondered aloud. "Game over? Because really, I appreciate the R&R but I'd like to get out of here and go get my kid and wake up my wife."

Raven had no answer. Falling into step, they strolled easily together down the sloping lawns, following the stream. At the bottom of the hill lay a raised pool where a fountain leapt up, shooting and spilling shards of fragile colors that glinted like diamonds in the night air. Just there, the full moon's light spread particularly wide, lighting up the manicured lawns but keeping the furzy edges for the shyer of the fair folk, quite like the meadow where Oberon's country house lay.

Down there, too, invisible yet unmistakable, music sprang up—sudden, lively, quick with joy and the deep undercurrent of a drum filling the air. Music for dancing, for tapping your feet, for joining in. In fact, it sounded rather like a well-used folk guitar and a bodhran, a battered tin whistle, and a fiddle. More to the point, it sounded exactly like Dinah, Tom, Brian and Morgan banging out *Dr O'Neill's*, the rollicking jig they generally used to open the first gig in a new place. In just about a minute-thirty it would bounce neatly into *Merry Maids* and after that gambol in to *Kid on the Mountain*, and by that time folks would be clapping along and starting to grin. In short order someone would be up and dancing, at least bouncing enthusiastically in time to the music. If not stopped, they would roll on through half a dozen reels and jigs until they had to halt for lack of beer.

The closer he got to the splashing waters the clearer the

music grew, and he realized he was smiling and his heart was lighter for the first time since all this adventure began. And when Ben looked, looked properly through the moonlight, past the rainbows shed so promiscuously by the fountain, he saw— he was so used to weird by now that it was hardly worth mentioning—Dinah and the gang doing their opening set on some kind of stage under strings of stars, and he was walking faster, almost dancing on the long grass.

Scattered under the trees where the hill rolled into flat meadow, he noticed tables made out of big wooden cable spools set on end, each with a candle burning in a jelly glass in the middle. Around each sat hay bales covered with brightly colored rugs and tapestries against the dews and damps, seating for the folk who came to listen, clap along, and dance.

Something like a make-shift bar resolved on the left, just where in his mind's eye he expected to see it: a rugged, much re-painted wooden structure that looked familiar, except that the last time he'd seen anything like it, he was a kid in California. The rich odors of Turkish coffee, spicy chai with the bite of fresh ginger, and something that must be, yeah, venison chili hung in the air to mix with the rich, damp smells of earth and trees at twilight. By candle flame and dancing waters, Ben breathed it in like the scents of home, and his smile just got bigger.

The booth was painted with what in this light was an ancient, fading red, and the counter strained under the burden of two huge coffee urns. A massive antique espresso machine took a place of honor, he knew, somewhere inside. To one side a glass case displayed pastries from honey-dripping diamonds of baklava to fanciful constructions of marzipan and magic, and a single, plain cake donut. Overhead in scrolling Moorish-style script floated a sign that had seen too many oak forest summers, which read: *Last Call: We Never Close*.

Behind the counter, Gaezel and others of her sisterhood flirted and laughed, their hair tied up in gypsy scarves, pouring drinks and dishing up food, golden hoops shining from their long, furred ears. There were other mortals here, too, as well as fae of all sorts. There was also more than coffee and tea to drink. Jewel-like pitchers and bottles with exotic labels stood ready for pouring wine, mead, and cider, lemonade and metheglin, and more besides. Ben half expected to see Aubrey behind the bar, but the faerie king was nowhere to be seen. Presiding instead was mighty Odin in a plain tunic and embroidered Moorish vest, with his braid over his shoulder, clapping along with the music and pinching the girls.

Ben's friends, who called themselves Faerie Reel when pressed for a name, had set up on a sturdy wooden platform covered with Persian rugs and draped with silken scarves. More instruments were ranged behind them at the back wall— they seem to have brought everything, including an empty chair and a harp—his harp, Moytura, whole and waiting for him, vibrating in the flickering light.

Gobsmacked, he stood stock still by the counter and watched them play, and in another moment he was tapping his foot, and in another his fingers were striking imaginary strings in the air in front of him. Dinah saw him coming from where she stood bowing a passionate fiddle. She caught his eye and gestured, her whole body swinging to point him toward the place they'd made for him at center stage, the waiting chair, the harp. Moytura, his harp.

Tears in his eyes, Ben shook his head and looked away.

"Raven, I haven't got time for this," he shouted over the sweet din just as the set crashed to its end and a shout rose up from the tables and down from the tree branches, crying out in their musical voices for more. Some of the faerie lights twinkling in the trees were real faeries who shrieked and turned fluttery somersaults in the air, applauding like crickets chirping.

"You've got all the time there is, sir," said Raven. "This place on the Borderland was made for you at my lord's command. Your friends were only too happy to come."

"So they're not...?"

"Enchanted, sir?" The boy smiled, reminding Ben again of a very superior butler. "Only by the prospect of gigging in Faerie, though I'm told there was some bit of doubt at the beginning. You'll notice they brought... well, everything, including the amplifiers and the drum kit."

"Electricity?" Ben said doubtfully.

"For that, there is a spell," said Raven, eyes crinkling with delight. "They are not the only musicians here tonight, as I'm sure you realize. Anything may happen, who knows?"

"And Moytura! My god! Raven, she was smashed! Wasn't she smashed?"

"Magic, Ben, remember? You must tell me if her voice has changed at all. And before you ask again, we are in a bubble, you might say, outside of time entire. Six mortal hours will pass here, eight if you can bear it, while no time passes outside, and hearts ease."

"But we're not…" Ben stammered, starry eyed, aching to play, aching for his family. "We're not finished! I haven't earned a break."

"You have had your heart broken, and while we cannot mend it, nor any hearts, you have earned the chance to mend it yourself. Follow your gift, Ben Harper."

"People keep telling me that," Ben said, threading his way through the tables to hop up on the little stage.

Two thoughts interlaced in his mind as his friends spilled out from behind their instruments to bury him in hugs and exclamations:

This is where I belong.

If only Mellis were here.

47
Command performance

It was Moytura waiting for him, his darling and his mistress, carved of English oak by a master to Ben's own design, with dragon scroll work in the pillar, inlaid in part with old gold, bronze and copper. Her bronze and amalgam strings hummed under the enormous tension that let him play loud and fast as he liked; if he reached for the string, it leapt to his fingertip, every time. Or when the mood was intimate and soft, he had only to touch and release. Coaxing the music from her was not so much playing as simply thinking it.

For being able to afford such an instrument, he was grateful to the career he'd chosen and now was about to abandon.

Was he about to abandon it? Wasn't he just taking a year off?

The thought made him jump a little, but he set it aside for later, turning Mellis's wedding ring on his little finger. When this was all done, they would talk. Just now, settling in the chair and rocking Moytura back into his arms, Ben thought he should play some music.

The silence grew around him as he sat and waited for the moment to form. Dinah and the others had gone for a beer and left the stage to Ben Harper alone, but they'd be back soon enough. The tables nearest the stage were crowded with the great fae, the most human seeming of their kind, with long slender limbs and jewel-like eyes, their murmuring voices sweet. Some had brought their mortal lovers, or those who were simply friends of the house. The two wild boys who had herded ponies on the moor were there braiding each others' hair and sipping chai.

Beyond the fairest folk, lurking in the trees and hovering in the air, the moonlight revealed flower fairies and green ladies, weedy looking goblins, a brownie and a wee, small man chomping on a pipe. All waiting, all hushed.

Now the only music in the faerie glade was the sparking of the fountain, and a few random fairies giggling like the sound of tiny bells.

Shh!
Okay!

Ben touched the strings, and because he was thinking of his wife and his life, he simply let the music come, improvising, soothing his heart until almost inevitably, he was playing Chris Caswell's *West Country Girl.* He was half way through the first chorus before he realized where Moytura had led him, so he let the harp have her way until the verse came round again and he could join in with the lyric of passion and loss.

And the longing grew. What dreams was she wandering in, he wondered, and how would he find her again?

> *"I've walked through your cities and I've wandered alone*
> *Across the deep water and through the high stone*
> *Though long are the traces I've traveled from home*
> *I will always return for my west country girl."*

Artlessly he segued into the high wild melancholy of Wild Swans, and Tom's guitar joined in, then the bodhran in Morgan's clever hands tossed off a cadence, and with a look he shifted gears and threw them into King of the Fairies that got feet tapping, as Oberon had meant it to when he gave it to the blind Irishman. Before he was quite done with that, Dinah's dulcimer joined in, and they were barreling into a set of reels that had no names, just the numbers on an old play list.

After a quick break, just enough to breathe and swap instruments a bit, they started again—just to be fair—with *The Faerie Queen* (O'Carolan's, not Purcell's, though bits of that came later) and for balance, the tripping tune about the big fae and the little one: *Sidhe Beg, Sidhe Mor.* It was a little, Ben guessed, like playing Danny Boy at an Irish wedding: it was probably a cliché but they wanted to hear it, and so they did. Three tiny faeries fluttered down from the over-hanging tree and perched on the high curve of Moytura's neck to listen.

Just as in mortal lands, he found, in Faerie a harper spends a lot of time in the eighteenth century with the music of blind O'Carolan. The man had produced hundreds of tunes, and the fae ate it up as if they'd written it themselves, and some of it they had. But there's more to the music beloved of immortals than old Irish tunes, and thanks to the clues Ben had found in the diary, they played and sang those too.

A double handful of songs later, Aubrey arrived. He strolled toward the stage swiftly changing a two-tone Ricky Ricardo jacket for a tie-dyed, knitted silk muscle shirt and butter soft leather pants that might have been painted on. With the blue-black hair curling on his sculpted shoulders, and even considering the slight points of his ears and the long, alien glitter of his eyes, he looked like the cover of a Rolling Stone. Dinah whistled, wide-eyed in fan girl appreciation; Morgan almost tumbled off the stage trying to get a better view.

Ben drew the set to a slammin' close and stood for the applause, happy for the chance to let the pads of his fingers cool, and thankful for the extended practice of the past few days. Moytura wasn't tired, and barely allowed time to let everyone take a bow, and acknowledge, wave or blow kisses at their king, before she was calling again.

But mortal musicians need a break, and Dinah was in danger of snapping a fiddle string, so they called a pause for technical adjustments (principally, more beer), and stood around for a while in the cool, shivering a little as the sweat dried and everyone caught their breath.

48
Take five

"Enjoying yourself?" said Aubrey when Ben hopped down to pay his respects.

Front row center, the royal box. His lordship nodded toward the hay bale next to him, an island of quiet in the busy courtyard of low laughter and murmuring talk and ears that still rang. Ben took the seat with a grin as well as the proffered drink.

"You know me way too well, your grace. Any requests?"

One of the fae gentlemen was trading guitar riffs with Tom, perched on the edge of the fountain. Dinah was sitting on the edge of the stage, swinging her feet, sipping a drink and staring around in wonder.

"It's the eve of Midsummer, and you have done very well. The night is yours to do with as you like."

"I'm honored, sir." Still doubtful, but certainly honored.

The king tilted his head slightly, launching the mysterious smile. "I told you the rewards would be worthy of you, didn't I? You're good, Ben Harper. You know that, I hope."

Ben sipped his drink, enjoying the cooling effect on his hands and the burn down his throat.

"I was thinking of getting into a few longer songs later, choruses you can sing along with. Will they sing along, do you think?" He gestured generally toward the odd assortment of his audience, fae and human, large and small, dainty and substantial, crooked and straight, winged and otherwise. "Can I ask? Who are all these people? I mean, I have all the books, but still ..."

"Oh my dear," Aubrey said glancing around. "There are

more fae in, well not in heaven but in earth certainly, than mortals have catalogued, even on Dartmoor. We were not all born out of hearth tales and moor mist, you know." He took a deep breath, shook back his hair, and met Ben's eyes. "But you're wondering which are the most perilous."

"That would be all of them," Ben said frankly, which the king rewarded with a slight smile. "No, I'm wondering if you invited everyone or only your own, I don't know, your own faction?"

"You doubt whether you and your friends are safe?"

"No, sir! God, no! But I haven't told you. Haven't had a chance, y'know. I met someone in my garden the other morning, just as I was leaving. Sort of a punk rock Goth biker chick faerie about so high, with a bad haircut and really big, uh, wings. Said her name was Pauly?"

An eyebrow lifted.

"She didn't do anything, that time, just whined at me like a Cockney shop girl. But then…" Ben went on to describe the other wolfish encounters with her, and Aubrey looked thoughtful.

"Onyx," he said after a moment. "She is to my queen more or less what Raven is to me, a good right hand. She is also, as I think you've guessed, more than she has shown you."

"Terrific."

"This place is open, yes. But the only power that may be expended here is whatever the music raises. My queen would be welcome—and I would be glad to see her. And any of her folk, as well. But she won't come, nor will they while we're at odds. And that's a pity." The pause grew until at last, he nodded toward the band, still tuning and fooling around, but mostly killing time. "I think they're ready for you."

Ben threw back the last of the lemonade as he got to his feet. "Silver acorn?" he said hopefully, wiping damp hands on his jeans. But Aubrey got up, chuckling in his other-worldly way, and slapped the harper's shoulder.

"Go play, human child. Lose yourself in the music, and play. Tomorrow, you have work to do."

49
The boy for bewitching them
❋

With bumpers of Aubrey's special lemonade over a lot of ice for inspiration, they jumped right into Banish Misfortune, which led into an endless string of jigs Ben could never remember the names of, but it got them up and dancing. Mind you, the fae in their insubstantial gossamer and gowns can dance with perfect grace, and without rest, as any number of mortal musicians have found to their cost. Still, his heart was so filled with the music and the fellowship, it was worth it.

They sang rebel songs and pirate songs, and a raunchy ballad or two, and the voices of Faerie lifted, laughed and sang along. They played bouncy favorites and stately reels, and on Ben's bright-eyed cue they dropped suddenly to an odd little waltz so strange that it brought the dancers down to sit on the grass and sigh over it. Then under his hands alone, the harp spilled out another melancholy tune set low and slow in the spooky old Dorian mode. And some few remembered that ancient mode from their youth in distant times and far away. One stood and sang a single chorus in a forgotten language, then turned suddenly and left with his face in his hands.

Their long sleeves and translucent draperies hushed on the grass as they leaned towards the stage or paced on the green, and small bells chimed in tune. Again some found their voices and trilled the verses in a strange tongue. Then in the silence that hovered after, Ben twisted them up into a country reel and shifted the mood again.

Behind and around him, Ben was aware of his friends changing instruments, sometimes changing strings, working the arrangements they all knew, jamming others to suit the moment and the mood. At some point Brian's bodhran had become the abbreviated drum kit, and the guitars went electric. Ben stopped long enough to take a long pull on a cold beer, flip a few of Moytura's tuning levers and lead into *Stairway to Heaven*—the full 8-minute version.

At last it was time to give up the harp for the electric bass and let Tom's lead guitar and Morgan's rhythm take point, while Dinah swapped her lovely old fiddle for the hot new electrified violin. They covered a little Police and little Peter Gabriel, and some mellow Phil Collins, Steeleye, Fairport, whatever came to them. And if they didn't remember the words, they made them up. The crowd went wild, even the ones in the powdered wigs and frock coats.

All night long Ben rolled along locked in with the music, locked in love with it, with the harp, and with the certain knowledge that inside it all was Mellis, honey golden Mellis whose ring was on his finger.

Then between one heartbeat and another, the light in the glade went golden, and Aubrey himself strolled down to the stage with a chiming 12-string guitar in his fist, and everything changed from the color of the sky to the shape of the weather.

In a breathless pause for the installation of more beer and lemonade, Aubrey whispered to one of his gentlemen who took up a guitar, another offered to relieve Brian on the drums, while his lordship bent over a silver flute and knocked out Jethro Tull's reworking of a Bach bourée. And when the band in its newly expanded form, fae and human, had all returned to their places, the King of Faerie stood forth and threw out the opening line of *Songs from the Wood*, and they found a whole album in them they hadn't known was there. By the time they got to *Fire at Midnight*, with Ben taking the lyric, the water in the forest fountain was dancing in the colors of other worlds and times, and mermaids frolicked in the rain.

He left the stage, then, before his voice could break, and collapsed on a hay bale at one of the little spool tables all the way at the back of the crowd and more than half in shadow. Raven ever useful brought him sweet iced chai in a shining goblet, which tasted as though it had been cooled in snow, and perhaps it had.

"Your fingers must be shredded," the boy said. "Wrap your hands around this."

Ben looked at him sideways and snorted, "My lord, we hardly know each other," but took the goblet anyway, swung around and sat up. Steam rose and disappeared where his fingers printed the silver. "It's late, isn't it?"

"Same time as when you got here, remember?"

"Yeah, okay, but how long have we been playing? Two or three hours, at least." Now it was Raven's turn to be delighted.

"Ben, you've been playing, all of you have been playing and singing and drinking beer and swilling Turkish coffee for almost five hours." Ben's eyebrows shot up. "His grace will doubtless let you go as long as you like, but I wouldn't go longer than eight. Human hearts tend to start failing after that."

Ben sighed and wiped his eyes. "You said I was supposed to mend my heart."

"And have you?"

He thought about it, shaking his head to clear the fumes that great music and great whiskey inevitably induce.

"When I met you," he said slowly. "I was angry, and scared, y'know? Already pissed off with the way my life was going, and taking it out on you—and Himself—so I couldn't even see what I was being shown. The opportunity I was being offered. What an asshole!"

Raven said nothing, though a wry smile played about his mouth.

"That's your cue to tell me it's okay, I had good reason."

"Is it?"

Ben went on with a sigh. "Okay, I thought I had good reason. That just makes it worse, I know. Since then, well…"

Oh god, he was about to get maudlin. So he sat up and took a long sip of chai, and another for good measure. "This stuff's really good. What's in this?"

Close call—avoided. "My god, did you see? When his grace decided to sit in? That was a heart attack! Wow!"

Now the time was leaving them behind, so Ben brought Moytura back to an emptied stage with O'Carolan's *Farewell to Music* and the one about the landlady, and half a dozen other melancholy songs that tore at the heart. Then Aubrey came down and sat on the edge of the stage more or less at Ben Harper's feet, with his thick sweet Turkish coffee in a painted wooden cup beside him, and added Dariole's silver-stringed voice to Moytura's, point and counterpoint.

After a while, he borrowed someone's lute, and Ben found a guitar, and they ranged through the Elizabethans—Morley, Gibbons and Dowland, galliards and pavanes and tunes they made up till the green glade was a candle-lit gallery and the dancers tall and small, even handsome Raven, drawn up again by the music and by starlight, moved through the figures stately and sprightly by turns, their dreamscape silks, paned velvets, or woodland leafy draperies murmuring and catching the light and throwing it back in rainbows. And finally they were done.

Well, not quite done. Gaezel, who had been curled up in a crook of the lowest arm of the sheltering oak, leaned down in a fall of moonlit hair and the drape of long, long sleeves tipped with bells, and whispered two words. And because one of them was "please", Aubrey nodded and hopped down to the grass. He collected his cup, turned and took Ben's hand with grace and thanks, and gave him the stage.

Ben Harper collected Moytura against his chest for the last time of the morning and gave them something no one, not even Mellis knew he had: *Greensleeves*. Not just the old tune everyone thinks is a Christmas carol, but the Ralph Vaughn Williams Fantasia, adapted for the Irish harp.

The strings sang and Ben's heart soared through the changes, the little bits of folk song that gave its lilt, and the sweetness of the refrain in its variations. Whether it was old King Henry VIII's plaint to his mistress or simply an ancient aire didn't matter; the swelling passion, the longing and heart's ease that came with it as it built and crested was like a rose opening in the heat of summer. And as one by one the variations and ornaments fell away again from the single thread, it became the silence of peace and utter joy.

When at last he stilled the strings for the final time, even the great fae sat wrapped up in each other's arms and unfamiliar passions. The king had left suddenly, without a word. And the bubble of suspended time broke into the star-filled dark at the bottom of Iveston common, and the fair folk, their coffee house, even the band were gone.

"Damn!" Ben said, sitting up suddenly in the dewy grass of midnight—still midnight, then, yeah—with heavy lidded eyes and wide awake. "Damn it!"

"What?" said Raven. Startled out of his own faerie reverie, he set to scanning the shadows for trouble.

"I was going to sing *Queen of All Argyle!*"

Raven whimpered and put his head in his hands. "Oh, human child, " he said softly. "Is that all you forgot?"

"I— What? Shit!" Almost but not quite hung over, astonished that it had slipped his mind, and on the verge of feeling cheated out of something he had paid for—more exhausted than he realized—Ben combed swollen fingers through his hair growling in frustration. Then looked down, his bleary eye captured by a glint of starlight. It's a hard enough thing to concentrate with the adrenaline still rushing and the ears still ringing, but he managed to uncross his eyes enough to see what was right in front of him.

Dew-spangled in the grass between his knees, a fat silver bell shaped like an acorn lay glimmering on a silver chain.

Tuesday

q

The Dragon Ring

50
Diamond Cottage

When he picked it up, the bell gave out a bright, surprisingly complex note that sang of refreshment and renewal, which it did. Ben slipped the chain over his head, and for the second time in he was not at all clear how many days, trudged up the slope to Diamond Cottage, guided through the thready mist by the lights from the office. From what he could tell, the windows had been repaired, and the garden restored as if nothing had happened. The air smelled of turned earth and flowers.

"Damn," he said, staring. "Y'know, it's a good thing we're half a mile from the nearest neighbor, or there'd be talk about this that even your boss couldn't stop! I don't even know what day it is. Do you?"

"No idea. Check your phone?"

Suddenly touched with a small animal panic, Ben pulled out the mobile and tapped it on. "What do you mean?"

Raven sighed and waited for Ben's breathing to slow again. "You do know it gets the time from a satellite, yes?"

"Of course I do, I... Oh." He checked. "It's just after midnight. On Tuesday. How did it get to be Tuesday?"

"Well, first it was 1763, and then it was Tuesday." The boy met Ben's glare with his usual insouciance. "And now you'll be wanting to answer that."

The phone chirped, and when Ben got over that surprise, he decided that midnight or not, he should probably pick up. It was Dinah, a little hysterical and deeply excited.

"Bloody fucking amazing!" she shrieked. Ben moved the phone away from his ear a few inches. "You were amazing, the whole night was bloody amazing, Ben, are you there? Okay, good, because Tom is talking about studio time. I've never felt so, so amazing! We could do it, don't you think? Ben? Seriously, I've got to write all that down. So much music I never even thought of before, I mean, what was that? I can't believe it's still just midnight, just like they said! I'm tingling all over! I can feel new songs just bubbling up, if I can only bloody remember it all. Get ready for the world tour, Yank! And that Aubrey bloke? Where did you find him!"

"Uh, Dinah? Dinah!" Impatient but stuck, he let the babbling go on with a tolerant smile. "Dinah, honey, that Aubrey bloke? You know who he is, right? I mean, they said…" But Raven was slowly shaking his head. No.

"Dinah, love, I've gotta go. Yeah, I don't want to wake Mellis up, okay? We'll talk later. Yes, it was bloody amazing. Call me tomorrow. Get some sleep. Yes. Love you too. Bye."

Raven suppressed a smile. "Policy. You know. A midsummer night's dream."

Thinking about that, Ben said, "Am I'm going to forget all this too?"

"Ben, I don't think even my lord can make that happen. You'll have to ask him later."

"Yeah, but… Never mind," he sighed. And shaking his head, he let them in by the office door, prepared to face the disaster they'd left behind, but caring only about getting upstairs to Mellis.

It took a moment but eventually it registered: with few exceptions, the room looked just as it had before the madness had struck. Most of the instruments were back in their proper places. The laptop was closed and quiet on the desk. The beloved old Gibson 6-string was back in its place of honor on a new stand with new strings, and when he picked it up and played an open G chord, perfectly tuned with none of its mellow voice lost. Now that was practical magic, he thought with relief. Even the *Tom Sawyer* had been restored to its pre-bitch-queen state.

Moytura, last seen minutes ago in Faerie, had been returned to her place where any movement of air would strike music from her strings, and where the setting sun would catch the gold, copper, and bronze laid in the sinuous carving and set it alight.

But one space remained empty. "The Martin?"

Raven gave a doubtful shrug. "They're working on it, but some things…"

"What happened to 'It's magic, Ben'?"

"A great instrument can be beyond even faerie skill to repair, especially a classic like that one."

"But Moytura?"

"Has in some part a magic of its own, they said. Plus, she was only thrown out of the window to a relatively cushioned landing, not bashed a few times over a desk. All in all a good thing, sir. The Martin was expensive but it may perhaps be replaced, Moytura would have been lost."

Enough of this, Ben thought, and flung that concern aside. "Fine, whatever. Where's Mellis? I've got to…"

"Right where we left her, Ben, as I told you."

Raven got out of the way as Ben bulled passed him up the narrow staircase and into the mellow lights of the parlor. It too had been tidied up, music and papers neatly laid where she could find and sort them herself. From somewhere, probably the music system, the mellow tones of a lute were softly playing and the room smelled lightly of violets.

And there where he had softly left her, stretched out in her long yellow dress, she lay as if she hadn't moved since they'd left. A little like Snow White. Frowning, Ben dropped to his knees beside her and touched her face and took her hands.

He spoke her name. Nothing happened.

He removed her wedding ring from his little finger and took his own back from her but that, however potent otherwise, wasn't part of this charm. He looked back over his shoulder at Raven who waited quietly, white hands folded.

"What do I do?"

The young man smiled lightly. "It's your faerie tale, Ben Harper. What do you think?"

Well, he could take a cue, if nothing else. Leaning over her still form, feeling the warmth of her body rising to meet his, he kissed her lips and sat back to watch her eyes flutter open like the princess in the story. The gentle smile that blossomed across her face, dimpling the corners, told him she had slept without troubled dreams, but in the next moment he saw the flash of memory, and he rocked back in a hurry as she sat up, shaking and pale.

"Oh my god, Ben! What did I… No, wait." Her look of hurt and apology froze, then subtly shifted. "What did she do? That bloody cow!" She sat back to look at Ben, taking her husband's face in her hands to examine the scrapes and bruises, already fading, as if they were new and bright. "Are you all right?"

"I'm fine, love," he said, slightly amused but wary as well. Her rare anger was best to avoid. And she was angry, that was clear.

Her breathing came quick and excited, but gradually improved as he drew the story out of her. A woman, she explained, had come to the door, an older woman with the bearing of a duchess, Mellis thought. Very polished and lovely, very sweet, said she was collecting for something, or taking a survey, or… Odd, what was it? No idea. Something to do with children, of course.

All she knew was that she, Mellis, had been just too happy to have the woman come in and sit down to a cup of tea, and oh they just talked and talked. Well, about her music. And combining a family and a career. And Dominic. Yes, mostly about Dominic. This was after she'd already found him sitting in the play box, fussing and refusing to eat, and just being a brat. The woman had laughed about that, and Mellis had too. In fact, she'd been just too, too happy for days, about everything.

"Does any of this make any sense?" But none of it made any sense, did it? "And then, somehow I knew you were here, downstairs. And suddenly I was just furious. Oh Ben, so angry with you! But then, it was like, like it wasn't my anger and I knew it, but I couldn't stop! I think— I don't know, I think I must have passed out for awhile. Next thing I knew, someone was holding a knife to my throat! Couldn't speak, couldn't do anything! What a nightmare!"

Her husband was shaking his head as he held her trembling hands and looking grim. "Titania," he said.

Where another woman might have been hysterical, Mellis was just righteously pissed off. And where some other woman might have burst into tears, she barked a bitter laugh.

"Really! Lady Grace, she called herself, I remember now. Dear, stately old lady. I suppose I'm grateful she didn't bring me a poisoned apple, too. Oh, Ben, next time you bring me a story about faeries on the moor, I'll believe you, I swear I will. But..." She fixed him now with a terrible look as her laughter fled. "She wants our son, doesn't she?"

"Yes."

"And that, that thing! That looked like him?" She shuddered.

"A changeling, love," Ben said cautiously, stroking her hair. "Nothing but driftwood and magic."

She was trembling, now, and her hands were cold. "Changeling? But there's no such... I mean, that's just a legend. It's ridiculous."

It was safe now to hold her, and she came into his arms while he crooned and hushed her. "It's all right, love. It's all right. We'll make it good."

He turned to Raven for confirmation and to make a delayed introduction. With a feeling like a punch in the stomach, Ben realized the boy wasn't there—vanished again—and swore.

Finally the trembling settled and she sat back, flushed but calm with a serenity her husband recognized for grim determination. She reached for a tissue from the box on the table, and blew her nose.

"So what do we do?"

He started to speak, then caught his breath, waited before saying, "Now, you're going to meet my friend Raven."

51
Buried treasure

Mellis snorted indelicately. It was a thing they said, shorthand for that dear friend everyone has who's slightly awkward in company, but precious nevertheless. She knew what he meant immediately: Raven was a difficult friend, but a worthy one.

"You've grown a beard," she said, and reached up to touch it, soft and curling under her fingers.

He'd forgotten about it in all the mayhem, but "Yeah, I guess I have," he said.

"Very piratical."

"Almost Viking!"

"It's gone," Raven announced cheerily. The difficult friend was trotting down from the upper floors looking particularly pleased with himself. "The stock. Brown Meg didn't know what to do with it, but I did. Sparrow will never even know it was there, except that you tell him. And nor will anyone else."

Mellis frowned, and wasn't it adorable. Ben could hardly stop smiling and looking at her, even though there was so much of dire importance yet to do.

"Stock," she said flatly.

"The changeling. It went back to being a few ugly pieces of wood, and now it's gone. I'm Raven, by the way." He stuck out a hand and waited while she took it, carefully.

"How d'you do. And this changeling— thing?"

"Of no matter, now that it's gone," Raven said airily. "A trick of the queen's."

"My queen?"

"No, madam. My queen, I'm afraid. Ben, haven't you told her?"

"Been trying. Can't get a word in."

"Never mind. Brown Meg—that's your brownie, ma'am—has set up some food in the kitchen. If you'll come through?"

"My what? I have a—a what? Well, I have missed a few things, haven't I?"

There was nothing else for it but to follow the rich smell of mushroom omelets and home-made *frites* into the kitchen with its massive table and windows facing the high moor. The late rising moon was peering grey and hag-ridden through the misty landscape, just visible from where they sat.

"She says," Raven counted off the points on his fingers. "You need your strength, what were you thinking staying up all night, Mellis must be all used up, things like that. In a deep Devonshire dialect, I'm afraid."

"You spoke to her?"

"Obviously. Anyway, please be seated, Professor Powell."

"Just, just Mellis, please." She mouthed at Ben: Brownie? Then waved it off. It would wait.

And so began the midnight lecture in surprise and a little confusion which Raven was fairly efficient in clearing up. Ben let the kid explain, which saved having to talk while eating both his omelet and Raven's, since the boy didn't seem to eat significantly, and Ben's reserves had been seriously depleted by a shocking amount of liquor and An Extraordinary Gig. A gig he seriously wanted to talk about, but it would wait. Mellis was already disappointed at having missed so much and annoyed at having to be rescued like a damsel in distress.

"And that's pretty much that," Raven said at last, buttering a muffin with honey.

"So," said Mellis thoughtfully, sipping her tea—perfect tea by the way, just the way her granny made it. "What Ben needs to do—what we need to do—is figure out what has become of the gold in the arm ring, is that it?" Both men nodded, and she knew it was true. "Somehow, everything has come back to us. Nice work, love," she added in her trademark professorial tone.

Ben hung his head, but he was grinning. Wonderful, sensible Mellis was back. It would all be all right.

"Yes," he said. "It's all around us, somewhere, probably

right in front of us, and we'll slap our heads and feel deeply stupid when we find them. Y'know really, you're taking this part very well. Why didn't you believe me the other day?"

"Oh Ben, really? You know it sounded completely mental. You were babbling on about piskies and Oberon and lemonade and quests, and the phone ringing in Fairyland! What would you have thought?"

"Yes, all right, you're right. I would have called Terry the Shrink myself. So why believe us now? Is it because Raven's so cute?"

"Is he?" She gave the slender, boyish face an appraising look and poured more tea. Then she shook her head and said, "That's not it, no."

Raven chuckled and gave a courtly nod. "Madam," he said.

"It's simple really. Now that you tell me calmly what's been going on, the logical necessity is to believe you. For one thing, you never lie to me, even over little things, you're such a dear man. Secondly, I am witness that something has certainly been done to me and, good lord!" Scanning the sparkling kitchen, "To my house. Finally, my son is missing, and that's no small thing, but you tell me he's safe. I'd like to confirm that, if you please. My family are being used and abused, and that will not do. So." She set the china teacup in the saucer with a click. "What do we do? What did you learn that will help us find these things?"

"Well— Where are you going?" said Ben, as she jumped up from the table.

"Getting paper and pencil, of course. To take notes. I know you, too busy to take notes, so now we'll have to retrieve it all from your exceedingly tidy memory." She was gone, but just as the two men were sharing a shrug, her tousled head popped back around the door. "Diary, please?" Then she vanished.

"Crap, I knew she'd want to see it!"

He was thinking of the rude jokes and worse. He'd slung his jacket over the back of his chair, so he grabbed it now and dug out the little book that had brought him so far. As before, all the frenetic movement had halted on any pages no longer in use. Notes that had lain in multiple layers had settled into illegible scrawls, and even the neat copperplate script had faded, as though written long ago in rusty inks. Some of the rudest remarks were simply gone, but Gaezel was still there, oh my yes. Hopefully Mellis would laugh.

The new pages were very rough—perhaps the gremlins had partied too heartily—and the only new drawings simply sketched the three artifacts as he remembered them: laid out to show where they belonged relative to each other, as they might have been by the Wessex Antiquarian Society, had they known. Below each piece was a word in Old English, first in the runes that appeared on the piece, then a simple translation in the neat copperplate hand: (male) child—me—he made. *The boy made this*.

The only other new notes were a list of some Norse myths and motifs, some musical notation, and the first few lines of Beowulf. Nothing so far was crying out for his attention.

"Hmm," Mellis said, sitting down with a spiral notebook and a ball-point pen.

Ben shoved the book across to her; she flipped through it quickly, stopping now and then to frown or chuckle.

When she got to the genealogy, she said "Dad will want to see this." And when she turned the page on Gaezel she said, "Hmm. Really."

Ben said quickly, "I think you're supposed to get mad. They think it's hysterical."

She smiled her knowing smile and moved on. "All right, you said you could hear or read the story, the history I guess, of where each piece has been."

"Right."

"Let's start, then," she said with her usual brisk efficiency. The terrors of the previous day were parked, for the moment, where they could do no immediate harm. "Oldest first."

52
Dragon tales

With some diversions and a few consultations with Raven, in
the end the history of the reliquary came out in more or less
coherent English. Fortunate, as it was both the longest and the
busiest story of the three.

Bishop Wulfhere's little surprise had remained part of the
treasures of his Church, although stored with the bishop's
personal traveling alter. It had been lost through carelessness,
found by chance, and cracked early in the Wars of the Roses,
lost again and found like King Richard's crown under a
hawthorn bush. Rehearsing it aloud for the first time, Ben
could see it all in swift detail, like a movie unrolling in his mind:
the birdsong on the heath, the smell of fires smoldering in the
ancient airs, the metallic taste of death.

Salvaged and repaired, handed down, the box had become
part of a nun's dowry who was destined to be an abbess. Ben
registered both her innocence and the cynicism of the
Cistercian monastery to which it later came, St Swithin's finger
bone long since replaced by a crystal vial said to hold a dram
of Our Lady's breast milk, miraculously renewed every year
until the dissolution of the monasteries under Henry VIII. The
chant of cloistered monks came down to his mind's ear across
the centuries as he spoke; he stopped to listen until realizing at
some point that only he could hear it.

Eventually by the usual underhand means it had come into
the hands of Sir Thomas Cromwell who hoped his king would
like it. Great Harry had in turn given it as a gift (false relic sold
separately) to a Throckmorton, whence it came to Plymouth.
It had been sold a few more times while managing to stay in

fairly good shape though the rock crystal walls were starred with cracks. The set jewels, of course, had been prized out and sold, replaced with glass, which were gouged out in turn and discarded with disappointment sometime before the Civil War. A Parliament soldier barely missed smashing through it with his hobnailed boot while clearing bodies out from behind a cannon-blasted royalist wall. Ben flinched at the sound of the cannon's roar and the crash and tumble of brick and stone. It was a Dartmoor man who had shoved it into his buff coat against orders and taken it home to his wife, in whose family it had remained until very recently.

"And apparently," Ben said over his shoulder, having gotten up to stare blinking out at the buttery moon. "Somebody gave it to us. Wedding present, maybe?"

Mellis was frowning at the diary sketch, notes abandoned, as if trying to remember what it reminded her of. "Half a minute," she said, sitting back with a start. "I know that box!"

"Eh?"

"Seriously, I do. It was, yes, it's… Oh this is too easy!" Her chair was still spinning as she dashed out of the kitchen, and Ben had done a double take before realizing he should bring the diary and follow her. Raven brought up the rear.

When they'd bought the cottage, Mellis had claimed what the realtor called the "formal sunken dining parlor" as her music room. Here she kept her desk, her own instruments, and the baby grand piano. Because it was her own work room, off limits to her famously organized husband, and because it was only just big enough for everything she needed, it was a controlled riot of boxed papers, music scores choral and symphonic, and awards, mementos and the framed BAFTA nomination for a film score. Even Brown Meg had understood it was not to be touched, although miraculously it appeared to be dust-free. And that's where they found her, burrowing through the layers on her desk.

"Y'know," observed Ben the Organizer, not for the first time. "They found the fabled city of Troy under only twenty-six layers." As always, she ignored the implication.

Raven added, "Much deeper and paper starts turning to

diamonds, you know."

They both halted and stared at him as if he had dropped from the moon. "A joke!" said Ben. "Who knew?"

At last Mellis emerged from the bottom layers, clutching a dull gold box with clear glass sides looking like a piece of French ormolu ware. The ancient enamel in the dragon's head had long ago been chipped out and at some places painted back in with... was that nail varnish? But it was there, its inter-lacing traceries and the rune of victory worn almost smooth with generations of handling. The once consecrated container of sacred relics real or hopeful, now held a few No. 2 pencils with erasers chewed or perished, a dried out stick pen, a spool of green thread, plus odd bits of string, a pearl earring, and half a sequin.

"Found it!" she cried, practically hopping up and down like a cheerleader. "I knew I'd seen it before, bit of a pencil sketch doesn't really... Don't you remember? Dinah and Tom put it up at a jumble sale in the village, and I bought it for a fiver. That was when you Now-or-Never'd their barn, remember? I can't imagine they knew how old it was. It was just an old box they weren't using, crusted with dirt, had to go. I mean, I suppose we all knew it was an antique of sorts, but my god! It belongs in the British Museum or something." She gasped suddenly and stared at Ben with huge eyes. "I've been using a thousand-year-old work of art for a pencil box!"

Just in time, Raven stepped in to neatly pluck the reliquary out of her hands before she dropped it from suddenly nerveless fingers. While they were still staring at each other in awe, he cleared his throat and mentioned diffidently that there were still two more pieces to find.

"All right, all right, yes," said Mellis, still beside herself. "Oh my giddy aunt, I knew you were telling the truth, but— oh my!" She paused, catching her breath at last. "Oh very my— it's real"

Raven also had the pen and note pad, so they sat down in the nearest folding chairs and started in on the next object of interest. This time, he volunteered to take notes.

Briefly Ben told over his adventure with Jack Greengage,

leaving out the humiliating panicky bits for now, then backed up to give the complete history of the middle fragment. It had been flung back through time not quite as far as the first one, lodging amongst the gold of a Wessex nobleman's treasure trove, who applied it to a daughter's stingy portion on her marriage to a minor knight.

Again he was transported in his mind as the tale unwound. When the Normans came, he was the lady's liegeman burying a sack containing her last hoard of coins and bits and pieces of treasure in the field by the river: the fragment, a chain, a chalice, a cross. Much later he saw it dug up by chance, then the finder killed by a jealous neighbor who took away a few coins but reburied the rest to retrieve afterwards.

Then that fellow marched away to serve his lord on the field at Agincourt and never returned. The gold, its rough covering rotting away, lay in silence for another two centuries, while the river changed its course and the tree was felled. Until at last, most of it was turned up by Jack Greengage's plough in the spring of 1599 and taken to London where it was melted down and remade into jewelry—including Bessie's wedding ring, Ben was happy to report—also a brooch enameled with violet, and a chain of linked enamel flowers. It had all remained with Jack's descendants and eventually come down to Mellis through her mother. So the detailed genealogy in the diary was a clue after all.

Mellis, idly spinning her wedding ring on her finger, grew wide-eyed. Catching her look, Ben's jaw dropped just slightly. "Oh you have got to be kidding me."

"What?" said Raven, dotting a final i in his neat old-fashioned handwriting.

"A ring, a brooch, and a chain with little flowers on it?" said Mellis. "Most of the enamel is all worn or broken out, and the chain..."

"But," Ben said. "That's just some old crap costume jewelry from the..."

"Play box!" they said together, and both were on their feet.

"Wait!" Raven snapped, looking at both of them a little sternly. "Tell me what you're thinking, and where it is."

Ben gulped, caught up in the enthusiasm. "Upstairs in Sparrow's room, there's a painted box, his play box, full of old scarves, dressing up clothes and odd bits, wooden sword, plastic crowns, you know, for being knights and wizards and stuff."

"All rather Winnie the Pooh," Mellis added with a smile. "There's a cigar box in it with all sorts of beads and chains and things. Too nice to throw away, not nice enough to wear. Great for draping around the King of Muscovy or whatever."

"And now it appears it's the Cheapside Hoard!"

"Well, the Dartmoor Hoard, anyway." Their hands met and closed on each other, faces beaming.

Raven listened, nodded, and gestured at the piano, and the cigar box resolved in front of them. "That one?"

"That's it!" Ben fell on it, spilling the contents out on top of three copies of *Part Songs for Young People* by Mellis Powell. And there they were, battered and beloved, a long chain made of flat oval links joining tiny daisies of white enamel with sparks of something, probably crystal. "I played with these when I was a child," Mellis said in wonder. "How can they still even be... well, anywhere?"

The brooch was like a sailing ship, a model of the Golden Hind in miniature, with gaping spaces in the middle that had once, Ben could tell them, supported three garnets and a suspended pearl for a gentleman's hat. Jack had done well, apparently, with his found fortune. Ben poked around in all the old rings and earrings pushing pieces back and forth with a finger.

"And here it is," he said with a sigh. "This is what he wanted so much he was willing to brave the big bad old city, trust a smooth talking stranger, and run through the rain with an elf to get."

Bessie's wedding ring. It was locked in place as he held it up, three bands slipped together like a puzzle ring. But when Mellis took it out of his hands, the bands fell away from each other revealing the motto, a line on each of the outer bands and the tiny golden heart within.

> *My love is fix'd, it hath no range*
> *While I live it will not change*

"It's beautiful," Mellis sighed. "They're all so beautiful." She looked up at Raven, then at Ben. "Such a shame to have to destroy them."

"A greater shame to let your world fall apart, I think," said Raven, and collected up the three pretty pieces, flicking the cigar box with the rest of its treasures back to its home upstairs. "These trinkets can be reproduced, copied. Your lives cannot."

"I'm still not sure I understand all that."

Ben stopped her with a hand on her wrist.

"Don't," he said. "Sweetheart, just don't. It will only make your brain hurt. Here," he added, dumping out the contents of the reliquary. "Might as well keep them together."

"And the final piece, Ben Harper, if you please."

Ben took a deep breath and swallowed, then took a seat at the desk, letting his mind drift out across time and story once again. The last piece, the smallest and least traveled, had indeed been sold as part of a lot with all the other dusty antiquities from Diamond Hall. Fairly soon it had been melted down by a local craftsman, happy to have found old gold so cheaply, and eventually made up into sugar spoons marked with a monogram for someone who ordered but failed to pay for them, and was transported to Australia for debt. They had simply lain in storage for many years, unregarded, until bought at auction by a craftsman who had used them...

Ben stammered as he realized in horror what had happened, and where they were now.

"No, no!" he gasped, stricken. "Oh god, no! That's not fair."

"What?" Raven whispered back, the midnight eyes narrowed. Mellis only stared, preparing herself, but not for this.

"Randall Simmons bought them," said Ben in a bleak voice. "Randall, see, he did the decoration, the metal work." He choked, swallowed, tried again. "He melted down antique gold spoons for the gold inlays in Moytura."

And he wondered how he had missed it. Had she been trying to tell him this all along? He had never known how to listen before, but it wasn't important until just now. And now—

"Raven?"

But the fae lord was shaking his head without pity. "I don't know, Ben. Let's go down and see her."

"But!"

"Let us go down, human child," Raven said sternly. "Bring all the pieces together, and we shall see what my lord will do."

Mellis wrapped her arms around the husband she adored for his cleverness and his humor and the music that thrived between them, then took his hand.

"Come on," she said.

53
Midsummer morning

Once assembled in the office, Raven laid the reliquary with its treasures on the work table, and went to the side door. How odd, it was almost dawn. A pearly light filled the mist that swirled from the moor and gave the garden an eerie, almost primeval atmosphere.

"Wait here," he said over his shoulder. Then in a moment he shifted and shrank and shook his feathers, and when the door swung open, he flew off with a raucous cry, disappearing from sight almost at once.

"That is so disconcerting," Ben said, trying to laugh.

Mellis, who had apparently been thinking much the same thing, sat down hard on the old sofa. "If I were the swooning type, I think now would be a good time."

Except for a faint movement of air swirling in to just stir the harp strings, there was nothing but silence, though the light was strengthening.

Ben stood with his hands in his pockets, just staring dry-eyed at Moytura, his gaze caressing the lines and curves, the shining inlay of the gold in the dragons interlacing from the one head at the top to the other matching it near the bottom. He'd never realized before that the two fierce faces each bore a Nordic rune, just like the ones on the dragon ring: one for triumph, as he knew now, the other for peace. Morning light glinted on the strings, the neat mechanism of the sharping levers. For a few hours they had soared above the stars together, but such things never happen twice. There would be another harp perhaps as fine, but such a night would never come again.

"On the other hand," he said more or less out of the blue. "Maybe I'm being pessimistic."

"Oh Ben," Mellis moaned softly. "Your beautiful harp!"

When he turned to face her, his eyes were sorrowful but his jaw was set.

"Our beautiful son, Mellis. Our beautiful marriage."

"Would the world be so awful if Britain never became a great empire, though? Wouldn't millions of people have been happier? Who's to say we wouldn't meet eventually anyway?"

"For the world at large, who knows? But sweetheart, Aubrey showed me. You walked right past me without a look. I didn't even notice. We weren't the same people, it wasn't the same place. In that world, Moytura might never even be made, so what would be gained? But really, love, it's not our risk to take."

So he had, in the end, come around to seeing what the king of Faerie had been trying to show him.

"And not before time," said Aubrey from the garden door.

Ben jumped and Mellis looked up and smiled almost against her will.

"Oh my," she said, getting to her feet. He really did look like Rupert Everett, in an embroidered tunic of pale gold silk belted over beautifully tailored jeans, but mostly he looked like a king, with a golden crown nestled in his curling black hair. When he came to her, all warmth, and bent over her hand with an airy kiss, she suddenly felt like dropping a curtsey. So she did, just a little.

"Always a great entrance, sir," said Ben, coming forward and offering his hand, which Aubrey took as he had last night. "Where's Raven?"

"Waiting for you. You've done very well, Ben Harper, and Mellis Powell so have you." For once he began to sound like a creature from another world, so serious had he become. "There are perils still to face, but you have come through well so far. Now the pattern is closing and there's little time for niceties or, I fear, for sentiment. Bring the other pieces here, if you please."

Mellis summarily cleared the top of the bookcase under

the window. Ben opened the reliquary and removed the jewels, placing them in the cleared space, the box to one side, the harp to the other.

"Is this something we can watch?" he asked cautiously.

The mist was burning off rapidly in the garden, and over the back gate they could see Raven Tor at last, glowing in the distance where the Midsummer sun was rising. In seconds the light would come streaming through the office windows.

Oberon the king, who might be in some part Odin and uncounted other immortals, and looked it, met Ben's eyes with glittering blue ones.

"Yes. Yes, in fact, I think you must. Hold yourselves away a little, though, please."

Like good children, they went to stand with clasped hands behind the sofa, while Oberon faced the shimmering row of golden treasures. He raised his hands over them and began to sing, first just a single note sustained. Laser-like, the sun struck through the gap on the tor called the Raven's Eye, lighting up crystal and gold, collecting and folding their light into a brilliant globe that filled the room.

A thin, high note leapt from the golden box like a living thing; reaching out, he touched one finger to it, and another to the deep hum in the throat of the golden tracery in the harp, and the light enveloped him, his haunting, mellow voice moving through a pattern of making. Into this he wove together the tinkling trills from all the Elizabethan trinkets and jewels and bound them with the rest, until the song began to take shape. His voice wove them into a harmony that rose above his moving hands and blossomed, unfolding like a poem in suspended time.

Above his hands, in a glowing ball of music and magic, sinuous shapes began to form, to coalesce; a spinning disk whirled out fiery threads that found and snagged and chased one another until, interlaced and intersecting, dragons came. Threads became serpents, a dozen small creatures with scales of red gold and white fire, salamanders bickering and snapping in the flame. Held within the music, they swirled hungrily through the figures of some ancient dance, catching their tails and swallowing up one another, until only two remained; long and sleek, they tumbled about each other, chased and joined and twisted in the superheated air, yet the chord would not resolve. It wanted a note, a new voice to cool, shape, and bind them, and time was short.

So with a thought, Oberon bade Moytura's bronze voice come into the song as well; a deep harmonic sounded through the room. Ben Harper, sensing an irresistible invitation, and hoping he hadn't already sung his voice to pieces, came in to keep her company, to anchor the progress of the spell. Obeying a similar impulse, Mellis floated her clear true soprano in a descant over all until the beauty of it so ravished her, hot tears filled her eyes and fell, unnoticed while her tone held true.

Voices moved as the spell evolved, hers above, his below, the king's a sweeping anthem that carried them inexorably through to coda, resolution, and home at last. The sun processing in its stately way through the arc of the sky, the beam from the tor swept on. One by one each gilded voice fell away, then the man's, and the woman's. A single word sounded, alone and clear, and the king held out his cupped hands.

With a pure bold chime like the ring of a broadsword, a heavy arm ring of braided gold with dragon finials fell out of the air and into the waiting hands of the king of Faerie. Where the hard-won artifacts had been lay a few contorted scraps of crystal and glass, and an Irish harp,

Silence crashed over them, and Ben blinked wildly, blinded for the moment by an impossible vision seared into his brain.

"Well," said Mellis, with tears in her eyes. "Who says singers can't jam?"

Oberon turned to her looking refreshed and energized, quite contrary to her expectation, and laughed out loud. "I don't know, madam. Who would say that?"

"Oh, everybody!" she laughed, to her own surprise, and decided it was time to sit down now. Happily, the sofa was still right there.

"Well, we know better, don't we?"

But Ben was only looking at one thing. To his speechless

delight, the harp stood unharmed and perfect, still vibrating slightly with the memory of enchantment. Deeply impressed, he came around to check her condition. Then he saw the twining dragons in the pillar that gleamed with bronze and copper, but no gold.

No, wait.

"Now that is magic." He was already running his hands over the polished curves still warm with sun and power, hardly daring to touch a string, reassuring himself that she was all right.

"I thought we could spare a bit for the eyes, you see?" said Aubrey pointing there, and there. "Guthrum will never notice."

"Oh yes, yes I see. Thank you." More or less speechless. For everywhere that gold had been now shone, albeit less brilliantly, sinuous lines of faerie-made bronze just a little on the copper side. "It's brilliant! And you're right, the old pirate will never know the difference."

"I think you'll find the sound unchanged," Aubrey said placidly, but anyone could tell he was pleased. "Tell me if it needs any adjustment. And then, of course, there's this."

Gently, he handed the dragon ring to Ben. It was hot to the touch, polished bright and humming. Holding it, turning it over gingerly in his hands, the harper could feel its stories swarm together and interlace, hearing his name, faint but true, at each point where its story intersected with his. Then all at once, his face that had been so somber a moment before split into a lively grin, and his laughter bubbled out unchecked.

"Dude!" he sang out. "Sparrow!"

"What?" said Mellis and Oberon in their separate tones of surprise.

"I know what it means. The legend, the words on each piece. See, here it says, in Old English like you showed me: 'The child me made'. The bishop thought the child meant the son of God, but it's not. Mellis, my lord, don't you see? The boy made me. Our boy. Our Sparrow made this. Aubrey, that's what he was doing with Gwydion. They were braiding lengths of gold and singing over them, remember? Sparrow doesn't just want to be a wizard. He wants to be a maker. This is his first piece, and Gwydion signed it for him. How? I have no idea!"

Weary beyond measure but giddy with joy, he collapsed next to his wife, giggling just a little hysterically.

54

By the king's command

"I don't suppose we can bring Dominic home now?" Mellis asked, still vibrating with the unexpected passion of magic.

"No!" both men chorused, Ben apologetically.

She rocked back and sat down again, while the king went on in a no-nonsense mode she recognized.

"He's still in great danger. The only place I can protect him is exactly where he is now. Any other option risks his safety and the safety of those with him."

"Then, can you take me where he is? He must be terrified." Her excitement was rapidly being replaced by an edgy anxiety.

"It is my hope that he is not. The last time we looked in on him, he was happily engaged in childish activities with some of the finest gentlemen of my realm. You can't go to him because the enchantments surrounding his twist of my world can be broken only by Ben with certain tokens which he has, I hope, obtained." He threw a glance at Ben, who nodded. "Those who are within that safe zone cannot come out until he does. Thus Sparrow's safety is proof against both coercion and treason. Only his father has the means to enter from without. Even I cannot, unless—"

"Unless?" Ben said doubtfully.

"Oh Ben, don't make me say it. Very well, unless you are dead."

"Dead!"

But Oberon scoffed. "Do you read all the dangers on a prescription bottle? Of course not."

Ben considered what the king was not saying, then nodded. What else could he do? Eventually he said, "What I really don't understand, forgive me, is why you've taken such measures. Why do you care so much about my family?"

With a slightly pained expression the king looked away. "Let it be enough that I do. Perhaps some day, when you're drunk enough, I'll tell you. For now, they are in danger principally because you are in my service. So I must be responsible for them."

"Oh! Wait!" It finally dawned on Mellis what else he had said. "You looked in? You can look in on him? Then I can see him, can't I? Why can't I see him?"

"Yeah, can we see him?" said Ben. "It's been, well I don't really know how long it's been almost a week. Come on, sir. For his mother's sake."

Aubrey blew a sigh of impatience. "Very well, turn on the computer and listen to me." Ben moved to comply. "I take it you have all three of the tokens you were told to collect?"

"I do," Ben nodded, and drew out the acorn sweetly tinkling on its chain. "There's this." And the nail was in his.... yes, in the coin pocket of his jeans. And the leaf was still folded into a page of the diary which was "Upstairs, in my jacket. I'll go—"

His Majesty snapped his long fingers and held out his hand, and in a shimmer of air the worn leather jacket was draped from his finger tips. "Fetch it out please. Mellis, you may press Control G whenever you're ready. Ben, this is essential. Give me the tokens please."

"There he is!" Mellis squealed. "Oh! What's he doing? What's going on? I can't hear anything." She muttered, tapping at keys, then put on the headphones and smiled with relief.

With the tokens in his hand Aubrey did something and said something, and handed them back a few seconds later, all now linked together on the chain: leaf, nail, acorn. Ben stared, astonished again, even though he'd seen far greater magic just minutes ago. Then he bent his head and Aubrey settled the chain around his neck.

"If you want to change your clothes or anything, do it now. I have to get you out of here quickly."

While his human operative hunted up a fresh shirt, and found the one Brown Meg had laid out for him, Oberon snapped out his orders. Ben was not to lose track of the silver chain and its burden. He was not to wear it over any mail armor he might find himself in, but keep it under his shirt or tunic. He would slip back into the time stream in medias res shortly before he was needed. And for the love of everything don't forget to take the ring!

Yes, he trusted Ben to do exactly what was required. No, he was not going to try to explain how Sparrow had made the dragon that Odin gave to Guthrum's ancestor long before Sparrow was born, and it wasn't important. "Time. Mobius strip. Leave it."

"Excuse me?" From the desk, Mellis sounded un-characteristically frantic. "I think there's something wrong here. They've all gone inside."

The two men converged round the screen and saw immediately what she meant. The pleasant glade that had been Sparrow's classroom was grey with storm clouds and tossed with blowing rain. No surprise, perhaps, that it was empty of people, but it was not a good sign.

The worse the weather surrounding the haven, the nearer Titania's anger.

"Did this just start?" When she nodded, Aubrey reached in for the controls that shifted the viewer left and right, then moved in on a sturdy flint-roofed cottage that had not been there before. "That's not good."

He spoke a word and displayed the interior, which looked slightly familiar, as if Gwydion and Taliesin had raised it from some design of Sparrow's. Sparrow himself seemed to be happily explaining plastic architecture to a supernaturally patient Gwydion while playing with the Legos of a thousand worlds. Mellis recognized the location immediately. "Oh, that's from—

"I know what it is," the king snapped. "Though they are beset they are still safe, and choose not to alarm the boy. I was afraid this might happen, however. My sweet queen took Dominic's true name from you, my dear, when she had you in her power. What a surprise that must have been to her!"

"Oh my god, you mean it's my fault?"

"It is the queen's fault, never doubt it. And now, though she can bring her power to bear on the haven I created, we have some time. Some, but not much. And that means you must be off at once. Do you remember the way?"

Compressed lips twisted up a grim, lightless smile. "I could walk it blindfold. Wait! Sir, is Mellis safe?"

Oberon turned to Mellis with a slight and courtly bow over her hand. "All will be well, Ben Harper. You have my word on it."

This time, at least, he could leave his wife while she was aware of him going, so he kissed her, and said, "Be right back. I love you."

"I love you!"

"Go!" With that, Oberon wrapped darkness around Mellis and himself like a cloak and they were gone.

Wednesday

9

55

Wessex, Christmas 876 AD

❋

Now Ben had to compose himself. He knew the path, yes, but what was the most efficient way to come to it? No time for sightseeing, nor being chased by wolves; he must enter the scene in time and not a moment later.

"No," he whispered to himself. "It's all about the music, isn't it?"

Moytura was larger than Dariole, the king's harp, and was not held or played the same way, but she was a harp, and the two had sung together such a little time ago. Raven had said she had a magic of her own, and the king just minutes ago had called it forth. Surely some of that magic must remain for him to draw on.

Lightly, lightly he touched a single string and launched a note so fraught with enchantment that for a moment he was lost in it. And then he knew.

It took only seconds then to lift the harp over to the comfy chair and seat himself on its edge. Leaning her into his shoulder, he struck one tone then another from the middle range, keeping it simple as he had in the Saxon court. And while he played, he set that image before him: the beast-carved pillars, the hall lit by torches and the blaze of a central fire with the smaller ones crackling, driving back the shadows along the painted walls; the give and hiss of the rush-covered floor beneath his stained riding boots.

In his mind's eye he peopled that vast room with fierce, sturdy men in their tunics and bright mail shirts, hair braided or shaggy or hacked off at the shoulder. And at the top of the room, nearest where he sat himself with Dariole on his knees, a long table, scribes scratching with care at precious parchment under the clean white light of candles borrowed from the Church with only mild complaint from the Bishop; priests murmuring in the corner.

The smells, then: the scent of those candles honeying the air already laden with too many bodies too close together, anxious and eager, under-washed and under-slept; the heady aroma of roasting meats.

Without any sense of transition, of gates or doors, he knew he was Brand the Gleeman picking out strange melodies on a silver strung harp, felt the gentle weight of steel ring mail beneath an embroidered woolen tunic. All the while, three feet away a barbarian warlord fidgeted, and facing him, the thoughtful, ascetic man of twenty-five summers who would be called Alfred the Great.

Tenderly, Ben lifted his fingers from Dariole and stilled the strings. Raven, who had been making a serving girl laugh behind the king's chair, suddenly stopped toying with her long blond braid and looked over, as if sensing the subtle alteration. Understanding came then as he too shifted into the new pattern, and he winked. Ben nodded, and scanned the room afresh, this time shutting out the songs and stories all around him to focus on the one about to unfold.

The question still seemed so simple. How difficult could it be to agree to stop fighting and exchange a few hostages? But he already knew it wasn't.

The rich smells of sizzling pork and beef floated up from the massive kitchens, together with the sweet scent of honey mead flavored with bilberries, bringing the touch of Christmas and Yule into the room. Outside, a snow storm was battering the walls of the mead hall and cold winds whistled through the chinks between the stout shutters and oiled hides that covered the windows. That was new, that wind. Guthrum was starting to look uncomfortable, though that look may have been only the everyday consequence of the weals and scars on his face and arms, and a trickle of sweat under his arms.

Ben set the harp down on its painted deerskin bag and leaned it against his stool, within reach. This time it would be best not to leave it behind. When the king at last rose from the table, Brand Harper did as well.

Alfred stretched and nodded to Ben that he had stopped at just the right time, as if recognizing a cue, as if it had been planned. And perhaps it had. The secretaries had all put down their pens.

"Are we finished then, lord?" the king said at last. "Or do we continue to haggle like fishwives on a market day?"

"It is not for you to say so, Alfred Aethelwulfson," Guthrum rumbled, leaping to his feet. "We are done when I say we are done!"

Hot eyes scanned the company with a challenge as hostile as when he arrived. The room had become quite silent, though Ben could hear knives and daggers whispering, eager to be drawn, axes and swords calling from their hangers for release and battle.

"Well?" said Alfred, showing neither fear nor impatience nor any attitude at all.

"It remains but to swear our oaths, as I told you," said Guthrum. "On Odin's ring."

Here we go, Ben thought, touching his fingers to the golden dragon ring that his son—his son!—had sung into being with Gwydion ap Dôn more than a thousand years from now. The ring he had helped to remake not an hour ago. Though the words made no sense, they lightened his mind.

Alfred smiled his stately, kingly smile and snapped his fingers. The bishop strode forward with the long silk-wrapped box in his hands. At the same time, Ben took the step that put him at Alfred's side, holding the dragon ring out to him.

"My king," he said softly.

Smoothly, the ring passed from Ben's hand to Alfred, who offered it to the Northman who had demanded it. The bishop did not look at all pleased. Anyone could tell he had a sermon ready, which sputtered instead and died.

"And so," said the king of Wessex, not surprised at all. "You have your heirloom, as you were promised. For you know," and here a telling glance was directed at the bishop, "a Christian man is bound to keep his word once given, no matter by what token he takes his oath."

Startled into a gruff silence, Guthrum shifted his look from Alfred to Wulfhere to the harper to the king again. With little grace he snatched the arm ring to examine it, turning it over and over in his hands, noting the weight and markings. Rudely he threw it to one of his men, a grizzled one-eyed veteran with grey streaking his plaited hair, and demanded the lore master read the runes inscribed there and compare it to his knowledge of this thing that had been lost before he was born.

Ben stood forward, drawing by instinct on his store of obscure knowledge and notes from the faerie diary. And incidentally on his personal acquaintance with the parties involved. "I assure you, lord, it is Odin's Gift, as it is called," he declaimed. "I know this, for it was shown me in a dream."

All heads turned his way; only Alfred the thoughtful appeared unsurprised, knowing as he did the quality of his skald.

"What's this?" bellowed Guthrum and the bishop together, and most of the hall besides..

"What sacrilege is this?" Bishop Wulfhere added with a sneer.

Well, Ben thought, what is an adventure without a little risk? "I swear it on my life, lord," he said, cheating out to address the hall as well as the great lords on the dais. And when the murmurs began to die, he went on.

"In my dream, a Raven spoke to me in an ash tree. And when I awakened and went into the wood, I found that same ash tree and beneath it, between two stones, lay a casket bound in silver, black with age. Without opening it, I took the casket to my king, as the Raven bade me do. At the king's touch, it flew open, and lo! This lay within it. Is it not Odin's ring that you wished brought to you, Lord Guthrum? Is it not the one thing in Midgaard—which is Middangeard as we Saxons say it—on which you will make your bargain with him?"

The bishop was in a state, but Raven was a black-clad pile of grins.

Grumbling and muttering filled the hall, for Ben had found his acoustic sweet spot, and no one had missed a word.

Struck almost speechless, Guthrum turned at last to speak to his lore master. Nods and grunts and shrugs, and the older man put the ring on the table.

"That was Odin's raven, then," he said grudgingly. "In Odin's tree. And so it must be as you say. But will a Christian swear on this ring, Alfred King?"

"He will not!" spat Wulfhere, sensing the situation had slipped away from him. He almost slammed the reliquary down on the oaken table with perhaps less reverence than passion. Oh, even the heathens could see how much he wanted to damn the harper for a liar and a traitor, to insist that the true ring had been destroyed, beaten into God's weapon against their enemies. But you could also see him calculating. How much credit was he willing to spend with his king to do it?

A similar calculation had already been run in Alfred's more sophisticated imagination. Calmly, he said, "I see no reason why you, Guthrum Dansker, should not swear on what is sacred to you, and I shall swear on what is sacred to me, and so we seal our bargain." Idly, he flipped the silken coverings to either side of the crystal casket. "And see how my craftsmen have made the lock on Saint Swithin's reliquary a mate to the serpents on your ring."

And note too, Ben thought, how Alfred managed everyone by not acknowledging the dragon as Odin's at all. He had the Church's support and, as a man of true faith and of state, he was not about to squander it. The Viking, putting his tongue between his teeth, nodded grudging agreement.

Each lord touched his own talisman with his left hand, and reached to take the other man's right, forming, as the Christians saw it, a cross with their limbs. Guthrum noticed, but didn't care. His plans were already laid.

The Dragon Ring

56
Diplomacy

"One last thing," said the wily Dane just before their fingers quite touched. And this actually caught Alfred off guard. For a moment, the only sound in the room was the crackle of the fires, and the bright chime of an ale cup crashing to the floor.

Ben's heart dropped. They had come to the point, he knew, where any sharp practice beyond the normal bounds of diplomacy would open the chink Titania needed to explode into the room and destroy everything he had worked for, for no better reason than to be contrary. He could sense the potential for that explosion growing with the coiled tension in the room.

"Give me," said Guthrum, "your harper and your boy among the hostages."

The court erupted with objection until Alfred shouted them down. "Lord, the matter of hostages has been settled. You have already named six of my nobles and as many of my kinsmen. It is late in the day to take my harper from me, and my shield bearer too."

"I will return half of the others to you even now. Knowing as I do how precious these men are to you, the peace will surely hold."

Now Raven saw that it was his turn, and stepped up looking earnestly boyish and proud. "I am not afraid to stand for my lord's honor."

"And I am eager to do so," said Ben, eyes bright as if with hidden knowledge. "How blithely I shall bide the time in the company of Guthrum the Dane seeking out new songs and tales of heroes to divert the great lord from his cares. If I may send to my wife, I will be happy to go, once the Yule feast is past."

He hated to do it, and Raven may have been reluctant in some part, too. When they left, whoever stood in their places would have to go with the Danes. And they would die if Guthrum proved false. Whatever happened, happened.

Grinning broadly, the battle-proud Viking agreed. Messages might be sent, feasting might be had. "Let the Yule bring peace," he said grandly.

His men chuckled and nodded with him. Alfred looked relieved and pleased. His men in turn filled the hall with strained laughter, and took their hands from their weapons, calling for mead and ale. Again, the leaders of two obscure corners of an unregarded quarter of the fire-lit world each placed a palm on their respective talisman, and again they reached to clasp each other's hands.

Ben could feel the air vibrate like the string of a harp, the golden thatch of the roof tremble. The lords clasped hands and spoke their oaths, lengthy and elaborate and filled with sincerity and the names of their gods. Still the tension didn't pass, but rather built, an ill-struck note growing louder to those who could hear it but diffuse and confused as if searching for its critical mass.

To cover his unease, Ben backed away from the oath-taking and shouldered Oberon's harp. While he did so, he also touched the three tokens concealed beneath his tunic, clutching the acorn to make sure the bell made no sound. Raven, following his lead, joined him looking grim.

Alfred said, "So say I, Alfred, king of Wessex in Christ's name."

"She's here," the boy said quietly. "Or nearly so. We should..."

Bishop Wulfhere pronounced a benediction in Latin, tracing the sign of the Cross in the air three times over the crossed hands of his king and his enemy whether he liked it or not. It was done.

"Go!"

Too late. Thunder and a crack of lightening at once

exploded over the hall.

"Liars and betrayers! Traitors and magicians!"

The noise was worse than Ben remembered: the rending sound of earthquake and hurricane, and a shriek like a woman's sorrow but more horrible, and when all eyes looked upwards, they saw, all northern men drawing on a common lore, a Valkyrie screaming on the wind, hovering at the painted roof tree: a woman with eyes like hot coals, with skin as white as snow, a raging mouth the scarlet of heart's blood. She was not, to any of them, the queen of Faerie but a raging demon, a giantess.

"Thordis," some cried.

Titania, crazy and screaming and lashing out beams of power that turned first one smug young priest and then another to pillars of ice. The caring, maternal queen who had spared seventeen schoolboys had vanished, utterly.

"The harper will betray you, Guthrum Sitricson," she intoned. "He is already foresworn!"

That was wrong. That was altogether wrong. There was no treason, no lies that Ben knew of. He had done his job, accomplished his task, kept Alfred's word. But the Fae cannot lie, and suddenly Ben understood. Another man would be going with the Danes. The Fae cannot lie, but they can choose their facts.

And the racket was deafening. Men ran for their weapons racked for the truce along the walls and in outer rooms; those not struck down already shouted challenges and blame at one another. Shaken and furious, weary of peril and wrangling, Ben set his jaw and stepped forward into the emptying room with nothing but Oberon's harp in his hands, freed again and waiting. He looked up to the raging virago fluttering in the ribbons and rags of her fury and thwarted desire.

"Titania! " he shouted in his best outdoor voice. "Face me!"

Hysterical, she flung balls of snow and ice at the fire, at the doors, at anything that moved. A serving man froze in his ice-rimed tracks, but she paid Ben Harper no mind as if, overwhelmed by her fury, she had forgotten why she was there.

"Titania!" he called again. "Thordis of the Ice! Bridget of

the Fire! Queen of the Fae, I name you! You cannot deny me! Face me, damn it!"

On a shock of silence, the wind of her fury seemed to suck all the air out of the room, and all the torches went out. Men cried out in their fear of the dark, and halted where they stood. Only the hiss of labored breathing marked them..

"I'm here," Raven said behind him. The voice betrayed some nerves but courage remained.

"Remember last time?" said Ben, still staring up where she floated on her anger, illuminated by her anger and the threads of light from the hide-covered windows.

"I don't think this will be like last time, sir."

He could feel the movement as a sword whispered out of the scabbard at Raven's side, though part of Ben's brain wondered how that would help. Never mind, he thought.

The fire in the hearth hissed and steamed under its burden of snow, while the room grew colder and filled with acrid smoke. Above the hole in the painted roof, the storm continued to rage and blow, while Titania's eyes searched the room blindly, as if having spent so much power she had none left for ordinary senses.

"I am here, great queen," Ben said mildly, and struck one silver note on the harp.

Blind eyes indeed turned toward the sound, and she snarled. "So you are, human child."

He had been searching for the tune, for the harmonic that would let him cross into Faerie in two steps, but the noise of ice and wind had masked it, kept it from him. He had it now. Another tone bloomed from a silver string.

"Do you think to cross me?" the white queen cried.

"There is nothing here for you, my lady. You're too late. You must be gone and leave these men in peace."

"You dare to conjure me, Ben Harper, you babe, you pustule, you weed! You think your plinking music and your puny courtesies matter? That your tricks can hide Dominic the Sparrow from me?"

"I do, great queen." A sweep of silver notes. "He is my son, and the child of my heart. He does not belong to you!"

She threw back her head and shrieked a horrible cry of grief and despair, spun three times in the air and launched a flash of cold that would have shattered him on the spot. But Raven's sword was out, and it was no ordinary thing, no prop for an afternoon's adventure.

As quickly as the beam lashed out, the faerie blade met and caught it, and though it twisted in his hands, still he stood fast. And though he began to buckle and the blade too, yet he held and turned aside the killing beam.

"You!" she screamed. "You have had your last day of grace, boy!"

Another bolt flew and was blocked. Harsh on the last breath he had, Raven turned a strained face to Ben and gasped, "Now!"

Nine notes had already formed in his head, and now he struck nine notes from the elf king's harp, laughing the tune in her face, and like dolphins in the sea they twisted away.

The last thing Ben Harper saw of Anglo-Saxon England was torches moving in the darkness.

57

Somewhere in Faerie

There was no time, no traveling, no gates to open, no paths to walk or metaphors to push aside, only a prickling sensation of warmth and the echo of the last note still hanging on the air. Behind closed eyes, Ben realized that he was lying on a hillside cushioned by green grass fragrant as a new mown lawn, thick as a Turkish divan, and that someone very small was tickling his nose with a feather. He really needed to stick his landings better. Or maybe stop making them in dire circumstances. That would work, too.

He waved a hand at his nose and the tickling stopped. Began again with tiny giggles, followed by sneezes which, being his own, forced open his eyes.

Okay, not Santa Cruz. Underwater? Unlikely, though the watery blue that hazed the quick-charged air would have to be identified eventually. A sweet scent suggested bluebells.

And he wasn't cold, also good.

Flower fairies. That was nice, too. At least he had gotten where he meant to, more or less. Then his eyes focused and he forced himself to sit up, holding his head, and he swore. Raven, for whom these transitions were as natural as breathing, was lying next to him unconscious, still garbed in his Saxon tunics and leggings, the hilt of his shattered sword still clutched in one white hand. The faerie glow that should have shone even to Ben's idle gaze sputtered like a tallow candle.

Shaking his head to clear it some—bad idea, brain loose, focus!—Ben reached out to touch the boy's shoulder.

"Hey, kid." When Dariole on its strap caught him up short, he gently wrestled his way free, then turned on his knees to get a look at his friend's face. "Raven? Come on, mate, wake up."

But the eyes were closed, the lids faintly bruised, the breathing shallow, and the long tapering fingers when Ben took them were icy. When he tried to prize the sword from the boy's hand, it burned with cold.

Ben looked up, staring about in wild surmise at nothing but oak and spreading ash and holly trees rising out of bluebell slopes surrounding this one green patch. This was the usual moment for Aubrey to say something clever from two feet away just to make him jump, but there was no sign of anyone over five inches high. The only movement, a breeze that teased delicate music from the hyacinthine bells on every hand, rattling in the tops of the trees. Clouds like piled opals rolled and built with the intimation of rain on a tree-crowded horizon.

Bad weather. In Faerie. Not so good, he imagined. That would be Titania, venting her rage through the corridors of the world.

The moth-winged fairies buzzed about like worried flies making worried noises. Still blinking but not broken, Ben stood up and assayed the damage. No broken bones, though his head was pounding. Dramatic exits are like that, as he'd discovered, and he had been shouting a bit. Realizing what he'd shouted and at whom made his stomach turn over, but that would pass.

Rough week for heroes, came the wry thought. And it wasn't over yet.

The little harp that had brought them here was good too, as far as he could see. He picked it up and slung it over his shoulder, then looked again at Raven, still silent on the ground. Though the boy was slender, he would be no easy burden, and right now Ben's gift of direction was clearly on the fritz. Maybe it didn't work the same way in Faerie.

A yellow primrose faerie fluttered up and got in his nose, the curled petal hat and speckled face looking puzzled. Perhaps help wasn't that far away after all, Ben considered, if he could figure out how to ask for it. He backed away a step to give a respectful bow.

"Master Primrose," he said, very quietly so as not to blow the creature away. "I pray you find Lord Oberon, if you please, and ask if he would to come to us here. The Raven boy has been hurt by a blow from the queen and we are, well…" He could hardly bring himself to say it, "Lost. Can you tell him that for me, please?"

The little fellow consulted quickly with his friends in their piping voices, then as a tribe they turned and waved their cerulean blue and wild rose and violet caps at him and took off, popping out one by one each on a note like a toot from a tin whistle. Settling in to wait, Ben made Raven as comfortable as he could, then pulled off his jacket and rolled it up to place gently under the kid's head.

Ruefully he realized the kid was probably a thousand years old, maybe more. But there was something in the way he stood, or the changeable attitude somewhere between lofty arrogance and the deference of a first-class valet and, no kidding, the Gainsborough prettiness that let him think of Raven as no more than sixteen or so. That and his penchant for fancy dress, which reminded Ben of himself at that age.

What else could he do for him? He'd never expected to find himself wondering how to apply First Aid to an injured faerie—one of the few things his wacky education and career, not to mention his Red Cross card, had not in some way prepared him for. Lightheaded himself, Ben sat down cross-legged beside this ancient young man and just watched and waited. He hadn't eaten since midnight, whenever that was now; hadn't slept since… no telling. He was getting used to thinking of himself as exhausted, even when he managed to grab an hour's sleep. He didn't mind. He was protecting his family. Saving the world was just a happy side effect.

To beguile the time, he drew Dariole forward to settle it between his knees, and bent some thought to recalling one of the unknown tunes that had tripped from his fingers—good lord, barely twenty-four hours ago now. So many tunes that he had never played or never heard before. If you can name all the tunes you know… Well clearly, he didn't know enough tunes.

Now, searching his mind for the fae-spun melody, he let

his fingertips dance across the strings. Tentative at first then with more certainty, he felt the magic working. Little by little a song began to form, and the music came, and when it got to the end, he began again, drawing strength seemingly from the harp itself. On the next repeat he added variation, briefly wondering if Faerie minded its tunes being altered. Ornamenting the next variation, altering the fingering for a minor strain, he no longer wondered, he knew: still wistful as it was meant to be, beauty built on top of beauty as if Faerie itself sang through the silver strings, until Ben had to stop or he thought his heart would break.

He took a deep breath and held it, savoring the richness of the air, the fragrance of the bluebell wood, the tang of coming rain, then slowly blew it out. And while Ben sat in that vibrating silence, with his head resting against the shoulder of the harp, Raven began to stir. Just a bit at first, the long lashes fluttered and the bruised lids twitched.

"Play," he said. The voice was faint and rasping. "P— Please."

"Raven?" said Ben.

The long silence returned, then, "Music, harper, for my sake."

The music is all that matters, Ben thought. So he opened himself again and listened, really listened till the bells of Elfland rang in his ears and he began to play, not songs as such—not ballads or jigs or reels—but the music that came to him as a gift. And after a while, Raven opened his eyes and smiled a little wanly. A bit later, his hand opened to let fall the shattered remnants of a sword.

He had just begun to sit up with Ben's help when the fluting notes of the flower fairies returning filled the air. Hundreds of them fluttered and giggled and tumbled everywhere, surrounding Ben and almost engulfing Raven. They sang something silly in their light high little voices:

> *Home! Home! Home!*
> *Here we go, here you go, heel and toe!*
> *Come along, sing a song, ding ding dong!*
> *Home! Home! Home!*

Ben had become accustomed to simply walking or stumbling or even falling more or less seamlessly into Faerie on the wings (he cringed to say it) of song. This was— different. Tiny bells rang, birds caroled, colors swirled like a Disney transformation then stopped just before his stomach could rebel.

They had not changed positions, as such. Ben, his head spinning, still knelt in a posture of concern next to Raven, who was just barely holding himself off the ground on one elbow. But now Aubrey stood over them, Oberon in sooth, given the flashy medieval gear he wore and the delicate filigree of a golden crown shining on his brow. They had been taken to a grand but comfortable room in the king's Great House. It looked, in fact, just a little like Mellis's parlor at Diamond Cottage, but much, much larger. Ben had no time to notice as he unshouldered the harp and set it aside.

"Well done, gentlemen. And my harp, too, excellent," Oberon said with approving smiles playing around his mouth. Then his face changed to alarm. "What's the matter with Raven?"

The message had apparently lost something in translation.

"It's all right, sir," said the boy hoarsely. "Really, I'm fine." He tried to sit up, but even with help he clearly wasn't fine. "The sword you gave me, sir. I'm afraid..." He held out the blasted hilt that had come along with him, and promptly fainted.

Oberon caught him up then spoke two quiet words, and Raven faded from sight.

"It's all right," he said to Ben's stunned expression. "You must have done something wonderful, my old son, while you were waiting for me to notice you were back."

"I played for him a little. Well, rather a lot, I guess. The kid blocked Titania's power shot, took it right on the blade, twice! And held it, too. Gave me the space I needed to get us out of there."

Oberon laid a hand on Ben's shoulder and walked him to a cushioned divan, inviting him to drink something and for godssake sit down.

"I tried to send the little folk with a message to you, sir, but I guess they had a better idea." He stopped for a swallow from a frosted goblet. Sweet, clear water had never tasted so good. "She wouldn't listen, your queen."

"But you were in time for Alfred and Guthrum, and they made their pact."

"We were. They did. Y'know it was funny, really. It was almost like Alfred knew who we were. Or who I was, at least."

The king's inhuman eyes were hardest to read here in his own place, holding mysteries Ben would have to be satisfied never knowing. "He is a man of singular abilities, the king Alfred, extraordinary for his times. It's a pity, of course. Guthrum will betray him soon enough, and overturn the truce."

"So I almost died—Raven almost died—for nothing?"

Outrage quailed in the face of that mysterious, knowing smile. "Not for nothing, no, Ben Harper. Or should I say, Brand the Gleeman. Guthrum will turn and even prevail for a time, while Alfred will spend some months living rough, and come out of it hardier and more determined than ever, and better able to bring men to him. And then..."

He stopped pacing and smiled apologetically. "That's more than you care about, I know. Enough to say you did what was needful—with grace—and repaired the damage you had caused. In fact, you handled yourself very well, you know," Oberon said, or Aubrey perhaps, now that he was wearing pleated linen pants and a loose silk shirt. "Ben Harper, diplomat."

Waving off the compliment, Ben nodded thanks, cautious with his tongue for a change.

"Ben the showman, more like." He had done what they went out there to do, and all was well. Or would be soon. "Y'know, sir, the queen is not a happy woman, erm, faerie. She wasn't going to give up Sparrow just because she failed to screw up your plans for Alfred. But as pissed off as she was, I have to tell you, sir, she sounded... I don't know, not just angry. Not just crazy, either."

Now it was Aubrey's turn to look doubtful. "What do you mean?"

"I mean that what I saw, what I heard under all the screaming was more like grief."

The king said nothing, staring at his hands.

"You should have seen her at Iveston yesterday," Ben went on "When she, her shadowlings, Raven called them. She was angry, but with them, not with us. Sir, she helped us save a roomful of school kids and... This is more of that story I'm not drunk enough to hear today, isn't it?"

Not today. Aubrey raised his head and met Ben's eye. "Mellis is in my studio. She has been keeping her keen eye on Sparrow from there. You'll be wanting to go to her."

Immediately Ben was on his feet, not so weary that he wasn't ready to find his little boy and go home, even if it meant facing whatever new violence Titania threw at them.

58
The gathering storm

"So what happens now? I don't want to be melodramatic, but you do realize she's out there throwing a Force Ten tantrum, right now?" Rain was pattering against the stained glass windows, and a low rumble of thunder rattled the panes. "Is she on her way here?"

"Not here, exactly, no."

Walking quickly, they shimmered from the parlor into another room filled with screens and keyboards, computers and microphones, a mixer board and a classic Rickenbacker bass guitar in a stand. Studio, he'd said. Recording studio.

The near side of the room was set up for guests and conversation: a sleek Art Deco sofa flanked by matching chairs and a coffee table littered with magazines. The sofa faced a state of the art—which art wasn't entirely clear—wall monitor displaying a view into Faerie. Ben saw none of it, distracted as he was by the blonde in the flowing gown who cannoned into him and covered him with kisses, gasping her gratitude and anguish. Then for a long minute she just held him, with her head on his shoulder while he murmured reassurances and revelled in the feel of her in his arms, the smell of her hair.

When he held her away at last, he fell briefly into the molten gold of her eyes, and kissed her once, lightly. "Well, it's been a day," he said with admirable restraint. "How's our boy?"

"Come and see."

Aubrey was standing at the wall display, talking quietly with Gwydion. Shortly the warrior bard gave his salute and disappeared out of the picture.

"I thought ..."

"Magic, Ben, remember? He was talking to me as if I was there with him, not looking into this room. You might think of it as a hologram, though of course it's nothing of the kind."

"Can I see my son? Is he okay? Did he get his inhaler?"

"Oh Ben, you won't believe it!" Mellis said, still giddy with excitement. "He hasn't needed it, not once, nor his medication. And his lordship says..." She stopped, overwhelmed. "He says Dominic won't need it any more, ever. He's well! Show him, sir, please?"

With a nod, Aubrey turned back to the wall and passed his hand through the air across its face. Like changing the channel, the view shifted to the one Ben had seen before, the haven of safety and the flint-roofed stone house. The weather had gotten worse, the peaceful landscape storm-ridden and wind-wracked, trees and hedges tattered and torn. A sunless sky boiled with purples and reds. It looked like the end of the world. Mellis cried out in dismay.

With another gesture, they looked inside where even Sparrow's persistent good cheer had abandoned him. He huddled by the fire with the two extraordinary men who had his charge, looking scared but stalwart. He was dressed as they were in tunic and hose with a smart little mail shirt and steel cap. He might not have a sword, they had said, but a stout staff in his hand glowed with eldritch light. With his other hand he traced glowing patterns in the air, practicing. If he failed to get the right result, he would stop and shake out his hand two or three times, as if to throw off the error, then try again.

Ben stood with his arm around his wife and lover's shoulders, trembling. "Can we talk to him?"

"It's best not. If he sees you and cannot come to you, it will distress him, and you will be distracted." Aubrey waved again and the wall was plain grey stone.

"Well then," Ben said, controlling his despair with determination. "We'd better get to it, hadn't we. Sir?"

"I was going to send Raven with you," the king said, frowning. "I'm not sure, now. But I can't go myself."

"Why?" Mellis said. "What's the matter with Raven?"

"He took a little hurt on the last part of the mission. I

believe your husband's gift for music is what saved him. Had you done anything else, human child, I might have lost him for, oh, quite a long time."

"Like the last time? He said she—"

"Very likely. I didn't know he'd told you."

"Not much, but enough. It's funny. When we saw her in 1763, Titania treated him like, I dunno, like an unpopular relative. Today, when saw him, she really hit the G above high C and held it!"

"Ah," said the king. "Hmm." He paced away with his hands behind his back.

Mellis persisted. "I don't understand. Isn't he, aren't you all immortal?"

The tolerant smile Oberon turned on her was at least as good as her own, and much older, and she flinched a little from it. You could forget, for a while, what he was, but something would always come back to remind you.

"Yes, Dr Powell, we are, as far as we know. Which means that for us a 'long time' is a very long time indeed. She is not over fond of the kid, as Ben calls our Raven. And being deeply injured, well— We do not take injury in the same ways as mortal men, and women, do. And nor, as you can see, do we easily let go of offense. Well, there's nothing for it, Ben. You've just returned and must venture forth again. I cannot come with you because, as you remind me, I have my wife to manage. And you cannot go alone."

"Sure I can! Just tell me what to do."

"No!" Mellis might have been the shortest of the three but she was not used to being cosseted, rescued, or disregarded, as her faculty had cause to know. "I'll go."

"Mellis!"

"Mellis what?" she demanded of both men equally, and for her purposes "men" was sufficient unto the day for both of them. "He's my son too. I'm as fit as you are. And you are not going without me."

"If Raven were here…"

"If Raven were here, I'd still be going with you, so just get me some proper clothes instead of Great Grandmama's maiden rescuing outfit, and stop being an idiot."

Ben paused, waiting for Aubrey to lay down the law as he had before, but the faerie king simply waited and watched them both, a light amusement hovering about him.

"Aren't you going to say no? Isn't there something here she should be doing? Like staying out of trouble?"

"You can't govern your wife?" the king asked with amusement.

"Govern your wife?" she said quietly. Dangerously. Then she punched Ben in the arm and said, "Silly ass," and turned back to Oberon. "Forgive me, my lord. That was rude. I need my own clothes back, please. Or if you can, something more practical. This gown is lovely, but I am most assuredly not a damsel in distress."

He nodded and she looked down expecting, well, not expecting to be a Warrior Princess in a short skirt and leather armor. "Charming, your majesty. Try again, please."

When they had stopped laughing, the team of Harper and Powell in something approaching expedition gear sat down at Aubrey's suggestion to the light meal that Ben desperately needed, and to listen to the storm building outside.

"Unusual weather we're having, eh, you're grace?"

The king was scowling at the wall monitor again. Time and again he passed his hand through the air, and wherever he looked the same picture resolved: rains and winds, frightened folk huddling in their caves and howes and hollow hills, their music silenced. The sky had turned a slaughtered crimson, and thunder crashed.

These are the forgeries of jealousy! The words Ben had dreamed all those nights ago, coming home to Oberon's door.

Looking strangely anxious, Aubrey sat down with them for the few minutes he felt he had to spare, and said: "Very well. I would I had not to— That is, I wish I didn't have to send two mortals out in this, so I will give what aid I can. Give me your hands."

Which they did, joining them all in a tiny circle—a triangle, really—like the shape of the king's little harp. "I did not say no to Mellis, because two people are needed. Happily I did not set the spells so that one must be fae. And you two, bonded as you are, share a magic my realm cannot match."

They both nodded acknowledgment and even thanks, blushing a little, and a pale faerie glow began to form around all their joined hands.

"Ben Harper, you see clearly and you cannot get lost. Your real gift, though, is neither of these but the music that is your soul. You know this, and so, I think, does your wife." Ben inclined his head again, resisting the urge to share a look with her, but the glow had reached their hearts.

"Mellis Powell, you are clever. You have perfect pitch. She never forgets a tune once she's heard it, did you know that, Ben? But your true gift is your passion—for music, for your husband, for your child."

"Yes," she whispered as the glow reached her face.

"These tasks will require you to try the depths of those gifts, both of you. The tasks I have set to break the spell are not hard but they are a challenge, and require you both. Now," said Oberon, like a captain giving final orders before a battle. "There are three tasks. You have the tokens."

"Right here," Ben said, pulling it out from under his collar, shaking the bell. The pure chime for a second pushed back the hiss of the wind.

The king of Faerie nodded his approval. "There are three doors. You will need one token for each door. When the last door opens, the barriers to Sparrow's haven will fall away.

The three of them were at this point cloaked in a glow not generally seen within the borders of the faerie realm itself, but only by the gifted mortal in his own world, and then only at great need.

"I have lent you what virtue I may for the task," said Oberon, and letting go their hands he rose, allowing himself the lofty diction of faerie tale. "Now we must to our separate tasks depart. Are you ready?" They both nodded. "Ben Harper, which way do you go?"

The circle broken, the glow subsiding, Ben stood up, considered and looked, really looked around the windowless, doorless room. And there it was. Not a golden thread or anything he could describe, just a certainty that the path lay straight before him. He held out his hand to Mellis, who took it firmly.

"Ready," they said together.

59
Elsewhere in Faerie

"Damn it," said Mellis with annoyance, tripping over a tree root. "I should have asked for rain gear."

It was more wind than rain, but annoying enough. The sky in its perpetual morning blue, was barely streaked with red here, so close to Oberon's great house. And yet it was raining. Granted, the rain was the kind of annoying patter that a Dartmoor native hardly acknowledges unless they're lost on the moor, or locked out of the house. But the moor was for the most part open, with known dangers: thick sudden fogs, sucking quagmires, rushing brooks tumbling over falls of stone, patchy cell phone service. And the odd ravening Hound. The Faerie wood had all of that, plus open meadows hidden behind ancient, close growing trees; huge oaks clutched with mistletoe, the white berries cloudy overhead; spreading ash and beech and elm; tangles of holly, and now and then stands of apple trees heavy with fruit, and woodbine twining through the branches.

"And a hat!" she added.

The path when they started had been clear and open, Ben thought, while clambering once again out of a stony stream bed. The flowers and greenery tossed in a gentle summer breeze. Fluttering woodland faeries and groundling fae disguised as landscape had kept them company, surprising and delighting his wife as he had known they would, in air alive with their bell-like voices. Swinging her arms as she walked, Mellis started singing.

"I've waited longing for today,
Spindle bobbin and spool away!
In joy and bliss I'm off to play
Upon this high holiday!"

A folk song, good for walking, with a chorus for Ben to lend his harmony. Then some even older rounds, and an Elizabethan catch that was only naughty when the two voices crossed with their offset lyrics, which made them giggle.

But all too soon it had become less play and more like slogging through the Old Forest with hobbits, only without the murmuring trees. So far. And the musical accompaniment of the little folk had left them, except for an occasional phrase in a minor key that came from nothing they could see. Oberon's kingdom was retreating to a corner. Who knew what was being left behind.

Though there was no path they could see, they walked quickly, Mellis keeping her thoughts unusually to herself. Ben found her silence unsettling. He wanted to ask if she was scared so she could say yes and he could say it was all right, but she was soldiering on over hillock and ditch, climbing over boulders and taking the sudden drop with only occasional swearing. Bitching about the rain was probably a sign of deeper concerns, or maybe the rain was getting down her collar. Usually they talked about everything, but she wanted to be a hero and, to be honest, so did he.

"Feeling lost?" he said into her silence. "We're not, you know. Though I wish I had my walking stick."

He paused, wondering if it would simply appear in his hands.

Apparently not.

"You never get lost," she said, almost off-hand. "So no, not worried."

Then a minute later while skirting a dark, leaf-masked pool she snarled with annoyance as the wind began to pick up, and the raindrops got bigger.

If Titania was attacking Sparrow's stronghold with her patented weather witch temper, it would get worse the closer they got. And in this place where the time never moved beyond a late breakfast, the day grew dark, even where the forest canopy opened to the sky, no longer blue but bruised with red and violet.

"Well, that's odd," said Mellis rather suddenly.

So many odd things and just one stood out? Their faerie escort had left them. So far, he hadn't wanted to mention it.

"What's odd, then?"

She pushed a low hanging branch out of her face with annoyance and it smacked her back with small, wet leaves and something that must have been alive. She swore creatively.

"Somehow I thought Faerie would be more, I don't know, more pleasant."

He chuckled and held the next branch for her to pass under safely. "Unicorns? Purple mushrooms?"

"Perhaps. And less like, well, England on a rainy day."

"I don't think this is normal," said Ben. It wasn't a Faerie he was familiar with either.

His wife started to chuckle, appreciating the understatement, and kept walking even though one foot sank over her heel in something squishy. Oak leaves and wet loam. At least the boots fit, and came away without much effort.

"Do you really remember every tune you hear, the first time?" he said later.

"Hmm," she replied, just before one foot came up against some barrier she couldn't see and went right out from under her. She gave a little shriek and tried to catch herself on the other foot, but the ankle gave way. Both feet went up and her butt went down, and she could have killed Oberon for providing her with a Lady Explorer costume, an adorable but useless Banana Republic trumpet skirt instead of trousers.

Ben was there in an instant, muttering and blaming himself. "I should never have let you come."

"Let me? Hark at you! It wasn't up to you in the end, was it? Now, help me up and— Look, a lovely log to sit on. And *ow!* And just let me catch my breath. Oh!"

Her breath, which had been coming quick and fast, betraying more pain that she was letting on, suddenly stopped.

"What's that, then?"

She was staring at something over his shoulder.

She waited, but he persisted in examining her foot with that sweet, worried expression instead of looking where she wanted him to, so she sighed and tried another tack.

"You never get lost, darling. Does that mean you always know when you've arrived?"

That made him look up and grin. "London was a bit awkward, but I found it."

In the uncomfortable twilight of the wood, Ben felt for his gift, then looked where she was pointing and smiled. "Oh, you mean the invisible door?" Automatically, he patted his jacket and found his glasses. That might help. "Yep, that's a door."

The wood was lovely, dark, and deep and old, impossibly old. The lowest branches of the oaks were twenty feet over their heads, and the earth beneath greener than such a wood would have been in mortal space. Weals of angry red and white streaked overhead in what they could see of sky, and a dank wet smell surrounded them. Except right in front of them.

"Oberon—why do you call him Aubrey, by the way? Anyway, Oberon said there are three doors."

"Yes," said Ben, examining an invisible door as well as he could, all things considered. "Yes, he did."

A space, as ordinary seeming as any other space in an enchanted wood, was outlined in leaves and vines like a leafy garland bent, more or less, into an arch like a door in a monastery. The garland itself was tightly woven of withy and runners of oak, bound together with ivy vines, chased with oak leaves and acorns. Oak leaves, good sign! No hedge expanded from either side; no stone or brick or anything but open air with dull sunbeams and dust motes sifting between the raindrops.

He could see through the arch, no question, to the whole rest of the landscape beyond, but when he put up his hands to it, the resistance from empty air was startling. It was as solid as if the whole oak tree, and not just a few withies, stood in his way. He tried walking around it. That worked just fine, but it didn't matter. The task was to open the doors; walking around them wouldn't serve. He stood back and, figuratively at least, scratched his head.

"What if we look in the diary. Or is that the same as asking for directions?"

"Uh, yeah," he said, examining the arch more particularly. There was something he was supposed to notice, obviously. Or not so obviously, he thought, with the usual sense of irony. "I mean no, it's not, and yes, it might help. But I haven't had time to look at it since I got back from the Dark Ages and, y'know... Those are oak leaves, right!"

"Why yes, they are," Mellis said matter-of-factly from her seat on the mossy log. And when he continued to contemplate the arch. "Book, please."

When she had it in her hands and flipped to the active pages, she raised an eyebrow and muttered. "This is so odd!"

Ben laughed shortly, knowing how she felt.

"Yeah, it is. You just have to read everything. If something is going to be useful, it just— is."

"I think there must be a variety of possible actions for any situation and your little friends know more about the possibilities, probabilities, and plausibilities than ..."

"Welcome to Faerie, dear." He waited. "Anything?"

"Oh, well I think this means ... Look for a bare oak branch. You know, like a new twig or something, ahh, with something missing."

"And when I find it?"

"Oh! The oak leaf, no question. It's not meant to be a trick. Everything on this page is about oak leaves, and new growth— and, oh dear, a crossword clue I wish I'd never seen."

"As far as I can tell, the cruder jokes are just goblin humor. Wait, here's something."

It was hard to tell one particular bare stem from all the stems in a cluster of frilled leaves and capped acorns woven and latticed like a Christmas wreath, but when he looked properly, there it plainly was.

"One day I'm going to do this looking thing without having to be an idiot first."

He drew out the tokens on their silver chain, happy to see them all still in place. When he tugged it gently, the Saxon oak leaf came away as if it had never been attached. Like magic.

Smiling, Ben reached up into the curve of the arch, standing on his toes while managing not to slip. Stretching, he touched the stem of the leaf to a raw nubbin on the branch from which it must have come. With the tiniest gleam like the spark of a diamond, the leaf became one with the stem, and the barrier melted away leaving only an ordinary garden gate, standing open.

"Oh my!" Mellis exclaimed.

Ben, grinning, walked through and disappeared.

60

Nancy Drew

"Ben!" she yelped.

But he popped back into view almost immediately, holding a hand out to help her up. "Wait till you see what's on the other side."

Limping only slightly and without complaint, Mellis followed her husband into a starlit landscape, a broad glade ringed with trees, where a chattering spring tumbled in stepped cataracts down to a reflecting pool. The fountain in the middle splashed prettily, but without the dramatic colors he had seen the last time he played here.

As their eyes adjusted to the gloom, Mellis exclaimed again, "What is this place?" at the same time that Ben snorted, "Déjà vu all over again."

The coffeehouse was empty, and the hay bales and platform stage were bare and damp, but the moon was still full flooding the glade with light, and the grass was still springy under his feet.

"You've been here?" she asked.

"Tell you later, love," he said, shaking his head. "You should have been there."

"Sorry. Couldn't make it. Enchanted, y'know," she said in her all-purpose posh accent, and took a seat by one of the spool tables. "Maybe we should just go to the diary straightaway," she added, flipping it open to where she'd left off, and tilting the pages to read by moonlight. "More silliness. That old rhyme about 'for want of a nail'."

"Got the nail!"

"And a drawing of a— it's some kind of box. I can't tell

whether it's a casket or a steamer trunk. Old fashioned, brass bound maybe? Very Nancy Drew."

"Hmm," Ben mused, searching between tables and around hay bales. Maybe behind the stage? He listened for a distinctive voice as he had listened for the dragon ring, but this place was utterly silent, waiting for stories but not keeping any.

"You know?" Mellis called when he disappeared behind the platform. "Nancy Drew? *The Secret of the Brass Bound* ...? Oh, never mind. Anyway, it's a box of some kind."

Nope, nothing there. At least it wasn't raining, for now, and Ben wondered how Oberon was progressing with his queen. Every change in the weather was probably significant, but he had no time to read it. And they really needed her under control by the time the last barrier came down, or it would all go to hell.

"Okay," he said, reappearing from behind the backdrop. "I have been here before and I don't remember a box. But I was a little busy."

Standing center stage, arms folded and looking determined, he scanned the glade from the hill top, farther away and steeper than he remembered, down to the fountain. It was dimmer now, and quieter, without the glimmering fae and their friends large and small singing, dancing, and making music with Dinah's band. The tree tops were dark, reflecting starlight from their glossy leaves, but no faerie glow. Every shadow might be the hump of a domed lid.

And there was Mellis in the middle of it all, the spark of his life. He blew her a kiss, which she caught and returned, then he looked again.

"Sweetheart?" he said, with a sudden grin. "Whatcha sittin' on?"

Mellis jumped up and looked down. It had been the only thing that wasn't too wet to sit on, muddy skirt notwithstanding.

"Well, isn't that interesting," she said dryly. "It appears to be a brass-bound box."

In a hop and two heartbeats he was at her side, wrestling the box out of the shadows by the leather handles on each side.

"Can I help at all?"

"I don't suppose you brought a flashlight—I mean, a torch."

Knowing a rhetorical question when she heard one, Mellis just sat down again on the nearest hay bale, damp or not. "Maybe there's one inside."

"Funny. No, there's something inside, but of course, it's locked." Ben sat back on his heels and considered, looking closely and not seeing whatever he was supposed to see.

It was quite like an old-fashioned dome-lidded steamer trunk but smaller, about the size of an ordinary foot locker, or a treasure chest. The whole thing had been covered first in soft leather then bound with wooden bars, the bars laid down with decorative metal work. Not brass-bound: gold, that shone in the starlight when everything else was dull with dew. In the empty panels between, the leather had been fancifully carved and outlined in golden nail heads.

The one thing it was missing was a lock or keyhole, though there was a catch, thoroughly sealed. Of course it was.

It was all about the music, right? Bringing out the silver chain Ben first tried ringing the acorn bell. Too easy. Well, obviously. Music was common to every denizen of Faerie, but only Ben could solve this puzzle. That left the nail. An iron nail none of this Realm could bear to touch except Odin, the god of an Iron Age; Odin, who had set the spells.

"What are you thinking?" Mellis asked quietly.

"I think we need some light," he answered slowly, then looked up at her smiling. "Take my hand, please."

I will give you what virtue I may, Oberon had said.

Hands touched, a spark snapped, and they both let go with a squeaked, "Ah!"

But there had been light, too, as Ben had hoped. A bark of nervous laughter, and they tried again.

Again she laid her hand in his, withstood the first sparky shock, and this time held on as the air began to hum and a light to grow.

"Yes!" Ben cried. "Excellent. Thank you, your Grace."

Eagerly, anxiously, they knelt and held their joined hands

above the box like a lantern. It would be awkward, maybe, but it was just the magic assist they needed.

"How long will this last?" said Mellis.

He couldn't answer, looking closely, counting nail heads, tipping it up one-handed to examine back and sides for every detail. And suddenly, there it was in front of him as if painted in bright colors: an empty hole in the pattern just the size of the square-headed nail Jack Greengage had lost from his second-hand boot.

With a lopsided smile, he brought down the light, kissed her hand and let it go. The light winked out, leaving them blinded but only for a moment. Ben found the nail without needing to see it, and it came away from the chain as easily as the leaf had done.

For a moment he feared he had lost the spot in the persistent after-image, but no. With a blink or two and a sigh of relief, his vision cleared. Then leaning forward, he pressed the nail into the hole in the carved leather panel.

With a click, the lid popped up slightly, the chest open. With trembling hands—it was chilly, okay? Certainly not nerves. She lifted the lid till some mechanism within stopped it going any further back.

Ben stared with alarm. "It's empty!"

"Empty?"

"No wait, I'm wrong. Just a second." The light that showed him an apparently empty container was coming from inside the box. He reached in carefully and, eyes shining, pulled out a silver hammer the size of a toy between two fingers.

"Ooh, you scared me, Ben Harper. That's not funny!"

He smiled a little sadly and reached to touch her face. "Sorry," he said, stealing a quick kiss. "I was scared myself for a second. But look!"

Perplexed, she looked and said "That's lovely, Maxwell. But what do we do with it? What about the door?"

"Ha, I think finding this was the whole point. Look, the light is changing. The box is the second door!"

And it was. As if dawn were rising, the glade lightened and shadows fled. Even the milk-pale moon, fixed in the sky like a painted backdrop, was fading to a translucent paper white blossom. The wind was rising though. They had pushed the rain off a little, but the Queen of Air and Darkness was pushing it back.

The light changed and bubbled up at the edges in colors seen only in Faerie. Ben found himself staring up to the top of the hill, far away where, in some other creation of Faerie, a hedge maze stood and past that, Diamond Hall. Today, though, that gate was gone and in its distant place, a tall pair of doors, cut and carved in pure crystal, almost invisible but for the rainbows called from them by the dawn.

"And that would be," Ben said, nodding toward it, "the third."

There was no path, but a few yards of open space lay between the edge of the steep spillway and the dark wood that reached long roots and over-hanging branches to its bank; no path, just long grasses laid flat by rain and wind, slippery as a mountain of glass. The grade was sharper than he remembered, and though the way was apparently clear, there was no reason to assume it would stay that way.

"This is going to take a while."

Hand in hand they started up the hill. Mellis's ankle argued with her, but she wasn't about to stop or stay behind.

At the first cataract the rain came again, and the angle of the slope increased. A few dozen yards later, another cataract chuckled over stone, and the rain was faster, harder, too. No fat lazy drops dewing their hair and clothes, but sharp and slantwise with anger behind it: Titania was fighting to take what was theirs, though she might easily lose interest once she had it. Did she truly want Sparrow just to annoy Oberon, or was there more to it? What made their discord so terrible?

Ben shook all that away. It didn't matter. Let Oberon manage his wife; it was time to go get their Sparrow, though Titania throw everything at them she had. With luck, and with the king's gift brought to bear, she had less now than before.

But still, not nothing.

61
Storm Force Ten

The hill was much steeper than it looked. The only rest came with the terraced layers a few feet deep carved out with each cataract in the tumbling brook, marked by patches of flowering clover. But if they stopped to rest for long, tangling vines slithered out of the surrounding wood to snag their feet and drag them down.

While he kept hold of her hand, the vines drew off, and to some extent the rain. But if one of them stumbled and hands parted, they lost ground again, and the storm beat at them. He helped her when he could, but the wetter they got, the harder it was to hang on. There was no singing, and no conversation in the rushing wind, just muttering and encouragement, and cries when one fell.

With every painful step, it got colder until the rain turned to sleet. The wind drove gravel and dirt and wild leaves at them, bitter smelling and sharp-edged, stinging their faces and hands, and something tiny with wings that might have been a dragonfly, or a fairy. When that struck his face like a bug on a windshield, Ben scraped it off with irritation, shouting into the wind.

Irritation turned to frustration and finally to something like anger. Already exhausted, the harder he worked toward his goal, the more impossible it became. Pausing on a terraced bit of clover, the white heads beaten down by this storm, he cast a longing glance at Mellis. Her fair hair was dark with rain and slicked around her face. Her wonderful face.

"You okay?"

"I knew I should have asked for a jumper!" she shouted

over the wind and hissing rain. She looked like hell, clothes soaked through and plastered to her body, but damn, she was almost laughing! Ben got a hold of himself, at least for a while.

He had no idea how long it took, but he felt like Sisyphus every step of the way. "Do you want to rest?" he said, struggling with despair.

She shook her head. "We're almost there!"

"I'm freezing! It gets harder as we go, we should rest. Your ankle is all purple, look."

She looked down, frowned, and looked up again. "Yes?"

"Oberon's bloody gift." He held up their joined hands, but the glow was clearly too feeble to be of any use. "I know he said this one was the hardest, but I don't think he took the queen's weather magic into account."

"We can't give up now!"

"Not giving up, just..." He coughed, blinded by rain and long effort. Running trembling fingers through dripping hair, he said, "Y'know, as faerie tales go, this one deeply sucks!"

She searched his face, drawn with care and lack of sleep, but still capable of a smart-ass remark in the midst of all this. Faerie tales, my god. And then suddenly, Mellis knew exactly what to do.

"That's it! He said we have our own magic, Ben, you and me. So we make our own happy ending!" Impulsively, she threw her arms around the love of her life. "I love you, Ben Harper!" she cried, and kissed him soundly.

Startled but happy to comply, Ben held on and kissed her back for his love and need, and at last for pure joy. As if on cue, the wind died and the battering rain, and with it, the feeling of panic that dragged on them both. "Well!" he sighed, holding his wife to his heart. "You Dartmoor girls always have just the right answer, don't you?"

She smiled and let him go, futilely brushing the leaves and trash off her dripping skirt and trying to smooth her soggy blouse. "You Yanks know what to do with it, don't you?" Then brushing his lips lightly just once more, she added, "Now, then. One last surge?"

They broke apart, both laughing a little hysterically. He

stopped when he saw her eyes go wide.

"Uhm, sweetheart?"

And when her bright eyes turned to his curious ones, she nodded over his shoulder. This time he simply took her direction and turned around. They had arrived, and the crystal gate glimmered before them spanning the bubbling spring in its pool.

Was it really that easy, Ben wondered. Or had something else happened?

"How?"

"Welcome to Faerie, my lady."

Ben shook himself and came back to the moment, turning to study the doors that spanned the spring. Two panels formed an arch, like doors in a Gothic cathedral. Each was carved or etched with half of a spreading oak tree, the branches and leaves swelling and twining and budding into acorns as Ben and Mellis watched.

"Perhaps you hit it with the hammer," she said thoughtfully.

"It's too beautiful. We can't be meant to shatter it. Besides, this is the acorn."

"Then what is the hammer for?"

"I don't suppose there's anything in the diary?"

Silence, and the awkward sound of Mellis swallowing nervously. "Diary?" She stared at him miserably.

"No teasing, woman, I thought that was understood."

"But I don't have it!" Hot tears sprang into her eyes as she turned to look the long, long way back. The stage, the tables, the hay bales were so small and far away, with snow covering everything at the base of the hill. "I must have put it down when we, when we made the light. Oh Ben!"

"Well, well," drawled a harsh Cockney voice above them. "If it ain't Jack an' Jill. Lucy an' Ricky? The Doctor an' somebody?"

Ben sighed and looked up. Pauly, of course. Tats, piercings, raggedy black rimmed wings lazily beating the air. No, wait, he realized with a touch of hilarity. Not Pauly. Quick, what was her real name? What had Aubrey told him? Bloody hell, it was probably in the diary!

He wanted to howl with frustration, but instead he struck a careless pose and said, "Oh look, dear. It's the Goth Fairy."

"You mean, if I put a Goth under my pillow, she'll bring me a penny?"

"Something you're missin', dearie." Titania's minion said, punctuating her remark with a hearty snort. "And a lucky thing I 'appened by, innit?"

"What could you possibly have that... Oh, of course!"

Ever the opportunist, the bitch had the diary between her black-varnished fingertips, and from her special vantage point over their heads was dangling it over the spring and gliding gradually downhill and further away

"Ben!" Mellis sobbed.

Sometimes an answer appears only when you stop looking for it. Positively tingling with pleasure, Ben snapped his fingers, pointed at the Titania's Goth girl, and commanded: "Onyx, give me that book!"

Before she could draw another breath, she had flown forward and done that very thing, which Ben then handed carefully to his wife. The faerie practically exploded with fury.

"Bloody bastard!" she bellowed. "That's cheating! That's..."

"Onyx, go away. Now."

Poof. The last clouds vanished with her. Sky blue, temperatures mellow, almost home.

"Damn, why can't they all be that easy?"

Mellis wanted to laugh, but couldn't. "Who was that?"

"Another long story. Not important right now. But I had her real name, and that's what counts."

"No," she said in a small voice, holding it out to him. "It's too late, love. Look, it's ruined."

His expression fell but he shook it off. It didn't matter. Folding his hands around hers, he closed the covers over swelling pages. "Sparrow will love it." he said, and dropped it into a pocket. "We don't need it, now. We are very smart people with very special gifts, and how hard can it... We'll figure this out."

So he pulled out the acorn bell again and shook it, tentatively. A sweet chime came from it that lightened their hearts and made them smile in spite of everything. It also made the crystal door quiver slightly, but nothing else changed.

"Wait!" said Mellis suddenly, staring in wonder at the gate as if it had spoken to her in French. The beginnings of the glimmer of an idea started to blossom across the English rose of her face. "I think, maybe... Oh my god, two inspirations in one day! Oh, I am brilliant! Don't give up, love, I know what to do."

He bent his head, sighing.

Mellis said, "There's always music in it, isn't there." It wasn't a question.

"Honey, a funeral march is music."

"So is 'Banish Misfortune.' Just listen. I think everything Oberon said while we were joined was important. He was clear that we each have our gifts. You have followed yours," said the music teacher, gently taking the silver chain from around his head. "We have used his. Now it's my turn."

She held up the chain, letting the acorn slide down to the bottom, suspended between her two fingers. It swayed just a little as it fell and the silver glinted in the strengthening light.

"The task was not to find a bell, they said nothing about a bell. They said acorn. A seed, you see? The door is the tree. We must plant the seed and make it grow. Now," she went on, sounding awfully pleased with herself. "For today's lesson in harmonics, young Benedict. Strike the acorn with the little hammer, please."

He stared at her quizzically, but fetched the silver hammer, barely the length of his thumb, from his pocket. Thinking a moment, considering distance, angle and windage, he pulled out his glasses and put them on, then looked again. That was better. With a fond glance at his wife, he focused on the acorn, and gave it a tap.

The tiny blow drew forth a note so fine, filled with such joy, so much greater than the simple shaking of the bell had done. And instead of fading away, the tone grew until the crystal door trembled, and the air brightened around it. Then the note faded, and the light dimmed. Mellis, far from looking disappointed, had gone quite pink with excitement, as if poised on the brink of a brilliant discovery.

"Hush!" She held up a hand before her husband could speak. "One more time a little more firmly, Ben, please. Strike the acorn."

So he did, sure and sharp; the same silver note rose and swelled and grew in volume and power. And before it could reach the top of its voice, Mellis took a breath and added her clear soprano to it, at an interval a third above. Harmony began. Then she nodded at Ben and his eyes lit up. The tone was building, and he had a part in it, too.

Alive and aware, he added his pleasant baritone in his own octave, a third tone up again, and so raised a simple, perfect chord so perfectly blended it became like a single voice calling from outside of time, from mind alone, making and growing from the seed to the growing tree that was their passion and their joy. And finally, the silver note melted away leaving only the perfect mating of their two human voices. The crystal doors thinned, sparkling, into diamond rainbows, then nothing at all.

62
Dartmoor

Sparrow's safe haven suddenly looked remarkably like the Raven's Eye as the summer morning of Faerie blended into the long midsummer evening of Dartmoor. The only wind now was the green-smelling breeze murmuring across the tor, and the only ringing, the five bronze bells of St Michael's tolling Evensong.

"Mummy!" Sparrow shrieked, only a few feet away and wreathed in smiles. He threw off his steel cap and tossed away his weapons and ran towards his parents, both crouching to receive him. "Dad!"

There were exclamations and hugs, happy tears and multiple kisses all around as the little boy leaped lightly into his father's arms. "Pixies, Dad! I told you. Teacher said no, but I was right. And it was so cool!" No halting in his speech, no labored breathing. Impossible, but true.

Ben hated to release him, but let Mellis take the boy to swarm with fuss and kisses when he saw through damp eyes that they were not alone. He thought he ought to say something to the extraordinary gentlemen who had been his son's guardians, but for a change, he had no words. Gwydion took his hand briefly, looking grave but pleased, while Taliesin bowed. Then both were gone.

"Well done, Ben Harper," said a fair and utterly unfamiliar voice in the usual place, two feet behind him. Taking a deep breath, he turned to face the King and Queen of Faerie in their splendor. Both Mellis and Sparrow took no notice. In fact, Mellis stood up with her son's fragile little person in her arms while he was showing her something he'd made, and started the walk down towards the village and home.

"Wait!" Ben called, reaching out to her.

"You'll catch her up, never fear," said Oberon. He was dressed as he sometimes was in gorgeous silks and brocades, short belted tunic and long, dagged sleeves, with the twinkling filigree of his golden crown on his brow. And by him, leaning on his arm, his queen contrite and sad in a grass green gown, the color shifting as if lit by other stars, the diamond coronet crowning the curling white-gold hair. Primroses, never seen in this part of the moor, sprang up under her dainty gilded sandals.

Ben took a step back, uncertain of his safety. The king put out a hand to assure him.

"Give my lady's grace a moment, please. Madam?"

She came forward full of sweetness and bent her knee and then her lovely head, curtseying to him in all humility. And when she rose, she offered her cool, long fingered hand, which Ben took and graciously kissed.

"So, " he said, then cleared his throat and started again. "So, we're good?"

The king of Faerie nodded regally, then bent over his queen's hand, and dismissed her. She faded in a gentle sparkle of light. Then he heaved a sigh Ben found hard to interpret.

"Yes, for now."

"Wait, that— that was an apology? For trying to, y'know, for almost... For everything?"

"Yes, Ben, and as good as any mortal man is likely to get from her. And you accepted it."

"Did I? Oh," said Ben, just a little annoyed. "I suppose I did. And well, yeah, just as well. The last thing I need is a permanent issue with the Queen of Air and Darkness."

That made Oberon smile.

"I prefer to think of her as the Queen of Love and Beauty."

Together they started walking the spiral down from the standing stones. To the several casual ramblers they encountered, he nodded a friendly greeting, his lordship just another vaguely familiar face. No one noticed the fabulous costume or the vague glow that hovered about him except Ben, who suddenly asked, "Speaking of permanent issues with the queen, where's Raven?"

"Recovering nicely," said Oberon. "Cursing the Saxons, the Queen, and everyone charged with tending him. Not you. You did very well by him, you know, as by everything else in your charge, once you got the hang of it."

Ben almost thought he heard a snappish voice behind a, what, a curtain, saying "I'm standing right here!" but it was probably his imagination.

"You'll see him soon, I think," the king went on. "In his own time, of course." He paused while they walked a little further, and then said casually, "There's something else you want to ask me, Ben. Are you waiting for me to tell you what it is?"

Ben grimaced painfully, halting on the path to face him. "About Titania? Yeah. How did you get her to do that? What made her apologize? What did you do to her?"

"Not tonight, human child. There are old pains between us, and old sorrows. For the time being, her temper is bound with a slender chain, though I don't suppose it will last. I have her promise, for now. But that is not your real question."

Not drunk enough, okay. "No, that's true. The real question is about Sparrow. Is he going to be all right?"

"Oh, of course!" Oberon said with an airy gesture. "A very brave boy, and a credit to you both, seriously."

"I guess what I really mean is, will he remember all this, or am I looking at years of therapy?"

That really did make Oberon laugh out loud, and his garments shifted again to stylish, comfortable Aubrey's. "As with your musical friends, Sparrow's memory will fade until it is no more than a pleasant dream that he sometimes revisits in his sleep. The magic he learned will prove to be card tricks and sleight of hand that will drive his teachers mad. Oh, he'll still see the little folk when it pleases them, until he is too old to believe in them."

The rock star who was the king of Faerie added soberly, "But if that time doesn't come, Ben. If he doesn't outgrow us, send him to me when he is sixteen. I'll see what else can be made of him, if he wishes it."

Hmm. Scary, but okay.

"Oh!" Aubrey snapped his fingers, remembering. "I'm also told he wants a puppy."

"Really! We've never had that option before, y'know, pets. What about Mellis?"

"I think she wants a kitten," his lordship nodded. "She was brilliant, you know. Gwydion designed that final charm himself, and he was always one for complicating matters. But Odin said the last one had to be hardest, which of course is true. Anyway, you can discuss it all with her tonight, and praise her and make love to her. But in a day or maybe two, well, she may talk about it for a while as a film you saw together, or a nightmare that turned pleasant in the end. Then daily life will over-print it with the usual things. Her love for you has been strengthened, if anything, and that will remain."

Okay, life would be simpler without this episode at its center.

"And what about me?"

"You!" Startled, Aubrey clapped hands on both Ben's shoulders. "Oh Ben, there's nothing in the world, yours or mine, that can take this from you. You are the heart of it. You were at its center from the moment we met at the pub. And if you don't object, we may even meet there again. If Dinah doesn't mind me sitting in from time to time."

Ben chuckled, letting out the breath he hadn't been aware he was holding. "I don't think she'll mind, sir. Especially if she's not to remember."

"Well," said the king. "Maybe a tune or two. She's heard the bells of Elfland now, and that seldom leaves a musician alone."

"She thinks we should go into the studio, do some recording."

"Why not? I know a little about recording studios. Don't look so shocked. We'll talk."

They walked on a little further down the hill in companionable silence, Ben's mind still crowded with questions he hardly knew how to ask, not knowing where to begin or what might get an answer, until they halted again just where the path turned off the tor and became the paved road through Iveston. Oberon, who was Aubrey, who might still be Odin and even a little bit of Raven, turned to him then and took his hand in compliment and comradeship.

"Follow your gift, Ben," he said.

Then all that was left was Ben at the bottom of Raven Tor, with the hint of a tune in his head, and a scent of violets.

THE END

OBERON

Sound, music! Come, my queen, take hands with me,
And rock the ground whereon these sleepers be.
Now thou and I are new in amity,
And will to-morrow midnight solemnly
Dance in Duke Theseus' house triumphantly,
And bless it to all fair prosperity.

About the Author

Maggie Secara started out wanting to be an archaeologist. Then a reporter, then an international spy, a poet, an opera singer, a novelist, a historian. She ended up being a bit of each, earning a Masters in English and becoming involved with historical costume and improvisational theatre. When all those passions came together at once, she decided to be a novelist again, and so she did. Her short fiction has appeared in a variety of publications, including New Realm, Unsung Stories, and Daily Science Fiction.

Maggie lives in Los Angeles, California, with one adoring husband, two goofy cats, and half a million English words to toy with.

You can find Maggie in all these interesting places:

Facebook	facebook.com/groups/maggiesworlds
Twitter	@MaggiRos
Tumblr	maggie-secara.tumblr.com
Pinterest	pinterest.com/maggiros
Website	www.maggiesecara.com

If you enjoyed this book, please consider leaving a review to aid other readers in their choices.

www.ingramcontent.com/pod-product-compliance
Lightning Source LLC
Chambersburg PA
CBHW072112250626
47159CB00007B/2411